A LESSON IN LOVE

"Talking to you," she said slowly and very deliberately, "is like trying to find one's way out of a maze." She rose swiftly to her feet and made to push past him.

It took very little effort to tumble her into his lap. His hands slid beneath her mantle and came to rest under her arms, brushing her intimately. He ignored her sharp intake of breath.

"What a slowtop you are," he murmured, and his lips, warm and open, lightly traced the line of her jaw. "Haven't you been listening to a word I've said? You belong to me. How am I to convince you of that fact?"

"With great difficulty," she answered. But he could see mischief lurking in the depths of her eyes.

"I don't suppose you're familiar with Aristophanes' theory on love?" Without waiting for her answer, he went on. "He believed that lovers are born joined but that the gods separate them at birth. They wander the earth, lost and lonely, till they find each other again."

"That's sheer myth," she retorted.

"So I believed. Until tonight. Now I'm not so sure." His tongue lightly flicked her ear. "Wouldn't you like to test the truth of Aristophanes' theory?" he coaxed.

"How?" Her voice was barely audible.

His mouth, gentle yet unyielding, closed over hers. He deliberately allowed her to taste the blatant urgency of his hunger . . .

Fallen Angel

ELIZABETH THORNTON

ZEBRA BOOKS
KENSINGTON PUBLISHING CORP.

Also by Elizabeth Thornton:
  Bluestocking Bride
  A Virtuous Lady
  The Passionate Prude

ZEBRA BOOKS

are published by

Kensington Publishing Corp.
475 Park Avenue South
New York, NY 10016

First printing: May, 1989

Printed in the United States of America

For "auld lang syne"

to my dear and "scattered friends"

Ellen Kemp Black
Jean Milne Irvine
Alison Adam Peerce
Rena Simpson Sharp
Heather Graton Still

and to my family in Scotland

Andrew, Constance, Alison, and Aunt Ess

Chapter One

The girl by the long sash window raised one edge of the heavy velour curtain and gazed steadfastly along the graceful sweep of Drumoak's gravel drive. A fine hoar frost had transformed the threatening aspect of the avenue of winter black oaks, fashioning them into a lace tapestry of incredible delicacy, and the dusting of snow which had fallen during the night dashed in a mad dervish against the small frosted windowpanes, driven by the blasts of cold air which habitually swept up the waters of the Firth of Forth to buffet Drumoak's grey granite walls.

Madeleina Sinclair, "Maddie" to her intimates, let the curtain drop from her fingers and she half-turned back into the saloon. Familiarity with Drumoak's commodious though sparsely furnished front parlour had inured Maddie to the uniform shabbiness of the place. Her eyes were drawn to the inviting blaze of coals in the grate, but she resolutely remained at her vigil by the cold window.

"It will be dark soon. He should have been here by now," she observed, and her eyes flashed a question, as if seeking confirmation from the other occupant of the room, but the lady's head was bent assiduously over the knitting in her lap.

Miss Nell Spencer, a handsome woman who looked to be a year or two shy of forty, carefully counted her stitches before favouring Maddie with a reply. "A watched kettle never boils," she said patiently, and looked reprovingly over the rim of her spectacles when the girl gave a sudden, unladylike snort. "Maddie!" she warned with a cautionary shake of the head, and she reinforced the admonitory tone with a quick frown. "Your Papa will be here directly. Now stop prancing about like an angry kitten and sit down and converse with me in a civilized manner."

Maddie pirouetted away from the window and made a great show of seating herself gracefully and decorously with the air of one well practised in such niceties, but her expressive and intelligent brown eyes twinkled perversely.

"That's better," said Miss Spencer, well satisfied with the ladylike demeanour her niece could show to the world when it suited her. "Now tell me what you have been doing today."

"You know what I have been doing. Oh, very well. I made a stab at that famous speech from Euripides's *Medea.* You know the one. It begins, 'Of all things that live and have intelligence, we women are the most wretched species.'"

Miss Spencer clicked her tongue, and her knitting needles flew a little faster. "Why do you squander your time on such a labour? There are perfectly good translations available for the asking."

"Time is one thing that I don't lack. Besides, it's a matter of accuracy. It's true, I assure you. You don't think for a minute that Malcolm's father prepares his sermons directly from the Bible? Of course he doesn't! He goes to the original texts which, as you know, are in Hebrew and Greek. It's merely to clarify interpretation. Any scholar worth his salt goes to the primary sources."

Miss Spencer was not at all sure that she had known that the original texts of the Bible were in Hebrew and Greek, but she refrained from saying so. "But in your own case, to what purpose?"

"If I'm to help the girls at Miss Maitland's with the production of the play for next Founders' Day," said Maddie reasonably, "it is essential that I understand Medea's character and motivation. Her revenge on the man who wronged her, you must admit, was a trifle excessive."

"Oh? What did she do?" asked Miss Spencer, interested in spite of herself.

The answer that sprang to Maddie's lips was instantly rejected. Murder and infanticide, she knew, were not suitable subjects for polite drawing-room conversation. After a moment's consideration, she replied tactfully, "Medea brought her husband's house to extinction. Even in those days, men, so it would seem, were preoccupied with carrying on their line."

"It's just as well they are, or there would be few married men in our acquaintance."

"Aunt Nell! What a shocking thing to say!"

"But true, nevertheless," retorted Miss Spencer, not without a certain degree of smugness. "Time you learned to exploit that fact and find yourself a beau, my girl, instead of filling your head with Greek and Latin and goodness knows what else. You would do well to remember that gentlemen feel threatened by girls who are brighter than they are."

"'A woman, especially if she have the misfortune of knowing anything, should conceal it as well as she can,'" quoted Maddie with a straight face.

"I beg your pardon?"

"It's a line from the novel I've been reading, *Northanger Abbey,* by an unknown lady."

"Books again, Maddie? Nevertheless, the author of that sentiment knows a thing or two. You should heed her."

"She is being facetious, Aunt Nell."

"Nonsense. Only you would say so. If you want to catch a husband, you had better forget that you ever heard of Greek or Latin."

It was an argument that Maddie knew she could not win, and she diplomatically refrained from reminding her aunt that the last thing she wished for was a husband who would in all likelihood stifle her individuality. She adroitly turned the subject.

"Do you think she'll be with him?"

Miss Spencer's busy fingers stilled on her needles. "Who can say what governs the conduct of such a woman? Duty should impel her to accompany your father. She is his wife, for God's sake."

At Maddie's pained expression, she added more kindly, "But there's nothing to stop us hoping that she will again find some pretext for remaining in London. That way, we shall all be more comfortable."

The rumble of coach wheels on the driveway was clearly

audible, and Maddie sprang to her feet.

"He's here, Aunt Nell! Papa is here!" and she made a dash for the closed double doors that gave direct access to the front entrance of the house.

"Maddie!" The word was a command.

The younger woman stopped suddenly in her tracks, ran the fingers of one hand through the crop of her copper curls in a familiar gesture of distraction and her brown eyes under the thick fringe of dark lashes and delicately arched eyebrows widened.

"Papa is here," she said forcefully, though a little breathlessly, but when she moved toward the door again, she walked serenely with a slow, stately grace, conscious of her aunt's oft repeated dictum that a well-bred young lady of nineteen summers should conduct herself at all times with a decorum befitting one of her advanced years.

Miss Nell Spencer watched approvingly as her niece made a dignified exit. But once beyond the parlour doors and out of sight, she had little hope that her headstrong charge would heed the tutoring she had so patiently and painstakingly imparted in the year since Maddie had graduated from Miss Maitland's Academy for Girls in Edinburgh. In that short space of time, Miss Spencer, Maddie's self-appointed companion and mentor, had done her best to impress upon her niece that there were more important accomplishments in life for a girl to master than the academic trivia she had studied under Miss Maitland. Miss Nell Spencer deeply regretted that her brother-in-law, Donald Sinclair, had not seen fit to send her late sister's only child to her own alma mater in Bath where she would have been instructed in the feminine arts so necessary for a young lady of quality. She heard Maddie's melodious voice cry an excited greeting and Miss Spencer's thinned lips relaxed into a half smile. That greeting, she knew, would have been more restrained if Maddie's young stepmother had alighted from the carriage. Not a soul at Drumoak would consider that jade's absence anything less than a special dispensation from heaven. Nor would the presence of Donald Sinclair excite anything stronger than a tepid pleasure, save to the daughter he so shamefully neglected and whose love he so little deserved.

Miss Spencer adjusted the spectacles on the bridge of her

10

patrician nose, and she smoothed the smart lace cap which adorned her neat coiffure. For a lady who was fast approaching forty, she possessed an uncommonly girlish figure, straight backed and slender, which was shown off to advantage in the warm, long-sleeved frock of blue kerseymere which she had chosen to wear to stave off the interior chill of Drumoak's drafty halls and chambers. Though her gowns were not of the first stare, their unmistakable cut, with meticulous attention to fabric and detail, distinguished the wearer as a lady addicted to quality, good taste and, particularly in the colder climes of Scotland, uncompromising comfort.

She picked up her knitting needles and glared distastefully at the work in progress. The sigh of frustration which escaped her lips was edged with impatience. She hoped she would never again have to knit another pair of bedsocks for her niece. The child was nineteen years old! If she had her way, the girl would be shopping in Bond Street for silk stockings and ribbons, and lengths of the finest gauzes and smooth satins to be made into fashionable dresses and breathtakingly beautiful ball gowns. Comfort should be the last thing on a young girl's mind! But Maddie had humbly asked her aunt if, in lieu of the silk stockings she had promised for her birthday, she would be kind enough to knit a pair of bedsocks to keep her toes warm during the long winter nights. Maddie cheerfully owned to being hopelessly inept with any sort of needlework. Her aunt wasn't fooled for an instant. She knew that it was lack of attention, not aptitude, which was responsible for the girl's want of accomplishment. Why, in some circles, Maddie, for all the warmth of her compassionate nature, would be considered positively *farouche*.

It was time, decided Miss Spencer as she furiously attacked each stitch on her knitting needle, that Donald Sinclair was brought to a sense of his iniquity. Before he removed to London, to the fashionable life of ease—and vice, if rumour was to be believed—in which he indulged amongst the beau monde of English society, she meant to have it out with him. It was intolerable that he spared scarcely a thought or a groat for Maddie who was so cruelly banished, at the whim of her stepmother, to the lonely wilds of Scotland. Maddie deserved better. And if Cynthia Sinclair was reluctant or ineligible to

11

introduce Maddie to a wider circle of acquaintances among whom, hopefully, a suitable husband for the girl might be found, then she, Nell Spencer, would be more than happy to take the girl to her grandfather and do everything that was necessary to launch her into society.

She glanced at the clock on the oak mantel. It would be a good hour before father and daughter would admit outsiders to their intimacy. She would wait until the vestibule was clear before going to tell Janet that dinner would have to be set back an hour or so. Her mouth tightened. That old crone, she knew, harboured a grudge for the shifts which Donald Sinclair's extravagant young wife had put Maddie to since his remarriage five years before. Dinner might very well turn out to be a dismal affair.

Janet, basting the Christmas goose in the back kitchen, heard the deep accents of their long-absent master as he came through the front entrance and she mumbled into her chin that she wished he was a lad again so that she might skelp his backside and make him mind his duty. Big Duncan, who was pushing through the back door with an armful of firewood, was equally succinct in his condemnation. He spat angrily into the black iron grate and swore that he'd happily break Donald Sinclair's bloody neck, aye and that o' the English *beesim* he'd taken to wife, if the wee lass hadn't made him promise to be on his best behaviour for the fortnight her father would be in residence.

Janet looked up from her domestic labours and said sharply, "She's with him, then?"

"No! Thank the Lord!" averred Duncan hastily. He grinned. "So ye can unearth a' those gewgaws ye've been burying this past sennight. Drumoak is safe from her greedy eyes and paws for a wee while yet."

"What gewgaws?" Janet sniffed. "She's already plundered the house o' everything o' value. If there was anything left, d'ye no think she'd be here in person to stuff it in her pockets or cart it away? Aye, and sell it later, I've no doubt. A 'lady' in her position maun have pin money to squander."

"One o' these days, the master will find himself up to his neck in the river Tick."

"Bankrupting Donald Sinclair is the least o' that foreign *beesim's* sins," said Janet sourly, and she lifted the lid of the

12

black iron pot to add boiling water to the *cloutie* dumpling that had been simmering for hours at the side of the hot coals.

She could forgive Donald Sinclair the folly of his infatuation for a woman half his age. He wasna the first man and he wouldna be the last to make a horse's arse o' himself over a pretty face and a ripe body, but what she could not forgive was the shabby way the pair o' them had treated Miss Maddie, casting her off as if she were some poor relation, out of sight, out of mind, whilst they pursued their pleasures in the fleshpots of London.

From a hook on the wall, she removed a wooden spurtle and vigorously began to beat the lumps from the savoury roux she had prepared earlier as a base for her parsley sauce, the invariable accompaniment at Drumoak for all fish and fowl. She would have preferred to vent her anger in some sympathetic ear, but she had no wish to confide her thoughts to Duncan. She sliced her grandson a quick glance, her expression hovering between affection and regret. Appearances, she knew, could be deceptive. Though the lad was bonnie to look at, he was inclined to be simple-minded since he had taken a ferocious beating from Black Douglas up at Balmedie. The mill had gone on for over twenty rounds and put paid to Duncan's promising career as a fighter. But he was still as strong as an ox, and fiercely loyal to the wee lass who had nursed him back to health. It wouldna do to get him all fired up over the slights the poor wee thing had endured at the hands o' her wicked stepmother.

She jerked her head in the direction of the faggots Duncan was stacking at the side of the hearth. "We'll need a sight more than that to keep us warm this cold spell."

He gave one of the damp logs a vicious kick with the toe of his booted foot. "You're no forgetting that the home wood was cut down last year to pay off the master's gaming debts? You tell me where to find kindling and I'll go fetch it."

"I should have smothered him when he was a *bairn*," Janet said, then folded her lips together as if to prevent herself saying more.

"Can I hae one o' those sweet-mince pies?" asked Duncan, and in the same breath reached for one of the pastries which was cooling on the long trestle table, and before Janet could answer, he had stuffed it into his mouth.

"Och, away and help Jacob with the master's boxes." Her voice was tart, but it gratified her to see Duncan so obviously enjoying her handiwork. He reached for another and she waved her spurtle under his nose. "Go on now! Ye're just in my way here. And see that ye keep yer tongue between yer teeth. Miss Maddie will no thank ye if ye miscry her father."

"Aye," he answered automatically, but his look was less than kindly. He muttered inaudibly under his breath, and dragged himself from the comfort of the warm hearth. As he pushed through the kitchen door, Janet's soft voice halted him.

"Och Duncan, remember it's Christmas Day. Donald Sinclair was once young himself, and as bonny and blithe as Miss Maddie is now. We maun forgive and forget, for auld lang syne!"

Dinner that evening proved to be a more congenial affair than the ladies had anticipated. The Christmas goose and pudding were done to perfection; the coal fire in the small back dining room burned brightly in the grate, Janet having been well warned not to bank up the fire with vegetable parings, as was the custom at Drumoak, to conserve their diminishing supply of coal in the coal cellar; and the absence of Cynthia Sinclair, who had remained in London for some vaguely specified reason, could only be regarded as an act of grace. Without the overbearing presence of her sharp tongued stepmother, Maddie relaxed her guard and openly enjoyed her father's company.

But Maddie was not wholly at ease. She listened idly as her aunt inquired after mutual acquaintances in London, but her eyes travelled slowly over her father's face and form, trying to discern what was different about him. She had never seen him cut such a dash, she decided, as if money were no object. His garments were of the first stare; a diamond pin reposed in his intricately folded neckcloth; and as for the gifts he had showered on them earlier that evening, she was sure she did not know how they were to be paid for. Still, he could not quite look her in the eye.

She tried to dismiss her uneasy thoughts. She was imagining things! Donald Sinclair had always been a fastidious dresser. Her aunt would say that he was trying to keep up with a wife who was twenty years his junior, and Maddie suspected that that was the truth of the matter. She watched covertly as he reached for the brandy bottle for the third time since they had sat down to dinner, and her uneasiness increased. She wondered if there was more to her stepmother's absence than her father had intimated.

"Don't frown, Maddie! It doesn't become you."

"I'm not frowning, Papa. I'm grimacing. I've just bitten down on one of Janet's Christmas favours. I may have chipped a tooth."

Maddie brought the silver dessert spoon to her mouth and, with as much delicacy as she could manage, extracted a small wad of paper.

"Good God, I'd forgotten about the favours in Janet's Christmas pudding. Well, come on girl. Tell us your fortune."

Maddie carefully unwrapped a small silver object and held it out on the palm of her hand. "A baby," she said, then added mischievously, "Perhaps I'm to have a little brother or sister."

"No!" The word was almost an expletive. Aware of the sudden tense silence, Donald Sinclair relaxed against the back of his chair. "No," he repeated more softly, "and it's just as well."

Maddie exerted herself to pass over the awkward moment. "Wait, I think I've found another." Again, she unwrapped a small object. "A ring this time. Now whom do I know who is about to be married?"

"Mayhap it's yer own wedding." The quiet words came from Janet who had entered silently to place a pitcher of hot pouring custard on the table, an accompaniment for her *cloutie* dumpling which these English *sassenachs* insisted on calling "Christmas pudding."

Miss Spencer frowned. In her father's house in London, a servant would never dare join in a conversation as if he or she were part of the family. Such familiarity was unthinkable. But at Drumoak, the servants were a law unto themselves.

"Look, Janet, a baby, too." Maddie held out her palm to display both tiny trinkets.

"Well, see that the ring comes afore the *bairn*, young lady, or I'll skelp ye myself."

"It's only a game, Janet. Besides, there should be more to

15

life for a woman than marriage and babies."

Maddie wished she could take back the incautious remark but only her aunt's sniff of annoyance betrayed that her words had found disfavour. She hastened into speech before she was asked to explain herself.

"Well, come on, you two. What's your fortune for the coming year? There are lots of favours still to be discovered in Janet's pudding."

"I've got the key." Miss Spencer looked hopefully at Maddie. "Does this mean we shall be removing to a new house?"

"Janet would say so. Or it might mean that you are going for an extended visit."

Miss Spencer's eyes wandered to her brother-in-law. She squared her shoulders. She coughed, and finally, before her courage failed her, she said with quiet precision, "Donald, would you permit me to take Maddie to my father's house in London for a visit? He's an old man now, and deeply regrets the estrangement that has kept his granddaughter from him all these years."

"What?" Donald Sinclair tore his gaze from the small object in his hand which had claimed his attention.

Miss Spencer, a little more flustered, repeated her request. "Well, will you?"

"I don't see why not. We'll talk about it tomorrow, shall we?"

Both ladies stared open-mouthed at the man whose attention was once again claimed by the object in his hand, unaware himself of the different emotions he had aroused in his companions. Miss Spencer was flushed with elation, but Maddie, always sensitive to what lay beneath the surface, felt her stomach knot. Donald Sinclair and his father-in-law had not been on speaking terms since her mother had eloped with the Scottish country squire, a northern barbarian in her grandfather's eyes, almost twenty years before.

"Papa, what is it?" Fear lent urgency to her voice.

His laugh sounded strained and hollow. "I've got the lucky angel," he answered, and he opened his clenched fist to reveal the small silver favour which nestled in his palm. "The last time that was dished up to me was before I met your mother.

16

Here, you have it. Perhaps the Sinclair luck is about to turn." He grasped Maddie's wrist and pressed the favour into her open hand.

"It doesn't work that way, Papa," she said with a tease in her voice, trying to lighten his mood. "Fate has given you this favour. You cannot refuse it or give it away. The Sinclair luck is with you for the next twelve months."

He grasped her fingers and deliberately closed them around the small token, and he said very softly and seriously, "Nevertheless, Maddie, I want you to keep it for me."

Their eyes held, but after a moment, Donald Sinclair looked away, as if he wished to evade Maddie's searching gaze.

"Stuff and nonsense!" interjected Miss Spencer brusquely. "You Scots are so superstitious! Why we send missionaries to India, I'll never know. You're only a hairsbreadth away from being heathens yourselves. Your Celtic heritage, I don't doubt."

"And you English are always so superior," Maddie shot back, embarking on a topic which she knew would set the sparks flying from her aunt's patriotic hide.

"You are half English yourself, Maddie, as you should be proud to own."

"Proud? To admit that I have blood ties to the most rapacious race on God's earth? No, thank you. I prefer to conceal that misfortune behind my Scottish heritage. Pity you have no such claim to respectability, Aunt Nell."

Within minutes, the gauntlet was taken up and for the remainder of the meal their lighthearted banter gave evidence of the ancient rivalry which had long existed between their two nations until an accident of fate had given them a common destiny.

Though Maddie kept up an amusing flow of conversation she was far from being the carefree creature she presented to her companions. Her eyes, beneath the concealing veil of her lashes, became more and more anxious as she studied her father through the evening. His mood swings became extravagant, shifting from unrestrained mirth one minute to self-absorbed silence the next. That he was well fortified from the brandy bottle was not in dispute, but Maddie devined that his fever-bright eyes betrayed a more sinister origin.

17

When it came time for them to retire for the night, she linked her arm through his and offered to walk him to his chamber. Once over the threshold, she detached herself from his arms and went to sit on the straight-backed chair which flanked the blaze of logs which Duncan had kindled as they dined. "Papa, what's wrong?" she asked without preamble.

Her softly spoken question seemed to strip away the vestiges of his pretense. He lowered himself on the edge of the bed, shoulders hunched, and he stared blankly at his clasped hands.

"You're so like your mother, do you know that, Maddie? She always knew when I was shamming."

"Am I?" This was a new tack and one she had not been expecting. She could not remember when her father had last spoken to her of her mother. In the five years since he had remarried, his conversation had been all of Cynthia, his new bride. Latterly, his expressions of admiration had given way to excuses for her unprovoked vituperation, and pleas for Maddie's understanding of a situation he was powerless to control. And when he had begged her forgiveness when circumstances made it impossible for the two women to live permanently under the same roof, Maddie had given it without reserve. She was not one to repine for the impossible. She had no more liking for the woman who was her stepmother than Cynthia Sinclair had for her. It was enough that her father loved her, though she sometimes wished . . .

"She would be so proud of you if she could see you now. You've grown into quite a beauty. Do you know that?" His voice was husky with emotion. "Whatever happened to the skinny little brat who, I once swore, would turn my hair a premature grey?"

"She's still here, Papa, under the grown-up finery and acquired polish—much to Aunt Nell's regret."

"She's taken you in hand, has she?"

"With a vengeance!"

"If only things had been different . . ."

"I know," she said softly, uncomfortable with the rush of guilt she heard behind his words. "But don't imagine I'm unhappy. I'm not. Naturally, I wish I could see you more often, but I've resigned myself to what must be. No, really! I mean it! I have my own life to lead now. I know that."

"You haven't had much of a life since your mother died."

"Don't say so!" She sounded genuinely shocked.

He looked unconvinced. "Five years at that school for girls in Edinburgh, what was it called?"

"Miss Maitland's Academy. I was very happy there, and since you've brought up the subject, I might as well tell you that—"

"And then here at Drumoak, with only the sheep for company."

"You're forgetting Aunt Nell. And don't forget Malcolm. I still see him in the holidays. He should be home for the new year."

"Malcolm? Oh yes. The vicar's brat."

"The minister's son. This is Scotland, Papa, or had you forgotten? We don't have vicars here."

"He's at Oxford, is he?"

"No. St. Andrew's. He left Oxford after a year."

"I vaguely remember. Didn't he complain that the undergraduates spent more time in the coffee shops and bawdy houses than they did at their studies?"

"Something like that."

"How could I forget that this is Scotland, where even the shepherd thinks that schooling will make him the equal of his master?" He lowered himself to rest on one elbow. "Are you in love with him?"

"Who?" Her wide eyes had the look of a startled deer.

"Malcolm, of course!"

"Don't be ridiculous! We've known each other since we were infants."

"It's just as well. Your grandfather has someone picked out for you." He pushed himself to his feet, and walked unsteadily to the tall mahogany dresser which stood against the window wall. Maddie's eyes followed him and her lips tightened imperceptibly as she watched him fill a glass from a decanter of amber liquid.

"You saw Grandfather in London?" Her surprise was obvious.

"I did. Though only the direst necessity could have compelled me to seek him out."

"What necessity?" She heard the desperate edge in her

voice, and forced herself to speak in more modulated accents. "What necessity, Papa? Tell me!"

He sank slowly into the depths of the feather bed and took a long swallow from his glass. After an interval, he said, "You need someone to look after you, Maddie."

"Someone to look after me?" she repeated blankly.

"A husband."

She looked at him for a long moment, and then she laughed. "Are you trying to get rid of me, Papa?"

His voice was slow and no longer distinct, and Maddie had to strain to catch what he said. "No. I am simply trying to provide for you the best way I know how," and he tipped up the glass in his hand, draining the fiery liquid.

Maddie's chin lifted a fraction. "I may have something to say about that."

He seemed to have lost interest in the conversation. His eyes closed wearily and the empty glass slipped from his fingers. It fell with a soft thud to the threadbare carpet.

Maddie rose to her feet and came to stand over him. "I don't wish to be married," she said forcefully.

"You don't understand," he mumbled under his breath. "You have no choice in the matter. I've done the best I can, under the circumstances."

"Papa, what are you talking about? What circumstances?" Fear constricted her throat.

He made no answer, and she touched him gently on the shoulder. "Is it Cynthia? Has something happened? Tell me Papa!"

Her words must have penetrated because his eyes opened slowly, but he stared past her. "Cynthia?" he asked stupidly, and then he laughed, and the sound of it tore at Maddie's heart. "Deceitful bitch! You're a fool. Deveryn won't have you! Not even when you're free of me. To him, you're just a warm willing body. But I've told you all this before. Go to your lover, then! See if I care."

Maddie hardly knew what to say. Though she was shocked, she could not admit to any real surprise. On the few occasions she had been in the company of both her father and her stepmother, she had observed an utter want of consideration and affection in Cynthia Sinclair for the husband who was so

20

patently enamoured of his young wife. And on one occasion, she had opened a closed door to hear her father's voice raised in anger. She had shut the door stealthily, but not before she had hear the word *slut*. At fifteen, the word had meant nothing to her.

One hand went out and she smoothed back the tangle of curls at his temple. His dark hair was shot with silver, and lines of dissipation were carved into his once handsome face. She felt a sudden overwhelming pity, but could not determine whether it was for herself, or for her father, or for a world which had lost its innocence.

At that moment, he seemed to her to be a broken man. "Papa! Oh Papa! I'm so sorry."

He had difficulty focusing on her. "He's taken everything from me." The words were spoken so softly, she could hardly hear them.

"Who Papa? Who has taken everything?"

"Your grandfather . . . Deveryn . . . damn them to hell." He reached for her hand. "Maddie! Maddie! Say you forgive me!"

"Of course," she answered soothingly, and tears welled in her eyes.

"I don't deserve your tears. Save them for yourself. Send Duncan to me, and kiss me . . . one last time."

She brushed his brow with her lips. It was pointless to linger. With a last anxious look at the inert form on the bed, she went in search of Duncan.

The following morning, at dawn, before the house stirred, Donald Sinclair was wakened by Duncan and he went for a solitary swim in the arctic waters of the Forth. He never returned. His clothes, neatly folded, with his boots on top to weigh them down, were found among the sand dunes.

At the coroner's inquest, Drumoak's housekeeper, Miss Janet Ross, testified that in days gone by, the master and other young bucks of the area had been used to disport themselves in such manner on Christmas Day for a lark, but that the tradition had gradually died out with the advent of a younger, more circumspect generation. It was presumed that it was an attack of nostalgia that had cost Donald Sinclair his life. A full sennight was to pass before the tides washed up the body, far from Drumoak. The coroner, as expected, brought in a verdict of accidental death.

Word of the tragedy was sent posthaste to the widow in London, who immediately set off for Drumoak. It was remarked that Miss Madeleina Sinclair, throughout the ordeal, conducted herself with laudatory fortitude.

But inwardly, Maddie seethed. How different now was the interpretation she placed on every inflection, every expression, every careless word of her father on that last unhappy night which was indelibly impressed on her mind. She kept her own counsel, however, and concealed her pain behind a frozen impassive countenance. Not for the world would she reveal her suspicion that Donald Sinclair had taken his own life.

By degrees, pain gave way to anger, and anger to an implacable hatred. The name "Deveryn," though she spoke of it to no one, became a torment to her, and to design a fitting torment for her tormenter afforded her more comfort than all the conventional expressions of condolence which were pressed upon her.

Chapter Two

The Viscount Deveryn checked his team with a negligible movement of one wrist and drove his high steppers through the Stanhope Gate and into Hyde Park at a fair clip.

"Deveryn! You drive to an inch." The hackneyed flattery was uttered by a feminine voice at his elbow.

Deveryn inclined his head gravely. Only an intimate would have been able to tell his companion that the ghost of a smile on the viscount's frankly sensual cast of countenance was the one he habitually assumed to mask his boredom with present company.

The lady, a certain Dolores Ramides, an opera dancer with Covent Garden, was blissfully in ignorance of this fact. She tossed her dark ringlets in an attractive though selfconscious gesture, and adjusted the fox capet on her shoulders, a parting gift from a former admirer, wrapping it more securely round her swan-like throat.

To be taken up by the viscount in his curricle was something of an honour. Apart from his four sisters, who were nothing out of the ordinary, only the beauties of both the beau and demi-mondes were ever granted that privilege. Miss Ramides was highly gratified. Even the weather seemed to conspire with her. The chill in the air on that late January afternoon was just what was required to bring out the new fox capet with matching muff and high poke bonnet which graced her charming person.

"Oh Deveryn, look. There's Teddy Banks and Gerry Cooke. I do believe they're going skating on the Serpentine. What fun!

Do say we may return another day and try it."

Miss Ramides tensed imperceptibly as she waited for the viscount to respond. She knew herself to have made a bold suggestion. Deveryn had yet to intimate that she would play any part in his future, immediate or otherwise. But she had hopes, not without some foundation. It made her bolder. She laid one elegantly gloved hand against his sleeve. "Do say we may, Deveryn, please?"

"It's possible," he replied non-committally, though there was no lack of civility in his tone.

At her escort's short answer, Miss Ramides, wisely, smiled to hide her resentment. The viscount was known to give short shrift to encroaching females who made demands upon him. And really, when she thought about it, she was sure she was making progress. It was she who had been invited to drive in his open carriage when other ladies of her acquaintance would have given their eye teeth to come within arm's reach of him.

She thought of Mollie Drake, and she smothered a giggle. Poor Mollie had spoiled her chances of snaring the viscount by committing an appalling blunder. Mollie, unfortunately, was clever. Though she had been well-educated, and could quite easily have found a position as a school mistress, the excitement of treading the boards and the luxury of life on the fringes of the ton as some well-breeched lordling's paramour held greater appeal for her. Deveryn had been attracted to Mollie's flaming beauty. What a pity that, thinking to impress his lordship, Mollie had opened her lovely mouth and capped one of the viscount's quotations from Shakespeare. She had thought to captivate him with her superior intelligence. Poor Mollie had not known what was generally acknowledged—that the viscount abhorred clever women! No wonder! His mother and four sisters were reputed to be unashamed bluestockings! The gentleman was obviously suffering from a surfeit of clever conversation. His tastes ran to something quite different. Miss Ramides thanked her lucky stars that no one could accuse her of being a clever woman.

As Deveryn embarked on a flow of easy conversation, she relaxed against the leather squabs and let the liquid sound of his voice, low and indolent, fill her with pleasure. Her eyes became drowsy and shifted to take in the unusual spectacle of

Hyde Park crowded with pedestrians and open carriages on a fine afternoon in the middle of winter. But though there were scores of smart phaetons and dashing curricles which were tooled by handsome young gentlemen who threw her shamelessly admiring glances, her eyes were most often drawn to the man at her side.

Jason Verney, the Viscount Deveryn, attracted as much attention as did the lady in his carriage. How could it be otherwise? Miss Ramides asked herself. The man was simply divine. He boasted a beautiful head of fine, flyaway hair the colour of new minted gold guineas; eyes like aquamarines, or was it sapphires?—she could never be sure; gold-tipped lashes that fanned those wide-set enigmatic eyes with heart-stopping effect; and finely sculpted bones which gave him the look of an English thoroughbred. But it was that mouth, she decided, which had earned the viscount the soubriquet "fallen angel": full, generous lips tucked up slightly at the corners, but on rare occasions breaking into a slow smile which could melt the ice in the coldest feminine heart. It could very easily make a woman forget that she was playing hard to get. Her ruminations were interrupted by a languid drawl.

"Dolly, don't stare so. I'm beginning to feel like the fatted calf that's been selected for the return of the prodigal son."

Miss Ramides regretted that she had never mastered the maidenly art of blushing. Nevertheless, she batted her long curly lashes and dropped her eyes in a fair counterfeit of confusion, and she hid her pretty face behind her enormous fox muff. The ghost of a smile returned to the viscount's bored lips.

"Gawd luv us, guvn'or! It be her ladyship, yer mother with yer sister." The shrill cry of warning came from his lordship's young tiger, a cockney lad, who was perched up behind.

A crested open landau approached the viscount's curricle from the opposite direction. Miss Ramides quickly glimpsed two elegantly gowned ladies, though their costumes, she noted with a degree of satisfaction, were not of the first stare. She affected an interest in a stand of trees on the far horizon.

The carriages drew level. The viscount's mother, the Countess of Rossmere, had a welcoming smile on her face. As her interested gaze took in her son's travelling companion, the smile gradually faded and she also affected an interest in the horizon. But Deveryn's young sister, a schoolroom miss of sixteen years or so, was not so shy. She looked with avid interest at the "lady" who accompanied her brother, and as the carriages passed, she was seen to wink broadly at the viscount.

"Minx!" he said under his breath, but his lips twitched.

The chance encounter with his mother and sister, though unfortunate, in no way disturbed his lordship's equilibrium. A single man approaching his thirtieth birthday, so he surmised, must be allowed to sow a few wild oats. His mother, though scarcely approving, knew how to turn a blind eye to the occasional opera dancer or lightskirt she might chance to see in her bachelor son's carriage or on his arm in some public place. Had the countess but known it, Deveryn's purpose in escorting the beautiful Dolores to the park when it was sure to be crowded was calculated to spare pain, not only to his mother but to an innocent man he felt he had in some sort wronged.

Deveryn wished to scotch the ugly rumours which were circulating that he had taken up with a married lady who moved in his own circles. Such a thing, he knew, would scandalize his family, and confirm the worst suspicions of the lady's husband, though as yet her name remained a mystery. Deveryn meant to keep it that way. And, he reasoned, the best way to scotch an old rumour was to start a new one.

There was one other reason which spurred the viscount's determination to be seen escorting a bevy of beautiful women around town. The affair with Cynthia Sinclair was long over. He wished to convey that message, not only to all the tittle-tattlers of the ton, but to the lady in question. He could not now say what had possessed him to break one of his own cardinal rules—to eschew married women, virtuous or otherwise. And Cynthia Sinclair must certainly be numbered among the latter. The husband, as he understood, had removed to Scotland, but the lady was proving something of a nuisance. Hence the drive in the park with the most coveted prize of London's demi-monde. Deveryn was resolved that Cynthia Sinclair must be brought to the realization that her persistence in pursuing him would not be rewarded—quite the reverse.

As the viscount's curricle neared the frozen water of the

Serpentine with its plethora of noisy skaters, Deveryn was hailed by the occupant of an equipage very similar to his own. Lord Blanchard, of an age with the viscount, gave him a very good day, and the lovely who was seated beside him greeted Deveryn's companion with only a little less cordiality.

Lord Blanchard's tiger was instructed to go to the heads of his lead horses, a very fine pair of matched bays. The two ladies were assisted down and, as they took a short stroll on the frozen grass verge exchanging commonplaces and surreptitiously casting hard calculating glances at each other's elegant costumes, Lord Blanchard came round the side of the viscount's rig.

"My thanks to you, Jason, for putting the sweetest little goers in my way."

Deveryn's eyes lazily flicked to Blanchard's handsome team. "Don't mention it, Toby. Glad to be of service."

Blanchard seemed to be having some difficulty framing his next observation. Deveryn's languid eyes beneath their hooded lids became a shade brighter.

"Jason, I hope you don't mind . . . what I mean to say is, I don't wish to give offence . . . Dash it all, Jason, you know what I'm getting at! Am I or am I not at liberty to offer my protection to Miss Roland?" Blanchard's soft brown eyes came to rest on the pert little redhead who walked the turf with Miss Ramides.

Deveryn kept his expression grave. "I know of no reason why you should not."

"You've no objection?"

"No, why should I?"

Blanchard looked to be immensely relieved. "I thought as much. But at White's last night the betting books were open, and some hefty wagers were made on which little ladybird would finally capture your fancy. Miss Roland's name was among those mentioned."

The viscount looked amused. "How many are on the list?"

"Four, as of yesterday."

"Only four? I must be slipping."

Blanchard's expression was faintly quizzing. "I say, Jason. What's your game?"

"No game."

Blanchard's face brightened. "You wouldn't, by any chance, care to put me in the way of a little inside information?"

"Toby, a word to the wise. If I were you, I shouldn't bet on any of them."

Lord Blanchard looked blankly at his friend's impassive countenance. After a moment, he shook his head and chuckled. "Jason! You're outrageous. Shall I see you at Watiers for dinner?"

"Indubitably!"

"Do you see your parents soon?"

"Yes, on Sunday for the obligatory dinner *en famille*."

"Convey my compliments to the earl and countess."

"Of course."

The ladies returned and Lord Blanchard very gallantly handed them up to their respective carriages.

A couple of turns around the park were sufficient for Deveryn's purpose. In other circumstances, he would have acted with more discretion. To flaunt his inamorata had never been much in his line. But it pleased him to think that his liaison with the mysterious married lady, like yesterday's news, was already forgotten.

There were but few things in his life that the Viscount Deveryn regretted, and his affair with Cynthia Sinclair was one of them. The regret was not for himself, nor for the lady, but for the husband who had been so negligently cuckolded. It should never have happened. Nor would it, if Deveryn had not been misled into thinking that Sinclair and his wife went their own separate ways quite amicably. It had suited Cynthia Sinclair to promote that piece of fiction.

He had severed the relationship the day he had observed Sinclair at White's, drinking himself into a sodden stupor. It was Toby Blanchard who had volunteered the information that rumour was rife that Sinclair's wife had taken a young lover.

"Well, 'twas to be expected, don't you know?" Toby had commented. "She's twenty or so years younger than Sinclair. Poor bastard! I think he really loves the jade."

Deveryn said nothing, but he felt a rush of pity for the empty hulk of a man who was intent on drowning his sorrows. But with Deveryn, where there was pity, contempt was not slow to follow.

A week later, he was to tangle with Sinclair at Watiers. The man was obviously in his cups and spoiling for a fight. Deveryn had wondered, fleetingly, if Sinclair suspected him of being his wife's lover. That notion he soon dismissed. A wronged husband was more like to call him out, not sit down at a faro table where his enemy held the bank and lose everything but his shirt to him.

It put Deveryn in a very delicate position. With anyone else he would have simply pocketed his winnings and walked away without a backward glance. Fortunes were won and lost every day in the gentlemen's clubs in St. James. But some vestige of conscience, or something he could not name, would not let it rest. When Sinclair returned from Scotland, it was Deveryn's purpose to contrive a rematch and lose everything back to him. Only then would he feel shot of the whole sorry affair. After that, Sinclair was one name he hoped never to hear of again.

He dropped the incomparable Dolly at the theatre in good time for that afternoon's matinee performance. When he made no attempt to make a future engagement, the lady could not quite hide her disappointment. Even Deveryn wondered at his own lack of interest. Beautiful women, like thoroughbred horses and fine Sevres porcelain, had always been one of his passions.

He returned to his rooms in Jermyn Street to dress for an evening on the town. Martin, Deveryn's valet, noted that his master was in a thoughtful mood. It would have shocked that old family retainer to the core if he had devined that the viscount was reflecting that life of late had become so jaded that Sunday dinner with his family had become the bright spot on his calendar.

Dinner *en famille* in the Verney household was habitually an informal affair. The rigid etiquette which prevailed in the dining rooms of the high sticklers of the ton were, by mutual consent, eschewed in that family in favour of a very free and easy converse. Other grand houses in town might boast of an *haute cuisine* which few could equal this side of the English Channel. Such things meant little or nothing to the Verneys, or so the countess averred. At her board, sparse courses and plain fare were the rule. She reasoned that an *haute cuisine* might very easily distract from an occupation at which all the Verneys were known to excel. In that household, debate, or "family squabbling" as Deveryn once affectionately disparaged it to his newest brother-in-law, was honed to a fine art. And truth to tell, at the conclusion of many a dinner, few would have been able to recall what had been consumed only minutes before.

There were not many outside the bounds of this unusual family who could be comfortable in such circumstances. As the three elder Verney girls had acquired husbands over the years, it had afforded the viscount no end of unholy amusement to observe the horror of each of his brothers-in-law when first introduced to the manners and modes at his mother's table. To politely confine one's conversation to the person on one's left or right hand was considered the stupidest kind of folly. One joined the debate and argued one's point of view with vigour, or one was left to vegetate in silence. No topic was consciously selected. No subject was considered too trivial or so elevated or delicate that it could not be argued with relish. Most often, a casual remark made in passing was taken up and within minutes, the battle was joined. Though Deveryn might sometimes cavil at the bland dinners and highblown conversation which were to be found in his parents' residence in Manchester Square, it was remarked that he rarely subjected his family to the slightly contemptuous cast of countenance which he commonly presented to the world.

The countess was highly gratified that evening to have three of her five offspring and one son-in-law sit down to dinner. By virtue of the nuptials of the three elder daughters and Deveryn, the eldest of her brood and the only son, having set up his own establishment long since, the Verneys considered themselves a scattered family. Lady Sophie, at sixteen years and still in the schoolroom, was the last fledgling left in the nest, as her mother would have it. Lady Mary, the third girl, and her husband, Mr. Max Branwell, a darkly handsome young man in his mid-twenties and the latest addition to the Verney ranks, made up two of the party. Though married for only a six month, the young couple had come up to town to travel with the earl and countess to Dunsdale, the earl's seat in Oxfordshire. There was to be a family reunion when the two eldest girls with their husbands and children would make up the rest of the party.

Conversation was all of the absent members of the family whom the countess missed dreadfully, especially the grandchildren. By degrees, interest shifted to the newlyweds and to their new home in Hampshire. The countess, behind the screen of her long lashes, watched the young couple with interest. The earl observed her ladyship's small smile of pleasure and rightly devined that the mother of his children was well content.

The covers were removed. The port and glasses were brought out. But the ladies did not excuse themselves and repair to the drawing room as they would have done if more exalted company had been present. Conversation momentarily lagged.

It was a chance remark from young Sophie which proved the catalyst for the debate which followed. She merely observed that her best friend's sister was soon to be married, an innocuous remark which passed without comment. She named the groom. A tepid interest was kindled.

"Roger Templeton?" repeated the countess. "That rakehell? Juliana's wits must have gone a-begging to contemplate a match for her daughter with the likes of that rakety young ne'er do well!"

"He's very rich," disputed Sophie, "and handsome too."

"And completely ineligible as a suitor," declared the countess with crushing finality.

"What makes you say so?" demanded Sophie, her petulance rising. "All the girls are mad for Roger."

"Yes dear, I'm sure they are, but from what I hear, it's mutual. The boy is not ready for marriage yet. He merely thinks to do his duty by providing an heir for his aging sire."

"Careful dear," reproved her husband with a chuckle, "You'll give Jason the notion that he's free to remain a bachelor indefinitely." He exchanged an amused glance with the viscount. So close was the resemblance between father and son that a stranger, seeing them for the first time, could have made the connection easily. "I have a whim to dangle the next in line to the title on my knee before I die."

"So do we all, dear. But the point I am making is that it were better for a man to choose a wife for love, rather than her suitability to be the receptacle for his heirs." The countess was known to call a spade a shovel.

"Why are men so fanatically committed to propagating their line?" The earnest question was asked of the table at large by Lady Mary.

Like all the Verney girls, who took after their mother, she was small in stature, of somewhat sallow complexion and owned that her rather nondescript crop of light brown hair, which was cut and curled in the current mode, was best described as "mousy." Such failings in their parts was scarcely noted in their sum, for all the earl's clever daughters boasted what their papa was used to call "countenance," hazel eyes alive with intelligence set in finely sculpted bones which made an arresting impression. Nevertheless, the countess was sometimes heard to sadly express the sentiment, when her eyes idly wandered to the handsome figures of her husband and son, that she and her lovely daughters would show to better effect if they had not been saddled with a couple of demi-gods for relations.

Lady Mary's eyes came to rest on her brother and she repeated her question. "Well? Why do men set such store in begetting heirs?"

"How should I know?" Deveryn parried. "I didn't invent the tradition. It seems to be handed down from one generation to another as a sacred trust, more's the pity."

"By men, of course," his mother exclaimed. "I think it must be instinct. Men marry for heirs, women marry for love. Well, there's some Greek play, I forget the name of it, which shows the folly of men's logic. The betrayed wife revenges herself on her husband by bringing his house to extinction."

"How does she do that?" asked Sophie.

"I forget," replied the countess evasively.

"Well, you're wrong about Roger," said Sophie, ruthlessly bringing the subject round to what most interested her.

"Georgie said that when Lottie and Roger saw each other, it was love at first sight."

Mr. Max Branwell opened his mouth and spoke without thinking. "Piffle! There's no such thing!" and he groaned inwardly when he realized that it was he who had opened with the first salvo. He waited in some trepidation for the counteroffensive to begin.

The countess crushed her napkin in her hand and threw it on the table. "My dear Max, just because some things are beyond your ken does not signify that they do not exist. I have never been to China, nor am I like to be. If I were to deny its existence, I should make myself a laughing stock."

Deveryn took pity on his stricken brother-in-law and interjected humourously, "What, Mama! Did you fall in love with *pater* at first sight?"

He looked down the length of the table at his father and grinned wickedly. The earl, whose attention was focussed on her ladyship, was seen to smile enigmatically.

"Certainly not. I found your father a loathsome creature, not without just cause, I might add."

The earl and his countess exchanged a long challenging look, though from experience, the other members of the family did not doubt for a minute that their parents were in perfect charity.

Lord Rossmere passed the port decanter to his son-in-law. "Not in front of the children, dear," he droned. "Personal reminiscences of that nature should not intrude on after dinner conversation."

"Am I to understand, Mama," asked Lady Mary, "that Roger Templeton has now become an eligible suitor simply by virtue of having fallen in love with Lottie?"

"Of course. Love makes all the difference in the world."

"Love," murmured Deveryn absently. "The currency of poets and philosophers since the dawn of civilization."

"And theologians," remarked Sophie daringly, remembering the vicar's homily that morning on a text from St. Paul.

"Romantic love," mused Mr. Branwell, quite forgetting that he had made up his mind that on no account would he ever again allow himself to be drawn into a debate by his clever

Verney in-laws. "Idealized by the poets, trivialized by the philosophers."

"And the theologians," added Sophie sagely.

"Poets, philosophers, *and* theologians," declared the countess, "with few exceptions are misogynists at heart. Well, look at Byron, Socrates, and St. Paul. You can't tell me that they liked women."

"You're generalizing dear," reproved the earl.

"What about troubadors and courtly love?" interjected Mr. Branwell with an unaccustomed show of heat.

"Codswallop! They didn't know women at all. They set us on pedestals. Men, very stupidly, though conveniently, I might add, throughout history have divided the members of my sex into two distinct classes—good women and the other sort. The one they marry, and the other—well, you know what I'm getting at. Romantic love, real love, cannot flourish in such a climate."

The countess's knowing glance came to rest on her son. Deveryn acknowledged the hit with a slight inclination of the head, but he did not pick up the gauntlet his mother had thrown down. Mr. Branwell did that.

"But there *are* two sorts of women!" he exclaimed flatly.

His wife's hazel eyes flared to a dangerous hue. "That's all you know! It is men who make these distinctions and set women against each other. Given my druthers, I'd rather be 'the other sort!' To be a mere receptacle for producing some man's heirs doesn't appeal to me at all."

The earl's cool voice soothingly prevailed. "I think 'love' just got lost somewhere in the shuffle. You ladies seem to think that you have a monopoly on the subject. If given half a chance, I think that we poor males might attempt a rebuttal to all the charges that have been levelled against our sex." He looked a question at his son.

"Don't look at me," said Deveryn and put out a hand, palm up, as if to ward off an attack. "Since I disclaim any experience of the phenomenon," he continued outrageously, "I declare myself a skeptic and leave it to those who know better to convert me to their dogma." He raised his glass in salute to his mother. "To be perfectly frank, Mama, I'm not at all convinced that China is not simply the figment of some rich cit's imagination. I've yet to see any profits from a certain trading company in which I invested rather heavily some time since."

From such modest but promising beginnings a full scale attack was soon launched. But beneath the viscount's easy cajolery, and blandly offered commentary, the countess, a perceptive and watchful mother, sensed a cynical persuasion which troubled her a little.

As Deveryn shrugged into his heavy greatcoat and accepted his hat and gloves from the porter before departing for home, the countess descended the graceful sweep of the Adam's staircase and presented him with a slim volume.

"Greek philosophy, Mama?" The eyebrows shot up "I should have expected a small tract from the Bible." The countess was known to be devoutly religious.

"Milk before meat," she countered with a faint smile. "And don't forget, it was a work of the pagan philosopher, Cicero, which led to St. Augustine's conversion. Read it, though I know you're familiar with the work. I thought you might be especially interested in what Aristophanes has to say."

Her cool lips lightly brushed his cheek. "Now be a good boy, and don't get into mischief." It was a parting comment that Deveryn had been used to hearing from his mother since he was in short coats.

"I'll try." Even the response, he thought wryly, was automatic. He slipped Plato's *Symposium* into his coat pocket and fervently hoped that the work was in translation. His Greek he knew to be shockingly in want of exercise.

When Deveryn climbed the stairs to his rooms above the apothecary's shop in Jermyn Street, he almost choked on the stench of roses that permeated the air. Only one woman of his acquaintance used such a sweet cloying perfume.

"Damn!" he muttered under his breath, and pushed into his lodgings. He impatiently stripped off his outercoat and gloves and handed them to his man.

"It's all right, Martin. I know I have a visitor," he said curtly, waving aside his valet's apology, and without another word, he followed the trail of perfume down the hall and into his study.

Cynthia Sinclair, looking ravishingly elegant, turned as the viscount entered. She quickly replaced the Sevres porcelain figurine which she had been examining, and looked up with a melting expression.

"What are you doing here?" he demanded peremptorily. "And without benefit of abigail?"

The melting violent orbs hardened a trifle under the harsh assault. "Jason," she said baldly, "Donald is dead."

For the first time, he noticed that she was decked out in black from wrist to throat, and the gown was more demure than he had ever seen her in.

Though her words shocked him, not a flicker of emotion showed on his saturnine countenance. "My condolences," he said simply. "Won't you sit down and tell me how and when it happened?"

He pulled out a chair and she accepted it gracefully. But he did not seat himself near the lady. He moved to the fireplace and leaned an arm along the length of the marble mantel. One booted foot came to rest on the rim of the brass fender.

The fire had been allowed to die down, but the room, of moderate proportions and boasting an ornate black and green Aubusson on the floor, was still quite warm. Cynthia Sinclair, who had never before dared enter the viscount's hallowed portals, had already taken inventory of the room's accoutrements and bric-a-brac. Though she thought that it was a very respectable room, it was more old fashioned and restrained than she preferred.

"You have a fine collection of Sevres porcelain," she observed conversationally.

"Thank you."

His pose was deliberately aloof.

Tears welled in the violet eyes, and trembled on long, lush lashes. "Don't be cruel, Jason. I need you now, more than ever."

Deveryn's rigid stance relaxed by degrees and the expression in the cold blue eyes warmed slightly. "You've had a shock. Let me get you a glass of sherry."

This was soon done, and he resumed his former stance, though there was now nothing of hostility to be observed in his manner.

"Now tell me what happened," he said gently.

With a great deal of persistent questioning and a little patient leading, the viscount was finally in possession of the main facts of the case, namely, that Donald Sinclair had lost his life in a swimming accident in Scotland—in December of all months, for God's sake.

After several moments silence, while the widow wept copiously into her lace handkerchief, Deveryn offered, "Naturally, I'll do everything in my power to help you. Tell me what it is you wish from me."

The tears dried, though the lips still trembled.

"Jason, do you mean that? Will you stand by me in my hour of need?"

"What do you have in mind?" he asked politely, though there was a wariness in his eyes.

The pouting lips parted slightly, and Deveryn watched as the tip of her pink tongue slowly moistened her lower lip. Familiarity to the gesture had inured him to its sensual potency.

"Donald made a new will. Well, you know how wild he became when he found out I had a lover. There was no reasoning with him. He has cut me out completely, I'm sure of it."

"But there must have been some sort of marriage settlement."

"Only a verbal one. He promised me Drumoak at his demise. You need not look so surprised. I was an orphan and without dowry when he married me. There was no guardian to see to my interests, then, and no one now to be troubled about my unhappy fate. Jason?" Her voice turned husky. "He told me that you had taken everything from him—that he had given the deed to Drumoak into your own hand. What do you mean to do with it?"

"It was always my intention to return it to your husband. I have no desire for a property in Scotland."

"In that case, you can have no objection to handing it over to me."

He took his time before replying. "I seem to remember that

37

there is a child—a daughter by his first marriage."

"Yes, Madeleina, a spoiled brat of a chit, a haughty creature, but no child. She's of an age with me, perhaps a few years younger, and she set her father against me from the first."

"But surely, under the circumstances, she will see that you are provided for from the estate."

"She won't, you know. Nothing would please her more than to see me destitute and begging for my bread on the streets of London. Girls like her, pampered from the cradle, have no notion of the shifts we less fortunate women are forced to just to stave starvation from the door. Well you must have known that my only reason for marrying Donald was to put a roof over my head and bread on the table. It's a sordid tale, I know, but not uncommon, surely?"

He found her conversation distasteful and her disloyalty to her late husband revolting, but he merely said, "Still, the girl has some claim on her father's estate, and I cannot simply hand over the deed of the property to you without some investigation."

"You needn't think that Madeleina will be without resources. Her maternal grandfather will take care of her."

"Who is he?"

"Samuel Spencer. Do you know him?"

"Not personally, but I've heard the name somewhere."

"They say that he's well-breeched, and there are no male heirs to inherit."

"Nevertheless, I think I should get in touch with your husband's solicitor. Do you know who he is?"

"Someone in Edinburgh. He'll be at the funeral and afterwards, I suppose, the will will be read. Oh, I shall die of mortification, I just know it. These Scots are very close, you know. To them, I've always been an interloper. They've never accepted me."

And then the tears dropped in earnest. Though they left him unmoved he was willing to own that it was a weapon the lady employed with consummate skill.

He watched the performance impassively, his eyes cooling to boredom, the impenetrable half-smile becoming fixed on his lips. It never occurred to him that the grieving widow was in need of comforting. After a moment or two, he said with a hint of impatience, "Come! Dry your eyes. I don't intend to throw you to the wolves, you know."

Other men in his position, he knew, would simply send the deed on to the solicitor in Edinburgh and wash their hands of the whole affair. He wished that he might, and could scarcely understand the impulse that prompted him to become actively involved in the woman's affairs again.

Her shoulders gradually stopped heaving. The handkerchief was laid aside, and she peeked coyly up at him through the matted spikes of her wet lashes. The appeal of those enormous, amethyst pools fringed by soot-black lashes was powerful. Deveryn was not unmoved by the picture she presented. Cynthia Sinclair's intensely brooding beauty was not in question. But the appeal was all to his senses. Now that she was free, a hot and heavy affair he would have entered into without regret. But the lady had set her sights higher. He was sure of it, and it made him cautious.

Cynthia's eyelashes fluttered nervously, and her eyes dropped to her clenched hands. The impassive expression on the viscount's face was not the one she had hoped to see. She smiled to hide her disappointment, and thought that he would be a very difficult fish to net. But the task, she believed, was not beyond her.

Her lips parted and she asked breathlessly, "You'll help me?"

"Why not?" And he abruptly pushed himself from the mantel and closed the distance between them.

"You'll give me the deed to Drumoak?"

He took her by the hand and she unresistingly rose to her feet. For a moment, she thought he meant to take her in his arms, but he merely led her to the door.

"In all conscience, I cannot do that. But with your permission, I propose to escort you to your destination in Scotland."

Her mouth fell open, and Deveryn permitted himself a small, genuine smile. "I intend to be your advocate, you see. No one shall take advantage of you as long as I hold the trump card."

39

"The trump card?"

"The deed to the property."

He escorted her into the vestibule and had her wraps brought. He could see that his offer had momentarily deprived her of speech.

"I'll make all the arrangements," he said smoothly. "Be ready to leave at first light tomorrow. Oh yes, one more thing. I'd be obliged if you would travel in company of your abigail. Apart from wishing to guard your reputation, you'll be glad of the company. I myself intend to spend a good part of the time on horseback."

She laid a hand on his arm and hope kindled in her eyes as she looked up at him. "Why are you doing this?" she asked softly.

He regarded her with an inscrutable expression for a long moment, then said very deliberately and cruelly, "For old time's sake. Nothing more."

Her hand dropped, and the smile on her face died.

When the door finally closed upon her, Deveryn returned to his study and poured himself a stiff drink. After a few quick swallows, he sat down at the desk and threw off a terse note to his mother informing her that he was obliged to delay the projected sojourn into Oxfordshire. He had it sent round immediately to Manchester Square.

Having done this, he unlocked the bottom drawer of his desk and withdrew some papers. In his hand, he held the deed to Donald Sinclair's property in Scotland and the vowels for the sum of money which Sinclair had lost to him at Watiers. He pocketed the deed to Drumoak and absently replaced the vowels in the desk drawer knowing that he would never see them redeemed.

He shut the desk drawer with a snap and quickly penned a note to his man of business giving him *carte blanche* to act for him in his absence. He left it conspicuously on top of the desk, knowing that Hepburn would find it first thing in the morning when he arrived for their weekly appointment. By that time, he would be on his way to Scotland.

Though it meant foregoing the reunion with his family at Dunsdale and put him to no little inconvenience, he felt he owed Cynthia Sinclair some recompense for their short-lived affair. A fortnight out of his life did not seem too heavy a penance to pay to satisfy the pangs of conscience. Still, it would give the gossipmongers something to tattle about, and cancel his strategy of the last month to allay the suspicions of the ton. A line from Scotland's bard, Robbie Burns, came to mind. "Man proposes, God disposes." Somehow it seemed appropriate.

Chapter Three

Deveryn threaded his way through the throng of customers in the White Horse's crowded lobby, and he made his exit through the main door. He delayed for a moment on the front steps, his windblown locks warmed to a lambent glow by the light from the oil lantern which hung from a bracket on the wall of the porch entrance. A couple of locals, their collars turned up against the rising wind, eyed the tall greatcoated stranger with veiled interest, and sidestepped him neatly. As they pushed into the welcoming warmth of Inverforth's only inn, their muffled greeting was carefully neutral. Before the door closed behind them, the din from the taproom wafted through to Deveryn's ears. It was Saturday night in the thriving metropolis of Inverforth, he thought with a cynical twist of his mouth, and it was evident that every able-bodied male in the indifferent parish, from farm labourer to squire, was bent on drowning his sorrows, or celebrating his good fortune, with his likeminded neighbours. God, how these Scots could drink! Not that he blamed them. Wresting a living from the land was a wretched enough business at the best of times without having the burden of Scotland's miserable climate to endure.

He stepped out of the shelter of the porch and struck out along the high street towards the blacksmith's forge. If he wasn't mistaken, there would be snow before morning. He cursed under his breath. Not for the first time since he had set out on this ill-advised journey, he wished he were in the bosom of his family at Dunsdale, and damn if he could understand the impulse that had made him forgo all the comforts and pleasures of home to escort his erstwhile mistress to this Godforsaken neck of the woods.

His eye was attracted to the faint light that illuminated one of the stained glass windows of the parish church. It was then that he recollected the reason for the sorry pass he was in. His favourite brother-in-law, the vicar, would roast him unmercifully if he, Deveryn, ever admitted that it was an attack of Conscience which had swayed him to a course of action he found distasteful in the extreme. He might have known, he told himself with a resigned shrug, that Conscience and Comfort were, in essence, incompatible.

A light sprinkling of snow began to fall, and he hunched his shoulders. In his eagerness to escape the toils of Cynthia Sinclair, he had inadvertently left his hat in the private parlour where they had earlier dined. Wild horses could not drag him back to retrieve it. Though there was not the slightest necessity for it he had determined to check on the smashed carriage wheel which had come to grief in one of the many potholes that turned the Edinburgh to Inverforth thoroughfare into a facsimile of Swiss cheese. Even if the blacksmith had forged a new rim, weather conditions made further travel impossible for the moment. It made an overnight stay at the White Horse inevitable. The thought soured his temper to a new low. He turned his collar up and cursed again. The snowflakes, like damp petals, fell with increasing vigour.

Maddie felt the shock of them as they beaded to moisture on her lashes. She checked Banshee with a slight touch on the reins and she turned her face upwards to test the density of the cold blast of icy crystals. She hesitated. Apart from the occasional light from a cotter's snug cottage hugging the rise, the darkness hung about her like damp cotton wool. The muted roar of the breakers as they surged against the shoreline warned her that an easterly wind would soon whip itself into a fine fury.

If the threatening storm broke, Maddie did not doubt that Aunt Nell would talk herself into a royal dither, quite unnecessarily, when she discovered that her niece was not behind Drumoak's stout stone walls. In normal circumstances, Maddie would have turned Banshee's head and made for home.

She had no wish to occasion her aunt the slightest anxiety on her behalf. But Maddie was beside herself. Duncan had given her the intelligence before dinner that Malcolm had arrived home from the university in St. Andrew's and was, even now, at the manse on the other side of the village. His intention was to wait upon her on the morrow. But Maddie could not wait.

In the week since her father's funeral, she had bottled her emotions—and such emotions—dark, turbulent passions which were strange to her, and frightening in their intensity, all the more so because she hid them from the world behind a tranquil facade. With Malcolm, there was never any need of pretence. He was never shocked by the secrets she revealed, never put out by any of her perplexing questions, and there had been many of those in the last years as she had grown to womanhood. His calm good sense was as dependable as the Bank of Scotland. Even before her mother's demise, it was always to Malcolm she had turned. He was only a little older than she, but his knowledge and experience of the world far surpassed hers.

"Oh Malcolm," she sobbed on a shaky breath. She drew up the cowl of her mantle to protect her face and she dug her heels in, urging the mare forward in the direction of the sand dunes. Banshee snickered then threw back her head and howled like one of the creatures of the night she was named for, and she stretched out her long smooth limbs to eat up the three miles between Drumoak and Inverforth.

If they followed the shoreline of the River Forth's broad inland estuary, even in a snowstorm, it was highly unlikely that any harm would befall them. Maddie salved her conscience with the thought that Janet and Duncan between them would be able to convince Aunt Nell that she stood in no danger, since horse and rider were used to traversing every hill and hollow around Drumoak even in the most inclement weather.

As she came round the corner of Inverforth's squat, red brick tollbooth at a slow canter, Maddie caught sight of him. He was a hundred yards ahead of her, on the main thoroughfare, almost level with the iron gate that gave entrance to the parish church. As he passed the lighted window of one of the cotter's houses, his fair hair seemed to burn like the halo of one of the

45

angels she had once seen in a Rembrandt painting. She almost threw herself off Banshee's back and went stumbling after him.

"Malcolm!" The wind tore the cry from her throat. She clutched her cloak more closely to her and ran after him. "Malcolm!" she called again, this time more desperately.

Deveryn heard the muffled sound and turned on his heel. The lantern over the wrought iron gate which gave onto the church yard was behind him, but its light did wonderful things to the face of the young woman who stood trying to catch her breath only an arm's length away.

It was only a trick of the light, only a trick of the light, his brain told him dispassionately, that gave her such an otherworldly appearance; only a trick of the light that turned her dark eyes to pools of mystery with the look of desperation he had sometimes seen in a deer just before the hunters closed in for the kill. Her cheeks were wet with tears, or snow, he could not say which, and her lips, so soft and vulnerable, trembled with the effort to regulate her breathing. It was only a trick of the light, his brain told him, but his heart constricted uncomfortably in his chest.

She straightened and made a pathetic attempt at a smile, then she walked straight into his arms as if she belonged there.

"Malcolm, oh Malcolm, I have needed you so," she said softly into his throat, and Deveryn thought that Malcolm, whoever he was, must be the luckiest man in Christendom.

Her head lay against his chest, the snood of her cloak just brushing his chin. Her arms went round his waist. For a moment, he did not know what to do with his hands. He rested them lightly on her shoulders. To hold her thus seemed like the most natural thing in the world.

With something close to reverence he moved his hands, sliding them slowly from her shoulders, testing every small bone in her straight spine, leisurely stroking the hollows of her waist, moulding the soft flare of her hips.

She tipped her head back and the snood of her warm, woollen cloak fell to her shoulders, uncovering her hair. In the dim light of the lantern, it had the rich tones of copper; in the light of day, he thought, it would brighten to warm sherry. He itched to bury his fingers in the fiery depths of those silken tresses.

"Kiss me, Malcolm, and make everything better. Just like

when we were children."

He wondered how Malcolm would kiss her, but it never occurred to him to enlighten her about his identity. He brought his lips to within an inch of hers and he could feel her breath, sweet and warm, mingling with his own. He held back, forcing her to take the initiative.

Her lips were cool and dry, and quite without passion, their touch as light as the snowflakes which melted against the heat of his skin. From a woman who was no relation to him, it was the most chaste kiss Deveryn had ever received in his life. At the first touch of her lips, his senses came fully alive. As that cool, dispassionate kiss lingered, he felt the heat of it, scorching, racing like liquid fire from his lips to his loins.

In the space of a single heartbeat, Deveryn lost his bearings. He was no longer aware that he was in the middle of the high street of some obscure hamlet with a turbulent breeze whipping at his coat and forcing wet snow down his collar. Cynthia was forgotten, as was his purpose in being abroad on such a wild night, and if such things had occurred to him, he would have consigned them all to perdition. In that moment, the only reality he was conscious of, wanted to be conscious of, was the rightness of the small warm body which was pressed so closely to his own. It was as if every fibre of his being, every solitude in his soul, instantly recognized the woman and responded to her in welcome. The cynical turn of his mind, which was almost second nature to him, might never have existed, so little impact did it make on the wave of wonder that swept through him.

"Open your mouth," he whispered, and she obeyed him without question.

The tip of his tongue, slow and persuasive, traced the outline of those inviting lips, then he gently moulded them to his own. He felt her stiffen slightly, but she made no move to draw away, and it registered in his mind that her confidence in Malcolm was something quite out of the ordinary.

He could taste the innocence on her tongue. That she was so totally ignorant of a man's passion and the ways of love brought a surge of tenderness and—he could scarcely credit it in himself—a fierce possessiveness that he recognized as primitive in origin. It was a new experience for Deveryn. As

47

the kiss continued, he savoured the novelty of emotions he had scarcely believed existed.

When he felt her trembling in his arms, he slowly brought the kiss to an end. That he should let her simply walk away, out of his life forever, was unthinkable.

"Malcolm?" she queried, and he heard the confusion behind the word.

"Come." He gave her no chance to deny him. One arm slid around her shoulders and he turned her head into his chest to protect her from the elements. She followed his lead blindly, and he half-dragged her at a run through the iron gate and up the stone flags to the great door of the church. He pushed it open and they entered the narthex. The lights from the sanctuary scarcely penetrated to their lair. There wasn't a soul in sight. It suited Deveryn's purpose admirably.

He turned her in his arms and said simply, "Kiss me again."

"Malcolm, no." He could tell that she didn't want to hurt Malcolm's feelings. The darkness hid his smile.

His hands tangled in her hair and he brought her face up. "Kiss me," he repeated softly, with a little more force behind the words.

Her hands spread out against his chest, but she allowed him to capture her lips just the same. When she melted into him, he released her and cupped her head with both hands, kissing her quickly and urgently.

He let out a shaky breath, and he laughed. "Damn if China doesn't exist after all! Who would have believed it?"

Her crop caught him a glancing blow across the chest. One backward step and she was out of his arms.

"You're not Malcolm." She spoke without heat, but he knew that her eyes were flashing fire.

He hoped she would not try to use the crop on him again, because then he would have to take it away from her, and the last thing he wanted to do was hurt her. "I never said I was."

"You're English!" Her tone was faintly accusing.

"How can you tell? Is my accent so noticeable?" He knew that it was.

His calm, good humour seemed to infuriate her.

"No. It's your quaint way of turning the truth on its head to justify your actions. I believe it's a talent that all the English

48

are born with."

The jibe made no impression on him. "You're English too. Though perhaps I do detect a certain softening of the vowels, now that you mention it. It's very attractive."

"Silver tongued, too. That doesn't surprise me." She paced toward the sanctuary, then swiftly turned on her heel. "Please let me pass. I must find Malcolm."

His back was to the door. He folded his arms across his chest and braced one shoulder against it. "I can't let you go like this. If I frightened you, I'm sorry."

"You didn't frighten me," she answered with forced calm. "Now may I go?"

At this last, he cocked one eyebrow. "Aren't you just a little bit intrigued by the man you shared that kiss with? And *such* a kiss, let me tell you. You felt it too, and don't try to tell me otherwise."

Her pacing slowed, and she looked at him as if seeing him clearly for the first time. Even in that shadowy interior, the creature's beauty and grace were undeniable. The semi-darkness should have robbed his blond locks of some of their lustre, but the faint rays of the candlelight penetrating from the sanctuary touched his shapely head in such a way that his hair, windblown and tousled, seemed to glow with a life of its own. It intensified her first impression that this was no mortal man but an angel. Only the sensual slant to his mouth detracted from the original impression. A carnal angel, she thought with a start, and her breathing slowed, became shallower.

"Why did you kiss me?" She scarcely recognized the hoarse voice as her own.

"What a singularly stupid thing to ask!" Though she had turned her head so that her face was in shadow, he knew that she was frowning.

"Malcolm will tell me," she answered at length, and Deveryn burst out laughing.

"Does Malcolm know everything?"

"By no means." He could tell that a ghost of a smile was on her lips. "But he understands the things that have to do with the sexes."

He was surprised at his own curt words. "And who might

Malcolm be?"

"A friend. A neighbour. I've known him for ages."

"He can't help you. You're frowning again."

"How can you tell? It's so dark in here."

In one swift push, he was off the door and had caught her by the wrist. "Let's go into the sanctuary where there's some light. No don't pull away from me. Really, I won't hurt you."

Without waiting for her reply, he propelled her through the archway and forcibly pushed her into the back pew. She moved over with only a slight show of reluctance when he made to sit beside her.

His lips twitched when he saw her eyes, frankly curious, move slowly over him. "That's better," he said. "Now we can see each other. Do I meet with your approval?"

Hectic colour heated her cheekbones, but she did not drop her eyes from his. Her chin came up and she said in a creditably cool voice, "You're not a bit like Malcolm. Only the colour of your hair is similar, though by no means the same. I don't see how I could have made such an error. You are broader and taller, and . . . ," her lips turned up slightly at the corners, "quite old."

"Oh, I'm 'quite old', am I?" he asked in an amused tone. "I'll be thirty on my birthday. How old are you?"

"Nineteen. But only just. Why?"

"That means a guardian. But we'll get to that later. What's your name?"

For the first time the girl's expression became guarded. "I'm not at liberty to say."

"Ah!" he said knowingly. "You've been well-schooled. But not well enough, or you wouldn't be here now, alone and with a total stranger. We shall discuss that later also. Tell me, have you ever been to Oxfordshire?"

"No. Why?"

"We'll be spending a great deal of our time there. How about London?" He was enjoying himself enormously.

"Yes. But I didn't care for it. Do you always speak in riddles?"

"Forgive me. Am I going too fast for you? I can't seem to help myself. Wouldn't you like to kiss me again?"

"What? Here? In God's house?" She looked around furtively.

"Why not? Doesn't God approve of kissing?"

"I don't know. I've never thought about it. I'll have to ask . . ."

"Don't say it! You'll never have to ask Malcolm about anything again. You'll come to me if you want to know anything. Especially," one long finger tilted her chin up, "especially," he repeated softly, "if it concerns what transpires between the sexes. No, don't be frightened." His hand, warm and reassuring, caressed the nape of her neck. "What are you thinking?"

He thought he detected a glint of amusement in the depths of her eyes. But he might have been mistaken.

"What I think," she answered in clipped accents, "is that one kiss has addled your brains."

"Two kisses," he corrected. "And that's only part of the story. Wouldn't you like to know what's happened to the rest of my anatomy? Ah, I think I see a blush coming. Does that mean that Malcolm has been before me again? Tell me, does he stand in the role of a brother to you?"

She gave his question some thought. "Possibly. How can I say? I've never had any brothers or sisters. He's my closest friend."

"You're not betrothed to him by any chance, are you?"

"No. Why?"

"Breaking a betrothal is a messy business. I should probably have to call him out."

She stifled a giggle. "Do you always talk this way to strange ladies?"

His bark of laughter was as immediate as it was spontaneous. The girl hushed him furiously, and that made him laugh all the harder.

"Have you ever been to Almack's Assembly Rooms?" he asked at length when the bout of laughter had subsided.

"No. Though I've heard of it, *ad nauseam.*"

"If you had, then you'd know that it's not *comme il faut* for the sexes to have any sort of converse that couldn't be broadcast by the town crier. But to answer your question, no, I

51

have never before in my life talked to any female, with the possible exception of my mother and sisters, so openly and frankly, whether highborn or lowborn, not even to the occasional lightskirt I've had in my keeping."

She blinked rapidly, and Deveryn cocked his head, his look speculative.

"Don't tell me! I believe, yes I do believe, that I've been before Malcolm at last."

"What's a lightskirt?" She asked seriously.

He answered in the same serious vein. "A woman who gives a man sexual favours for money."

"Oh!" she said, and fell silent.

He possessed himself of one of her hands and gently nipped it between his teeth. "I can tell that you can hardly wait to run off to Malcolm to explore this subject of lightskirts. What is it you wish to know?"

When she remained obstinately silent he said in a matter-of-fact tone, "Come. I'm perfectly capable of answering any of your questions. Try me."

"I was merely wondering," she said stiffly, "if Malcolm ever had a lightskirt in his keeping. If you can answer *that*, you must be a clairvoyant."

He smiled. "How old is Malcolm?"

"Two and twenty."

"Then the answer is yes."

"You can't know that!" Her indignation was very evident.

"Not absolutely of course, but it's more than likely."

"Why is it?"

Because, my little ignoramus, it's almost *de rigueur* for any young buck to have dealings with the muslin company, else how can he prove to his friends that he is a red-blooded male? Besides," he added with amused tolerance, "the practice has its compensations."

"Logic isn't your forte, is it?" she intoned at her most haughty. "But I won't argue the point with you. I really can't stay longer. You must let me pass."

"Don't you want to know if I have a lightskirt in *my* keeping?"

"Not particularly."

"I shall tell you anyway. As it happens I'm quite unencumbered at the moment, or rather, I shall be when my business in this neck of the woods is concluded. Does that reassure you?"

"Talking to you," she said slowly and very deliberately, "is like trying to find one's way out of a maze. Thank you for the lessons. I'm sure Malcolm will be able to clear up any misunderstandings."

She rose swiftly to her feet and made to push past him. It took very little effort to tumble her into his lap. His hands slid beneath her mantle and came to rest under her arms, just brushing the swell of her breasts. He ignored her sharp intake of breath.

"What a slowtop you are," he murmured, and his lips, warm and open, lightly traced the line of her jaw. "Haven't you been listening to a word I've said?"

She held herself stiffly, but she did not struggle to free herself from his embrace, and Deveryn said very softly into her mouth, "You belong to me. How am I to convince you of that fact?"

"With great difficulty," she answered, and he could have sworn that inwardly she was laughing at him, though her expression remained grave.

"What an unromantic girl you are!"

"I've never pretended otherwise."

"Don't you believe in love at first sight?"

"Balderdash!" But he could see the mischief lurking in the depths of her eyes.

His smile was self-deprecating. "It does happen, you know." She looked to be unconvinced and he said with a slight show of impatience, "I don't suppose you're familiar with Aristophanes's theory on love?" Without waiting for her answer he went on, "He believes that lovers are born joined but that the gods separate them at birth and they wander the earth, lost and lonely, till they find each other again. Only a few fortunate ones ever do. The unlucky ones learn to make do with second best—again and again and again."

"That's sheer myth," she retorted.

"So I believed. Until tonight. Now I'm not so sure." His tongue lightly flicked her ear. "Wouldn't you like to test the truth of Aristophanes's theory?" he coaxed.

"How?" Her voice was barely audible.

"Open your mouth to me and I'll prove that we are two halves who have found each other."

Her lips parted slightly and Deveryn, like a connoisseur savouring the bouquet of a rare vintage wine, brought his lips to hers and inhaled deeply. He wrinkled his nose. "You smell like . . . what is that scent? I can't quite place it?"

"Apples," she answered, and he thought he heard a challenge in her voice.

"Of course," he replied blandly. "I should have known that no ordinary scent would do for you. Tell me, do you drink it or sprinkle it?"

She smiled at this last, and said in a more natural tone, "Actually, I store it, or Janet does—the apples from our orchard, I mean. The clothes press in my chamber is the driest place in the house. Janet wraps the apples in paper and lays them down for the winter."

He chuckled. "Do you know what an extraordinary girl you are?"

It was her turn to laugh. "I like your choice of words. 'Extraordinary' has a nice ring to it. I'm used to thinking of myself as, well, slightly eccentric. Janet would tell you that I was *fey*."

"You don't have to explain what she means. I think I knew it from the moment you walked into my arms. We have such a lot to learn about each other. Still, we have a whole lifetime ahead of us to make our discoveries."

Her jaw dropped.

"That's better," he breathed and his mouth, gentle yet unyielding, closed over hers. Deliberately, by slow degrees, he patiently fed the first small flame of her awakening desire. Even so, the sudden flare of his own passion surprised him. He checked it ruthlessly, but not before he had betrayed himself.

She made a weak attempt to evade his embrace, but he would not permit it. One hand moved to her nape and stilled her head. The other slipped the front fastenings of her cloak, easing it back so that only the thin fabric of his shirt and her gown was between the heat of their skin. He ignored her soft gasp of protest, and eased her breasts against the hard wall of his chest.

"I want to feel your heart beating against mine," he soothed, and his lips followed the path of his gently caressing fingers from her eyes to her chin. His thumb slid under the collar of her frock. "Your pulse is throbbing madly in the hollow of your throat," he murmured. He loosened the top buttons of her gown and he opened the bodice. "Feel your pulse," and he captured her fingers and pressed them against her throat. His lips followed and he brushed them over the exposed skin. Her head fell back on his shoulder. He could feel her body shudder as her breath caught in her throat. Every pore in his own body told him that he could easily bring her to the point of surrender. His own checked passion exploded through him.

One hand closed over a softly heaving breast, moulding it with voluptuous pleasure. Her feeble movement to drag his hand away was easily parried. He wondered at the primitive drive throbbing at every pulse in his body, urging him relentlessly to make this woman his. His need to convince her that he was fated to be her mate surprised him as much as it delighted him. He had never thought to commit himself so totally to any woman. In spite of a string of past mistresses and so called "love" affairs, he felt, in that moment, that he was less knowledgeable of the mysteries of love as the girl in his arms. He longed for her to initiate him into them.

When his head came up to take her lips again, he deliberately allowed her to taste the blatant urgency of his hunger. When she began to return his kiss with equal ardour, he forced himself to drag his lips away.

For a long moment he held her close as he fought for control. It would be only too easy to carry her off to some private place and complete what he had begun. The girl was in no condition to deny him anything. But that would defeat the purpose of the exercise. He wished only to demonstrate, though irrefutably, that by some happy accident of fate they had been permitted to find each other—on such a night, and in Inverforth, of all places!

But the temptation to make love to her in earnest, to forget that there was some point to the exercise, was almost irresistible. Deveryn resisted, not without some reluctance, drawing on reserves of control he had not needed in an age.

"I've been waiting for you all my life, I think," he said against her hair. "You can argue against my logic till you're blue in the face. I knew from the moment you stepped into my arms that I would never let you go." His laugh was faintly self mocking: "Now do you understand?"

Her answer was to hide her face against his shoulder. It did not displease him. He smoothed her tumbled curls and cradled her as if she had been a child. It brought to mind the rush of tenderness he had experienced when he had first looked into her sad eyes.

"Now that that little matter is settled between us, my love, will you not tell me what brought you out to seek Malcolm on a wild night like this? When I first saw you, you looked so . . . forlorn."

Her head tilted back, and her eyes, dark and liquid, gazed unblinkingly into his. In their depths he saw confusion, but also a childlike trust that brought a jolt of feeling which seemed to lodge itself in his throat. His arms tightened about her, and he wondered how he could bear to give her up to her guardians till he could claim her for his own. "Tell me," he coaxed softly.

She spoke haltingly. "Have you ever hated someone you don't even know?"

"I don't believe so. Hatred is such a powerful emotion. Are you sure that you don't simply dislike this person?" He feathered her damp hair with his fingers.

"Oh no. I know what it is to dislike someone. This is much stronger. It hurts."

She was so patently honest and innocent. He shifted her in his arms till she lay curled snugly against his chest. "Tell me about it," he murmured in the voice he was used to employ to his young nieces when their safe world turned suddenly ugly and they had run to him for comfort.

"I know it's wrong to seek revenge. But it's all I can seem to think of."

He wisely held his own counsel and waited for her to continue.

"Everyone has a weakness. Did you know that?" she queried softly. "I intend to discover the weaknesses of my enemies and exploit them ruthlessly."

Though her words were fierce, she reminded him more of an angry kitten than an avenging fury. He kept his lips grave, but he wondered what tempest in a teacup had provoked her to such a passion, and who, in her small provincial circles, could possibly be cast in the mould of an enemy.

"Did someone . . . hurt you badly?" he asked gently, and his thumb lightly teased the lobe of her petal-soft ear.

"Oh no!" she answered, nestling closer. "I'm thick skinned. I don't bruise easily. Really."

Her tone was wistful, with a trace of sadness, and it came to him that her denial was nothing more than bravado, a fragile pride to cover pain. It was her defense, he was sure, against a world that had dealt with her cruelly in the past.

Though he wished to say so much more, he merely said in a soft undertone, "Tell me about it, from the beginning."

The words trembled on her lips, but before she could utter them, the door behind them ground out a warning. It was pushed open and soft footfalls entered behind the cold draft.

"Yer lordship, yer lordship, are ye here?"

Deveryn recognized the voice of the blacksmith's boy. "Damn!" he said under his breath, and quickly detached Maddie from his arms. "Don't move from this spot till I return. No need to give the locals a sight of you and set their tongues to wagging. I'll be back directly."

As his long strides carried him toward the narthex, the blacksmith's boy appeared in the archway.

"Lord Deveryn! Mistress Serle said she thought she saw ye come into the kirk. My master sent me to find ye."

"Out boy! You can give me your message outside!" His harsh tone brooked no argument, and the boy slunk away. Deveryn waited till the door had closed behind him.

He spoke over his shoulder. "This won't take long. The blacksmith is repairing the wheel of my carriage. If you're a good girl, I'll take you home in style."

"Deveryn? Is that your name?"

He turned to face her. She was standing in deep shadow in the centre of the aisle.

"No. It's my title. Jason Verney, the Viscount Deveryn, at your service," and he inclined his head slightly, then pivoted on his heel and made to follow the boy out of the church.

"No! It can't be! *You* cannot be Deveryn!"

Again he turned. "Oh, oh! Has my reputation preceded me?" His voice gentled. "Don't let it trouble you. I swear, from

57

this moment on, I'll be a reformed character."

"Wait!" She was almost pleading. "It cannot be so uncommon a name, surely?"

"Sweetheart, we shall talk of this later. But you must know that peers of the realm, with few exceptions, rarely share the same title. I shan't be more than a minute or two."

He found the blacksmith's lad shivering on the doorstep. The youngster brought the intelligence that his lordship's coach was fit for the road. Deveryn, slightly shamed by his former rough tone, pressed a shilling into the astonished boy's palm and told him to convey his thanks to his master.

It took only a moment to retrace his steps to where he had left the girl. She was gone. On the stone floor, beside the pew where he had left her, was her leather riding crop. He made the connection immediately. He sprinted out of the building and down the stone flagged path. As he pushed through the iron gate, he heard a shrill whistle from one end of the street and her mount's answering whinny from the opposite direction. As the horse brushed past him, he made a grab for the bridle, but missed it by inches.

To give chase was undignified and pointless. She had the foresight to put as much distance as possible between them. As her mount reached her, she scrambled on its back and checked its pace with a firm hand on the reins. He watched, motionless, as she brought the restive beast round to face him, the wind whipping about the folds of her cloak, the snood shielding her from his gaze. He had the urge to call out, to say something that would compel her to return, but he knew that it would be useless. She had set her mind against him. As she wheeled her horse, and shot forward into the shadows, the thought consoled him that it would be no great labour to discover her identity. Nevertheless, that she had not committed herself to him without reservation was a bitter pill to swallow. For a moment there, he had been so sure of her. He did not believe, however, that once he found her, she would hold out long against him. Her guardians, he thought without conceit, would be falling over him to secure the match. He was the Viscount Deveryn, independently wealthy, and heir to a great fortune and title of some note. There were no obstacles that he could foresee to obtaining his heart's desire.

58

Chapter Four

Maddie could never afterwards remember that wild ride home between Inverforth and Drumoak. Fortunately, her mount needed little direction, for Banshee was used to carrying her mistress on this favourite haunt along the southern shore of the Forth estuary. Maddie was scarcely conscious of the muffled drum of Banshee's swift hoofbeats on the wet sand, nor the ferocious spray from the breakers which saturated her heavy mantle, drenching her to the skin. As Drumoak's welcoming lights came into view, she automatically urged her mount over the sand dunes to the path which traversed the east pasture, her mind still burning with the name of the man whom she had encountered outside the church. Deveryn! Her thoughts chased themselves in wanton confusion as impressions of his conversation, his confident assumptions and his persuasive lovemaking pressed in upon her. Deveryn—the name she hated above all others!

What she said to Janet and her aunt as they divested her of her wet things, remained a mystery to her. She knew that she conducted herself with little semblance of composure and that she had no satisfactory explanation to offer for the state she was in. But the ladies clucked over her like two mother hens and she was put to bed with one of Janet's potent hot-toddies. The whisky burned her throat, but it had the desired effect of bringing her out of shock. As her teeth stopped chattering and she returned the empty glass to Janet, whose watchful eyes were shaded with anxiety, it occurred to Maddie from all the remarks she heard that the ladies had devined that she was suffering from delayed shock at her father's sudden demise. It suited her to let them think so.

As Aunt Nell hovered around the bed making soothing noises, Maddie heard Janet's rough voice say in warning, "Dinna *fash* yerself, Mistress Spencer. The lass will be the better for letting her guard down. It disna do to bottle yer feelings the way she has done this last fortnight."

Janet then turned her full attention upon her young mistress. "There, there, my wee lamb. Old Janet is here to look after ye. Hush now and go to sleep. Things will look better in the morning."

Maddie's eyes obediently closed and the last thing she remembered before sleep overtook her was Janet's hushed tones and work-roughened hand as it smoothed back the damp tendrils of hair from her brow.

It was still dark outside when she wakened. On the mantel, a candle was burning low and there was a feeble glow in the grate. The faint but pleasant aroma of the slow burning peat fire tickled her nostrils. She tensed in expectation of that first wave of grief which habitually assailed her every morning since her father's tragic death. It came, but muted, and overlaid with a confusion of emotions which were as unfamiliar to her as they were discomposing. Deveryn! The word seemed to drum in her brain.

She threw back the covers of the tester bed and stalked to the clothes press in search of her warm dressing gown. It was on its usual hook, just inside the press door. She wriggled into its warm folds and tied it snugly around her waist. Apples, she thought, and went still.

She brought up one arm and buried her nose in the soft sleeve of her dressing gown. She inhaled deeply. Apples, she thought again, and let out a slow breath. Deveryn! Oh Deveryn! Memory flooded her and she was overcome with a wave of longing.

She walked to the long sash window and looked out. It was still snowing. She wondered where he was and what had brought him into Lothian. Very tentatively, she began to examine each separate impression the man had made upon her, from the first moment she had caught sight of his hair shining like an angel's halo in the lamplight, to that last look of appeal he had thrown at her the second before she had dug her heels into Banshee's flanks and fled from him.

She could not believe that the man who had held her so comfortingly in his arms and who had brought her body and heart alive with that sweet unfamiliar ache could be the man she was sworn to hate. The man who had treated her father so shamelessly was worse than a felon. One day, she swore, she would be revenged on him. But he could not be *her* Deveryn. Every feeling revolted against such a conclusion. It had been the first shock on hearing that hateful name which had thrown her into such a panic.

She sat down at her dressing table and absently began to run a comb through her hair. Was she half in love with this Deveryn? She thought it very possible and she smiled to herself. He was like no other man she had ever known, but then, for a girl of nineteen years, she was singularly lacking in male acquaintances. Not that it mattered. If she had been acquainted with a thousand eligible young gentlemen, she would have instantly recognized that Deveryn was special to her. Oh no, she told herself again with increasing confidence, *her* Deveryn could not possibly be the man who had been responsible for turning Donald Sinclair into a broken shell of a man.

She rose to her feet and began to stride about the room in some impatience. Her Deveryn was gentle, compassionate, amusing, clever, bold—very bold, she amended, and smiled again to herself—the epitome of everything that was best in the English character. Her heart told her so. He was an English gentleman and there was no higher enconium a man could aspire to.

A soft laugh fell from her lips and she turned back to her dressing table. She rummaged in the top drawer and pulled out a folded lace handkerchief. She shook it out, and three small trinkets fell into her open palm. Reverently, she laid the silver charms in a row on the highly polished surface of the dressing table—a baby, a ring, and an angel. She picked up the angel and stared at it for a long moment. She thought that a little polish would soon rout the tarnish.

He had intimated that his reputation was slightly tarnished. Much she cared! She would forgive him a hundred lightskirts—

a thousand, if necessary. If only . . . if only . . .

She damned the impulse that had goaded her to run away from him. If only she had waited to hear his explanation! Deveryn! Surely there must be others of that name! She knew of a river Deveryn though she could not remember if it was north or south of the border.

Outside, the sky was beginning to lighten, but not so that it made an appreciable difference to the interior of Maddie's chamber. She took a taper from the mantel, lit it from the lone candle which was beginning to sputter in its pewter sprocket, and lit several more candles around the room. Sleep was the furthest thing from her mind.

Deveryn, she thought again, and wondered how she should contain her impatience till she could go to him. Though she had no notion of where he was to be found, she was confident that Malcolm would know where to begin to look for the viscount. She determined to ask for his help when she saw him at the church service in a few hours time. Perhaps Deveryn would be there. She looked at the clock on the mantel. Only four hours to wait. She used the great iron tongs to position a fresh block of peat on the dying embers of the fire, and then she settled herself in the faded damask chair slightly to one side of the large stone hearth. Moment by moment she began to relive every minute of the encounter which, she was sure, had changed her forever.

As it turned out, Maddie's hopes for meeting up with Deveryn at the church service were to be dashed. The fall of snow during the night made the roads treacherous, and Aunt Nell decided not to chance the carriage on the three mile trek, especially as Sam, Drumoak's lone shepherd, had predicted more snow to follow. Morning prayers were held in the front parlour with the servants also in attendance. Maddie longed to saddle Banshee and go tearing off to Inverforth, but she knew better than to suggest such a thing. This was the Sabbath, and in Scotland, it was observed to the letter. Still, she was grateful that modes at Drumoak were less rigid than at some other households she could name. She had the freedom to read any book she cared to choose. In some staunchly Presbyterian families, only the Bible, the Holy Bible, was considered appropriate reading for the Sabbath. But time hung heavily on her hands. Maddie could not settle to anything. After lunch, she retired to her chamber to work on her translation of *Medea*. She managed only a few lines before sleep claimed her.

In the middle of the afternoon, she was wakened by Janet's urgent voice calling her by name. Maddie quickly smoothed her dress and ran a comb through her unruly crop of curls and swiftly left her chamber. She was halfway down the long staircase, when the front door was opened by Duncan, and a tall greatcoated stranger stepped inside the vestibule in a flurry of snow. He removed his curly brimmed beaver, and ran a hand through a mane of dishevelled blond hair. Deveryn! Maddie's steps slowed and faltered to a halt. She steadied herself with one hand on the smooth oak handrail. Deveryn looked up and caught sight of her. She heard the hiss of his breath as he expelled it softly.

"You," he breathed, and came toward her.

Joy leaped to her throat, and she had to suppress the urge to fling herself down the last few steps and into his arms. A moment later, she was glad that she had not obeyed that first, rash impulse. A movement caught her eye. Her gaze shifted and she watched with something close to disbelief as Cynthia Sinclair made her entrance. In her form fitting, black redingote trimmed with black Russian sable, Cynthia's dark beauty was riveting.

Maddie stumbled and would have fallen if her hand had not tightened instinctively around the handrail. She swayed, but forced her knees to straighten and hold her. Fortunately, only Deveryn was aware of the slight movement, for the hall seemed suddenly to be thronged with busy people who had come from different parts of the house to help with the boxes or greet the visitors.

Maddie heard Deveryn's voice, low and urgent, close to her ear. "What is it? What's wrong?"

From reserves of pride she was scarcely aware she possessed, she dredged up a cool intimidating smile. "I beg your pardon. So clumsy," she murmured and brushed past him, her hand outstretched to greet her late father's wife.

"Cynthia," she managed, "it's been such a long time," and she touched her cold lips to the proffered cheek.

The introductions were soon made and the party removed to

the front parlour where a blazing coal fire had been kindled. Though Maddie's mind was reeling from the shock of discovering Deveryn's connection to her stepmother, she managed to remain neutrally polite. But it cost her something. She knew that she was unnaturally quiet and was aware of her aunt's anxious scrutiny. She longed to run away and lick her wounds in private like some creature of the wild, but pride kept her riveted to her place.

It took a few minutes to make sense of what was being said around her. Cynthia asked some questions about the funeral which Miss Spencer took it upon herself to answer. There was a pause, and Maddie heard Deveryn's cultured English accent as he explained his presence at Drumoak. He passed himself off as an acquaintance of the Sinclairs in London, and implied that he had been on the lookout for a hunting lodge in Scotland when word of the tragedy to Donald Sinclair had come to him. To accompany the bereaved widow to her destination seemed little enough to do in the circumstances, so he averred, especially when he himself was just about to set out for Edinburgh. His glib explanation was accepted at face value, though Maddie could not suppress the slight curl of her lip.

"Please accept my condolences on your father's death, Miss Sinclair," Deveryn intoned in a quiet aside to Maddie.

She heard her own voice calmly return some indifferent commonplace, and marvelled at her composure. It was, she decided, like playing a character in one of the school plays at Miss Maitland's. The thought revolved in her mind. When she finally brought her eyes up to look directly at Deveryn, she had herself well in hand.

"Perhaps you would care for some tea?" She was careful to include Cynthia in the question.

"Or perhaps something stronger," Cynthia responded pointedly. "Sherry for myself, and brandy for Lord Deveryn?" She turned to the viscount. "Donald always kept a fine cellar of your favourite cognac. And I remember your habit of having one drink before dinner. Indulge yourself while you may. There's not much at Drumoak to excite the palette of a connoisseur. You'll find our plain country fare a far cry from what you are accustomed to."

Deveryn's eyes flicked an apology at Maddie, though he

noted that it was Miss Spencer whose expression was patently affronted. "Thank you, but tea will be fine," he drawled easily. "And truth to tell, I'm accustomed to plain fare at my mother's table. Besides, it's always been my policy to follow the old maxim 'When in Rome' etc. No, really, I'm looking forward to sampling your Scottish cuisine."

"Good," said Maddie dryly, nettled beyond endurance by his English condescension. "I'll inform Janet that there's no need to defer the black pudding for another evening."

"Black pudding?" queried Deveryn.

Cynthia shuddered. "I hope you're funning Maddie. It's a barbaric dish. No civilized person would deign to let it pass his lips."

"Now you've got me interested. What is it?" asked Deveryn.

"Porridge, uncooked, of course, with the entrails of an ox, minced very fine," intoned Maddie with biting exactitude, "and soaked in the blood of the animal. It's very good for one, and a relic, I suppose, from the days when we Scots were cannibals."

Maddie unconsciously rolled her tongue inside her cheek and the viscount suppressed a chortle. Cynthia's complexion, he noted, had paled to an unflattering shade of grey.

"When the Scots were cannibals?" murmured Deveryn with exaggerated politeness. "And when was that, would you say?"

"About the same time we practised human sacrifice, give a year or two," drawled Maddie, "though it was before my time, I collect. Janet could tell you more if you're interested."

"Maddie," interjected Miss Spencer in determined accents, "you were going to ring for tea?"

Maddie rose and obediently pulled the bellrope at the side of the mantel. The gesture, she knew, was wasted effort. Until her aunt had descended on Drumoak to act as chaperone to her motherless niece, no one had ever used the bellpull which every room boasted. Maddie was not even certain whether they worked or not. Certainly, no servant at Drumoak had ever been summoned by a pull on a bell, in her memory. After a moment, she excused herself and went in search of Janet.

When she returned, conversation was all of court circles. It was evident to Maddie that the viscount moved in the upper reaches of polite society. Cynthia and Aunt Nell, she noted, seemed to hang on the viscount's every word.

The conversation held no interest for Maddie, and she was glad when the tea trolley was rolled in and she could busy her hands in pouring tea and offering round Janet's butter scones and shortbread. Her glance sliced to Cynthia. The cool violet eyes were narrowed on her. It had yet to be determined who was mistress of Drumoak. For the first time Maddie wondered what provision her father had made for her in his will.

She heard her grandfather's name on Deveryn's lips and she made an effort to concentrate.

"As soon as things are settled here," intimated Miss Spencer confidingly, "Maddie and I shall remove to my father's house in London."

"That is not my intention," said Maddie sharply. She saw the look of pained surprise on her aunt's face and said in a more gentle tone, "Scotland is my home, Aunt Nell. I have no wish to leave it."

"Surely it was settled between us, Maddie?" Miss Spencer's voice coaxed. "And if your father named Grandpapa as your guardian, you may have no choice in the matter."

Maddie shook her head. "I don't think so, Aunt Nell. I'm sure Papa told me once, a long time ago, that he had named Mr. Moncrieff as my guardian."

"And how shall we find out?" asked Deveryn, concealing his interest behind a mask of politeness.

It was Miss Spencer who answered him. "The solicitor is due to come up from Edinburgh as soon as we send word that Cynthia has arrived." She turned to Cynthia. "Did Donald ever say anything to you about Maddie's guardian?"

"No. But then he wouldn't."

"I don't care who is appointed my guardian," interjected Maddie firmly. "I intend to remain right here in Scotland."

"Who is Mr. Moncrieff?" asked Deveryn.

"The minister of St. Ninian's, our parish church at Inverforth," replied Miss Spencer absently.

At the mention of the church, a faint blush stained Maddie's cheeks, but she said calmly, "I scarcely know my grandfather, but the Moncrieffs have been like family to me."

"Well, the question is academic, till the solicitor gets here," interposed Deveryn. "Don't get too attached to Scotland, Miss Sinclair. London isn't so bad, you know. And there's some very fine country within a day's drive—Oxfordshire, for instance." And he flashed Maddie a bold smile.

Maddie drew a steadying breath. The man was insufferable. She thought to depress his pretensions and turned her eyes up innocently to meet his. It was a mistake. She found herself drowning in their cerulean depths. Silent words touched her, offering warmth, comfort and a promise of things to come. Heat seemed to spread over her skin. She put up one hand to her throat. Only Deveryn noticed her distress, and though his lips remained grave, Maddie was sure that it was laughter which brightened his eyes to the colour of the sky on a clear summer's day.

Deveryn bit into a scone to hide his smile. It amazed him to think that the electricity which seemed to crackle between himself and the girl went unremarked by their companions. Cynthia, who had bored him in the past with childish displays of temper when his eyes had strayed to other women, seemed totally oblivious of his compulsive attraction for the slip of a girl who sat very much on her dignity pretending an ignorance of what he intended for her future. Guardians, indeed! As though he gave a rap for them! It was only a formality, and then the girl who had captured his heart would be under *his* protection.

Conversation shifted to Drumoak's neighbours, and though Deveryn was careful to contribute his share to the conversation, he found that he could listen with only a small portion of his attention while he unobtrusively contemplated the girl across the tea trolley.

Not a beauty according to the fashion of the day, he supposed, though there was something very arresting about that vibrant colouring. Her hair, he noted, was just as he suspected. In the light of day, the muted fire in each silky tendril kindled to a burnished copper. Across her straight nose, there marched a sprinkling of freckles, an adornment which the females of his acquaintance would regard as a positive affliction. On Maddie he thought them adorable and wondered if there were others concealed beneath the drab mourning dress. It would be his pleasure, he decided, to uncover them one by one. But it was her eyes, those intelligent and eloquent dark mirrors of her thoughts which gave the girl her real claim to beauty. Though he was sure that he had discerned a welcome in them when he had first stepped over Drumoak's threshold, he was aware that a protective veil had been drawn over them. A few moments alone with the girl, and he would soon shatter the fragile defenses she seemed intent on building against him.

It was Miss Spencer who abetted the viscount in his design. "No let up in the storm. I think we're in for a week of it. I hope, Lord Deveryn, that you don't intend to travel the roads in this unsettled weather?"

"Only the three miles to Inverforth. I think I'll hole up there till the worst of it is over."

Miss Spencer was suitably distressed. "Please, don't even consider it! Our hospitality at Drumoak may not be extravagant, but it exceeds anything you're likely to find in Inverforth." She looked to Maddie for confirmation.

"Oh quite," said Maddie, though her voice lacked conviction. "But we shan't be offended if you have pressing business elsewhere that requires your attention."

"Thank you," returned Deveryn dryly. "How could I refuse such a generous offer? To be perfectly frank, a stretch in the country is to my taste at present, and, as you say, Inverforth's inn has little to recommend it."

It took only a few moments to make the necessary arrangements, and his lordship's carriage was on its way back to the White Horse to collect his valet and baggage. Duncan accompanied the coachman since it was deemed that his escort in a stretch of road which was unfamiliar to his lordship's lackeys might prove invaluable in the treacherous conditions which prevailed. They returned within the hour by which time Maddie had already given instructions to prepare rooms for the guests and lay a fire in the grate.

The tea things were cleared away and Maddie offered to show the visitors to their respective chambers. She was loath to let Cynthia have the master bedroom—the chamber which had once belonged to her parents, but not to do so would have raised awkward questions. Deveryn's room was in the other wing of the house, as far from Cynthia's room as Maddie could contrive.

She reached the head of the staircase ahead of Deveryn and Cynthia and turned to wait till they drew level with her.

"Your room is in this wing," she said to the viscount, and took a step away from him.

"Oh, ladies first, I think," he responded with a look of determination in his eye.

Maddie tried not to show her distaste when it occurred to her that Deveryn wished to ascertain where her stepmother would be sleeping.

The same thought occurred to Cynthia and she flashed Deveryn a brilliant smile. They strolled behind Maddie. "Donald didn't put much money into this old house," she said confidingly, slightly shamed by the shabbiness of the threadbare carpets and faded wallpaper. "We were never here. There didn't seem much point to it."

Deveryn said something suitable, though he had long since drawn his own conclusions about how Donald Sinclair spent his money. Since entering Drumoak, his contempt for the man had grown apace. It made his blood boil to see the shabby environment which had been provided for the daughter whilst the wife lived in the lap of luxury.

As Cynthia stepped over the threshold of her chamber, Deveryn made her an eloquent leg. Maddie swung away to hide the contempt which she was sure was showing plainly on her face. A moment later, her wrist was grasped in a firm hold, and she was brought up short. She made a weak attempt to free herself, but Deveryn's grasp tightened. Maddie stilled.

"Sir?" she asked, and stared pointedly at the hand which was clasped so securely around her wrist.

Deveryn shook his head and a tendril of blond hair fell across his forehead. "What a complete hand you are! Cool as ice, and as prickly as a hedgehog! Who would suppose that last night, in my arms, you were as warm and affectionate as a lost puppy?" There was a smile in his voice.

Though her insides were shaking like one of Janet's bramble jellies, Maddie was very proud of her performance, and managed, in slightly affronted accents, "I beg your pardon?"

The viscount moved off along the corridor and Maddie was obliged to move with him. "Why did you run away from me last night?" he asked softly, and he halted before a portrait which hung in a particularly dark corner of the passageway. Anyone catching a glimpse of them would think they had stopped to admire the artist's work.

"I never saw you in my life before today," said Maddie in a fierce whisper.

The exaggerated sigh which fell from Deveryn's lips was overlaid with impatience. "The smell of apples," he drawled, "is strong in my nostrils."

"Oh!" said Maddie, and her face took on a wary aspect.

"And I've met Janet," he added for good measure.

"Janet?"

"You mentioned her last night."

"I don't recall . . ." she broke off and looked up at him. Her lips thinned. "Janet is not an uncommon name in this part of the world."

A slow grin spread across his face. "I should advise you to abandon that tack," he said gently. "You left me any number of clues to your identity. And I don't suppose you're suffering from an attack of amnesia. Now, shall we begin again? Why did you run away from me last night?"

Maddie's pulse soared and her throat went dry. For a fleeting moment, she was tempted to give in to the soft persuasion of that beguiling voice and unburden herself completely. The impulse died stillborn when she chanced to look up at the portrait they stood under.

It was a picture of herself as a child of six or seven years painted in far happier circumstances. She was dressed for riding and proudly sat the back of the first of a long string of ponies that her father had supplied for his equestrian daughter over the years. A wave of nostalgia swept over her.

Her mother, as she remembered, used to chide her father for spoiling her, and had complained in fun that she was beginning to feel jealous of her own daughter.

"Whom do you love best, Maddie. Papa or me?" her mother used to ask, and Maddie's solemn reply was unwavering.

"I love you both EXACTLY the same," and she had wondered at her parents' peal of laughter and her father snatching her in his arms and throwing her high in the air till she shrieked for him to stop.

The question and answer became a family ritual, and though Maddie could not then fathom what prompted her parents to repeat the question over and over, she was wise enough to know that her answer pleased them both unreasonably.

"Maddie is so loyal," her father used to say, and she would skip away thinking that she was the centre of the universe. When had she discovered, she wondered with a quick stab of pain, that she was a mere speck on an insignificant planet signifying nothing? She felt the sting of tears at the back of her throat and swallowed hard.

Her voice, when she spoke, was in the cultured neutral tones that five years of elocution lessons at Miss Maitland's Academy invariably inculcated in the pupils of that establishment. "I ran away from you because you frightened me. You would not release me when I asked you to. When the opportunity presented itself, I grasped it."

He looked at her for a long considering moment. "That's not it," he said levelly. "There's something else. You've heard my name before, haven't you? What have you heard?"

"Nothing good," she was moved to answer on a rash impulse, and she wrenched her hand from his grasp. She took a step backwards.

"I can tell you are going to try to make this hard for me," he said, and waited in vain for her to take up his challenge. "There's no need, you know. I am not the same man I was . . . oh . . . a second before I met you. Don't ask me how I know, I just do. Maddie?" he reached for her, but she jerked away. He let her go.

"I'll give you a little time to get used to the idea," he said reasonably, "but you will learn that patience is not one of my virtues."

His unshakable confidence was an insult in Maddie's eyes. "Frankly, I'm not interested in hearing about your virtues or your vices. I have more important things to occupy my thoughts."

He laughed. "Maddie, don't be frightened. Really, there's no need. I shall be as gentle a lover as you would wish me to be."

"Are you asking me to be your lightskirt?" she goaded, and his smile of affected patience rankled her all the more.

71

"You learn very quickly, don't you? I suppose I have only myself to blame for introducing you to that word." His eyes went suddenly serious. "Don't provoke me, Maddie. You'll discover that I have a ferocious temper. I hope you never see that side of my character. Really, you won't like it."

"Dinner," she intoned coldly, "is at five. You can't miss your room. It's the last door at the end of the hall." She picked up her skirts and left him with a perfect view of her straight back.

His eyes, bright with laughter, followed her as she slowly descended the long staircase with a dignity that he was certain was assumed for his benefit. When he saw that she had no intention of further acknowledging his presence, he turned on his heel and made for the door she had indicated.

It occurred to him that Maddie might have heard something of his affair with Cynthia. He hoped she had not, but the thought scarcely disturbed him. It was evident to him that Maddie was abysmally ignorant of the ways of the world. In all probability, the girl exaggerated the importance of such women in a man's life.

Perhaps she believed him fickle or unable to form a lasting attachment. The thought brought a grin flashing to his lips. Was it only the day before yesterday that he had been of the same opinion? He marvelled at the turn of events which had converted him from his cynical persuasion. Her appeal to his jaded palette mystified him as much as it amused him. Maddie was scarcely in the style of the sophisticated women of the world who had attracted him in the past. And really, he knew nothing about her, though that would be soon remedied. It was that air of vulnerability which she had unwittingly revealed on their first meeting and which she now took such pains to conceal which had ensnared him, he decided. No, that would not do. There was no explaining it. But it was frightening to think that the girl had suddenly become as necessary to him as the very air he breathed.

As his valet bustled about the room shaking out his master's fine tailored garments, hanging them in the commodious mahogany press, Deveryn stretched out full-length on top of the feather bed, his hands clasped loosely behind his head.

As was to be expected, this room was in no better case than

72

the others he had observed—scrupulously clean, and smelling of beeswax, he was willing to concede, but reinforcing that first impression of genteel poverty which had been so evident from the moment he had stepped over the threshold of the house. Maddie, he mused, would be quite overwhelmed when she discovered the estate to which she would be raised by her marriage to the Viscount Deveryn.

Chapter Five

The storm which was forecast by Sam, Drumoak's shepherd, was to last for several days. Drifts of snow whipped up by the persistent winds from the Firth of Forth made the roads impassable in places. No visitors came to call. There were no excursions to the village, no carriage rides in the countryside to relieve the long hours of tedium. Though it would be an exaggeration to say that Drumoak was completely cut off from the civilized world—Maddie always managing to exercise Banshee along the sands of the Forth Estuary—it was close enough to the truth to force the residents of the house to fall back on each other for conversation and amusement during the long winter evenings.

Maddie was at first dismayed at the prospect of entertaining the two people she most detested in the world. She did not see how she could behave naturally in the circumstances, and was certain that she would betray herself before very long. Her fears were groundless. It was Deveryn who made the forced confinement easier to bear, and where the viscount exerted himself to please, he could not fail to charm.

Though Drumoak was a house of mourning, he gave it as his opinion that there could be no harm in bringing out the cards for a quiet game of whist, or opening the piano for some music of an evening. Maddie soon discovered that Deveryn's preferences carried more weight than her own, which surprised her a little, especially with the servants, for the abstemious Scots were known to look askance at any form of frivolity and they regarded card-playing as an invention of the devil. But Deveryn had become the favourite of the hour.

This was borne in on Maddie one evening as she rose from the pianoforte after accompanying herself in a particularly haunting melody—a lament for the Scots who fell as they fought the victorious English on the bloody field of Flodden. Deveryn and Cynthia were playing a quiet game of picquet and Aunt Nell sat roasting herself at the coal fire, her knitting needles clicking furiously.

Deveryn's eyes met Maddie's with a silent question.

"I'll find Janet," she told him, "and arrange to have tea brought in."

"No need for that," he said. "Pull the bellrope."

"It doesn't work," Maddie explained.

"Nonsense! It works for me. Martin, my valet, always answers to its summons."

"English ears," said Maddie dryly, "must be different from Scottish ears."

"Are you admitting, Miss Sinclair, that English ears are better?" he asked quizzically.

"Not better, my lord. Merely boxed more regularly, I don't doubt." And she injected a touch of malice into her drawl.

His eyes laughed up at her as he stretched and uncoiled his long length from the confining chair. He moved toward Maddie with slow, feline grace. "Watch it, my girl," he said in a soft undertone. "You're outnumbered here by your English enemies three to one. And don't think I wasn't aware of the veiled insult in that last folk song you performed so charmingly. If anyone's ears are going to be boxed, I shall make certain that they are yours." He sauntered to the bellrope and jerked on it impatiently.

Maddie sank back on the piano bench and smiled to herself. The smirk was wiped from her face when Janet entered after a few minutes.

"You see?" said Deveryn quietly in her ear as he brought his teacup for her to refill. "A little perseverance is all that was necessary. A tad more English confidence is all you lack," and he grinned from ear to ear.

Maddie could not suppress her own answering grin. It died when her unwary glance caught the look of cold calculation in her stepmother's narrowed eyes. It was evident to Maddie that it would take very little to make Cynthia jealous. The woman was obviously in love with the viscount. Having reminded herself of Deveryn's connection to her stepmother, Maddie had little difficulty for the remainder of the evening in retreating behind a wall of glacial reserve.

Nevertheless, honesty compelled Maddie to admit that she had occasion to be grateful to the viscount for smoothing over several awkward moments with her stepmother when the two women came to points over the running of the household. Maddie could scarcely contain her impatience for the reading of her father's will. The uncertainty about her future was having an inevitably unsettling effect upon her. And Cynthia's confident assumption that Drumoak would pass into her hands brought Maddie's temper flashing to the surface. It was Deveryn who adroitly managed the two hostile women, to Aunt Nell's heartfelt relief.

By degrees, Maddie's painfully uncertain feelings for the viscount resolved themselves into a reluctant toleration, tempered she knew, by an admiration she could not suppress, try as she might. Under the circumstances, it seemed expedient to declare a truce until such time as Deveryn and her stepmother had quit Drumoak. Maddie was also sensible of the ancient claims of hospitality which enjoined a host to offer protection to strangers who shared his hearth. Though her ultimate design for revenge was temporarily set aside, it was by no means abandoned, so she told herself.

Such were Maddie's thoughts as she wheeled Banshee in the direction of the sand dunes on the first fine morning that she had enjoyed in several days. It was her intention to push on as far as the village if it were possible. A full sennight had elapsed since Malcolm's message had been delivered to her, and, with a thaw setting in, she was hopeful of finally making it through to the manse. But how different were her thoughts on this occasion from that other time, only seven days before, when she had been desperate to share her sorrow with the playmate of her childhood. She was conscious of a new constraint in herself which, in some vague way, had its origin in the night she had unwittingly walked into Deveryn's arms. That Malcolm had been displaced in her affections was not something Maddie was willing to acknowledge.

"Wool gathering, Miss Sinclair?"

Maddie's head came up and she slanted a glance at the rider who had silently overtaken her. Lord Deveryn, in skintight beige pantaloons and black riding jacket looked more handsome than any mere mortal had any right to, thought Maddie, and her eyes swept him from golden crown to mirror bright hessians with their dangling tassels. His mount, a massive black stallion, who looked as elegant and well-bred as his master, stamped restively as if impatient to be off. The stallion sidled closer to Maddie's mare and nuzzled her ear. Banshee's tail switched, and without warning, she pulled back her lips and nipped the huge beast on the neck. It reared up, but Deveryn brought its head down with iron control. Banshee whinnied and Maddie, her eyes bubbling with laughter, tried to suppress a giggle. She snorted.

"Like mistress, like mount, I don't doubt," said Deveryn, and he flashed Maddie a singularly charming smile. "Where are we off to this morning?"

"I," said Maddie, striving in vain to keep her lips straight, "I have it in mind to pay a morning call on the Moncrieffs." She had hoped to inject some ice into her voice, but knew that she had failed miserably. Deveryn's mount, she noted, was eyeing Banshee with covert interest, but that mischievous female had pulled back her lips in readiness to administer a biting setdown to the encroaching brute. Maddie found she could not restrain her laughter.

"Whoa, 'Thelo. Mind your manners and the lady will ignore you." Deveryn cocked a sardonic brow at Maddie. "Like master, like mount," he intoned with a suggestive smile.

"So I noticed," Maddie retorted, but for the life of her, could not keep her expression severe. She gave up the attempt. "Oh, come on, I'll race you to the causeway," and before Deveryn had time to gather his wits, she showed him her heels.

She expected him to best her, and was not well-pleased to find herself the winner of the contest. They dismounted and, finding that they could not easily traverse the wooden footbridge to the village, turned back to walk their mounts along the sands.

It was Deveryn who broke the silence which had fallen between them. "Why so glum? I thought you would be delighted to win our race."

"So I should have, if I had won it fairly. Why did you hold back?"

"To please you, though I can see I have failed in my laudable objective."

"Should I be flattered by such condescension?" asked Maddie crossly.

Deveryn laughed. "Oh Maddie. The more I learn about you, the more I . . . admire you."

"Ah," said Maddie gravely, "it were wiser if you would defer your opinion till you come to know my character better, my lord."

"Then by all means, let us rectify my ignorance. Tell me about yourself!"

"What?" She looked startled.

"I want to know all about you."

"What, for instance?" Her tone was guarded.

"Oh, I don't know. Anything will do. What was the first word you ever uttered as a child?"

"Are you serious?"

"Of course I'm serious. One can deduce a lot about a person's character from such small clues. Well?"

She gave him a glance full of mischief. "Are you sure you want to know?"

"Of course!"

"No."

"I beg your pardon?"

"No. That's the first word that ever passed my lips. My mother told me that it gave me enormous power."

"I can well believe it. It still does."

"What was the first word you ever said?" and she flashed him a quelling frown.

"After that, I don't think you'll believe me."

"What was it?" she encouraged.

"Yes!"

"'Yes' was the first word you ever said as a child?" She was genuinely amused. "You're making that up."

"Yes," he responded gravely.

"I might have known it!"

"I wonder if our children will be conventional and say the

usual 'mama' or 'papa?'"

"Don't!" she said with a note of distress.

For a moment, she was sure that he meant to take her in his arms, but he merely captured her hand and laced his fingers through hers. "What is your first memory as a child?" he asked softly.

"I . . . I don't remember!" She was acutely conscious of the warmth of his hand in hers and regretted the impulse that had made her strip her gloves from her fingers.

"Think about it—your very first memory as a child."

"I remember that my father used to throw me up in the air and catch me," she said quickly.

"Did you like it, or were you terrified?"

"Both."

He turned to face her. "Did he ever let you fall?"

"Of course not." She was angry at herself for the short breathless answer.

"Neither shall I ever let you fall. Your fears were as groundless then as they are now."

The compelling warmth in his eyes, which he made no attempt to conceal, flustered her more than she cared to admit. She hastened into speech. "What of your family? Were you born and raised in Oxfordshire?" And she moved off, though she could not shake free of his grasp. He kept pace with her.

"Yes. I am the oldest and the only son in a family of five. Only my youngest sister is at home. The others are all married and have moved away."

"Four girls? I'll wager you were spoiled rotten," she said with so much smugness that Deveryn was constrained to smile.

"Now why do you say so?"

She grinned. "It shows!"

"In what way?" he demanded, and Maddie could not be sure if the indignation in his voice was real or feigned.

"You're so sure of yourself. You think the sun rises and sets at your whim. I'll bet you were never beaten as a child! I can just see it now—you like an eastern potentate with the girls in your family waiting with baited breath for some small suggestion to fall from your lips. I'm sure you never suffered from a lack of bedsocks!" she finished cryptically. "Well, am I right?"

He laughed. "You wretched girl! Closer than comfort! But my sisters call me Jason, as I wish you would, though only in private of course till I speak with your guardian. But that last remark about bedsocks is completely mystifying. What can you mean by it?"

Maddie ignored the allusion to her guardian and stated gaily, "Ladies are always busy with their needles, and fathers and brothers are usually the recipients of their efforts, so it seems to me."

"Not in my family! My mother and sisters are strangers to the domestic arts, more's the pity. Not one of them can sew a fine seam. They're bluestockings, every one of them." He went on in an outrageous undertone. "I'll leave it to you to spoil me with handmade slippers and gloves and so on. But Maddie, no bedsocks, if you please."

She ignored this further provocation and merely observed, "It's obvious you've never lived through a Scottish winter. If you had, you'd know that bedsocks are man's greatest invention after the wheel. What's a bluestocking?"

"What? Oh, it's a term to describe clever women, like my mother and sisters. You know, those ladies who eschew silk stockings and so on because their minds are set on higher things!"

"Don't you like clever women?"

"They bore me to death—with the exception of my mother and sisters, of course," he added as an afterthought.

Maddie's expression was arrested. "How odd!" she said, and lapsed into a meditative silence. After a moment she asked tentatively, "You're not much interested in books and so on, I take it?"

"Certainly I am. But one wants something quite different in the conversation of a woman. Intelligence is necessary, of course, that goes without saying. But what man wants a steady diet of intellectual prosing?"

She could not suppress a smile. "Very few, I should imagine. It must be very difficult for you living in a household of bluestockings."

"Save your pity! I haven't lived at home in years. Besides, my sisters are mostly married and looking after their own households now. So my father has only two clever women to manage—my mother and young Sophie."

It was more the tone of his conversation than the words themselves which conveyed an impression of a close-knit family which looked with a tolerant eye upon the foibles of its individual members. Maddie could not help remembering her own lonely childhood.

"I always wanted a sister," she said wistfully.

"You'll have four of them, very soon, I promise you."

For a moment, a very fleeting moment, she surrendered to the temptation and imagined herself as part of a family such as Deveryn had described. It seemed to Maddie that she would have everything she had ever wanted in her life. She would also have Deveryn, the man who had wronged her father.

She pulled herself together and said mendaciously, "Thank you for the offer. But such clever girls as you describe would probably terrify the life out of me."

"I'll be there to protect you," he answered suavely.

"Thank you, no." A chill crept into her voice. "We were talking, as I recall, of our very first memory. I believe it's your turn."

His smile, though tender, conveyed an amused tolerance that did not endear him to Maddie. "My first memory is when my sister was born. She is two years younger than I. I shall never forget the morning my mother put her into my arms. That was the first miracle I ever experienced. The second was at Inverforth when you walked into my arms. I want another miracle, Maddie." His eyes were soft and sombre. "I long for the day when I cradle our first child."

She dragged her hand from his clasp and stood looking up at him, her bosom heaving. "No!" she exclaimed, but the picture his words conjured flashed into her mind, and she felt her womb contract painfully. "Never," she said through gritted teeth.

She saw the anger gathering in his eyes. "Why are you so stubborn?" He had her by the shoulders. "Why?" he demanded.

"You know why!"

"It's Cynthia, isn't it? You've heard something. Forget her Maddie. She means nothing to me. She never did."

She drew a deep steadying breath. "Then it's true." With

everything in her being, she wanted him to deny it.

"Cynthia," he said with an indifference that sounded callous to Maddie's ears, "and women like her have nothing to do with us. Nor will I tolerate an inquisition into my past. Don't ask for the sordid details. In this, I will not indulge you."

Though his words incensed her, she preserved an icy front and spoke with as much dignity as was in her power to command. "You are mistaken, Lord Deveryn, if you think I am interested in your past. I take leave to tell you that your future holds even less interest for me. Perhaps," she added very softly and with a suggestive lift of her brow, "my own past does not bear close scrutiny either. But neither is my past or future any of your business. Kindly remember that."

His eyes flashed with a sudden anger, but he had himself well in hand. "What a provoking girl you are! You're determined to keep me at arm's length. Pretending to an experience you lack is not the way to do it, Maddie. But there, I told you that I would give you a little time to get used to the idea of marriage to me. Shall we continue our walk?"

Maddie took refuge in silence. She held herself stiffly, her eyes staring straight ahead. The viscount, however, soon drew her out of herself by asking knowledgeable questions of the houses in the area which had been designed by the architect, John Adam, and there were many since the Adam family was Scottish. To her chagrin, Maddie found that she did most of the talking, and what was worse, became so involved in defending the merits of Georgian architecture that she forgot that she was intent in depressing the viscount's ambitions.

She gave him a quick, searching glance as they came within sight of the path leading to the east pasture. His blue eyes, so innocently expressive, stared calmly back at her, and Maddie's suspicions were confirmed.

Piqued at her own gullibility, she quickly hoisted herself onto Banshee's back and waited with a show of indifference for Deveryn to mount up. The return to Drumoak was made in silence.

The horses were soon stabled, and Deveryn followed an unusually quiet Maddie as she stalked ahead of him to the back of the house. As she laid her hand on the latch of the door that gave entrance to the back kitchen, they were both startled by a ball of black fur which came streaking round the corner of the house. The ball launched itself at Maddie's feet where it lay panting.

"Good grief! I think it's a dog," exclaimed Deveryn.

Maddie sank to her heels and embraced the shivering creature. "Kelpie!" she cried. "Kelpie! Where did you come from?" It was then that she observed that the animal at her feet, under the coat of matted hair, was painfully emaciated.

Deveryn squatted beside Maddie and gently scratched Kelpie's ears. "Easy girl, I won't hurt you," he said in a low, soothing voice, and his fingers splayed out as he probed beneath the filth infested coat of hair. The animal whimpered, but the viscount did not halt his careful perusal. There was the shimmer of tears brightening Maddie's eyes as she watched Deveryn's sure hands.

"The poor beast has taken a whipping recently," said Deveryn shortly, "but fortunately there are no bones broken. She'll be as right as a trivet with a little coddling and a week of regular meals. Still, someone has a lot to answer for."

"Will Fraser!" ejaculated Maddie. "This is his doing! I'll horsewhip him for this piece of cruelty. There, there, darling. You're home now," she crooned and tried unsuccessfully to lift the exhausted animal into her arms. After a moment, she looked up at Deveryn. He saw the appeal in her wide eyes. He looked ruefully at his immaculate coat and pantaloons and gave a resigned sigh.

"Allow me," he said, and easily performed the service for Maddie. He settled the dog comfortably in his arms and asked mildly, "Who is Will Fraser?" and followed Maddie as she pushed into the back kitchen. Janet was at a long, scrubbed trestle table chopping vegetables. Behind her, on top of the black iron grate, a pot of boiling water hissed furiously as steam escaped the loose-fitting lid. When she saw the animal in Deveryn's arms, the housekeeper threw down the chopper, and her hands splayed out against her hips.

"Ye'll no take that beastie into the house, Miss Maddie!" she said, her voice rising querulously.

"Oh Janet, it's Kelpie, and she's hurt." Maddie's face was set in mutinous lines.

Janet's arms fell to her sides and she came forward to peer at the animal. "Kelpie? It canna be!"

Deveryn pushed past the two women and deposited the shivering animal on the stone hearth. He was rewarded for his thoughtfulness by a warm tongue licking his hands. He straightened and said in a calm, deliberate tone, "I want to know what's going on. Who is Will Fraser and whose dog is this?"

"It's my dog," said Maddie quickly.

Janet shook her head and gave the viscount a speaking look.

"Janet, whose dog is it?" he asked, ignoring Maddie's impassioned declaration.

Janet could not meet Maddie's eye. "It was Maddie's dog once, afore her faither lost Kelpie to Will Fraser on the turn of a card."

"My father had no business to game away what did not belong to him!" Maddie burst out furiously. "Kelpie was mine! I trained her from a pup. Will Fraser tried to buy her from me, but I wouldn't sell her. What he couldn't get by honest means, he got by trickery!"

She brushed past Deveryn and went down on her knees at the hearth. It was obvious that Kelpie, no less than Maddie, regarded the reunion as a joyful homecoming.

"Who is Will Fraser?" Deveryn asked of Janet.

"He's the shepherd over at Cumbernauld," she answered, her troubled eyes still on the girl who was examining her pet closely. "The master was in his cups, so they say, when he met Will at the White Horse at Inverforth last summer. Kelpie was waiting for him outside the taproom door. It was a sorry business. The next morning, he tried to find Will to buy the dog back, but he and Kelpie had vanished into the hills."

Maddie's head came up. "With good reason! He knew that I would never give up my dog, especially to the likes of him."

She had risen to her feet and was busy about the kitchen opening doors and rattling crockery. Within moments, she had prepared a bowl of meal with scraps of mutton and dripping. It was obvious to Deveryn that the girl knew her way around the kitchen and he wondered idly if this was where she was to be found each afternoon when he had scoured the house for her in vain. He tried to recall how many servants he had observed and knew for a certainty that it had been no more than three.

He was aware, for the first time, of how much extra work he and Cynthia had imposed on the small household and resolved that the weight of that labour should no longer fall on Maddie's thin shoulders. His eyes followed her as she set the earthenware bowl before the ravenous dog.

She glanced at him over her shoulder. "Some shepherds train their dogs with kind words and rewards. Not Will Fraser! His dogs learn their lessons from kicks and blows. He's a sadistic master."

"But why would he go to so much trouble? Surely there are other dogs available, and much handsomer specimens, I shouldn't wonder," he said unthinkingly as he eyed the heap of scruff on the hearth.

Maddie shot Deveryn a look of withering contempt. "Handsome is as handsome does," she quoted, and her eyes insolently swept over the viscount's elegant figure. "One wants more than beauty in a work dog. A sheep dog must be intelligent, obedient, and easily trained. Kelpie is all of that. My mistake was in being gulled into letting Will Fraser put Kelpie through her paces."

"Aye, ye were showing off that day," said Janet with a sage nod of her grey head.

"I was proud of Kelpie," protested Maddie, "and it was Sam who bragged about her to Will Fraser."

A faint frown of puzzlement creased Deveryn's brow. "This matter is easily settled, surely? A guinea or two in the shepherd's pocket should smooth things over."

Maddie's hands gently stroked the matted hair of her pet. Kelpie, who had collapsed in mute contentment before the heat from the grate, began to purr remarkably like a kitten under the tender ministrations of her mistress. A smile lifted the corners of Deveryn's mouth.

"Will Fraser won't give Kelpie up for a few guineas," said Maddie. "It's not just another work dog he wants. His heart is set on winning the sheep trials next summer. Kelpie is his best hope of that ever happening. If he dares to show his face here," she went on in sudden heat, "I shall take my whip to him."

"Ye'll do no such thing, Miss Maddie," Janet cried out, her alarm at Maddie's threat demonstrating to the viscount that she knew it was not an idle one. "He'll have the *sherra* after ye in a jiffy. The wee dog belongs to Will now. Ye maun make up yer mind to it with good grace."

"Over my dead body!" retorted Maddie.

"Ladies, ladies!" Deveryn interposed. "May I prevail upon you both to leave this matter in my hands? This is men's business. I make no doubt that Will Fraser will think twice before he makes an enemy of me."

"He's not to be trusted," said Maddie with dogged persistence. "He'll take your money and he'll steal Kelpie from under our noses. I intend to keep her by me night and day until that snake follows his flock into the hills."

"Ye'll do no such thing." Janet glowered her displeasure at Maddie's intent. "That wee dog may be your darlin', but she could be mangy or flea infested for all we know. I'll no have her *biding* in my clean kitchen and I make no doubt that yer aunt will no *thole* her in the house. Duncan will look after her, and she'll make her home in the stables, where she belongs."

Maddie protested, but the most she could win from Janet was the favour of allowing the dog to be bathed and doctored before the kitchen fire, and with that Maddie had to be content.

She went upstairs to change out of her riding habit. When she came into the kitchen again, she was surprised to see that the viscount was there before her. He, too, had changed, but his elegantly tailored jacket of dark blue superfine was carelessly draped over the back of one of the kitchen chairs. The sleeves of his white linen shirt were rolled up to the elbows. Before the hearth was a small tin tub half filled with tepid water.

"Shall we begin?" he asked with a smile in his eyes.

Maddie could scarcely believe that he meant to help her in so menial a task. She nodded in mute astonishment and removed a voluminous bib fronted apron from a hook at the back of the kitchen door and quickly donned it. When her eyes dropped to the hearth, she saw Kelpie was no longer there.

"The victim is under the sideboard, I believe," Deveryn explained, and joined Maddie as she dropped to her hands and knees before the solid oak piece which had a scant foot of clearance from the stone floor. Underneath, in the dark cavernous depths, cowered Kelpie showing a perfectly healthy set of white fangs.

"She never did like bath night," said Maddie with a laugh. "But once she gets in the water, she really loves it."

"No doubt," responded Deveryn with an answering twinkle. "It's getting her there that's the problem."

"I've had practice," intoned Maddie confidently. She went to the larder and brought out a slab of cheese. She cut off a thick slice and kneeled down at the side of the tub extending her hand palm open. After a moment, Kelpie whined, then dropped to her stomach and crawled from her hiding place, her brown eyes warily watching the proffered hand. As soon as she took the tidbit from Maddie's palm, Deveryn swiftly lifted the black wriggling body and dumped it in the tub. Kelpie swallowed the cheese in one gulp and looked up at her captors with sad and sorrowful eyes.

"Is that how you plan to manage me when we are married?" asked Deveryn, flashing a wicked grin.

She turned her luminous brown eyes upon him and asked guilelessly, "With cheese?"

"Oh no," he answered, and playfully flicked her nose with a careless finger. "I meant with treats, of course," and he laughed at the sudden blush in Maddie's cheeks.

But Maddie found that it was impossible to sustain her displeasure against Deveryn. She was deeply sensible of the debt of gratitude she owed the viscount. For one thing, he had shown himself solicitous of Kelpie's welfare. And he had made the offer to intervene on her behalf with Will Fraser, useless as she thought the gesture to be. Furthermore, to maintain an icy dignity when the two of them were engaged in bathing an unwilling, squirming ball of misery into submission was beyond Maddie's power. Her laughter was as spontaneous as Deveryn's as Kelpie drenched them, time and time again, with the soapy spray from the churning bath water.

It was Deveryn who put the finishing touches to Kelpie's toilette. As Maddie held Kelpie's head in her lap, she watched his strong hands smooth a healing salve on the cuts and abrasions which covered the small body. Kelpie made no move to resist the viscount's capable touch, as if sensing that her destiny was secure in the powerful, masculine hands that tended her.

As Kelpie was led away by Duncan to a warm box which had

been made ready for her in the stable, Maddie's smiling eyes came to rest upon Deveryn. He was vigorously brushing the lint and excess of dog hair from his skin tight beige pantaloons. The top two buttons of his shirt were undone and the sleeves rolled up at the elbows. The exertions of their labours with Kelpie had soaked the front of his shirt and it clung to his muscular frame like a second skin. At that moment, he caught Maddie's amused look. He answered with a disarming grin of his own, and one hand swept back the swath of wheat gold hair that had fallen across his forehead. At the unconsciously boyish gesture, a small pang twisted Maddie's heart.

"I haven't done this sort of thing since I was a boy," he said negligently.

"You look like a boy," she told him and swung away to pick up the heap of wet towels on the floor.

He bent down to help her and their hands touched. "Maddie, you're good for me, do you know that? I haven't felt this alive in years."

At his words, she felt the blooming of pleasure. They stared at each other, wordlessly. She knew that she swayed towards him. But the door opened to admit Janet, and the moment was lost.

Chapter Six

The temperature had warmed and Deveryn was persuaded that it would not be long before the roads were passable once more. He had no intention of leaving Drumoak, however, until he had words with Donald Sinclair's solicitor. He was in a fever of impatience to discover who Maddie's guardian might be so that the matter of their marriage might be speedily settled.

He rode out over the links after lunch and reached Inverforth with little trouble. A small detour took him to the cottage of Will Fraser and his mother. It took him only a few minutes to complete his business. By a careful combination of blatant bribery and subtle threat, Deveryn soon convinced the young shepherd that it would be in his best interests to cut a wide swath around Miss Maddie Sinclair in future.

He returned to Drumoak in very fine fettle, determining that on the morrow, or on the next day, he would send his coachmen to Edinburgh to fetch the solicitor. Not finding Maddie, he wandered into the library, not very well stocked in his opinion, where he was joined by Cynthia, to his great dislike. With Cynthia, there could never be any comfortable silences, nor conversation which did not originate in the latest *on dits* about some member of the ton. Since they had been absent from town circles for a fortnight or more, conversation gradually flagged and soon died altogether.

The viscount was on the point of making his excuses when Cynthia's next remark riveted him to his place.

"Now that the thaw has set in, I expect we shall be seeing a good deal of Maddie's beau. I hear he's come home to stay."

The words dropped casually from her lips as she turned the pages of an out-of-date copy of *The Edinburgh Review*.

Deveryn relaxed against the cushioned back of his commodious chair and spoke with equal negligence. "I wasn't aware that the girl had a beau."

Violet eyes widened fractionally as they gazed guilelessly into his. "Weren't you? I thought I mentioned, oh aeons ago, that Donald had warned Maddie of the ineligibility of the connection."

Deveryn cast back in his mind, and a remnant of some forgotten conversation came into focus though still hazy at the edges. Of course, at that time, three months ago or more, Maddie had been just a name to him. It wasn't likely that he would remember what was said about a chit that held no interest for him. Things were different now. "I'd forgotten. I believe you did mention something. What was it?"

Under that hooded, neutral stare, Cynthia became restless. Her eyes dropped, and her fingers became involved in arranging the folds of her elegant, sarcenet mourning gown. "Donald was infuriated by the gossip about Maddie and a local boy. Some of it was quite nasty. Personally, I thought he should have encouraged the match. The boy's family is poor, but their connections are quite respectable. Donald, of course, would not admit to the truth of the stories that were circulating."

Deveryn brought his hands together, the tips of his fingers barely touching. "I'm all ears," he said, in an amused tone. "Who is the lucky man?"

"Malcolm Moncrieff. He's the vicar's son, and older than Maddie by a couple of years. They've been in each other's pockets since they were in leading strings."

"It seems to me that their connection is closer to kinsmen than lovers."

"That's what Donald thought at first, and perhaps they were until Malcolm went away to university. It was a case of 'absence makes the heart grow fonder' I suppose."

"I don't think I follow."

The journal was laid aside, and Cynthia braved a direct glance at those blue eyes brilliant with an emotion that was held in rigid control. There could be no turning back now.

Beneath the concealing folds of her gown, her fingers tensed.

"They were too close for Donald's comfort. Some poacher found them together at one of the *bothies* that the shepherds use for shelter when they're driving their flocks down from the hills. They weren't very discreet. That's why Donald came back every summer and Christmas—to keep an eye on Maddie when Malcolm was sure to be home for the holidays."

One brow arched, and he drawled, "Why did Sinclair not simply have the girl with him in London? Why leave her here at all?"

Cynthia looked to be slightly pained by his words. She touched the tip of her tongue to her dry lips and her head lifted. "I know what you're thinking and you're wrong, Jason. I wanted Maddie with us. But the girl preferred to remain at Drumoak. Donald was an indulgent father. Whatever Maddie wanted, she got."

The viscount's bored eyes travelled the shabby interior in a slow, appraising circuit, missing nothing, and finally came to rest on his elegant companion. "An indulgent father?" he repeated, and there was just enough bite in his voice to give the lie to his dispassionate expression. "Appearances can be deceptive, I suppose." He rose to his feet in one smooth, cat-like motion and, for a long moment, stood gazing about him. The cynical curl of his lip, more pronounced than ever, twisted the generous mouth into a parody of a smile, cold and intimidating.

"If the boy is a pauper, I don't wonder that her father forbade the match. What kind of life would the girl have? With her lack of fortune, they wouldn't have two pennies to rub together."

"She would have the sort of life that she prefers," Cynthia returned, striving for calm. "Malcolm has prospects. He's studying for the Bar. They would make their home in Edinburgh, where Maddie has friends. She went to school there. We did have her in London with us for a time, you know. She was miserable."

"I shall be the first to wish them happy," he responded with imperturbable civility. "Though, of course, the girl's guardian may not care a straw for my felicitations."

He left her then, the cool mask of indifference staying with him till he had gained the hall. He went immediately in search of Maddie but was not to meet up with her again till dinner time.

He was sampling Donald Sinclair's fine French brandy when the object of his thoughts pushed into the parlour, her cheeks a trifle warm from her last minute exertions in the kitchen, and one hand combing her fiery hair in a gesture of acute distraction.

She spoke in calm, deliberate accents, and though she addressed the company in general, her eyes were only for Deveryn. "Dinner is served," she said, then added a little breathlessly, "Janet asked me to make the announcement." Miss Spencer arched her brows in a telling gesture. "Everyone knows we're short-handed, Aunt Nell," said Maddie with a candour that Deveryn was coming to recognize as typical of Maddie's transparent nature.

Deveryn offered Maddie his arm to take her in to dinner. "What's on the menu?" he asked *sotto voce* as she slipped into the chair he held for her.

"You're to be honoured," she responded, and his brows snapped together when he noted the sparkle that lightened her eyes to the colour of fine sherry. "Janet means to treat you like royalty."

The first course was a piping hot broth that tasted exceptional by any standards.

"This must surely be ambrosia," Deveryn told Janet gravely as she made to remove his plate.

"He means that he likes it," Maddie translated when Janet looked a question at her mistress.

With a shy smile, Janet replied, "Ye maun like it. That's no broth boiled from yer scraggy second day bones, ye ken. That were made from a fresh sheep's head."

The viscount kept the smile fixed on his face till the old housekeeper had retired. It was still there a moment later when he addressed Maddie between his teeth. "How fresh?"

"Very fresh—poor beastie," she intoned mournfully, but there was an irrepressible glint in her eye.

Deveryn's smile tightened fractionally. "I have an awful presentiment that this dinner is going to be one of the most memorable of my life."

Before Maddie could answer, Duncan entered bearing a platter with one lone sheep's head on a bed of tiny roast onions. Jacob followed at his heels with a sparkling silver tray loaded down with suet puddings and pies.

The sheep's head, complete with apple in its mouth, was set before the viscount. He looked it in the eye for a long moment. "Poor Yorick," he murmured softly and quelled Maddie's snort with a quick frown.

"You have the honour of carving the beastie," she said, looking pointedly at the carving knife and fork which Duncan had placed on the table before his lordship's place.

"So I observe. But how is it to be done?"

"Spear it with the fork and hack it to pieces as though the knife were a claymore. It's really not that hard."

As Deveryn set to work to demolish the sheep's head, Duncan waited patiently in the background to serve the delicacy as soon as this should be done. As the meal progressed, Maddie took it upon herself to describe each dish in detail to her honoured guests who soon discovered that the hearty appetites they had brought to the table had considerably dulled.

Janet entered and proudly placed a huge crystal bowl which was filled to the brim with whipped cream in front of Maddie's place. At her heels came Jacob, no less proud, bearing a platter of grapes and apricots which had been culled from Drumoak's small greenhouse the day before.

Maddie picked up an ornate silver server and ritualistically cut into the froth of whipped cream.

"What is it?" asked Deveryn as he watched Maddie dig to the bottom of the bowl with a silver ladle.

"A trifle," she said, and heaped a generous portion into a small china bowl. "That's the name of the dish, by the way, not a personal comment."

The dishes were distributed and everyone politely sampled the dessert, a rare and fancy treat which the plain Scots reserved for special occasions only. Maddie waited anxiously for the viscount's verdict.

"There's something in it which gives it a distinctive flavour. What is it?" asked Deveryn as he savoured the moist cake which was to be found beneath the layers of cream and egg custard.

"Glenlivet," said Maddie. "That's the best whisky that Scotland has to offer."

Cynthia leaned over the viscount, her breast carelessly brushing against his sleeve, and she retrieved a small cluster of black grapes from the platter that Jacob had placed in the centre of the table. She negligently dangled the grapes above her parted lips, her head tilted back, and she said provocatively, "Whisky and sheep are the only things worthy of note that the Scots export to England."

With mingled aversion and fascination, Maddie watched as her stepmother's sharp, white teeth nibbled on one of the plump grapes which brushed her mouth. There was something suggestive if not downright obscene about the gesture. Without volition, Maddie's glance travelled to the viscount. Stranger though she was to a man's passions, she knew intuitively that his senses were stirred. The fingers of his right hand toyed restlessly with the slender stem of his wine glass and a dark tide of colour had deepened his eyes to slate. He watched Cynthia as if mesmerized, like a *puir wee* rabbit watches a weasel before, too late, it realizes its jeopardy, thought Maddie; wrath, boiling and bitter, rose like bile in her throat.

Her gaze dropped to the trifle in her dish. Suddenly, all the joy had gone out of the evening, and the dinner she had spent all afternoon helping Janet prepare seemed to have been so much wasted effort. She picked up her spoon and forced herself to swallow a mouthful of whipped cream, painfully aware of the undercurrents that passed between Deveryn and Cynthia. Silently, vehemently, she denied that the game they were playing had any other effect than cause her a disgust that was nauseating in its intensity. She lied and she knew it.

Deveryn watched Maddie covertly out of the corner of his eye, and with no little difficulty, contrived to keep his lips grave. They had retired to the front parlour at the conclusion of a dinner that he had been at some pains to convey was the best it had ever been his good fortune to sample north or south of the border. Maddie had accepted his extravagant compliment with something less than grace, and had intimated that Janet would be delighted to hear him say so. Her indifference to the vagaries of his lordship's highly developed palette could not have been more evident.

She had been shocked, he knew, by Cynthia's blatant sexual overtures at the table, and more shocked by his own swift response, thoroughly masculine in nature, which he had wrongly supposed he had concealed. The trouble with Maddie was that she was abysmally ignorant of men. His reaction had been automatic—something any redblooded male would comprehend. The finer feelings had not entered into it. The girl saw too much and understood too little, he thought with a stab of impatience, and his eyes, carefully devoid of expression, came to rest on Cynthia as she rose gracefully from the piano bench. She moved in a rustle of silk skirts to take the vacant place on the faded chintz sofa beside the viscount. Deveryn swallowed the faint sigh that rose to his lips. Maddie's attention had not wavered since she had opened the book which she held up to the candle at her elbow. He wondered if she would deign to notice him if he began to show some attention to Cynthia. He discarded the notion as being unworthy of him. Maddie's feelings were fragile, and he would not hurt her for the world. In time, she would learn to trust the husband who intended to cherish her as if she were a piece of priceless Sevres porcelain. His eyes warmed with laughter when he observed her turn a page. It was the first she had turned in the half hour since she had sat down to read.

Maddie doggedly focused all her powers of concentration on the printed page in her hand. "Of all things that live and have intelligence," she translated for the umpteenth time, "we women are the most wretched species." Amen, she said under her breath, turned the page, and went on. But her thoughts this night were far from Euripides's wretched heroine, Medea, and her diatribe against men. They were all for little Maddie Sinclair whose emotions were so confused and lacerated that she scarcely recognized the distraught girl who presented, she hoped, a tranquil exterior to the world. Her sombre eyes, unguarded, lifted to meet Deveryn's mocking gaze.

Deveryn caught that forlorn look and it brought him to his feet. A rush of memory carried him back to their first

97

encounter under the lamplight outside Inverforth's church—Maddie and her sad, haunted doe eyes.

He made to take a step toward her.

But Maddie's expression transformed in that instant. She looked past the viscount, and the back of her hand went to her mouth.

"Malcolm," she said softly, then with more animation, "Malcolm!" and she was out of her chair and hurtling herself across the room before Miss Spencer had time to lay aside her knitting needles.

She came to an abrupt halt a step away from a young man who had entered Drumoak's front parlour unseen only a moment before. Deveryn would have recognized him even if Maddie had not given him his name.

His blond hair was cut rather short to be in fashion and was much darker than Deveryn's own sun bleached locks. His complexion was pale, indicating that he spent much of his time indoors, and though he was tall and broad of shoulder, he was far from having the viscount's powerful physique. His resemblance to the stiff backed figure who regarded him steadily from under heavy lidded eyes was only superficial. And his garments, well-fitting and of superior quality as they might be, lacked something of the distinction of that other gentleman's turnout.

Malcolm smiled warmly at Maddie, totally oblivious of the other occupants of the room, and held out his arms. Maddie walked into them as if she belonged there.

She tipped back her head and said very softly, "Kiss me Malcolm. I have needed you so."

The words were low and intimate, and uttered so quietly that only Malcolm could hear them. Deveryn saw Maddie's lips move, and knew instinctively what she had just said. As he watched that fair masculine head incline toward Maddie and saw the brush of another man's lips on hers, a jolt of fury, like a thunderbolt, shook him to the core. His hands fisted at his sides.

Deveryn, conscious that his mask of well-bred civility had slipped, ruthlessly checked the force of his temper. With unhurried ease, he stationed himself by the sofa, but his eyes remained on the couple who were locked in each other's arms.

Maddie's head was buried against the young man's shoulder and a spate of words, soft and soothing as if he had been comforting a child, fell from Malcolm's lips.

Cynthia, growing bold, said for Deveryn's ears only, "What did I tell you?" It was in her mind to say more, but she felt the tension in the man who stood so stiffly beside her and dreaded to invoke that fury against herself.

It was Malcolm who first became aware of the impropriety of their position. He looked over the top of Maddie's head and saw three pair of curious eyes watching them. One pair, he observed with some surprise, were stormy.

"Maddie," he said under his breath. When this had no effect except to make her burrow more snugly against him, he administered a light shake. "Maddie," he repeated, "you have guests, if I'm not mistaken."

Her head came up and she stood irresolute in the circle of his arms. Reluctantly, her arms dropped from his waist and she turned to face her companions.

"Miss Spencer and my stepmother you have already met, I collect," she said tonelessly.

Malcolm acknowledged the presence of the ladies with a polite bow.

Only then did she glance in the viscount's direction. Though she did not think him fit to tie Malcolm's shoelaces, protocol prescribed that it was he who must be addressed first. "Lord Deveryn," she said in a creditably calm voice, "may I make known to you a good neighbour and friend, Mr. Malcolm Moncrieff?"

Deveryn acknowledged the younger man's bow with a grave inclination of the head. A few civilities were exchanged and Lord Deveryn resumed his place on the sofa.

As was to be expected, it was the viscount who took command of the conversation. Without giving the least offence, he soon elicited from the unsuspecting young man at his elbow enough facts to form an accurate picture of his history and future prospects. Maddie hid her indignation behind a mask of polite indifference.

"So you think Edinburgh is the centre of the universe, do you?" Deveryn remarked to Malcolm in an amused drawl.

Cynthia laid one careless hand on the viscount's sleeve.

"What did I tell you, Jason? The Scots, more than any other nation in the world, are tied to the shores of home."

"I beg to differ," the viscount responded pleasantly, and in the act of stretching out a hand to select a bonbon from the crystal dish in the centre of the sofa table managed to dislodge the lady's hand from his sleeve. He flexed his fingers, allowed them to hover for a moment over the dish, then withdrew his hand as if he had changed his mind.

Maddie's eyes lifted to Cynthia's and surprised a look of smouldering resentment which was quickly concealed.

"The colonies," continued Deveryn, "as I understand, are populated with as many Scots as there are in their native land."

"That's an exaggeration, surely!" exclaimed Maddie, and for the first time since leaving the dining room looked directly into Deveryn's eyes.

"Perhaps a slight one," he agreed, and held her gaze, contriving in the space of a few seconds to convey a message of mingled apology and regret. Maddie quickly looked away.

"There was good reason to leave Scotland during the last century," she observed with some heat. "Our stand in support of the Stewarts was ruthlessly suppressed, and the Highlanders cruelly dispossessed of their lands."

Maddie knew her words were inflamatory. One did not, in mixed company of Scots and English, refer to recent history where the age-old enmity between their nations had twice in one century flared to civil war, more or less.

"That's ancient history, Maddie, and best forgotten," Malcolm soothed, and his hand fastened on her wrist in a crushing, cautionary grip. "Haven't we just joined forces, as one nation under one flag, to overthrow the designs of the Corsican upstart?" He turned to Deveryn and said in a confiding tone, "Maddie likes to be argumentative. Perhaps you've noticed?" He released her wrist and forced a laugh. "I think it's a national characteristic. And in this neck of the woods, we weren't even on the side of the Young Pretender."

"Nevertheless," said Deveryn in a tone all the more menacing because it was devoid of expression, "in some quarters such sentiments might be taken as . . . treasonable."

"In England, I don't doubt," flashed Maddie. "In Scotland, I'd be toasted as a patriot." She turned reproachfully on

Malcolm. "And since when did you take to calling Bonnie Prince Charlie 'the Young Pretender'?"

"Since I read history at university," he replied with energy. "A Scottish university, Maddie." He picked up the crystal dish of bonbons and said in a tone that brooked no denial, "May I suggest that you suck on one of these?"

Maddie looked at the proffered bonbons. Then she looked into Malcolm's warning eyes. "Oh, very well," she said, and popped a hard brandy boiling into her mouth.

"I don't wonder that Maddie has no desire to reside in London," said Cynthia with an arch look at Deveryn. "One shudders to think what affront she might give the high sticklers of the ton. My dear, you would be ostracized before you could say . . ."

"Scotland forever!" interjected Deveryn, and Cynthia burst into a trill of shrill feminine laughter. Malcolm tried unsuccessfully to smother a chortle. Though Maddie was mortified, she managed a weak smile, and she curled her tongue around the hard bonbon in her mouth. She was tempted to spit it on the floor and blister the ears of her mirthful companions with a lesson in history they would not soon forget. Deveryn seemed to read her thoughts and the boyish smile on his handsome face deepened into a taunting grin.

His eyes softened, and he took pity on her, drawing the attention of the others to himself.

When it came time for Malcolm to take his leave, Maddie detached herself from her guests. As she preceded him through the open doorway, his hand fell across her shoulder in an absent, brotherly gesture and Maddie's face lifted. She flashed him a questioning smile. The moment of intimacy was not lost upon Deveryn. Nor was he best pleased when Cynthia turned to him and said behind her hand, "I'll wager we don't see the girl for a good half hour. And nobody here seems to see anything improper in this exclusive attachment! The girl's in a fair way to ruining herself!"

A muscle tensed in Deveryn's cheek but he said with perfect composure. "You refine too much upon their friendship. I see nothing amiss in it. Be sure, my lovely, that you do not impute to others a failing which is natural to yourself."

"And to you!" she returned hotly.

His lip curled in that way that she so much detested. "As you say," he drawled, his voice devoid of all expression save a thread of something that might have been self-mockery.

On the other side of the parlour door, Maddie fetched Malcolm's woolen plaid and watched as he carelessly threw it across his shoulders, one end hanging loose at his back.

"Malcolm," she said softly, "I must talk to you."

"Of course. I'll ride over tomorrow morning and we can go for a walk along the shore."

"No! Tonight!"

He was on the point of remonstrating with her, but the sharp edge of urgency in her voice and the appeal in those soft, dark eyes stayed the words on his lips. "What is it Maddie?" he asked gently.

"I'll get my cloak," she said, and he could hear the relief in her voice. "The stable is warm. We can talk there. Besides, Kelpie came home. You'll want to see her. Don't scold me, Malcolm. I couldn't bear it. Really, no one will take exception to our being in the stable. Duncan or Jacob is bound to be about."

As it happened, neither Duncan nor Jacob was in evidence when they entered the brick building which was on the other side of the orchard. The stable was warm, as Maddie knew it would be, and had more horses in its stalls than Drumoak had seen in many a long year, most of them, she reflected with rising pique, belonging to his lordship and positively eating their heads off. She led the way to the tackroom where Kelpie, catching scent of her mistress, stood alert and silent, waiting impatiently just inside the door.

In a few moments she had related all the details of Kelpie's loss and unexpected recovery.

"I wouldn't put it past Will Fraser to try something desperate," she said, scratching the ears of an appreciative Kelpie.

"I shouldn't worry. If Deveryn said he would take care of the matter, you may depend on it, he will."

"You like him, don't you?" she asked and there was just enough suspicion in her voice to raise Malcolm's eyebrows a fraction.

102

"Of course. Don't you?"

"No . . . yes . . . oh, I don't know." Now was the moment she had been waiting for, the moment when she could unburden herself completely and share with the friend of her childhood the suspicions about her father's death and the part Deveryn had played in it. "Malcolm," she said and her voice sank. "Malcolm," she began again, but Maddie found to her consternation that the words could not be said. To expose Deveryn and his utter want of morality seemed quite beyond her power. Nor could she divine why this should be so, except that she felt, in some sense, it was a betrayal on her part.

Malcolm straightened slowly and looked intently into the dark confusion of her sad eyes. "What is it, Maddie?" he asked, and he captured her hands.

"Malcolm," she began for the third time, and ran the tip of her tongue over her dry lips, "I must tell you . . . what I mean to say is . . . I'm so very glad you are home. I missed you so," and she slid her arms around his waist and laid her head against his chest.

For a moment, he hesitated. He knew that the bonds of their long standing friendship must soon be loosed. It was inevitable. The thought saddened him. He enclosed her in his arms and drew her close, offering a silent, heartfelt comfort.

Though his own estimation of Donald Sinclair had never stood very high, he knew that Maddie did not share his opinion. To her, the man represented her one secure foundation in a very insecure childhood. Now that he was gone, there was no one Maddie was really close to. Except himself.

He tipped her head back and kissed her very chastely full on the lips.

"I trust I don't intrude?"

The lazy drawl startled the couple. They drew apart quickly. Deveryn stood framed in the doorway, his arms folded, one shoulder negligently braced against the door jamb.

Malcolm was first to recover his composure. "No, of course not, sir. Maddie was just showing me Kelpie."

"So I observed," returned Deveryn dryly.

A dark tide of colour rose under the younger man's skin. There was glitter in the viscount's eye that promised swift retribution.

"I'd best be going," Malcolm said hastily, highly conscious that a very improper interpretation could easily be placed on what had been after all a very innocent embrace. He thought to set the older man straight about what had just taken place. "Maddie was in need of a little comforting."

His words in some small measure seemed to have a conciliatory effect. Deveryn removed himself from the doorway and allowed Malcolm to pass. But his only comment was, "We shall see you safely on your way."

Under Deveryn's hard stare, Malcolm's fingers fumbled when tightening his mount's girth, and to Maddie's nervous flow of conversation, he replied in terse monosyllables. He thought, rather resentfully, that Deveryn's hauteur was a trifle excessive. But he assumed that the viscount saw himself in some sort as standing in the role of Maddie's guardian. The thought mollified him slightly.

When he rode out, he turned in the saddle and gave them both a small, stiff salute. Maddie waved back, and after a moment lifted her skirts to tread the path back to the house.

Deveryn's hands clamped on her shoulders. "Not so fast. You have some explaining to do," and he wrenched her round to face him. "Your conduct is inexcusable."

"Look to your own conduct!" she shot back, struggling to break free of his painful hold.

He turned her in his arms so that the light from the stable lamp illumined her features. He studied her angry expression for a moment, and then he said calmly, "Cynthia quite deliberately set out to cause trouble between us tonight. She is a clever, devious woman. She is also beautiful, and knows how to use that beauty to ensnare men. In an unguarded moment, my interest was caught, but only for a moment. I can't promise you that I shall never look at other women again, Maddie. But I swear that when I do, it shall be from a distance."

Irrationally, the one thing that her mind fastened on was the fact that he had called her stepmother "beautiful." Her own claim to distinction, supposing she had any, was in the breadth of her education but she did not think that Deveryn, or any man for that matter, would be impressed if he should learn that her command of Greek literature and philosophy was considered exceptional.

"If Cynthia is clever," she scoffed, "I must be a genius."

He laughed. "That's better," he said.

"What's better?"

"It gratifies my vanity to know that I am not the only one to be eaten by jealousy. But have a care, Maddie. You came within a hairsbreadth of having your pretty little neck wrung this evening. If I hadn't felt myself in some sort to blame for bringing your anger down upon my head, Moncrieff would be nursing a sore jaw or worse on his ride home tonight and you would be foregoing your morning gallop across the sands for a good sennight or more."

"Don't," she said between her teeth, "impute to Malcolm and me the depravity of your own relationship to my stepmother."

He kissed her then. It was almost inevitable that he would. He had some vague idea of offering her reassurance. But when his lips touched hers it was like flashfire—the spark to dry tinder, an instant, explosive conflagration flaring out of control.

He had found her in the arms of another male, and the spectacle had unleashed some dark and sinister emotion, some primeval drive that was not to be denied. With lips, tongue, hands, and body easily breaching her defences, he ground himself into her, branding her as his woman, claiming her as his mate. More than anything, he wanted to tumble her there, in the orchard, and enter her body, possessing her fully, irrevocably binding her to him. That the instinct was purely primitive in nature, he did not doubt.

Maddie could no more resist that fierce onslaught than she could resist a raging whirlpool. As if she were drowning, sucked into the dark, turbulent depths of his passion, she clung to him. In some dim recess of her mind, she understood the origin of his need to dominate her senses. Her own instincts took over. He belonged to her. She would make it so. Moulding her softness to his hard body, offering everything that was feminine in her to this maleness, unconsciously, she enticed him to do more.

Deveryn felt her surrender all through his body, and a fierce masculine exultation swept through him. Only then did he wrench himself from the embrace. For several moments, he stood motionless, visibly controlling himself. Maddie turned her face into the lapels of his coat.

When he finally had command of his breathing, he said, "Nothing is going to stand in the way of our coming together. You know that as well as I do. Deny it if you can."

She shook her head mutely.

He tilted her head back, framing her face with both hands. "Maddie, I wish we'd met under different circumstances, no truly," and he placed his thumbs against her lips when she made to argue with him. "What's done is done, and an ocean of regret won't wash out one moment of it. But don't ask me to regret Cynthia. If there had been no Cynthia, there would have been no reason for me to come to Drumoak. And if I had not come to Drumoak, how should I have found you?"

His hands slid down her arms till his fingers laced with hers. "You're shivering. This is really not the time or place to settle things between us. We'll talk everything out tomorrow."

She could not know what it cost him to let her go. He wondered at his own self-restraint and decided wryly that their nuptials could not come too soon for his comfort. To touch her, to kiss her, was to put himself to a test he had never before experienced with any other woman. It was a test he did not think he could safely weather again.

Chapter Seven

It was the heady perfume of roses, sweet and pervasive, which alerted Maddie to the presence of the other woman in her bedchamber. She was in her nightclothes, in the act of selecting a suitably dark frock for the day ahead, when the lingering fragrance of apples from the open clothes press was gradually overlaid by a stronger, less pleasant aroma. Maddie turned her head.

"Cynthia!"

Her stepmother stood just inside the door. Though the sky had long since lightened to dawn outside the window, and a lone candle burned resolutely on the mantlepiece, dark shadows still hovered in the corners of the room. Even so, Cynthia's elegance and beauty were clearly evident.

"May I sit down?" she asked, and at Maddie's mute nod, glided to the stool beside the dressing table.

Maddie's eyes narrowed on the elaborate coiffure of dark glossy ringlets which framed a perfectly oval face, and she wondered, with a stab of envy, how it was possible for a woman to appear so consistently without a hair out of place. Selfconsciously, she ran one careless hand through her short crop of curls and regretted, not for the first time, that papers and hot tongs could never induce her own wilful locks to lie just as she desired.

"Do sit down," said Cynthia.

The softly spoken command acted on Maddie like a douse of cold water. She became conscious that she had been staring, and a sudden warmth suffused her cheeks.

"Th-thank you," she managed, and obediently seated herself at the foot of the unmade bed, then was furious with herself for allowing the older woman to act on her as if she had been a tongue-tied miss just out of the schoolroom. She strove to compose herself.

"How old are you Maddie?"

"Nineteen."

"You seem younger."

Maddie felt the other woman's critical scrutiny, and she pulled the edges of her dressing-gown closer together. She did not take her stepmother's comment for a compliment, and she remained silent.

"I can give you ten years, you know," Cynthia continued.

"So I understand," Maddie responded, and a flicker of warning passed over her when she observed the smile, so patently solicitous, which touched Cynthia's cold lips.

There was an awkward pause, and Cynthia's eyes roved the room, coming to rest on the small miniature which hung above the cluttered lady's writing table. It was a portrait of Maddie's mother. She contemplated it for a few moments longer before turning her gaze on Maddie.

"Your father wanted me to be a mother to you. I'm afraid I never did have any talent in that area. Pity. But I don't believe in repining for the impossible. You never would have accepted me, you know."

"True. My mother's place could never have been filled by another woman." The foolish hope, at fourteen years, that her father's young bride would have made a friend of her was long forgotten.

"Then how fortunate that I never made the attempt." The retort was etched with amusement.

"I presume," said Maddie coldly, "that there is some point to this conversation?"

"I'd forgotten what a straightforward girl you are. 'Frank to a fault' your father used to say. The point I am making is this: you are sorely in need of a mother's guidance at this moment." A lift of one hand silenced Maddie's protest. "You aunt is an estimable woman, I don't doubt. But her experience of the world is sadly limited. Little as I relish the role, it falls to me to give you a word of warning."

108

At this point, Cynthia hesitated, and Maddie queried with mock politeness, "Yes? In your role as a woman of the world, you have some gem of wisdom to impart to me?"

There was an edge to Cynthia's quick reply. "Take my advice. Stick to young puppies like Malcolm. Deveryn is a predator. He devours little lambs like you for breakfast."

"If I'm not mistaken," said Maddie, parrying the thrust and lunging in her turn, "the viscount means to offer for me."

Cynthia's stricken look, quickly masked, was not lost on Maddie, but it did not bring the surge of triumph she might have expected. For some inexplicable reason, her ire was all for the absent Deveryn.

Cynthia took a few moments to consider Maddie's shocking revelation. When she spoke, her voice was soft, not scathing, not incredulous, but quietly persuasive.

"That it would be a triumph for you, I don't deny. A man of Deveryn's rank and fortune is expected to choose his consort from one of the noble houses of England. You would be the envy of other women. That goes without saying. But ask yourself, Maddie, whether or not you would be happy."

"Why shouldn't I be?"

"Come now! You're surely not such a green girl. In plain terms, your place in his life would be negligible; your purpose merely to provide the heir to continue his line. You would be one among many. I don't doubt that for the moment his palette is whetted by your . . . innocent appeal. That will soon pass. The appetites of such a man are soon sated. My dear, you would be miserable."

Cynthia had touched Maddie on a raw nerve. She knew that her experience of men was negligible. And never, in her short life, had any gentleman remotely resembling the worldly viscount come within her orbit. She had witnessed, only the night before, how easily he had been seduced by her stepmother. That he held a powerful attraction for Maddie also, as she did for him, was not in question. When he touched her, she could not think straight. But she wanted so much more. To be just one among many was not to be thought of.

Besides, nothing of any real significance had changed. She had sworn, wildly and a little hysterically perhaps, to be revenged on the man who had wronged her father. Having come to know Deveryn as a real person, she knew that she could no longer execute that design. Nevertheless, to be on intimate terms with the man who had driven her father to such lengths—she still harboured the suspicion that he had taken his own life—she knew could never sit well with her conscience. But she was not about to tell her stepmother so.

"Your concern for my welfare is most gratifying, though perhaps a trifle belated. You may be sure that I shall give your words the consideration they deserve," and she rose to her feet as if to indicate that the interview was at an end.

Cynthia was not to be dismissed so easily. She too rose to her feet. The curl on her mouth was clearly contemptuous. "Imagine yourself in Deveryn's milieu! Have you forgotten that you were like a fish out of water when you were last in London? Your manners and conduct may do very well for this provincial backwater, but I make no doubt that in polite society you would be considered farouche—an object of ridicule. Deveryn would soon come to his senses, to his great regret!"

The sneer in Maddie's voice matched exactly the older woman's tone. "That's as may be. But do you, dear stepmama, think yourself better fitted for the role of the viscount's wife? Or perhaps you don't aim so high? Are you reconciled to your place? As I hear tell, in spite of your ambitions, you've never climbed higher than his bed."

Cynthia's eyes narrowed. "So," she said consideringly, "your father told you about Deveryn and me."

Maddie did not deny it, but she was sorry that she had revealed so much. She remained silent.

After a moment, Cynthia shrugged philosophically. "It's as well that you know. Jason may want you for his wife, but it's to me that he will turn when boredom sets in. Think on it Maddie." Her smile was taunting. "The pleasure would be all mine."

It was a vulgar conversation, and Maddie could not understand how the older woman had come by such power to provoke her. In the five years since she had known her, she had thought herself immune to her stepmother's jibes. She was mistaken.

"So be it Maddie. It shall be an interesting *menage à trois,* if

110

you've resolved to have him—the daughter for his wife and the widow for his mistress. Even Deveryn's circles will be shocked, and that's saying something! I wonder how long you will be able to stomach the scandal?"

The door closed softly behind her, and Maddie thankfully sank down onto the bed. She was shaking! For some few moments she stared disconsolately at the new woolen bedsocks which peeped from under the hem of her cotton nightrail. A tear dropped to her lap. As though it had scalded her, she surged to her feet. She stalked to the window and opened it wide, breathing deeply of the pure, chill air uncontaminated by the stench of summer's roses. It occurred to her that the pleasure of cultivating that particular flower was lost to her forever. That thought seemed the most inconsolable of all.

She turned back into the room and began to pace restlessly. Her eyes were caught by a movement in the mirror. She halted. The reflection drew her like a magnet.

Maddie was used to glancing at herself in the looking glass each time she changed her garments. But never before had she subjected her person to such a cool, critical scrutiny. A young girl with a tangle of loose copper curls, huge dark eyes and a small square chin stared resolutely back at her. One hand went up to brush the freckles on the bridge of the small straight nose. They remained obstinately in place. Her brows drew together.

The garments in her clothes press brought even less comfort. In a fit of impatience, she reached for the dark, bottle-green riding habit and donned it quickly. Cynthia seemed to have an unending supply of black mourning gowns and garments. Maddie's means did not stretch to such luxuries. She tied a black silk ribbon around one arm and gave herself a cursory glance in the mirror. You'll do, she told herself severely, and made for the door.

She reached the stables without the alarm being given and gave Duncan a message for her aunt, excusing her absence on the flimsiest of pretexts. Let them make what they liked of it, but Maddie had determined that she would have some relief for a few hours at least from the discomposing presence of Deveryn and her stepmother.

Maddie's disappearance occasioned her aunt not the least

anxiety, though she admitted to a slight pique on not being told in person that her niece intended to spend the day with the Moncrieffs. With Deveryn, it was otherwise. He was at first amused at Maddie's stealthy decampment, conjecturing that this was a vain attempt to avoid the inevitable interview with himself. As afternoon gave way to evening, his tolerance began to wear thin. By the time dinner was over and still no sign of Maddie, his lordship's displeasure, silent and foreboding, was felt by everyone. He was on the point of saddling 'Thelo to go in search of her, when she rode in.

"Where the hell have you been?" he demanded and he turned to watch as she led her mare into its stall.

"Is Kelpie about?" she asked anxiously. "I've already asked Jacob. He says he hasn't seen hide nor hair of her all day."

"Don't try to turn the subject. I asked you a question."

She gave him a furious look and brushed past him. He followed her into the tackroom.

"When I ask you a question, I expect the dignity of a reply."

"What? Not now, Deveryn, please." Kelpie's box was empty. Perhaps Janet could put her mind to rest. She turned toward the door and halted.

He filled the doorframe, one hand braced on each door jamb. His posture was threatening, but Maddie was not in the humour to be intimidated. She had heard in the village that Will Fraser had taken advantage of the thaw to go into the hills for strays that had become separated from his flock. She knew that he would have had to pass close to Drumoak before striking out on the old drovers' road that would take him to Cumbernauld. And Will Fraser was not to be trusted. That thought had sped her on her way home. And now, there was no sign of Kelpie.

"I asked you where you had been."

"With Malcolm. We went for a ride to look over Dalmeny House." Her voice was edged with impatience.

"The Earl of Roseberry's new show place?"

"Yes."

As she tried to push past him, he caught her by the wrist. "Not so fast. I take it someone can verify this cock and bull story?"

"Like whom, for instance?"

112

"The earl for a start."

"The earl?" For a moment, amusement showed on her face. "Deveryn, you have a strange idea of the circles I move in. It's his housekeeper with whom I have a nodding acquaintance. Besides, the roads were impassable. What business is it of yours anyway?"

He ignored this last provocation, and said in a more controlled tone, "Your groom was with you, surely?"

"What groom?" She looked to be mystified by his question.

"Are you telling me that you have been in Moncrieff's company for most of the day without benefit of chaperone?"

"There's nothing unusual in that."

"Well there damn well ought to be!" He was practically shouting at her.

Out of the corner of her eye, Maddie caught a movement. She looked past Deveryn and saw Duncan entering the stable. It was evident that he had heard the viscount's voice raised in anger. Duncan's first look of surprise gave way to belligerence. He stood behind the viscount and said stolidly, "Yer wanted in the house, Miss Maddie. I'll take care o' Banshee."

Maddie felt the tension go out of her. Duncan was her self-appointed watchdog. No one would lay a hand on her in his presence, and she very much feared from the viscount's expression that he intended to do her bodily harm.

Deveryn turned slowly, and his eyes narrowed on the broad muscular frame of the other man.

Maddie said quickly, "Duncan, where is Kelpie?" and she tried to edge past the viscount.

"She were wi' Sam earlier."

"And where is Sam now?"

The big man shrugged his shoulders. "I dinna ken, miss. Mayhap he went to the hills to look for sheep."

"That can't be right. All our sheep are accounted for." On an afterthought, she asked, "Was he alone?"

"Nay. Will Fraser was wi' him."

"My God. Kelpie *is* with Will Fraser. He's taken her to Cumbernauld."

Her first thought was to mount up and make for the shepherd's bothy that lay six or so miles along the drovers' track to the small village of Cumbernauld. She sliced a glance at Deveryn and her resolve faltered.

"Will Fraser has taken Kelpie to Cumbernauld," she said with quiet desperation. "I'm sure of it."

His answer was to grasp her by the elbow and thrust her toward the open door of the stable. "Kelpie is with Sam. You heard Duncan. I've already told you that I fixed things with Fraser."

Duncan moved to block their exit, his huge frame tensing for action. The viscount's insolent gaze swept over him. "You'll get out my way, man, if you know what's good for you."

Not a muscle moved in Duncan's face, but his eyes fastened on Maddie, asking a question.

Duncan's brute strength was proverbial in Lothian. She was sure that Deveryn must have heard something of it. She was equally sure that it would weigh little or nothing with the viscount if the big man got in his way.

"Let us pass, Duncan," she said softly, and the big man moved aside. His relief was patent.

The interview which followed with Deveryn and her aunt, Cynthia looking on as an interested spectator, was strained and awkward in the extreme. Little was said by the viscount, but his silence at every excuse which Maddie offered for her conduct conveyed his censure. Even Aunt Nell was made to feel the bite of his displeasure. When she tentatively admitted that her chaperonage of Maddie had been sadly lacking, Deveryn said nothing to dissuade her from her opinion. The matter of Kelpie and Will Fraser was brushed aside as being of little consequence, and Maddie gave up trying to convince Deveryn that the shepherd was not to be trusted.

Once in her room, she gave vent to her temper. Cushions were knocked to the floor, books and papers swept from her small desk, and her riding boots stripped from her feet and thrown furiously into a corner. Having relieved the sharp edge of anger by these small acts of defiance, Maddie flung herself down on the bed and lay staring up at the ceiling.

Not only did she find Deveryn's high handed ordering of her life intolerable, but to add insult to injury, no one had thought to ask her when she had last eaten. And while they had gorged themselves silly at *her* board, she, the mistress of Drumoak, was left to starve. If she had been a small child and sent to her room without supper for some minor infraction of discipline she could not have felt more humiliated.

Deveryn understood nothing! Nor would he listen! He had blown up over a trifle—a petty disregard for conventions which were never observed to the letter save in the polite world of London. Good God! It was common knowledge that the morals which prevailed among the higher reaches of the English aristocracy were as free and easy as those of the lowest bawdy house in Edinburgh's Lawnmarket! And he had the temerity to call her to account. Hypocrite!

Her dog had been stolen. And Deveryn imagined that Will Fraser could be bribed by a purse and intimidated by the consequence of a viscount. This was Scotland, for God's sake!

More than once, she strode to the door intent on confronting Lord Deveryn and forcing him to listen to reason. Dammit, she needed his help! But her courage failed her.

By morning, Will and her dog would be miles away. Tonight they would get no further than the bothy at the ford over the River Esk. Neither Deveryn nor all the king's men could stop her going after Kelpie. For a moment she thought of enlisting Duncan's aid, but decided against it. Deveryn would damn anyone who lifted a hand to help her. The danger was minimal. She would take her riding crop of course. But Sam, her own shepherd, she hoped, would be there. She thought that she could make it back by morning and no one the wiser.

Downstairs in the front parlour, a pall had settled like one of the insidious winter fogs that creep in from the Firth of Forth. The viscount was seen to be making heavy inroads into the bottle of brandy which Cynthia had procured for him after Maddie's ignominious retreat to her bedchamber. The burden of conversation was, for the most part, left to the two ladies.

A less clever woman than Cynthia would have been at some pains to discredit her absent rival, especially after so recent a contretemps. A glance at Deveryn's brooding expression satisfied Cynthia that the viscount's thoughts were feeding his anger. She listened sympathetically as Miss Spencer lamely defended her niece's frequent lapses of propriety and forbore to smile when Deveryn's lips grew grimmer. That the aunt was damning Maddie even further in the gentleman's eyes was very evident to Cynthia.

When the tea trolley was brought in, it was Cynthia who acted as hostess, dispensing tea and biscuits to the manner born. She was in her element.

"I wonder if Maddie had any dinner?" Miss Spencer mused aloud. "Perhaps I . . ."

"A dish of want will do that chit a world of good," interjected Deveryn with a ferocity which had Miss Spencer retreat behind the thick lenses of her spectacles.

Though there was much that she might have said in rebuttal to his lordship's harsh rejoinder, she wisely kept her counsel. It was a relief when Janet came in to clear away the tea things, and she could finally make her excuses and retire to her room.

Though the temptation was great, Cynthia did not linger overlong. In answer to her query, she learned that the solicitor was expected on the morrow. She waited, hopeful that the viscount would give her some clue to what he intended to do about her husband's property. When none came, and he showed no interest in her next observation, she also withdrew and left him to his silent ruminations.

It was a good thirty minutes later when Deveryn stalked from the front parlour and made for the kitchen. Janet and a young girl he recognized as Cynthia's abigail were chuckling over some comment which had been made before he stepped over the threshold. Flat irons were heating on the stove, and on the table was a black silk frock which the abigail was assiduously pressing with a wet cloth and a hissing flat iron.

Deveryn addressed himself to Janet. "Where is this drovers' road that goes to Cumbernauld?"

She looked at him for a long moment as if he had spoken in a foreign language, then answered, "Ye'll no be going there in the dark o' night?"

"She wants her dog back," he replied, as if that remark explained everything.

It made perfect sense to Janet who had been given the whole story by Duncan before he had left earlier that evening to enjoy a pint with his cronies at the White Horse.

"Ye canna miss it," she said, looking at the viscount with unabashed interest as if seeing him clearly for the first time. "Beyond the stables, there is a track between two dry *staine*

116

dykes. Follow it for a mile and ye'll come to the old drovers' road. There's a bothy beyond the ford.''

It was all he needed to hear. With a curt farewell, he spun on his heel and left her staring.

Within a short time of leaving Janet, the viscount was dressed for riding and leading 'Thelo out of the stable. He followed the old housekeeper's directions to the track between the stone enclosures and mounted up. Though night riding was not one of his favourite pastimes, he had a soldier's disregard for what must be endured. The night was clear, the track ahead visible in the uncertain light of the moon. He had been used to worse in his advance across Spain with Wellington.

Though he thought that he had sent himself on a wildgoose chase, he never once slackened his pace.

Maddie was alarmed about her dog's fate. He regretted that he had brushed off her fears as if her feelings meant nothing to him. She must know that that was far from being the case. In some small measure, he meant to atone for what he was sure she had regarded as his callous indifference. It had been no such thing.

It was her intimacy with Moncrieff which had brought his temper to boiling point. Innocent though that relationship surely was, he would not tolerate the gossip that her disregard for convention was bound to occasion. Damn! It was more than that! And he knew it! He was as jealous as a green cat! Was there no end to the unfamiliar emotions this one young girl could arouse in his breast?

'Thelo stumbled, and Deveryn brought the stallion's head up with a sure touch on the reins. The track was climbing steeply, taking him away from the coastline. He hoped that Maddie would be suitably mollified by all the efforts he was making on her behalf. He thought of her snug in her bed. The picture warmed him as the damp wind caught the tails of his cloak.

But Maddie was not at that moment snug in her bed as the viscount surmised. She was up to her neck in the swollen waters of the ford into which she had tumbled when Banshee had come to grief on a concealed rock. She dragged herself to her knees and sobbed her alarm for her downed mare. When Banshee whinnied and rose on four legs, Maddie sank back in

117

relief. It was the horse who dragged her from her icy stupor, for Banshee was eager to leave the freezing waters far behind, and Maddie was still clutching the reins in her hand. The skirts of her riding habit were like a dead weight as she was half dragged the last few yards to the other side of the ford.

There was no light from the bothy, no welcoming aroma of burning peat lingered on the air. The place was deserted. Maddie did not know whether to be relieved or alarmed. She could not very well stand up to Will Fraser when she was as weak as a drowned kitten. On the other hand, it meant that she had come on a wild goose chase. She thought she might beat her dog when next she found her. At least she had the comfort of knowing that Kelpie was not in Will Fraser's possession. The shepherd was too acute to linger within reach of Maddie's retribution if he had harmed her dog. And conditions had not improved sufficiently to allow him to get far from home. He could be anywhere. And so could Kelpie. Maddie groaned and dragged herself to her feet.

It took only a few minutes to pen Banshee in the open lean-to at the back of the bothy. She found a crock of meal which she knew was reserved for the drovers' dogs. In the circumstances, it was the best she could offer her tired mare.

The bothy itself was a low stone structure with a thatched roof. The door was half falling off its hinges. There was no need to trouble herself about trespassing. The bothy was held in common, belonging to no one, belonging to everyone, and used mostly in emergencies when a sudden mist or fall of snow caught the shepherds off guard in the hills.

Maddie's first task was to get a fire going in the grate. It took her a good half hour. Only then did she light the oil lamp and take stock of her surroundings. To one side of the fireplace was a plain deal table with an assortment of chairs. On the other side, along two walls, were a series of built-in cots covered with sheepskin pelts. A large wooden chest and an assortment of stone crocks and blackened cooking utensils made up the rest of the furnishings—not all the comforts of home by any means, but welcome nevertheless.

She stripped to her chemise and draped her habit and cloak over one of the chairs which she had dragged to the blaze of the fire. The blankets, she knew, would be stored in the large wooden chest to protect them from mice. In a moment, she had opened the lid and was winding a coarse woolen garment under her arms and around her shivering body. Only then did she inspect the stone crocks. As she suspected, they were filled with oatmeal, the staple of Scotland's shepherds—and armies—for centuries past. Though she was hungry, she decided to forego the gruel which could be easily prepared from a cup of the oats and a little boiling water. She had neither the inclination nor the strength to leave the shelter of the bothy to fetch water from the ford. In the last crock, among other things, she found a bottle of whisky.

She withdrew her booty and carried it to the fireplace. Remembering the efficacy of Janet's hot toddies, Maddie forced herself to sample the foul smelling liquid. She drank sparingly. After a while, the numbness began to recede and a delicious feeling of warmth spread along her skin. She drank some more, and decided that she felt considerably more the thing. After another swig, she felt brave enough to consider the implications of her position.

In another hour or so, she thought that she might be able to tolerate the ride back to Drumoak even supposing her clothes could not possibly have dried out by then. After further reflection, she decided that it was imperative that she return to the house before daybreak. Pneumonia she could face, but not the blaze of Deveryn's anger should he discover that she had spent a good part of the night alone, and again unchaperoned, away from home. If she had returned with Kelpie, she would have been vindicated. As it was . . . Her mind refused to finish the thought. She shivered and took another swig from the bottle to stop her teeth from chattering.

Chapter Eight

It was the draft of cold air on her bare shoulder which roused Maddie from her intoxicated slumber. She resisted the pull to wakefulness and snuggled deeper into the warmth of the heaped pile of sheepskin pelts on the cot. A shadow fell across her face and her eyes reluctantly opened.

The first thing she noted was the sheen on the blond head. She stretched in a lazy, natural, cat-like movement. "Malcolm?" she intoned sleepily, and smiled up at the man whose face was hidden in shadow. There was no answer. By degrees, her gaze became more focused. She noted the breadth of shoulder and the silklike tendrils of fine hair across the forehead. No, not Malcolm. Deveryn, of course. He had come to help her after all. Her smile deepened.

"I thought," she said with only the merest slur to her words, "that you weren't coming. What made you change your mind?" She had no idea how damning her words were.

There was no answering smile. "I'm sorry to disappoint you, sweetheart. I'm not Malcolm. Were you expecting him? Oh! Now I think I understand. Is this your usual trysting place?"

Her brows drew together. She was not deceived by the mildness of Deveryn's tone. He was angry. She struggled to come fully awake. After a moment, she pulled herself to her elbows.

"What are you doing?" she asked uncertainly as she watched him throw first his cloak, then his jacket onto one of the spare cots.

"What does it look like I'm doing? I'm undressing. It would

121

be a pity to let all that beauty go to waste." His eyes swept over her, insulting, damning.

There was no doubt in her mind. Deveryn was not merely angry. He was beside himself with fury. Her eyes dropped, following his gaze. The blanket had dropped to her waist and the fine linen chemise was plastered to her damp full breasts like a second skin. She hastily drew the blanket up to her chin, and swung her legs out over the narrow bed. The pleasant effects of the whisky, if that's what she had consumed, were beginning to wear off. Her courage seemed to ebb with them.

"Deveryn," she began with a show of boldness she was far from feeling, "I made a mistake. Will Fraser wasn't here. Now you can say, 'I told you so,' and we can both go home. All right?" Her look was hopeful.

"Wrong!" he said, coming to tower over her. A strong hand tipped her head back and she was forced to look into eyes as turbulent as a summer storm. "You can drop that innocent pose." He shook his head and smiled, feigning amusement. "You must have been laughing up your sleeve to take in a jaded cynic like me. Was Moncrieff in on your game? Well, no matter. Time to pay the piper."

He withdrew his hand and undid the gold studs at the cuffs of his shirt. Maddie's mind went reeling.

"If you're trying to frighten me, Deveryn, you're not succeeding." Unexpectedly, her hand grazed the half-empty bottle at her feet.

The viscount stripped off his shirt and seated himself on the adjacent cot to remove his boots. Maddie stole one swift glance then could not bear to look at that sleek, powerful torso. She flexed her own muscles. Nothing happened. Disappointment mingled with dismay. There could be no question of pitting her puny strength against his. Her hand on the neck of the whisky bottle tightened. Little Maddie Sinclair wasn't afraid of anything, she told herself resolutely.

"Trying to frighten you? On the contrary," he mocked. "After tonight, you'll be under my protection. Let Moncrieff or any man come near you, and I'll kill him."

"Under your protection!" she echoed, her indignation momentarily blotting out the fear she had newly disclaimed he had the power to provoke.

"I see you've heard the expression. Moncrieff, no doubt!" he sneered. "Make no mistake, Maddie, I don't share my mistress, or my lightskirt, with any man."

She tried for a reasonable tone and sounded, even to her own ears, ridiculously prim. "I don't wish to be your mistress."

Very deliberately and cuttingly, he said, "I've no wish for a slut for a wife. You can forget I ever offered you that position."

"I don't wish to be your wife either," she shouted, almost on the brink of hysteria. She had never seen Deveryn so coldly determined. Nothing she said seemed to have the least effect on him. Her mind began to grapple with the logistics of escape.

"Don't worry, I'll meet any price you name."

"Can't you get it through your head? I don't wish to be anything to you." Desperation lent urgency to her voice. "Don't I have any choice in the matter?"

"No! You don't," he said baldly. "To the victor go the spoils. I'll hold you against all comers."

He had stripped naked and Maddie felt that in removing his clothes, he had discarded the fragile veneer that kept him civilized. From his throat down, he was covered in a sheet of hair—not the pale, angelic gold of his head, but a riot of dark copper gold, like a ripe cornfield ready for harvest. The potent virility was overpowering, too much and too soon. She gulped. It was time to make her move.

"Jason," she said, low and sultry, modulating her tone to ape the siren's voice she had once cultivated when playing the part of Clytemnestra in a school play. "Jason," she said again, more softly, and she rose gracefully to her feet. She prayed that he would remain on the cot. If he were to stand, she would lose the advantage. A few steps took her to his side. Though it took all her courage, she put out one hand to touch his naked shoulder. The powerful muscles seemed to contract under her palm.

"Maddie?" he said, and his anger became muted, his expression uncertain.

"I can't fight you any more," and she smiled tremulously.

He expelled his breath slowly, and both hands went to the blanket, stripping it back to reveal the transparent chemise. "Maddie," he said again, and she heard regret, mingled with longing in the single word before she was dragged to stand between his hard thighs. His mouth closed over the raised peak of one breast. "God, Maddie!"

She brought up the bottle and swung it down toward his head. At the last moment, as if warned by a sixth sense, he jerked away, and the blow caught him on the shoulder, close to the neck. Maddie cried out and dropped her weapon. Deveryn was bent over, holding his neck, dazed from the unexpected blow. She clutched the blanket to her and ran.

There was no time to saddle Banshee. She led her mare out of the lean-to and scrambled on her back. Keeping her head well down and clutching Banshee's mane as if her life depended on it, Maddie urged the mare forward. A shrill whistle split the air, and out of the shadows, in front of her, loomed a prancing, snorting monster. It took Maddie a moment to realize that Deveryn had called up his stallion to block her path. Desperately, her heart beating frantically in her throat, she wheeled Banshee to face in the other direction, but Deveryn's stallion circled them, pinning them down like a sheepdog herding skittish sheep toward the pen, and the mare was too nervous to heed her mistress's bidding.

And then Deveryn was there, his hand grasping her bare ankle. Maddie tried to kick herself free, but his hand moved higher, fastening with paralyzing force on the soft flesh of her thigh. With a strangled cry of rage, she threw herself at him. It was a fatal mistake. Her blows were ineffective. She was lifted, high in his arms, and carried to the open door of the bothy. He dumped her roughly on the floor and fastened the latch securely.

"You bitch!" he breathed, and dragged her to her feet. His mouth, purposefully cruel, closed over hers, scorching her lips with the full flame of his anger. She tried to drag her head away, and that small act of resistance seemed to strip away the vestiges of his control. With a vicious jerk, he swung her round and pinned her against the door. Though she tried to shrink from the crush of his body as it pressed relentlessly against hers, her spine flattening against the hard, unyielding surface of the door, he would not permit it. His hand caught her hip, dragging her close to the lower half of his body, forcing her to accept the heat of his muscled thighs pressed intimately against hers.

There was never any doubt in her mind that his motive was punitive. There was nothing of the tender lover who had seduced her to willingness in the darkened nave of the church. His lips burned, his hands bruised, and he used his body like a weapon to subdue her. If it had been any other man, Maddie would have been terrified out of her wits. But this was Deveryn. That he could humiliate her in such a degrading way, making her feel all the implications of her helplessness, fanned her fury to boiling point.

Her puny strength was no match against his. His weight was smothering, permitting her little movement. But what little was left to her, she used to convey her utter contempt for the hurt he was inflicting. Her lips firmed and she pressed them ruthlessly against his until she could feel her teeth grinding his. Her hands clenched on his arms, her nails digging into the corded muscles which restrained her so effortlessly, and she jerked her small body spasmodically, straining against the hard planes of his length.

The change in him was subtle. By degrees, he began to absorb her anger into himself. His lips softened, his muscles relaxed and the cruel clasp of his hands gentled, moving over her back and hips with the sensuous touch of a lover. Maddie's anger flamed higher. He had frightened her half to death, called her vile names. And now he thought to insult her with enforced tenderness! If he cared for her at all, he would never have subjected her to this terror.

She pulled her head back. "Let me go, Deveryn!" There was no pleading this time, only a command.

The wish to punish her had been short lived. The satiny feel of her skin as it pressed intimately against his had aroused other, more compelling emotions. But it angered him that she would still resist when she had given herself freely to Moncrieff. She was an experienced woman. Nothing could change that. He would get over it, in time. But he would be damned if he would tolerate her missish rejection when she had been his for the taking anytime this past week. With bitter clarity he saw himself as a lovesick schoolboy in the throes of first love. Any other woman, he would have simply walked away from. This chit had enslaved him. By God, when he had finished with her, he'd make her *his* slave! She'd known the

125

fumblings of an inexperienced boy. When this was over, she'd know what it was to be pleasured by a man. Wordlessly, he swung her in his arms and carried her to the cot.

He threw himself on top of her before she had a chance to escape him. His mouth closed over hers with restrained savagery, persuasive, pleasuring, unyielding. When she tried to drag her head away to evade the scorching heat of that embrace, his hand grasped her chin, opening her mouth wider, and his tongue forced its way between her teeth to penetrate to the sweet moistness within. That one wanton act of possession had an electrifying effect on him. Deveryn lost control.

He reared over Maddie, his hands dragging at the straps of her chemise. She caught at his wrists to prevent him.

"Don't!" he warned, and there was something in his voice, not anger, not passion, but an unwavering resolve coloured by an emotion which Maddie could not name.

In that moment, she felt as if a hand had closed over her heart. She had credited him with a few redeeming qualities, not least a certain *tendre* for herself. She had been mistaken. Nothing seemed to matter any more.

Her hands fell away, freeing his wrists, and the chemise was swiftly stripped from her. She could not hold that unwavering stare, and turned her head away. Slowly, with deliberate possessiveness, his hands traced the curve of her shoulder, smoothed the indentation of her waist, the flare of her hips, and tested the taut muscles of her abdomen. He stilled and Maddie opened her eyes.

His head was thrown back, his eyes closed, his features carved in harsh lines, and beads of perspiration dewed his skin. In different circumstances she would have supposed that he had endured some unspeakable torture.

Conscience and passion fought for mastery of Deveryn. Doubt took hold in his mind. The girl was trembling, her hands unconsciously trying to shield herself from his gaze. He had known many women. If her innocence was a sham, it was an excellent counterfeit. Then again, she could be a consummate actress.

Without warning, his hands moulded themselves to her breasts, the soft pads of his fingers brushing against the sensitive nipples. The air in Maddie's lungs froze.

"Damn you, no," she cried out, shamed by her body's unexpected response, and flung his hand away.

Her wrists were grasped easily in one strong hand. He held them above her head, gently but forcefully, and he arched her back. His head descended, and she felt the soft pull at her breast as his lips and tongue played with her. A nipple contracted, then hardened as his mouth became more purposeful. Her body jerked, and she sobbed in protest. Her distress was ignored. Sensitive, skillful fingers and lips lavished her with slow, tantalizing caresses. Nothing had ever prepared her for this total seduction of the flesh. She discovered a new enemy that she was forced to contend with. Herself. Outraged will and rioting senses warred within her.

"Maddie, please! Let me!"

The hoarse plea acted on her senses more potently than an aphrodisiac. Her lips formed the word "no" but she became restless. Her breathing changed, became slower, less regular. Deveryn recognized the beginnings of her surrender. He released her hands and eased her legs apart. His hand slid to the silky auburn curls at the junction of her thighs. Unerringly, his fingers found her and pressed to the secret core of her femininity.

Pleasure, sweet and wanton, stirred Maddie's blood, and bone and sinew seemed to melt under Deveryn's sensual onslaught. Flame licked through her veins, heating her skin, engorging the most intimate and secret parts of her femininity. Her pulse soared. Breathing became difficult. She felt the world slip. Instinctively, she reached for Deveryn, seeking a more intimate joining.

His mouth took hers with compelling urgency, his tongue surging and receding in erotic tempo as his fingers sheathed themselves in her soft woman's core. Maddie writhed in an agony of sensation, her body arching rhythmically against his hand. Her hands kneaded the powerful muscles of his shoulders, communicating the depth of her need. Deveryn pulled back. Through passion dazed eyes, he observed the quick rise and fall of her full breasts. The small room seemed to throb with the tempo of their rough breathing.

He eased between her legs. With infinite tenderness, he pushed back the tendrils of curls which lay against her damp

127

cheeks. "Love," he said softly, "forgive me. This will hurt. But only the first time. I'll never hurt you again. I swear it."

The reassuring words were at first unintelligible to Maddie. A moment later, she grasped the full import of their significance. There had never been any doubt in his mind of her innocence. He had used her friendship with Malcolm as a convenient excuse to wreak his will on her.

His thighs settled against the lower part of her body, the demanding hardness of his arousal poised for the final act of possession. He braced himself on one arm.

Tentatively, Maddie stayed him, her hands spreading out against his shoulders. She stared up into the velvet, blue eyes, and she said softly and unflinchingly, "You're not the first, I thought you knew."

He closed his eyes. Instinctively, she shrank from the violence she could sense as the hard muscles of his body tensed. The explosion was not long in coming. His mouth curled in a cruel line, and with a feral snarl, he ripped through the delicate membrane, sheathing himself fully.

Maddie screamed as that rending pain sliced through her. Though she had achieved her object, though she had punished her willful body and cured it of its sensual addiction, the price was more than she had counted on.

"Maddie?" His voice was unmistakably etched with remorse, but still he remained inside her, unmoving, his male arousal stretching her unwilling body to accommodate him.

In her torment, her nails curled into claws and she flayed the rigid muscles of his arms and shoulders. He flinched but made no move to protect himself from her anger. Neither could she compel him to withdraw.

By slow degrees, the pain receded to an uncomfortable fullness. She averted her head and lay like a block of marble beneath the press of his weight. Only then did Deveryn try to coax her to passion again.

She was too spent from everything that had gone before to offer more than a passive resistance. But it was effective. She was deaf to his pleas, immune to the voluptuous caress of his hands, and finally unmoved by his bitter frustration. As he moved upon her, trying to draw a response from her unwilling body, her eyes closed. She concentrated on the pain of the violation she had been forced to endure. It was an effective antidote to passion.

When it was over, he left her abruptly and stalked to the fire. The silence stretched taut. Not for anything would she give him the satisfaction of hearing her whine like a whipped cur. Let his conscience flay him, if he had one.

In a moment, he was back at the cot, looming over her like an angry tiger who had discovered a kitten in his lair.

"How could you do this to me?" His eyes glittered with the strength of his emotion.

The words momentarily robbed Maddie of speech. She pulled herself to a sitting position and dragged one of the sheepskin pelts across her lap.

He repeated his question, but this time, there was no mistaking the hard anger in his voice.

He had frightened her half to death, forced her against her will, and now had the temerity to put her in the wrong. "I think" she retorted, "you have taken the words out of my mouth. *I'm* not the one who has anything to apologize for."

"You wanted me to hurt you!"

It was true, of course. She had known when she had uttered those taunting words that he would not be gentle. She had sought pain as a cure for . . . Her mind shied away from the word that formed on her lips.

"What you did to me was wrong," she parried. "Even if Malcolm was my lover, you had no right to . . ."

"You gave me that right."

"Never!"

"Yes, Maddie. If you're honest with yourself you'll admit it. I'm experienced enough to know when a woman's affections are engaged. I could have taken you anytime I wanted this week past. I held off because I knew you to be an innocent."

"Don't pretend that made a difference. It didn't stop you tonight."

"I was crazed with jealousy. I thought you had betrayed me with Moncrieff."

"Liar! Your words convict you. You knew that this was my first time!"

"I learned it only as I made love to you. I could tell that you had never been with a man before. By that time, it was

129

impossible to stop what I'd begun. God, Maddie, what else should I think when I found you naked and with that cub's name on your lips but that I had surprised you in a secret tryst?"

"If you had asked, you would have learned that I had fallen in the ford. I was waiting for my clothes to dry. And it's not the first time I've mistaken you for Malcolm."

"All this is beside the point," he interrupted. "When you said those words to me, and at such a moment, you knew what the outcome would be. Why, Maddie, why?"

There was a thread of something in his voice which gave her pause. She studied his face carefully. His expression was open, vulnerable. A rush of guilt, as sudden as it was inexplicable, surprised her. She squelched it.

"I saw no reason why I should conspire in my own ruin," she answered coldly.

"Your ruin?" He settled himself at the edge of the cot and grasped her chin firmly, turning her face up to the light. "I've never yet ruined a woman." She could tell that she had kindled his anger again. "Don't bandy words with me, my girl. Between us, such clichés are meaningless. If anyone has been ruined, it is I."

"That's preposterous," she countered.

"Is it?" I've never had a moment's peace since you forced yourself into my life. You've robbed me of my desire for other women; made me dissatisfied with my lot; cast a pall over my future when I think of it without you, and worst of all, you've made me act contrary to my own principles. What more can you do to me?"

"What more can I do to *you?*" she asked, outrage strangely mingled with contrition. He should be grovelling at her feet, not taking her to task when she was the injured party. "Damn you! You *hurt* me."

For a moment, his gaze faltered. When he brought his head up, the thick veil of his golden eyelashes effectively concealed his expression. "You're right of course, though I plead extenuating circumstances." A crooked smile played across his face. "I'll make it up to you, and that's a promise."

When she remained discouragingly silent, the smile gradually faded though the unrepentant amusement lingered in his voice. "I see. Nothing will do for you but sackcloth and ashes. Frankly, I've no taste for protracted penance and such like. Do you expect me to wear a hair shirt for the rest of my life?"

"Of course not!" Pride dictated the snappish retort, but nevertheless, Maddie was honest enough to admit, at least to herself, that she had expected more than an offhanded dismissal of the torment he had put her through.

She watched warily as he recovered the whisky bottle she had earlier used against him. He uncorked it and offered it to her. "Drink," he ordered. Then more gently, "It will do you good."

He waited till she had taken a few sips then put the lip of the bottle to his mouth and took a long, greedy draught. "I needed that," he said, and set the bottle aside. "What are you thinking?"

The words startled her. Her eyes, which had been staring into space, flew to his. Without thinking, she answered, "I was wondering what I should tell my husband on my wedding night."

She knew immediately that it had been the wrong thing to say. The glitter was back in his eyes and she could have sworn that she heard the hiss of his breath as he inhaled it through his teeth. For some reason, she thought her words had wounded him. It surprised her even more when she discovered that she did not wish to cause him pain. She put an uncertain hand on his arm. "Don't give it a thought. I shan't marry anyone under false pretenses."

"Tell me," he drawled, "are you saying this to annoy me on purpose, or do you have an unfortunate knack for saying the wrong thing at the wrong time?"

"I don't know what you mean."

"Forget it! Your sentiments are irrelevant now. As are mine. I told you. I've never yet ruined a woman. We'll be married within the fortnight. Now get some sleep. I'll waken you in an hour or so. By that time your clothes should be dry."

There was no point in arguing. Maddie recognized the ring of authority in his voice. She had heard that tone often enough in school from Miss Maitland in her heyday and knew better than test a temper which was unpredictable at the best of times. She

131

settled herself in the warmth of the soft sheepskin pelts. The thought occurred to her that she was behaving with remarkable calm under the circumstances. Perhaps she'd had too much to drink. The feeling of euphoria was not unpleasant. Her thoughts wandered. She burrowed deeper. Fleeces, she thought. Jason and his quest for the golden fleece. Medea's Jason . . . Maddie's Jason . . . The male of the species didn't stand a chance when he roused his womenfolk against him. "Have a care, Jason," she murmured drowsily. "Have a care." Sleep claimed her quickly.

The room was hot. For a disoriented moment, with her eyes closed, she did not know where she was. She felt the familiar softness of the sheep pelts at her back. The male scent of him filled her nostrils. He must be very close. She opened one eye, slowly and carefully.

He was crowding her to one side of the cot, leaning over her, and still not a stitch on him. She closed her eyes against the potency of that masculine appeal.

"Are you all right?" he asked. His gentleness surprised her.

For a moment, she was mystified by the question. Both eyes fluttered open. "I'm fine."

"You're not . . . sore—in pain?"

"Oh!" Comprehension dawned. She wriggled surreptitiously beneath the sheepskin. "No." Her surprise was evident. "No," she repeated with more assurance, but she could not prevent the blush that stole across her cheeks.

He smiled at that, one of his rare, unaffected grins which never failed to rob Maddie of that clarity of thinking on which she so prided herself. She found herself grinning back like, as she was later to furiously chide herself, a lovestruck moonling. If she had only kept her head and resisted that potent charm which he projected so unconsciously, events might have taken a different turn.

The back of his fingers lightly stroked her bare arm. "The pain was inevitable, Maddie. It's part of the price of being a woman. If it's any consolation, I've already donned that hair shirt, figuratively speaking. It's dashed uncomfortable, let me tell you. But I won't remove it till you give me permission."

And as if she had been completely castaway, which she knew she was not, tears gathered in her eyes and all she could say between gulps was, "Oh Jason!" "Oh Jason"—not even distancing him with his title!

"Don't love." His hand went to the nape of her neck and began a slow, gentle massage. His voice was husky with checked emotion. "I would give everything I have in the world to turn the clock back. I'm not going to ask for your forgiveness. I don't deserve to be let off so easily. I shall try to earn it by so filling your days with happiness and your nights with love that you'll forget the pain and sordidness of our first joining."

She could not doubt his sincerity. The habitual mask of inscrutability had vanished. His heart was in his eyes.

She was deeply affected. She wanted to throw herself in his arms and offer herself as consolation for the pain she saw reflected there. What prevented her?

She looked inward, trying to identify the blurred emotions which flowed and ebbed in such profusion. Guilt. Shame. Dread. Regret.

Deveryn was right. He could have taken her anytime this past week. It was his principles which had been her best protection. Her own had dwarfed into insignificance from the moment of their first fateful encounter. How had she allowed herself to give this man so much power over her—the man upon whom she was sworn to be revenged? Pain expanded and contracted in her chest leaving a residue of blessed numbness.

She drew herself up to a sitting position and eased back against the wall.

"What time is it?" she asked in as matter-of-a-fact tone as she could manage in the circumstances.

"We have lots of time."

She was mulling over his answer when she detected his smothered chortle.

"Strawberries, ripe and succulent," he mused.

"What?"

Her eyes followed the path of his intent gaze. The sheepskin had slipped to her waist, exposing the ruby red tips of her breasts. Under her horrified gaze, they seemed to swell and throb with a life of their own. Her glance sliced to Deveryn. Amusement warmed that faintly challenging expression.

His eyes leisurely swept over her, then came to rest on a

bared shoulder. "I've found one. I knew I would." One long finger brushed across her skin. Maddie shifted uncomfortably.

"Stop that." The warning was automatic.

"Stop what?"

"You know!"

"Don't you like me touching you?" he asked softly.

"Of course not."

His hand instantly lifted from her shoulder. Maddie made no attempt to cover herself with the sheepskin which lay across her lap.

Into the silence, she said. "What have you found?"

"A freckle." Again, his hand descended, a butterfly touch, tracing a circular pattern on her arm.

"Oh, is that all!" She couldn't think straight when his hands were on her.

"Are there more? I thought there might be. Where are they hiding?"

Their eyes held. He was watching and waiting. Cover yourself, Maddie's conscience told her sternly. Her heart gave her a different, contradictory message.

"Why do you want to know?" Her voice was almost a whisper.

"I promised myself I would kiss every last one of them when I finally claimed you for my own."

Maddie fleetingly thought of the horrid spots which had never quite faded from the oddest places on her person—a result of exposing her skin to the sun on those rare occasions when she had indulged in a nude dip in the river Forth on an intolerably hot summer day. He surely did not mean to kiss her THERE! A jolt of heat suffused her loins, and fire seemed to spread upwards from the tips of her toes to the ends of each curly strand of hair on her head. When his mouth descended, and his warm lips brushed her shoulder, she put out a hand in a half-hearted attempt to ward him off.

He captured her hand and brought it to his groin, curling her fingers around the silky length of his arousal. Maddie's heart stopped beating, then raced out of control. Against her express wishes, her thighs parted to the insistent pressure of his hand.

"Strawberries," he said, his mouth open and moist, closing over one throbbing nipple. "My favourite . . ."

The sheepskin was brushed aside and his lips coursed down, heating every inch of Maddie's already feverish skin.

"How many . . . freckles . . . are there?" she asked on a difficult breath.

He laughed softly before answering. "Not nearly as many as I'd hoped. I shall take steps to remedy that deficiency in future."

Future, thought Maddie through a passion-drugged haze. She would not think about that now. Tomorrow was a long, long way off. Touching. She craved it. Until that moment, she had not known the depth of her longing to be held. She was starved for physical contact. That Deveryn was using her for his own purposes—even that could not stifle the yearning which had taken hold.

When he stretched out full length beside her, she welcomed him. "Hold me, touch me," she breathed against his mouth.

"Maddie!" he groaned, gathering her in his arms and holding her close. His kiss was gentle and reassuring until she opened her mouth to him. The taste of surrender was on her lips. Passion exploded through him. His kiss deepened, urging her to accept the more complete possession of his body.

He dragged her leg over his hip. Slowly, ruthlessly battening down his desire, he entered her. When she cried out, he stilled. "Am I hurting you?"

She shook her head. "No. It's not that. But I don't think . . . I can't . . . you must stop."

"Maddie!" he protested, and eased deeper.

"Don't!" she implored, and her head began to move restlessly from side to side. "Jason . . . help me! Something awful is going to happen. I can feel it building inside me!"

Her words unleashed some instinct, some primeval force, deep within him. He surged against her, carrying her over on to her back. He braced himself on his hands and levered himself higher, savouring the deeper, more complete penetration. Then he began to move. When she matched his rhythm with her own arching body, he felt the pleasure burst through him like waves of liquid fire.

"I warned you!" she sobbed and in mingled ecstasy and distress, clamped her small white teeth on his arm.

Deveryn scarcely felt the bite of her teeth. Never had this

135

ultimate act involved more than the taking and giving of pleasure. Nothing in his past experience had ever prepared him for this overpowering need to brand this woman as his mate. His movements became rougher. At his hoarse command, she obediently wrapped her legs around his flanks, and he exulted that she would permit him whatever he desired. Her shocked gasp of pleasure brought a chuckle of triumph before the rippling waves of ecstasy claimed him. Never, he thought, as she writhed beneath his thrusting body and he took his own shuddering release, never had a woman ever meant as much to him as this one slip of a girl. They were one flesh. Until that moment, he had never understood the full significance of those simple words.

When it was over, the familiar rush of tenderness returned. He pulled to his side, keeping her fitted to his length. He showered her with unending kisses and lazy, calmly possessive caresses.

Maddie burst into tears. "I told you and told you," she said between sniffles, "but you wouldn't listen."

"Now what's troubling you?" He reluctantly uncoupled their joined bodies, but his ministrations continued unabated.

"I bit you," she mumbled against his throat. "I'm sorry! Truly! I don't know what came over me. I've never known myself to lose control like that."

He shifted his weight slightly to allow her to draw breath. On the deepest tenderness, he said, "Little ignoramus! That's how it's supposed to be." He planted a languid kiss on her nose. "More freckles," he added by way of explanation.

Her dark eyes stared unblinkingly into his. Then she took his breath away by saying, quite simply, "Thank you."

"For what?"

She was hard pressed to give him an answer. How could she explain that the void which had so long been a part of her, seemed, inexplicably, to have shrunk to manageable proportions.

"For . . . the comfort. I think I've been empty for a long time. I don't feel empty now." And she touched her fingers to the fall of blond hair which fell across his brow.

Though her words affected him deeply, he could not keep the smile from his voice. "Comfort?" he mused. "Is that what it is? Then I'm in luck. I've an insatiable need for comforting for a host of slights and wounds I've endured in the span of my thirty years. Let's see now. It began, I think, when I was three years old and nurse spanked me for . . . I forget the reason now." He kissed her long and deep. "And then," he went on, his voice turning low and husky, "there was the time I fell off my horse. That was when I was five or thereabouts. Comfort me, Maddie," he breathed, and capturing her hand, he dragged it down the length of his body.

"But I didn't mean . . . ," she interposed quickly. A slow, persuasive kiss cut her off in mid-sentence.

"Didn't you? Then let this be a lesson to you, my girl. Never, ever, put suggestions into my mind, however innocently meant, unless you are prepared for the consequences."

"But . . ." He wasn't interested in her explanation. Evidently, he had begun a new hunt for those horrid spots. She wondered if Jason had the odd freckle concealed on his person. It was her last coherent thought for some time to come.

Chapter Nine

The slight touch on her shoulder startled her into wakefulness. Janet's lined face came into focus hovering over her. Her eyes were shadowed with anxiety. Maddie's accelerated heartbeat slowly subsided. She was in Drumoak, in her own chamber, in her own bed. And she felt *awful*.

"I must have dozed. What time is it?"

She struggled to her feet and cast a swift glance around the room as if to satisfy herself that she had left the demons of her dreams far behind. Her eyes came to rest on the reflection in the cheval mirror. She *looked* awful. The riding habit she had worn the night before was creased beyond redemption and a small, chalk-white face with sooty circles under the eyes stared back at her.

The old housekeeper mentioned a name.

"He's here? So soon?"

"Aye. In the library, wi' yer aunt, waitin' yer pleasure. Yer stepmother has been sent for."

"I didn't expect father's solicitor to get here before afternoon."

"It is afternoon."

"Oh." Her eyes travelled to the clock on the mantelpiece. She calculated that she had slept a good four hours since she'd flung herself down on her bed in a state of exhaustion after Deveryn had brought her home. The story that he had concocted, that they'd been out for an early morning ride, had passed without raising an eyebrow. He was awake on all suits, that one. She supposed that a life of dalliance with other men's

139

wives made a man adept at getting out of tight corners. She should be grateful to him. But she wasn't. She was irritated.

"Tea and shortbread, I think, Janet, for my aunt and Mr. Forsythe. That should give me time to tidy myself. Oh, and if you would be so kind, one of your elderberry possets for me. I've wakened with a bit of headache," she explained with a weak smile.

"Headache," grunted Janet as she made for the door. "Mayhap I should make Kelpie a posset as well. That wee dog had the same look about her when she skulked into my kitchen at first light."

Maddie said nothing. But when the door closed behind Janet, she expelled a long sigh of relief. Janet's shrewd eyes saw too much. She might keep her tongue between her teeth when his lordship smoothly articulated his barefaced lies, but such constraint was not a courtesy she was like to offer the mistress she had nursed since she had been in swaddling clothes. Thank God that only the servants had been up and about when she and Deveryn had ridden in!

And Kelpie! Damn that dog! She had not known whether to be relieved or furious when her pet had come flying out of the stable door to greet them as if the hounds of hell were after her. She looked to have been rolling in every filth infested midden between Drumoak and Edinburgh. And the stench which had clung to the matted coat was foul beyond description. Maddie had been too angry to say one kind word to her wayward pet.

"Dunk her in the duck pond and tie her up," she had told Duncan tersely before stalking into the house.

"Don't be too hard on her," she heard Deveryn say in an amused undertone at her back as she reached the top of the stairs. "The pup is only a pawn in nature's game. Perhaps she merely answered the call of her mate. Even humans have been known to do as much."

The words had brought a fiery bloom to her cheeks. Now they were as pale as parchment. She pinched them hard. The improvement was almost negligible. Perhaps a good dunk in the duck pond was what she deserved as well. She tried not to think of how shamelessly she had responded to Deveryn's careful tutoring in a long night of passion. She failed, and colour flooded her cheeks.

"Oh Jason, what am I to do about you?" she said softly into the empty room. She felt warm and achy inside, and terribly frightened. "Damn you, Jason Verney. You've made me fall in love with you."

With swift, angry movements, she stripped to her chemise and went to the washbasin to sponge herself off with cold water. It brought to mind Deveryn's intimate ministrations of the night before when he had insisted on bathing her. Just thinking of those powerful masculine hands so gentle in love brought a flush of heat to her loins. She must have been as drunk as a lord to insist on performing the same office for him!

When Janet returned, she was doing up the last few buttons of her black bombazine. The posset was silently proffered.

Maddie brought the glass to her nose and sniffed. "What's this?"

"Hot toddie," said Janet baldly.

"But . . ."

"Whisky is the only cure for what ails ye."

"Oh." She drank it off without saying a word.

In the library, she found Mr. Forsythe and the ladies. Of Deveryn, there was no sign. Maddie was grateful for small mercies. She did not think she was ready to face him yet.

Mr. Forsythe was seated behind her father's desk. He rose to his feet as she came into the room.

Though she had had little converse with the man over the years, what little she knew of him was more than satisfactory. He was a contemporary of her father, and as she understood, had been at one time his friend. He was of medium height and of swarthy complexion. When she was a child, she'd imagined that he was a pirate. The thought brought a smile to her lips. Age had mellowed him, softened the harsh features. She'd learned long since that his interests ran to the scholarly, but she still held to the opinion that he would look in his proper milieu on the brig of a ship.

"Well Maddie, it's a sorry business that brings us together again. My condolences."

She murmured her thanks and accepted the chair that he held for her. "How are the girls?" she asked politely. As she remembered, Forsythe had been a widower for a number of

141

years. He'd never married again. Not like her father.

"Blooming. Perhaps you remember the eldest, Mary Anne? She goes to your old school after summer. I'm not wholly convinced that a formal education of the sort Miss Maitland espouses is quite the thing for a gently-bred girl, but I'm willing to give it a shot." He could not quite erase the pride from his voice. "Mary Anne is a remarkably clever girl. It would be a pity to deprive her of this opportunity—or so she has persuaded me."

Cynthia looked knowingly at Miss Spencer and raised her eyebrows in an I-told-you-so gesture. The message was understood by the older woman—the Scots and their inexplicable reverence for higher education, even for girls!

Miss Spencer rose to her feet and, in a lull in the conversation, excused herself. "I'm having the carriage sent round to take me to the manse. I promised Mrs. Moncrieff that I'd help her plan for the spring sale of work. No, no, you're not chasing me away," she disclaimed when Mr. Forsythe expressed a polite regret. "I've been looking forward to a quiet coze with Margaret all week, and I know you'll be anxious to have things settled as soon as possible."

The "carriage" was a one horse gig, but Miss Spencer, without design, employed the language of her girlhood. To her, all conveyances which ran on wheels and carried passengers were known by the exalted title of "carriage."

When the door closed on her, Cynthia addressed herself to the solicitor. "Before you begin, I should like to have my advocate present."

"Your advocate?" Forsythe asked, one brow arching.

"Lord Deveryn." And she shot Maddie a bright, victorious smile.

"By all means. I have no objection, if you think it's necessary." The solicitor's eyes, frankly curious, moved between Maddie and Cynthia. "It's not a complex will, however. I don't really see the necessity."

"Nevertheless," Cynthia interposed. "Lord Deveryn has offered to represent my interests."

The bold, challenging statement hit Maddie with all the impact of a ton of coal. She forced a cool smile to her lips, but she dared not trust herself to speak. That she could still

142

regulate her breathing, she counted as a small victory.

The bellrope was duly pulled and Deveryn sent for. When he strode in, Maddie sliced a glance at him. In his elegantly tailored superfine, he looked immaculate and disgustingly healthy. Also cheerful. Her lips tightened.

She watched with a jaundiced eye as he introduced himself to the solicitor. His handshake was firm, his manner warm, cordial, confident. The whole thing was obviously premeditated. It rankled.

"As to my presence here," she heard him begin to explain.

"We know why you're here, Deveryn," she interrupted. "Can we get on with it, d'you think? Mr. Forsythe has been kept kicking his heels too long as it is." Her words were ungracious, but she was past caring. It occurred to Maddie that the viscount's real purpose in coming to Drumoak was about to be revealed. She adjusted her guard. It was just as well she did, for when she lifted her eyes to his, the warmth in those twinkling orbs hit her like the blaze from a blacksmith's forge.

He inclined his head, the merest mockery of a bow, and strolled leisurely to the vacant chair beside her own. "Miss Sinclair. You look like death warmed up. You slept well, I trust?" The soft undertone was like a sensual caress.

"Tolerably," she managed, though she almost choked on that one word.

He flashed her a smile. She sent him a quelling frown. Mr. Forsythe cleared his throat. He began to read the last will and testament of Donald George Forbes Montagu Sinclair. It was dated February 1810, the day of his marriage to Cynthia. The document was simple and to the point. To Maddie was left the house and lands of Drumoak and all the rents which accrued thereto. The estate had been larger when the will had been drawn up. There were no tenants and no rents now to augment her meagre income. To the widow went an acreage in Upper Canada valued at approximately five hundred pounds. Last of all, there were various small bequests to old retainers.

"And that's all?" The furious question came from Cynthia.

"More or less."

"In other words, my husband has left me destitute."

"Scarcely that!" Forsythe turned back a page. "Perhaps I should have read the preamble. Ah . . . here we are. 'Having

143

settled upon my wife Cynthia Rose Foxe Sinclair the sum of ten thousand pounds on our marriage to be used for her sole use and at her discretion, I bequeath the remainder of all properties, revenues, and chattels as follows.' So you see, you were provided for, quite handsomely I might say, considering the value of your husband's estate.''

"Fool! That money was spent long since. What am I to live on now?'' She threw a beseeching look at the viscount. He silenced her with a cool, cautionary stare.

When he turned that taut, implacable profile upon the solicitor, his lips relaxed into a half smile. "Mr. . . . er . . . Forsythe? There is still the matter of Miss Sinclair's guardians to be broached. Pray continue.''

The solicitor recognized the will of iron behind the innocuous words. Without further prompting, he found his place. "Yes, of course.'' His eyes scanned the document in his hands. He coughed. "Here we are, and I quote, 'In the event that I should die before my daughter, Madeleina, reaches her majority, I appoint as her guardian, my younger half brother, Thomas Andrew Sinclair of Stonehaven, Kincardinshire.' Well, nothing could be plainer than that.''

"Oh nothing!'' said Cynthia with biting sarcasm. "How like Donald! His brother emigrated to Canada the very month we were wed.''

Mr. Forsythe gave a small sigh of regret. It was to the viscount that he addressed his remarks. "True. I remember mentioning that fact to Donald at the time. In spite of my misgivings, he could not be constrained to change the will.''

Deveryn uttered a soft expletive. "And Sinclair appointed no other guardian, not even when he knew that his brother was so far removed that his influence was bound to be negligible?''

"My lord, you know the answer to that question as well as I. To be fair, Donald thought that the day of his demise was so far distant that a guardian for Maddie was merely a formality. It's a common failing, and utterly human.''

"And improvident and unforgivable,'' said Deveryn.

The solicitor felt the personal censure in the biting words. He met the hard stare unflinchingly. He lowered his voice so that only the viscount could hear. "Maddie could not be worse served by a guardian in absentia that she was by her own father in his later years."

The shadow gradually left Deveryn's face. He acknowledged the words with a curt nod. Mr. Forsythe felt the tension ease.

Maddie rose to her feet. She had heard little of the exchange between the two men since the solicitor had disclosed the name of her guardian. Her relief was transparent to all. "I can't take it in. Uncle Tom to be my guardian! In my whole life, I only met him a couple of times. I understood that he was sent away with a cloud over his head."

"So he was," replied the solicitor, "though I've no information as to what peccadillo prompted his removal to Canada. He was a goodly number of years younger that your father and the black sheep of the family, as I understand. Also, quite unfit for the role your father chose for him. But Donald could not be gainsaid in this whim. As I recall, he seemed to think it would be a slap in the face for some other relative who stood to fill the slot."

"My grandfather," Maddie absently informed him. She strolled to the window and looked out at the avenue of old oaks. Life at Drumoak would continue as it always had, each day as safe and predictable as the one that went before. And as empty. She shied away from the thought. She had what she had always wanted. In time, she would forget Deveryn. She was sure that she was not the first woman to have said those words to herself. If others had forgotten him, so could she, for she had more reason. But oh, it would not be easy.

"Did you know your husband's half brother, Cynthia?" asked Deveryn in a quiet aside.

"Scarcely at all. Donald didn't have much to say about him, and what little he did wasn't good. Jason, about my claims to the estate . . ."

"All in good time. Trust me." He raised his voice. "Mr. Forsythe, it's obvious that the girl can't stay here." From the corner of his eye, he caught Maddie's abrupt movement as she spun to face him. He kept his gaze fixed on the solicitor's face and rose slowly to his feet.

Forsythe's eyes lifted to assess the formidable set of shoulders, the arrogant, indolent posture, the determined cast of countenance.

"Go on," he said cautiously.

"Since Maddie's father has failed to make suitable provision for her, it's up to you to decide what's best for the girl. May I suggest that you allow me to convey her to her grandfather in London? He is her nearest living relative here and would be well within his rights to contest this capricious disposal of his granddaughter's future.

"No!" Maddie's cry of denial might never have been uttered for all the notice Deveryn took of it.

"Think man!" he said persuasively. "She can't stay here."

Surprise held Maddie immobile for a moment. Then, in a flurry of skirts, she was across the room and had thrust herself in front of Deveryn. She flattened her hands along the top of the desk, bracing her weight to steady herself. Unconsciously, on the other side of the desk, Forsythe edged himself back in his seat, his head tilted as he looked up at her.

"Mr. Forsythe," she appealed, "I don't wish to leave Drumoak. This is my home. If you send me to my grandfather, you will be going against the express wishes of my father. I won't go! And you can't make me!"

Over Maddie's head, the eyes of the two men locked, Forsythe cleared his throat nervously. "My lord, you credit me with more authority than I deserve. I am only a servant of the law and must abide by my client's wishes. However, if Maddie were to consent to what you suggest, and until her guardian decrees otherwise, I would not cavil with sending her to her grandfather."

"You mean that the decision rests with the girl?"

"The choice is not mine to make, my lord," protested the solicitor.

Deveryn swore under his breath.

Maddie straightened. "Thank you, Mr. Forsythe," she said simply. Though she could not meet Deveryn's eyes, she half turned in his direction and said firmly. "This is for the best. I tried to tell you how it must be."

The line of his jaw tightened. "I won't accept that. Do you mean to let your father rule your life from the grave?"

When she did not answer, he asked her abruptly, "Where is this guardian to be found? Do you have his direction, or has he conveniently disappeared off the face of the earth?"

The sneer stung Maddie. "I can lay my hands on one of his

letters if you grant me a few minutes."

"Do so!"

Deveryn's terse imperative galvanized her into action. Without a word, she turned on her heel and made a speedy exit. Her father's personal belongings had been removed to a boxroom in the attic. It took her a good half hour to find what she was looking for. A little dusty and warm cheeked from her exertions, she sped into the library flourishing the yellowing letter in her hand. She came to a dead stop.

Cynthia and Deveryn were standing with heads close together, her hands absently fingering the lapel of his jacket. They turned when she entered. It was Deveryn who stepped away and cooly took the letter out of Maddie's hand.

A silent message seemed to pass from Deveryn to Cynthia. There was a moment's hesitation, then Cynthia threw Maddie a brilliant smile and brushed past her. The door closed softly. Maddie and Deveryn were alone.

"Where is Mr. Forsythe?" she asked, a little breathless from her headlong flight down the stairs.

"He's gone back to Edinburgh."

"Edinburgh?" she echoed foolishly. "What for?"

"His business here is concluded. I promised to convey the letter to him in a day or two. There's no hurry."

"Oh."

"Sit down Maddie." His expression betrayed no clue to what he was thinking.

With affected indifference, but obedient to the firm clasp of the viscount's hand on her elbow, Maddie allowed herself to be led to a chair. Deveryn's hand on her shoulder gently but forcefully pushed her into it.

He lounged gracefully against the desk, but said nothing till Maddie had composed herself. The light was behind him, his broad shoulders silhouetted against the glare from the window, his face in shadow. She suspected that he had deliberately arranged it so that she would feel the full force of his intimidating physique.

"You can't stay here, and that's final."

"Why—why can't I?"

"You've no one to look out for your interests."

"My aunt . . ."

147

". . . is an unexceptionable lady, but unsuitable for the purposes of a guardian. You draw rings round her, Maddie. That much has been proved. I shall escort you to your grandfather in London." He permitted himself a small smile. "He shall decide what's to be done with you. I've persuaded your solicitor to my opinion. So you see, argument is pointless."

She answered him without heat. "I don't think so, Deveryn. Really, it's better if I stay here."

"You'll do as I say." He said the words flatly, dispassionately, all the more lethal in Maddie's ears because of their underlying confidence.

"Mr. Forsythe said otherwise."

His eyes narrowed, his lips firmed. He surveyed her for a long, considering moment. Finally, in a voice as smooth as glass, he said, "Perhaps I'm not explaining myself very well. Let me put it this way. After what happened between us last night, it is imperative that I make amends. I don't know yet how this marriage can be managed without your guardian's permission, but I aim to try. It seems logical to put my case before your grandfather. I have no inclination to divide my time between London and Edinburgh. And your place is by my side."

His words revolved in her mind. Though they were passionless, she was not ungrateful for his concern. Nor would she hold him solely responsible for what had transpired at the bothy. Her own share of guilt was felt more keenly than she cared to admit, and involved far more than the loss of her virginity.

She had sworn on her father's grave to be revenged on the man who had wronged him. In less than a month, she was sharing his bed. Was she then to compound her betrayal by making the arrangement permanent? She could not do it, though she was sorely tempted.

Her eyes slid away from his. In a voice low with emotion, she tried to explain why she must refuse him. "I think I've told you before, how things stand with me. I could not reconcile my conscience with marriage to the man who . . . who—you know what I'm trying to say. As for last night, I do not hold that against you. My one wish is to forget that it ever happened. If you truly wish to make amends, you will leave here, and quickly."

She was unnerved by the protracted silence which followed. She chanced a quick look at his profile. His attention was held by a packet of papers which lay on the desk. He fingered them idly.

Finally, he said, "I wonder at this loyalty to your father, Maddie. The man must have been a paragon."

"He loved me," she defended quickly, hearing the thread of mockery in his tone.

"Did he?"

"I don't wish to discuss my father with you." She tried to make her words crushing, final.

"That doesn't surprise me. You're the only person I've come across who has a good word to say about him. He was selfish to the core, and deep down you know it. Look at this place!" he went on with a comprehensive wave of one hand, dismissing the poverty of her inheritance.

"That's not fair! When my mother was alive, things were different. It was after he married Cynthia that things began to change."

She jumped when he slammed his hand angrily against the desk. "Cynthia is a convenient excuse, and you know it! You forget, I knew your father in London. The man was a gamester, a profligate. He never gave you a thought. Now that I know more of him, I take leave to doubt that your mother was very happy either. And as for Cynthia, we both know . . ."

"I want you out of my house and off my property," she told him furiously. "You have said unforgivable things about my father. You know nothing about him. I won't listen to another word. Get out. I never want to see you again."

His hands clamped on her shoulders. "Listen to me well, Maddie. Drumoak is not yours. It belongs to me. Do you understand? Your loving father lost your inheritance."

His words made no sense to her. "You're mad!"

"I would not claim something I could not prove." He rose to his feet and retrieved the packet he had been earlier toying with. He tossed it into her lap. "The deed to Drumoak," he said coldly. "Lock, stock, and barrel. It belongs to me. See for yourself."

His air of quiet confidence persuaded her that he was deadly

149

serious. With uncertain fingers, she began to smooth out the documents he had so carelessly thrown at her. In a matter of minutes, she was in full possession of the facts. Scalding tears gathered in her eyes. Angrily, she blinked them away.

"What threat did you use to get my father to sign away my birthright?"

Deveryn uttered a soft imprecation. "I won it in a game of cards, if you must know. Surely that doesn't surprise you? Isn't that how you lost your dog?" He surveyed her bowed head for a moment, then tempered the violence of his tone. "How can you choose him over me when he has treated you so abominably?"

"I don't understand." Her voice held an oddly pleading note. "Why are you doing this? Why now? Why didn't you tell me that Drumoak was yours at the outset when you arrived?"

As if he were soothing a hurt child, he said softly, "I would not be telling you now if you had listened to reason. You leave me no choice. I am going to escort you to your grandfather, and that's the end of it."

"Then what will become of Drumoak?"

"That doesn't concern you, since it is no longer yours."

Her shoulders slumped, but only for a moment. She was on her feet, moving restlessly about the room, fighting to regain a modicum of composure. Only one thing kept her spine straight. Pride. That Drumoak was lost to her, and in such a manner, incensed her.

"What's mine and what's yours?" she asked suddenly.

"I beg your pardon?"

"If I'm to leave here, I must know what I'm permitted to take with me. My mother's miniature, for instance, my books, my dog? I've no wish to find myself locked up in the tollbooth for theft." To her regret, the break in her voice robbed the scathing words of some of their force.

He shook his head and said very gently and quietly, "Maddie, there's no occasion for this. I'm very conscious of my obligation to you. If you would simmer down, you'd admit that everyone's best interests will be served by what I propose."

The soothing words acted on her temper like a spark on dry tinder. "What exactly did you relieve my father of, Deveryn?

You said lock, stock and barrel. What does that mean?" she demanded angrily.

"If it makes any difference, the contents of the house belong to you. Otherwise, every stone, every blade of grass, every tree and leaf are mine. And," he added as an afterthought, "the herds and stock, of course."

"My father's cellar?"

"Yours, I regret to say."

He was relaxed, a conciliatory half smile playing about his lips. She knew exactly what she was going to do with the fine cellar he coveted before she shook the dust of Drumoak from her feet. The thought made her own lips curl slightly.

"That's more like it. You're a better loser than I gave you credit for."

"Deveryn, you don't know me at all. How soon do you want me out of here?" she taunted.

His brows shot up. "There is no hurry. As I said, I have to go to Edinburgh on business. I should be ready to leave in another day or so."

"I'll be gone by the time you get back."

Her words rekindled his anger. "Don't try it," he warned her. "You'll be packed and ready to leave when I return. Nothing more."

The calm assurance that he could order her life to suit himself after bringing her world down about her ears broke the tenuous thread of her self-control. Like a furious, spitting kitten, she turned on him.

"You're not my guardian, Deveryn. Neither is my grandfather. I'll talk to my solicitor before I'll let you drag me off to London without a fight. Drumoak isn't everything. I don't need it. I can make my own way in the world without help or interference from anyone."

"Fine."

"What?"

"We'll see Forsythe together." He folded his arms and regarded her calmly. "It's a useless exercise, but I'm willing to indulge you. Forsythe has already accepted my advice on this matter. But get one thing straight, Maddie. I don't give a jot for the man's sentiments. Come hell or high water, you leave with me for London."

151

A jumble of words trembled on her lips. She bit them back. She shook her head. Her throat was choked with all the unshed tears she had been forced to swallow since Deveryn had so carelessly sent her world spinning.

"Try to put yourself in my place," he said gently. "After last night, our marriage became inevitable. There's no going back now."

"Marriage? Are you mad? I wouldn't let you touch me if my life depended on it," she stormed at him.

"You let me touch you last night, and more," he told her with furious calm. "You liked what I did to you."

A fiery blush suffused her cheeks. "Last night I was drunk, or didn't you notice? If I hadn't been, do you think I would have allowed myself to be dragged into an incestuous affair? I feel filthy all over."

He grabbed her shoulder and shook her violently. She clamped her teeth together to prevent them rattling.

"What nonsense is this? What incestuous affair?"

"Mother and daughter," she said between gritted teeth. "You stand in the place of a father to me. If you legalize your connection with my stepmother, I shall call you 'Papa.'"

"Stepmother," he roared, "not mother. You're not related."

"And if, God forbid, I ever find myself shackled to you, Cynthia will call you her son."

He practically threw her from him. She stumbled backwards and fell against the chair.

"What a filthy little mind you conceal behind that innocent facade," he spat at her. "If you ever say such things to me again, I shall beat you senseless."

"I won't. Once I leave this room, I hope I shall never set eyes on you again."

"I could almost second that sentiment," he said viciously. "But as I told you last night, my own wishes, and yours, are irrelevant. Circumstances compel us to marry. My God, you're still a child. You belong in the schoolroom. I was mad to think that you were fit to be my wife."

With a small cry of anguish, she whirled from him and ran from the room. He let her go in angry silence. As the door closed behind her, he brought his clenched fist down on the desk top, rattling the brandy decanter and small glasses, sending one spinning to the floor. He bent to retrieve it and at the same time gathered the papers that Maddie had let slip from her fingers. He stared at the deed to Drumoak for some few minutes, then folded it carefully and thrust it into his coat pocket.

He felt drained of all emotion save a simmering residual anger. His fingers clenched and unclenched around the small glass in his hand. He filled it from the brandy bottle and drank it off in one gulp. The effect left something to be desired. He sank into the chair behind the desk and carefully replenished his glass to the brim.

The girl was utterly impossible and deserved a beating for the things she had said to him. He tried to sustain his anger against her but found the task beyond him. By degrees, he got himself in hand and began to sift through the scene that had just taken place. It did not take him long to uncover the real origin of his spleen. Maddie had chosen her father over himself. It was as simple as that. And it was intolerable.

She reminded him of a small chimney boy he had once been instrumental in removing from a brute of a master who shamefully misused him. There had been no thanks from the object of his benevolence. Quite the reverse. The boy hadn't wanted to be taken away from his sadistic employer, and had called down a spate of furious oaths on his benefactor. He'd heard that it was a common story. The familiar held a powerful attraction. The unfamiliar was something to be feared and avoided.

Which was another reason for his bile, he admitted ruefully. From the moment he had met her, Maddie had seemed as familiar to him as he did to himself, as though he had known her in another time, another place. There had been a rightness in their coming together. He had sensed it from the first. Until she'd learned his name, she had sensed it too. After that, she would never admit to what was between them.

He rested his elbows on the flat of the desk and cupped his glass with both hands. Absently, he dipped his head to inhale the bouquet. The aroma of brandy should have reminded him of grapes. Instead, he thought of apples. His mind, heart, senses were filled with this girl. And after last night, a bond had been forged between them which could never now be broken. He'd never felt this way with any other woman and he never expected to feel like it again. She was his. She had given herself to him without reservation, had accepted his claims upon her. There could be no going back. Not for him. Even now, he longed for the solace of her body to heal the ugly words they had said to each other in anger.

Impatiently, he drank down the brandy, scarcely conscious of the fiery liquid burning a path down his throat. For a long, considering moment, he gazed with brooding eyes at the empty glass in his hands. He hoped that once the deed was done, once he'd given Maddie his name, there would be some respite from the guilt which afflicted him so mercilessly. The thought made him restless. He slammed to his feet and abruptly left the room.

Minutes later, from her chamber window, Maddie watched as the viscount led 'Thelo out across the links. With angry fingers, she began to undo the buttons of the riding habit she had donned only moments before. Nothing would induce her to put herself in the way of falling in with Deveryn. If she never saw him again, it would be too soon for her, she assured herself convincingly.

She kept to her room, assiduously working on her translation of *Medea* between bouts of helpless tears. She did not go down to dinner, but asked to have a tray sent to her chamber. Instead, a curt message was delivered. The new master of Drumoak informed her that she would present herself for dinner or suffer the consequences. Maddie, reckless with righteous anger, ignored the threat.

Later in the evening, Janet, round eyed with worry, brought her mistress a covered tray. There was nothing on it but a slice of dry bread and a glass of water.

154

Chapter Ten

When Maddie pushed into the breakfast room the following morning, her confident steps slowed then faltered altogether. A swift glance, surreptitious and comprehensive, was not reassuring. Deveryn was alone. He was at the sideboard lifting the covers from a variety of dishes. The urge to bolt like a hare who has caught the first whiff of the fox was almost irresistible. Maddie resisted the temptation. But it took every ounce of her courage to drag herself to the table.

"You sent for me?" she asked with studied indifference. Inside, she smouldered.

He looked up with a smile in his eyes. "Hungry, Maddie?" What can I tempt you with?" And he added insult to injury by reeling off a menu of breakfast fare that she was sure would do credit to the kitchens of Carlton House. Her own housekeeper, she decided, had turned traitor. She sniffed.

The aroma of grilled kippers and kidneys tickled her nostrils. Maddie was ravenous. Also, rebellious. Pride won out. She would starve to death before she would accept a morsel of food from his well manicured hand. "Thank you no," she drawled. "I find I have no appetite this morning." Her stomach growled, low and long. Maddie was mortified, but tried not to show it.

The smile went from his lips to his eyes. "No appetite?" he asked amiably. "Come now, Maddie. What Scot worth his salt would turn up his nose when offered the ambrosia of the gods?" And he heaped a ladleful of thick, glutinous porridge into a dish which he playfully jiggled under her nose.

"I said I'm not hungry," she said stubbornly, her eyes

carefully averted, her nostrils pinched.

"Sit!"

The smile had left his eyes. To Maddie it was a victory, albeit a small one. She made a great show of arranging her skirts as she accepted the chair he held for her. The bowl of porridge was slammed down before her. She looked at it dispassionately and wondered how far she could push Deveryn before she went her length with him.

"Eat," he commanded.

She had gone her length with him. She picked up the spoon at the side of her plate and held it poised but motionless.

If there was one thing that Maddie heartily detested, it was porridge. Brose, mealy puddings, oatmeal stuffing, oatcakes, and haggis were perfectly acceptable. But porridge was different. In the whole of her life, the only time she had ever wanted it was when she ran out of glue and used it to paste cutouts in her scrapbook. Even then, the horrid stuff had failed her.

Her tongue seemed to swell to twice its normal size. Her lips refused to open. She stole a glance at the viscount. There was no relenting in his expression.

"May I have some cream?" she asked politely. Anything to delay the confrontation with her old enemy, porridge. He deposited the cream jug, none too gently, in front of her.

"And one of those little bowls on the sideboard?" He fetched it. "Where is my aunt?"

"Packing. She's delighted to be going home to London." He sat down facing her across the table. "I've already eaten," he said conversationally.

"What have you told her?" she asked.

He watched as she carefully poured the cream into the small porcelain bowl he had just handed her.

"That you're to go to your grandfather."

She dipped her spoon into the porridge then immersed it in the small sidebowl of fresh cream. Surreptitiously, she slanted the spoon at an angle and managed to dislodge most of the porridge. It was an old trick from childhood days.

"What's the point in that?" he asked, indicating the two separate bowls of porridge and cream. "Why not simply pour the cream over the porridge?"

"I'm not sure. I think it's because the porridge stays hotter this way. It's the custom in Scotland."

"Would you like some sugar?"

Her lip curled. "Certainly not."

"Of course. Scottish to the backbone!"

An awkward silence fell to be broken eventually by his long sigh of impatience. "Maddie, I'm sorry for yesterday. I'm sorry for the way everything came out. You were upset. You had every right to be. I see now that you were in shock. Perhaps I didn't explain things properly. Naturally, we'll come back here for holidays. Drumoak isn't lost to you, you know. You'll always be welcome here."

"Thank you," she said with crushing civility. She stared at the glutinous mass of porridge. More than anything, she wanted to pick up the bowl and dump the sticky contents on his golden head. *You will always be welcome here.* His condescension was insupportable. She'd cut off her feet before she'd step across Drumoak's threshold as long as he was master here. She almost told him so. But more than anything, she wanted to appear as cool as a cucumber. She raised the spoon and opened her lips.

"Maddie," he said, forcing himself to speak calmly. "I'm doing this for your own good."

She thought she would choke as the lump of glue slid slowly down her gullet.

He tried a different tack. "I'm off to Edinburgh this morning. I want you to come with me. I have business to attend to, but you could do a little shopping. Splurge on yourself. I can afford it."

"Thank you, no. I don't feel up to much this morning." Especially not the porridge.

"It would do you the world of good," he insisted.

"I think I know better than you what's good for me." She wondered if he would think she'd lost face if she were to ask for the grilled kippers and kidney. Her eyes went longingly to the covered dishes on the sideboard. She became conscious that Deveryn's tone was earnest, his expression grave. She made an effort to attend to his words.

". . . and Drumoak is not what you need, whatever you may think. Oh, I know, you feel safe here. This house is all you

157

know. You're afraid to leave it, afraid of what you don't know." He flashed her a rueful grin. "If you're honest with yourself, you'll thank your lucky stars that I came along when I did. In another year or two, you were in a fair way to becoming as wooly as the sheep that graze these hills."

Every fine hair on the back of her neck rose like the fur of a cat which had been rubbed the wrong way. *Thank my lucky stars. Thank my lucky stars.* She was so angry that without thinking, she tipped a full spoon of the hateful cereal into her open mouth. She froze.

"Trust me, Maddie," he went on softly, mistaking her silence for acquiescence. "You'll like our life together. I promise you."

She gagged, then painfully, agonizingly, choked down the porridge. Her stomach heaved and she opened her mouth, greedily drawing in air.

"Maddie, what is it? You look like a fish out of water." His hand reached across the table to grip her clenched fist.

The heaving gradually subsided and she shook him off. "Deveryn, don't you dare talk down to me as if I were a child! I'm a grown woman of nineteen years, and I SHALL have some say in the disposition of my future, d'you hear, I SHALL!"

"Sh . . . !" The smile was back in his eyes. "You're forgetting something, Maddie. I don't *always* treat you as a child. There are some areas where you have a natural competence. With a little tutoring you should do very well."

Her face was on fire. She did not know where to look. She gave up the pretense of eating and put up her hands to her burning cheeks.

"Please, can't we just forget that that night ever happened?" She was almost pleading with him.

He answered her carefully. "That I cannot do. Even you, naive as you are, must know that there are certain consequences to what we did together."

She looked at him blankly.

"Pregnancy, Maddie," he said dryly. "Babies are not found under gooseberry bushes, not even in Scotland."

"I never thought they were," she snapped back, her anger rising at his habitual mode of treating her like a child. She watched him from beneath slashed brows as he drained his cup.

158

Sudden inspiration came to her. She became involved in stirring the lump of congealed porridge in her bowl. When she heard the delicate chink of china on china, she lifted her eyes boldly to meet his.

"Rest easy, Deveryn. You don't have to marry me. I'm not . . . you haven't . . . there isn't the least likelihood that I'm breeding."

"What?" He scrutinized her carefully. No blush, no stammer, only a clear eyed determination. She would have to do better than that to gull an old hand like him.

"I don't understand," he said mendaciously.

Maddie swallowed. This was more difficult than she'd anticipated. Perhaps the viscount did not know about a woman's bodily functions. She tried to remember the words Mrs. Moncrieff had used on that long ago day when Malcolm had taken her to his mother because she thought she was dying.

"It's quite natural," she said seriously, "and nothing to fret about. Every month . . ." she faltered, her eyes narrowing suspiciously on the straight line of his mouth.

"Yes?" he intoned encouragingly. His eyes were as unclouded and as blue as a Mediterranean sky.

"Damn you, Deveryn. I am not pregnant. I am NOT! So you can wipe that smug grin off your face."

"Softly! Someone will hear you. I never said you were."

"Well, now you know I'm not!"

"If you say so."

"I do say so."

"All right!"

"You don't believe me!"

"What difference does it make?"

"What difference does it make?" She forced her voice lower. "Don't be stupid! We don't HAVE to get married now."

"Maddie, calm yourself. Whether you are pregnant or not is of the supremest indifference to me. Have some tea. It will sooth your nerves."

He poured her a cup and refilled his own. She delayed for just the right moment. He took a mouthful.

"How many women have you impregnated, my lord?" she asked artlessly, but there was nothing artless about her grin.

Deveryn choked. The scalding brew burned a path down his throat. It was a full minute before he could find his voice. "Maddie, for God's sake!" He coughed, then coughed again and brought his napkin to his lips. "None," he rasped out.

"None?" One eyebrow arched in a fair imitation of his own.

"None," he repeated emphatically. "I'm not a callow youth. I know how to prevent conception."

"I'm relieved to hear it."

He found her words mildly irritating. His eyes wandered over her. For a moment, he was tempted to let her take comfort in her false assumption. On reflection, he thought better of it. In the last twenty-four hours, he had quite deliberately cut the rug from under her feet. She had no one to turn to, nowhere to go but to him. To relent now would be to undermine his strategy.

"When you're an old married lady and have filled my house with children, I'll tell you how it's done. But till then, my love, I'll be doing my damndest to sire my sons on you."

"Then, the other night, you didn't . . ."

"No, I didn't. But by your own words, you have nothing to worry about." His lips twitched but he asked gravely, "Perhaps you do—"

"What? Oh no!" Then as an afterthought, "Might I have?"

"Possibly. But if ever you do without my permission, I shall wring your pretty little neck."

"Oh." Her hand went nervously to her throat.

He was on his feet and bending over her, one hand propped on the table. "Be ready in ten minutes. The carriage should be at the front door by then."

"What?" She couldn't think when he was so close to her.

"We're going to spend the day in Edinburgh."

"I thought I told you . . ."

"There may be papers to sign." He knew damn well that there weren't any, at least not for her.

"Papers to sign? Why didn't you say so?"

When she reached her hand to the doorknob, he remarked casually, "Janet tells me you positively loathe porridge. If you're a good girl, I'll buy your breakfast when we reach town."

She swung to face him, her eyes snapping. "You knew," she

160

accused, "all the time you knew. Then why?"

"To teach you a lesson. Maddie, you would cut off your nose to spite your face. Everything you have ever wanted is within reach. It's yours for the asking. Don't let pride . . ."

The rest of his laughing words were covered by the reverberations of the door as she slammed it smartly on exiting.

It was mid-morning when Deveryn's carriage pulled into the busy courtyard of the White Hart Inn in Edinburgh's Grassmarket. High above, impregnable, like a watchful, menacing sentinel soared the towers and battlements of the ancient fortress. A private parlour was bespoken and breakfast procured. Maddie was soon drooling over heaped servers of braised liver and kidney, poached yellow fish and the ubiquitous oysters, an Edinburgh staple, so Deveryn was told. But it was the fresh cod's roe, boiled to a pink perfection and newly in season which finally broke down her cool and distancing manner. He left her absorbed in the difficult task of making a selection from the cornucopia of Scottish delicacies. His explanation that he would arrange an appointment with the solicitor and be back within the hour scarcely registered, he was certain.

He found the landlord's directions easy to follow since the castle was one landmark which could rarely be lost sight of. Keeping it on his left, he passed the newly drained Nor' Loch on the south side of Princes Street, Edinburgh's most exclusive shopping district. It was a far cry from the more familiar and elegant Bond Street. He'd heard that the city fathers intended to plant gardens of flowers where the Nor' Loch's stagnant waters had so recently fouled the air. The fetid stench still lingered. On that grey, blustery, sunless January day, as he shouldered himself into the wind between long rows of smoke-blackened tenements which rose to seven, eight stories high, he thought it would be hard to find a more dismal spot on God's earth than this misnamed "Athens of the North."

Forsythe's chambers were soon located on Hanover Street. Deveryn presented his card to a red-haired, spotty-faced clerk. When his name was announced, the result was immediate as it was predictable. Three bent heads came up and he was

161

instantly bowed and scraped into Forsythe's inner sanctum as if he had been royalty. It left him amused and oddly piqued. His reception at Drumoak had been of a different order. Maddie, he decided, could do with a lesson or two on correct protocol.

After the obligatory handshake, Mr. Forsythe retreated behind his desk and indicated that the viscount should seat himself.

"Well?" demanded Deveryn without preamble. "Are you satisfied that my claims are legitimate?" And he removed the deed to Drumoak from his coat pocket and dropped it negligently on the leather-topped desk.

"Aye. There never was any doubt in my mind," admitted the older man grudgingly. Absently, he picked up the packet and tapped it against the open palm of one hand. "You've made a pauper o' the lass, there's no gainsaying. If her English relatives don't see fit to put a roof over her head, Miss Maddie will have to find some sort of gainful employment. I'm sure I don't know which one o' ye *scunners* me more, that poor excuse o' a man she called her father, or," he paused, his eyes insulting as they ran assessingly over the viscount's impeccable person, "or this fine specimen o' the English aristocracy who steals the bread out o' the mouths o' babes."

The belligerent words startled a laugh out of Deveryn. "Tush man, give your conscience a rest. 'Stealing the bread out of the mouths of babes' indeed! If you had seen Maddie as I last saw her . . ." A slow smile curved his lips. "More to the point," he went on, striving for sobriety, "I have every intention of seeing that Maddie is gainfully employed, more gainfully, perhaps, than she wants to be—as my wife," he hastened to add, rightly interpreting the stormy expression which had kindled in the other man's eyes.

For a long, uncomprehending moment, Forsythe stared at him. By degrees, the frown faded from his brow and he visibly relaxed. "Your wife," he reiterated blankly.

"My wife," affirmed Deveryn. He leaned forward in his chair and laid both hands flat on the desktop in a faintly menacing posture. "With or without her guardian's consent."

The challenge hung on the air as the eyes of the two men locked. A frisson of alarm danced along the solicitor's straightening spine. For one uneasy moment, it seemed to him that he'd just been challenged to a duel. Unexpectedly, he grinned.

"So ye mean to marry the lass?" he asked on a low, throaty chuckle.

Without knowing why, Deveryn found himself grinning back.

"If I can discover how it may be done," he confided, and resumed his former indolent posture.

Forsythe's shrewd eyes studied the viscount from beneath dark bushy eyebrows. He had made good use of his time since Deveryn had first stunned him with intelligence that Sinclair had lost Drumoak in a game of cards. A few words over a pint with the stewards of Lords Dalkeith, Roseberry, and of His Grace, Baccleough himself, had left him in no doubt of the integrity of the man who sat before him like a drowsy lion lazily observing the antics of an unwary antelope. By any yardstick, the man was wealthy. And he wanted to marry Maddie. Incredible! A question hovered on his lips. On second thoughts, he swallowed it.

"Ye don't need her guardian's consent," he said, breaking the silence.

"What?"

"Not if ye wed her in Scotland."

"Gretna Green? That's out of the question."

Those careless words raised Deveryn's credit even higher in the other man's eyes. Still, Forsythe was not forgetting that the viscount had put him through a most uncomfortable twenty-four hours before taking him into his confidence. Let him squirm a little, he thought.

"And what have ye got against Gretna Green?" he asked slyly. "It's a bonny wee place."

"Also notorious."

"And romantic," purred Forsythe, smiling broadly.

"Yes, but only for fortune hunters. I'm not of that ilk, as I've no doubt you've gathered from your sources by now."

Forsythe gave an appreciative chortle. "A wee dram is called for," he said, and extricated a bottle and two tot glasses from the bottom drawer of his desk. Deveryn dutifully accepted the proffered drink and nursed it idly as he considered the unholy gleam of amusement in the older man's eye.

163

"You know something I don't know," he offered.

"Aye."

"So." He sipped slowly. His patience was soon rewarded. "How much do ye know about Scots Law, Lord Deveryn?"

"Next to nothing."

"Och, for an educated man, ye're terribly ignorant."

"So my mother tells me. Get to the point." He drained his glass and set it on the desk.

Forsythe decided that his lordship's patience was showing signs of wear and tear. "In Scotland, any lad or lass over the age of sixteen years is free to wed without a guardian's consent by simple declaration before witnesses."

The viscount looked doubtful at this bald statement, and Forsythe went on to clarify. "Gretna Green is merely a convenience—the first haven across our mutual border for fleeing lovers. Of course," he went on, his Scottish burr becoming more pronounced by the minute, "the main obstacle is finding someone willing to witness the ceremony. Respectable folk, as ye may well imagine, look askance at such dubious goings on."

"A minister, a priest?"

"Highly unlikely, but not impossible. Then again, the banns would have to be read. That requires time."

"How much time?"

"Two months or more, an unnecessary delay if ye're pressed for time."

"Aren't there stipulations about domicile and such like?"

"Only in the case of an annulment or divorce. Not for marriage by declaration."

Deveryn casually leaned back in his chair and laced his fingers together. "Not a church wedding then. But I won't have her married over the anvil." He rolled his head on the back of the chair and gazed absently toward the light of the window. "A solicitor then, such as yourself, Mr. Forsythe?" he suggested quietly.

"Aye. Under certain stipulations."

A long pause ensued.

"Which are?" asked Deveryn softly.

Forsythe took his time in emulating his lordship's example. He settled himself more comfortably in his commodious leather chair. He brought his hands together in an attitude of prayer. "That the wee lass be amply provided for."

"I presume we are talking about marriage settlements and such like."

"You might say so."

"Done," said Deveryn coming upright in one easy movement. "Then let's get down to business."

He left the solicitor's office with a spring in his step and whistling the bawdy refrain of some long forgotten drinking song he had picked up in his carefree undergraduate days in Oxford. He threw back his head and laughed, feeling the first genuine easing of the remorse that had laid him by the heels since the night he had taken Maddie's innocence. The word *rape* flashed into his mind. He vigorously suppressed it, substituting the far more tolerable *seduction*. The thought that Maddie appeared to be untouched by that first brush with a man's baser, darker passions buoyed his hopes. Never, he promised himself, never would he ever again subject her to a side of his nature that made him a stranger to himself. He had never touched a woman in anger before. And that he should do so with the only woman he had ever felt any genuine feeling for, seemed totally incomprehensible.

A blast of cold air came whipping along Hanover Street and for the next few minutes he was engaged in a tussle with an invisible enemy who wrestled him for possession of his curly brimmed beaver. Deveryn bent into the wind, as if shouldering his way through a throng of people. God but he would never get used to these wild, North Sea winds! The air in Oxfordshire was balmy, the breezes gentle. Maddie would love it, given time.

But Maddie was not about to fall in with his plans without a struggle. She would fight him every inch of the way. His grunt of annoyance was swallowed by the wind. In other circumstances, he would have allowed her as much time as was necessary to overcome her objections. But time was of the essence. Moreover, a gentleman did not take his pleasure with a gently bred girl and leave her in the lurch. She might have at least given him credit for trying to do the honourable thing.

And he'd be damned if he'd allow Maddie to put him in the wrong over the business with her father. Such things were regrettable but scarcely of sufficient consequence to have him turned away like some misbegotten miscreant. And she was determined to misinterpret his motives with respect to Drumoak. Why couldn't she understand that he was doing everything in his power to make restitution? Hadn't he just instructed the solicitor to tie up the property in such a way that both Donald Sinclair's dependents would benefit? And wasn't he about to invest a considerable sum of capital to restore the place to its former prosperity? The girl was too proud for her own good. What she needed was . . .

He was past the shopwindow at the corner of Princes Street before the picture of shimmering satin penetrated his consciousness. He retraced his steps. The gown was elegant, a day dress and grey, but so pale as to be almost white. He knew enough about ladies' fashions to know that it was of French design and up to the mark on all suits. Perfect. He'd be damned if he'd let his bride marry him in black.

He returned to the inn with a large elaborately trimmed box under his arm. Maddie was in the private parlour he had reserved for the day, in the act of removing her pelisse. He noted with approval the glow in her cheeks and the sparkle in her eye.

"Where did you get to?" he asked and laid his burden carefully on the table which gave no evidence now of the feast Maddie had enjoyed an hour or two before.

She glanced at the box curiously. "I walked to my old school in Charlotte Square."

More to make conversation and to prolong the harmony between them than to elicit information, he observed, "I take it that your memories of school days are fond ones?"

"Extremely," she answered without elaboration.

His fingers seemed to be all thumbs as he attacked the knots of string around the box. "I suppose you picked up a smattering of this and that," he said, not really attending his own words, aware only that the knots were at last undone, the lid of the box removed, and the tissue paper thrust aside to reveal the skene of silk, looking like pale moonlight on a wintry night. He girded himself for battle.

"What's that?" she asked, her voice oddly wavering between awe and suspicion.

"Your wedding dress."

"My . . ."

"I've prevailed upon Forsythe to witness our vows this afternoon."

"Our vows?"

"We're to be married in his office at four o'clock."

"Oh." Her legs felt like water. Before they could buckle under her, she sank into the nearest chair. "Is that supposed to atone for all you've done to me?"

She was thinking of her father and the loss of Drumoak. Especially Drumoak. He was thinking of the night he had taken her innocence.

"If you like," he answered.

The words came out clipped and careless, as if he were indifferent to the mayhem he had caused in her life.

"And if I refuse?"

"I can't let you. In spite of that faradiddle you told me this morning, even now you might be pregnant with my child."

"Then we'll wait."

"It won't answer." He crossed the distance between them and cupped her shoulders with his hands. His voice gentled. "Once you go to your grandfather, you come under English law, Maddie. You cannot marry without the consent of your guardian. That might take months in coming."

Her mind sifted the puzzle with typical thoroughness. It became an impersonal exercise in dialectics. "If it becomes necessary, I suppose we could always come back to Scotland," she ventured at length.

"Stop arguing!" he roared. "The matter has already been decided. Anything might happen to me between now and then. D'you imagine that I'd let my heir be born a bastard?"

His anger shocked her. Also, his want of logic, not to mention his coarse language. If the child were born out of wedlock, she carefully substituted, Deveryn would *have* no heir. Wisely, she refrained from telling him so.

"I was only trying to help," she protested. It was obvious that Deveryn's first concern was for some hypothetical child whose future existence was highly improbable.

She watched in gathering resentment as he paced before her. Involuntarily, she jumped when he rounded on her.

167

"I've bespoken a chamber where you can change. There's a girl there now. She'll help you with your things. I took the liberty of buying you stockings and slippers and so on." He spoke in a tone that brooked no argument.

"I won't marry you and that's final," she argued.

She was still repeating those words as a granite-faced Deveryn threw her on top of the bed in front of the horrified eyes of the young chambermaid and threatened to tear the dress from her back.

She said them again, with less conviction, as he dragged her up the dark staircase to the solicitor's rooms. At the entrance, he spun her to face him. In tight-lipped silence, he adjusted the long elaborate puff sleeves of the highnecked spencer which matched the gossamer silk of the underdress.

"Fits like a glove," he grunted, and propelled her, without ceremony, into the outer office. Without hesitation, he moved to Forsythe's booklined inner sanctum.

The solicitor rose to his feet as they entered, a smile of welcome creasing his cheeks. In one stride, he was before Maddie and had grasped her gloved hand in his.

"Maddie," he exclaimed, "all grown-up and a beautiful bride. Your gown is magnificent."

"Oh," she said, her thoughts chasing each other in frantic confusion. She glanced down at her wedding finery. For the first time it registered that the frock which Deveryn had provided was uncommonly elegant and finer than anything she had ever possessed in her life. She touched her hands to the delicate fabric as if it were more fragile than snowflakes. The turned down collar of the spencer was decorated with a row of faced slits, the bodice heavily embroidered with white satin-stitched petals. The sleeves, in a series of diminishing puffs, reached from shoulder to wrist. A white satin ribbon to match the ribbons in her hair, was tied snugly under her bosom, and on the padded hem of her gown was a deep scalloped border with appliqued petals. Mr. Forsythe had not exaggerated. The gown was magnificent. Her eyes lifted to Deveryn's. "It's beautiful," she said softly. But she thought that he was more beautiful still in his dark, cut-away coat and beige pantaloons with matching waistcoat. Her eyes travelled to the spun gold locks which licked around the edge of his white starched collar.

She loved the way his hair fell across his forehead and the unconscious gesture of impatience as he brushed it back with one hand, as he was doing now.

"Ready?" he asked gently.

She met his eyes. There was no weakness in them, only a promise of some very unpleasant consequences should she persist in thwarting him.

"If you insist." And she wondered, in her heart of hearts, if that's what she had hoped he would do all along, and relieve her of the burden of her scruples.

"Then let's get on with it."

Forsythe called in two of his articled clerks to act as witnesses. Deveryn took Maddie's cold hand in his and squeezed it encouragingly. The solicitor handed each of them a slip of paper.

"You first, my lord," he said to Deveryn. "Read it."

The viscount obliged. "I, Jason Algernon Verney, do declare before witnesses that I take thee, Madeleina Elizabeth Sinclair, to be my wedded wife."

"Thank you. Now you, Maddie."

Maddie followed suit. "I, Madeleina Elizabeth Sinclair, do declare before witnesses that I take thee, Jason Algernon Verney, to be my wedded husband."

Forsythe beamed. "I now pronounce you man and wife."

Deveryn signed the marriage lines, but Maddie hung back.

At his look of enquiry, she exclaimed, "You're not going to tell me that *that* constitutes a wedding ceremony?"

Deveryn allowed himself a small half-smile. "Apparently in Scotland those few words are all that is necessary. What did you expect?"

"I don't know." But she did. She expected a wedding ring and flowers and the centuries old ritual that had bound countless couples together in the sight of God. And a husband she could love without reservation.

As if reading her thoughts, Deveryn observed, "There'll be a religious ceremony later, in the private chapel at Dunsdale. Now just do as the man says and sign the marriage certificate."

Maddie's expression turned mulish. "I don't believe it's legal," she prevaricated.

Before Deveryn could give vent to his impatience, Forsythe

169

diplomatically interposed, "Child, it's perfectly legal in Scotland. And once the marriage is consummated, no court in England would question the validity of your position as Lord Deveryn's wife."

"It's positively heathenish," she said crossly, but wrote her name just the same in a bold script where Deveryn indicated.

On the ride back to the White Hart, Deveryn broke into her reverie by asking in an amused tone, "Maddie, you do know what *consummate* means, don't you?"

Her eyebrows lifted and she drawled with what she hoped was chilling hauteur, "Naturally." She might have added, "What a thing to ask a Classics scholar!" but she kept her own counsel. The Latin derivative of the word was obvious, 'to complete, make perfect,' and hadn't Deveryn intimated that there would be a religious service at Dunsdale?

Deveryn patted her hand. "Good! When Forsythe uttered that word, I expected, well, fireworks, to say the least of it. Sometimes you're the most perverse chit!" And he folded his arms across his broad chest, tipped his black beaver over one eye and reclined with studied indolence against the leather squabs, whistling some idiotic ditty in a manner which Maddie could only describe as "cocky."

Chapter Eleven

Maddie climbed the steep stairs to her second floor chamber, highly conscious of Deveryn's soft footfall at her heels. She reached the closed door and spun to face him.

"How soon do we leave for Drumoak?" she asked in a creditably calm voice.

He was so close that his warm breath ruffled her eyelashes. Uneasily, her hand turned the doorknob and she took a step backward into the room.

"I can be ready in five minutes," she offered breathlessly, and quickly scuttled, crab-fashion, behind the protection of the door.

"What's your hurry?"

His hand shot out and splayed against the door, driving it hard against the wall. Maddie retreated a step.

"It . . . it will be dark soon. We should make for home while it's still light," she suggested.

He followed her into the chamber, shut the door firmly and turned the key in the lock. "Another hour or so won't make much difference. Besides," he grinned lazily, "I think we should explore all the specifics of how this marriage is to be consummated—to our mutual satisfaction." He had a good idea that Maddie hadn't an inkling of what the word meant except in general terms.

"Oh." Though his words were reassuring, they made no appreciable difference to the painful hammering of her heart. Quite the reverse. It wasn't the words, she decided, but the way that he said them.

171

He advanced, she retreated. He put out a hand to touch the ribbon in her hair, and she spun away from him.

"Oh!" She wished she could think of something intelligent to say. "They've lit the fire in the grate. And, and . . ." her eyes roved the room alighting upon basket after basket of rosy red apples. "Where did these come from?" Surprise and pleasure etched her voice.

"My doing. Do you like them? It was impossible to come by flowers at such short notice. In any event, I've discovered that the scent of apples is by far my favourite perfume."

He was at her elbow. Slowly, he reached out and fingered the ribbons in her hair. She inched away from him. He inched closer. She decided that it was time to introduce an air of reality.

"How thoughtful," she said, throwing him a grateful smile, and, in as natural a manner as she could contrive, she moved to one of the old fashioned armchairs flanking the coal fire and plumped herself down. "You wanted to discuss the consummation of our marriage," she invited.

One eyebrow quirked. "Discuss? Did I say that?"

She could see that her words had amused him. "The consummation of our marriage," she repeated more slowly, wondering if perhaps he'd had more to drink than the obligatory glass of champagne in the solicitor's office. "When is it going to take place?"

With a wicked twinkle in his eye, he reached for an apple and put it to his nostrils. He inhaled its wholesome and appetizing flavour. Tempting, he decided, just like Maddie. He could eat her whole. "Do you know, I believe I've developed a positive addiction to this humble fruit? Sooner than you expect, my love," and he tossed the apple away and sank to his heels at her feet, his hands balanced lightly on each armrest.

Very softly, his voice between tenderness and amusement, he said, "When and where do you expect it to take place, Maddie?"

"In the chapel, at Dunsdale. It's what you said."

"Aren't you overwarm in that spencer? Here, let me help you with it. Yes, go on. In the chapel at Dunsdale, I believe you said."

At the first touch of his fingers at her throat, she swallowed convulsively. Slowly, as if he had all the time in the world, he began to slip the buttons one by one. Maddie ruthlessly brought her thoughts round to the matter at hand.

"Mr. Forsythe implied that the marriage would be questionable until it is consummated."

"Mmm. Isn't that better?" His hands were at her shoulders stripping away the spencer with swift dexterity. Obediently, she followed his unspoken directions and slipped her arms out of the sleeves.

"And . . . and . . . to tell the truth I don't feel married with no vows spoken." Her eyes followed, mirroring her consternation, as he threw the spencer on top of the bed. His jacket soon followed. "Please be careful, Jason. The fabric is very delicate. It should be hung up before it creases."

"Martin will take care of it until such time as I can find you a maid," he soothed. "Your feet are cold." And before she could stop him, he had removed her white satin slippers and had raised her stockinged feet to his thighs. The warmth of his hands as he carefully massaged each arch and heel in turn seemed to spread upwards from her toes to the secret place at the juncture of her thighs.

"Sorry, I interrupted. You were saying something about vows," he reminded softly. "What else do you require to persuade you that our marriage is truly consummated."

His hands were very soothing, she thought.

"What? Oh, just the traditional things a bride expects on her wedding day, you know, the groom throwing a handful of silver out the coach window to handsel the marriage; flowers in the sanctuary; a wedding breakfast; toasts; well-wishers; a ring as a sign of our troth."

He made no answer, but studied one well-shaped foot as if he had just unveiled one of the seven wonders of the world. Around each slender ankle, he hooked thumb and middle finger. His absorption in her anatomy was unnerving. Maddie hastened into speech.

"And I always thought I'd carry a sprig of white heather inside the covers of my grandmother's catechism."

He was testing each bone and tendon with the pads of his fingers, but he asked dutifully, "White heather?"

"For luck."

"Catechism?"

"You know, 'What is the chief end of man?'"

He looked up, a devilish grin slowly spreading over his handsome face. Before he could comment, Maddie quickly interposed, "And don't you dare blaspheme, Jason Verney!"

"I wasn't about to," he said mildly. "I dare say I'm as religious as the next fellow."

She tossed her head. "That's what I was afraid of."

The grin intensified. She tried to ignore the rotation of his thumbs on the soles of her feet. After a considering moment, he said, "Do you know, I think my mother will adore you?"

If he had told her that she was the most beautiful woman of his acquaintance, Maddie could not have been more gratified. Praise seldom came her way. The Scots, taciturn by nature, deeply distrusted open displays of affection and flowery compliments. It was held that the English temperament was better suited to such foibles. Maddie, remembering that the happiest days of her life had been spent with her English mother, regretfully owned that in some things, the English were wiser.

His lips brushed her toes and her thoughts went scattering. "Please, Jason," she appealed.

With agonizing slowness, he rubbed the sole of her foot against his smoothly shaven cheek. His hand reached under the hem of her skirt, tracing a leisurely path up the calf of her leg to the back of her knee. "Your stockings are damp, Maddie. Your skin is chilled. Let me warm you."

Strange, where his hands touched, she felt as if she were burning with fever. Of their own volition, her eyes closed. She felt the release of the garter above her left knee, then the right, and beneath the lace hem of the frilliest drawers she had ever worn in her life, he eased the white silk stockings down to her ankles as if he were peeling away a layer of skin.

His hands left her. She heard nothing but her own irregular breathing, and the quick counterpoint of his deeper, harsher breaths. Her eyes fluttered open. He had removed his stock and vest. She watched mesmerized as he slipped out of the folds of his pristine white shirt.

"You haven't been listening to a word I've said." She wasn't sure if she'd spoken the words aloud. The sight of that broad

174

expanse of chest with its riotous mat of honey-gold hair, as it rose and fell in tempo to the erratic heaving of her own bosom did something curious to her insides. She was sure that she was melting and that in another minute, all that would remain of little Maddie Sinclair would be a puddle of water on the hearth.

His hands wrapped themselves around her ankles, but it was her nipples that contracted. Distractedly, she brought an arm to her bosom to quell the throb that had started there.

"I heard every word. When we get to Dunsdale, you shall have your traditional wedding with as much pomp and ceremony as you require. Will that satisfy you?"

She could not remember what she had asked for, not when his hands were kneading the soft pads of her calves, making rational thought impossible.

"Will that satisfy you?" he persisted.

"Y-yes."

"And what about me, Maddie? Don't you wish to know what will satisfy me?"

It seemed only fair under the circumstances. "Of course," she warbled.

"I'll show you. Raise your skirts."

"Wh-what?"

"Raise your skirts."

In answer, she gripped the arms of the chair and tried to rise. He prevented her by the simple expedient of sweeping her thighs apart and dropping to his knees. They were groin to groin. Maddie made a vain attempt to twist backwards. His powerful arms wrapped around her shoulders and he dragged her forward. He gave a low, throaty chuckle.

"Simpleton! Don't you know that the laws of the land are made by men? This is the only kind of consummation that means anything to a man."

He dragged the hem of her skirt to her waist.

Maddie closed her eyes against the spectacle of uncaring masculine hands desecrating the most beautiful gown she had ever had in her possession. This was no ordinary gown. It was a work of art. From the moment Mr. Forsythe had drawn her attention to its magnificence, she had harboured the whimsy of treasuring it like a family heirloom. A mother ought to have something to hand down to her daughter. Her own mother had been wed in little more than her shift.

She heard the soft rending of silk and her eyes flew open. A small tear had opened up along the seam of her bodice. She hopped from one foot to the other. "Oh, Jason! Please! No!" And she captured his hands and flung them from her.

Her rejection stunned him. "Maddie!" he protested. "Don't you want me to?" and his hands found the soft flesh above her knees and squeezed persuasively.

"Oh" she wailed. "Look at the creases. My gown was perfect when I walked into this room."

She pushed to her feet, and Deveryn sat back on his heels, his nose pressed tantalizingly close to her softly rounded stomach. He couldn't stop himself. His hands spread out behind her and he dragged her close. He buried his head in the lower part of her body and kissed her passionately with moist, wet lips through the silk of her gown. One tug brought her across his thighs, her knees splayed wide. He captured her hands and held them behind his neck.

"Jason, please, my gown," she mewed in his ear.

"I'll buy you a dozen," he grunted and eased her skirt to her hips. He shifted her in his arms till the valley between her thighs cradled the full length of his arousal. The protective clothing was ineffectual as a barrier. Each was intensely aware of the body heat forged by their mutual proximity. He rotated his hips, an invitation and a promise. Maddie clung to his neck and threw back her head in abandon. Her weak, strangled sound of pleasure drove his passion higher. His mouth coursed down her throat, and through the taut silk of her bodice he found a swollen nipple and grazed it with his teeth.

Maddie jerked. "Jason, it's my *wedding* gown," she entreated.

That her distress was genuine gradually penetrated his passion drugged senses. After a moment's indecision, he growled, "Damn if I can understand women," but his hands moved to her back and he laboured to release each tiny pearl button from its buttonhole.

"Now help me take it off," she implored, but her head lolled against his shoulder, her body boneless as if the gown were forgotten.

"Damn!" He wouldn't take the chance of being stopped

again. He shimmied the dress over her shoulders and peeled it from her. One swift toss and it fell on the bed in a heap.

She did a little jig of distress on his lap. He sucked in his breath and stilled her movements. "Maddie, for God's sake, have a care," and he nipped at her shoulder to reinforce his command.

She moaned, "Oh my gown, my beautiful gown. Please let me hang it up. I want to keep it for our daughter."

"We haven't got a daughter," he pointed out.

"No, but one day we may! Oh Jason, please?"

Comprehension slowly dawned. Hadn't his own sisters married in his mother's wedding finery, with a few alterations, of course, to allow for the changes in fashions? Maddie's distraction seemed more understandable. These trifles meant a lot to a woman.

With a smothered sigh of resignation, he lifted her effortlessly and dumped her in the chair. "Don't move a muscle," he told her, then stalked to the bed and removed the crushed gown and spencer. It took only a moment to hang them in the clothes press. Even so, when he resumed his kneeling position in front of Maddie's chair, he knew at a glance that she had gone cold on him. Her knees were glued together and the fingers which curled around the arm rests were rigid with tension. He thought she looked adorable in her frilly drawers and chemise.

His hands cupped her knees. "Open your legs, Maddie," he pleaded softly.

If anything, they tightened against him.

"It's . . . indecent and . . . undignified," she whispered, and her eyes wandered to the shaft of light streaming in the window.

His fingers found the ties of her drawers and inexorably began to release them. "You heard the solicitor," he said persuasively. "The marriage must be consummated—male fashion. Just close your eyes and think of, of . . . Scotland," he quickly invented.

She thought of Scotland then gave a little gurgle of laughter. Her knees relaxed a fraction. "That won't help," she said without thinking.

"Why not?" Surreptitiously, he wedged an elbow between

her parted thighs. His other hand trailed with studied idleness inside the loosened opening of her drawers.

Because, she thought to herself, *the emblem of Scotland is a lion rampant.*

Very deliberately, he touched his fingers to the triangle of auburn curls, softer than satin, at the apex of her thighs. She tightened her knees too late to prevent his gentle invasion. Her head arched back, and her thighs opened. He swept them apart. She was moist and ready for him, her body open to him. And he was done with gentling her.

Impatiently, he hooked one powerful arm behind her waist and hauled her bodily towards him, twisting, turning, till his back was braced against the chair and she lay just as he wanted her. One arm quelled her flaying arms and elbows, and his mouth cut off the words that spilled from her lips. His fingers found her and slipped inside the moist warmth that both excited and reassured him. She wanted him. Deliberately, he flexed his fingers and the girl in his arms tensed then melted, moulding herself against him, silently, unmistakably, inviting his fuller possession.

He released her mouth and he rested his forehead against hers, their breaths hotly mingling, his harsh and laboured, hers slow, shallow, painful.

"I don't know what it is you do to me," she told him on a thread of a voice she scarcely recognized as her own. "I find myself doing what I swore I wouldn't do."

"Good," he grunted. "That makes two of us."

He stripped her of her lacy underthings and tossed them aside. His hands went to the buttons of his trousers and he moved slightly till he eased them down, kicking them off to lie in a heap at his feet.

"I'm all yours," he said to her, his eyes dancing with wicked enjoyment. "What do you want to do with me?"

She hung her head. "Jason, I'm not very good at this."

"You're not a novice," he encouraged. "You know what I want," and his mouth dipped down to take full suckle at the breasts he had been so intently studying a moment before.

She cradled her hand to the silky length of his shaft. "Like this?" she whispered, sliding with the featherlight pressure he had taught her once before.

His fingers tangled in her hair and she was rocked back on her heels. "Maddie," he rasped, his voice a whisper of apology. "I meant to go slow," and his lips slanted across her lips in a hungry demand, his tongue delving and receding in her open mouth in an unmistakable rhythm that sent her senses spinning.

She was turning, turning like a kite blown about by the wind till he brought her to a safe landing. Languorously, she stretched out on the floor before the hearth. He knelt between her knees and nudged them further apart.

"You're wet for me," he told her with a grunt of satisfaction, and he settled himself against her parted thighs.

Passion put to flight all inhibitions. "What do you want me to do?" she asked throatily, and rotated her hips in deliberate invitation.

He braced his forearms on either side of her head. "I want you to say the words to me, Maddie," and he teased her bottom lip with the tip of his tongue. "You've never said the words to me," he breathed into her mouth. "Say them," and his hips rocked against her heated flesh in tantalizing arousal.

The silence seemed to throb with a thousand misgivings that kept her from him.

"Say it," he urged.

"I'm . . . afraid." She needed time to sort things out. Everything had happened too quickly. He demanded too much of her.

"Then say you don't love me."

"I can't."

With a kind of hopeless anguish, he thrust into her, filling her aching emptiness with his masculine complement. "I'll make you love me," he promised.

And then began the erotic dance as he taught her body the measure and counterpoint to match his rhythm, each thrust driving her pleasure higher, higher. With tender restraint, he held himself back till he felt her sudden leap to ecstasy. He followed, a mere heartbeat behind. Unfettered now, his movements became rougher, deeper, and as he spilled into her, he groaned her name over and over and over.

In blissful repletion, he slid from her and dragged her to his side. He trailed wet kisses from her eyelids to her ear and along

179

the underside of her jaw. "You do love me. You just won't admit it," he told her fiercely, and cradled her limp body more securely to his own. Maddie was strangely silent.

He raised on one elbow and looked down at her tousled head. "What is it, love? What are you thinking?"

"Splinters," she mumbled into his chest. He had to strain to hear.

"Splinters?"

"I think there's one embedded in my . . . posterior."

Laughter was quickly followed by dismay when he pulled to his knees and looked down at a hotly blushing Maddie. He could scarcely credit that he'd taken her on the bare floorboards in the middle of the afternoon. The girl was his bride, gently bred and innocent, and deserving of his utmost restraint. Yet here he was, again, abusing her abominably, as if she were the veriest trollop he had picked up at the Cyprian's Ball.

With infinite tenderness, he lifted her in his arms and carried her to the bed. He rolled her onto her stomach. As he knelt beside her, scrutinizing her derriere, Maddie hid her burning cheeks in the pillows. He saw at once the cause of her distress. Imbedded in the soft rise of one cheek was a wicked looking tack.

"Good grief, girl. You must have been in agony."

Maddie blushed even hotter. "No, I . . . I felt nothing till . . . till afterwards," she confessed in a small voice.

He was glad that she could not see the smug grin that creased his cheeks. There was something exhilarating in knowing that one's lovemaking could make a woman totally oblivious to pain.

He left her for a moment and returned with a washcloth and a bottle of brandy.

"This is going to hurt," he warned. She made no protest as he pulled the tack from her flesh, but when he poured the brandy into the small puncture, she writhed deeper into the covers.

A drop of dark blood oozed from the wound. He dabbed it with the brandy-soaked washcloth. Maddie squirmed. The bleeding seemed to have stopped. His eyes leisurely travelled over her, calmly taking possession of what he regarded as his private stock. She was small boned, perfectly proportioned, and totally female in her rounded contours and deeply carved valleys.

"Has it stopped bleeding?" she asked softly.

"No," he lied.

The scents in the room were intoxicating—a heady mixture of apples, brandy and most inflaming of all to his rapidly arousing senses, the pervasive scent of their lovemaking. His resolution to be a temperate lover for his bride began to wane. The struggle with his better nature was short-lived. "What the hell," he thought. He dumped the washcloth on the bedside table and climbed into bed.

Maddie turned her head on the pillow as his lips grazed her shoulder.

"What are you doing?"

Wordlessly, he lay prone on top of her, taking some of his weight on his braced arms. With the tip of his tongue, he traced a wet path from her ear to the throbbing pulse at the join of her shoulder. He heard the soft, liquid sound deep in her throat, and his body tightened, squeezing his lungs till his breath came hard and fast. He closed his eyes against the pounding in his ears and rested his bowed head on the shadowed hollow of her back. He breathed deeply, forcing himself to a slower pace. She was warm, soft and trembling beneath him. Her scent filled his nostrils.

"Maddie," he groaned, and he nudged the valley between her soft woman's thighs with his fully erect member. The message was unmistakable.

"Oh," she said, and buried her face deeper in the pillow.

His voice was low and ragged, a mere whisper of sound, gentling her fears, seducing her to accommodate his need in the age-old manner of the male with his mate.

"Let me!"

"Be generous, love."

"Trust me."

"I need you. I love you."

"Like this, oh yes, like this."

A touch, a gesture, and her smooth limbs and rounded contours were arranged for the perfect fit of his body. He locked one arm around her waist and raised her hips. Slowly, with infinite gentleness, he entered her from behind. Her head arched back on his shoulder. He began to move, rocking her rhythmically, voluptuously, sinking into her with deep, leisurely strokes.

"Jason," she warned, and tensed beneath him.

His arm slipped lower, locking her body to his. "It's all right, love. I want you to—"

Her cry of rapture, abandoned, full-bodied rose like the wail of a banshee to fill the room. Swiftly, he cupped her mouth with his open palm to smother her pleasure sounds. Her body convulsed, contracting around his pulsating shaft with hard, rhythmic spasms. Desire exploded through Deveryn. Bucking, rolling, in a frenzy of passion, he rode her to a quivering, breathless finish.

They lay for long minutes, panting, his mouth open at the nape of her neck where his teeth had administered several sharp nips whilst they revelled in the throes of their passion. He rolled from her and threw one arm over his eyes. No woman had ever affected him like this before. He was a skillful, considerate lover. Where did his art go when he laid a hand on Maddie?

God, he didn't care! He felt more alive than he had ever felt in his life.

Blindly, he reached out a hand and dragged her into the shelter of his body. Her breath tickled his armpit.

"You're damn good in bed for a beginner," he teased. "Also noisy." God, she could drive him to fever pitch with those pleasure sounds.

"And you're greedy," she disparaged with equal candour. And she hoped he would never lose his voracious appetite.

"Not at all," he countered. "It simply occurred to me that it were prudent to leave our bed somewhat less than perfect should the innkeeper ever be called upon to give proof that our marriage has been consummated.

They raised on their elbows and looked about them. The bed looked as if a hurricane had hit it.

He smiled in unholy appreciation and sprang to his feet. With arms above his head, he stretched, his muscles bunching along powerful shoulders and chest. He scratched one armpit, then the other, and leered at Maddie over his shoulder.

"I feel marvellous. How about you?"

A very delicate part of her anatomy smarted from the splinter he had so solicitously removed before tumbling her on the bed; she could have sworn, if she didn't know better, that a swarm of angry bees had descended on her neck; and her loins throbbed with an unfamiliar tenderness.

She glowered at him.

A wicked bark of laughter was her reward. "You'll get used to it," he consoled with unabashed masculine unconcern and strode to the washstand with a confident swagger.

Thirty minutes later saw Lord Deveryn handing Maddie, now restored to her blacks, into his waiting carriage. He followed her in, but did not immediately give his coachman the office to start. Maddie carefully stowed the box with its precious wedding gown under the flap of the front seat. She became conscious that Deveryn was waiting patiently till she should complete her task. She settled herself comfortably and threw him a questioning look.

"This will only take a moment," he began.

The intelligence that her husband intended to stay on in Edinburgh for another day or so to conclude his business with Forsythe, she accepted without demur. But the next calm disclosure rekindled every misgiving.

"Why must our marriage remain a secret?" she demanded, eyeing him with marked suspicion.

There were a number of cogent reasons. Cynthia was one of them. He did not relish the long drive to London in the close confines of the coach with a woman who, in some sort, might regard herself as scorned. He could remove himself from her spleen by the simple expedient of acting as outrider. But Maddie had to be considered. And there was a more compelling reason.

"In a word, your grandfather. He deserves the courtesy of being the first to learn of our nuptials. He is, after all, your closest male relative."

"That doesn't signify. To my knowledge, he's never concerned himself overmuch with my welfare in the past. I think you know how shabbily he treated my parents when *they* eloped."

"Precisely. I shan't make the same mistake your father did," he answered reasonably. "We're married. Period. Your grandfather can like it or lump it. However, I've no wish to provoke him unnecessarily. On the contrary, I'm hoping for his active support."

"Why should you care?"

"Not for myself," he explained patiently. "But for you. I wish to spare you any unpleasantness. There's bound to be talk. Your grandfather's acceptance of what is, after all, a *fait accompli*, should dispel some of the speculation, help smooth your entry into Polite Society."

The man seemed to have an answer for everything. She did not think that he was in humour to hear that she deplored the manners and mores of Polite Society and would deem it no great loss to be barred from its rarefied atmosphere. More to the point, her one brush with the ton had convinced her that Polite Society would not lament her loss by one whit less.

"Oh, very well," she agreed, suddenly resigning herself to the force of his logic. "I shan't say a word to anyone."

Deveryn smiled at Maddie's unaccustomed meekness. "Good girl. And now, there is one other small matter about which I must take you into my confidence."

He had chosen his moment with forethought. They were wed. The marriage had been consummated. They were in perfect amity, more, for in his own mind he saw their marriage as a love-match. And time was of the essence, for Cynthia might very well enlighten Maddie before he had a chance to explain himself. That could be disastrous. Still, he groped for words, trying to frame his thoughts in a way that would cause Maddie least offence. She sensed his difficulty and became alert. *Oh hell*, he thought, *there's no easy way to say this*, and he plunged into speech.

"When I see Forsythe tomorrow, I'll be signing papers on the future disposition of Drumoak."

"Yes?" She could not perceive the reason for his hesitation. Their marriage had removed Drumoak as a source of conflict between them, for the laws of the land stated unequivocally that what was his was his, and what was hers was his also, a cause for scandal to all thinking women. She wondered if perhaps he meant to make Drumoak part of the marriage settlement. That hope was dashed at his next words.

"Cynthia has some claim on the estate. I wish you would admit that."

Instinct made her cautious. "And if I don't?"

His lips tightened fractionally. "If you don't, it makes no matter, save perhaps to your own peace of mind."

A thousand thoughts circled in Maddie's brain. Sudden comprehension jolted her. "My God, you're giving it to her, aren't you? You're giving my father's house to *her*."

"Not exactly. Only a home for her lifetime or until such time as she marries. Eventually, the estate will revert completely to you or your heirs. So you see, Drumoak isn't lost to you. I think I've come up with an equitable solution."

Maddie digested his words in shocked silence. It was a moment or two before she found her voice. "That's what Cynthia meant when she told Forsythe that you were her advocate," she said weakly. "That's why you tore yourself away from London to come to Drumoak." Her voice grew stronger, more incredulous. "This whole thing has been premeditated. She didn't want my father, but she wants his estate. And you're going to give it to her on a platter! You always meant to!"

"Calm yourself, Maddie. Drumoak is scarcely Carlton House. We won't miss it. And you owe it to Cynthia, to your stepmother, to see that she is provided for. Your own conscience should tell you so."

He tried to take her hands, but she would have none of him. She threw them off and stared unseeingly out the coach window. Her eyes were very bright. For no reason he could think of, he felt like a cad. He fingered the silk of her skirt and said in a low, placating tone, "I've told you. We'll come back for holidays, put the place to rights, make it a show place, if you like."

"For Cynthia to enjoy? No thank you."

"It's not likely that she will be there," he reasoned. "Cynthia isn't interested in the estate. I daresay she may spend the odd month or two in Scotland when she has nothing better to do, but even that is doubtful." He tried to inject a note of humour. "Scotland isn't to everyone's taste, you know."

Maddie could scarcely make sense of what he was telling her. "You've just told me that Drumoak belongs to her."

"I can't see her spending much time there. London is her setting. It's the income from Drumoak which Cynthia is interested in."

"What income?" asked Maddie coldly. "We were scarcely self-sufficient."

He mistook her rigid control for calm and spoke carelessly, without thinking. "Naturally I shall provide Cynthia with an income until such time as the estate begins to show a profit. It's the least I can do under the circumstances."

"How very convenient," she said acidly.

"What?" Her tone left no doubt as to the state of her emotions.

"To pension off your mistress with the profits from your wife's estate! Very astute of you, Deveryn, though a trifle tight-fisted. And they say the Scots are parsimonious! Piffle! We can't hold a candle to you English."

His eyes flashed then faded to an icy transparency. Belatedly, he recognized that Maddie's temper was at boiling point. He had prepared himself for entreaties, persuasions, tears perhaps, but not this unwarranted display of venom. Moreover, he found her immutable antipathy to Cynthia childish and petty. And that she was determined to misunderstand him when his motives were as pure as a fresh fall of snow cut him to the quick.

"Don't take that tone with me, my girl," he said, unconsciously adopting her tone, "or it will be very much the worse for you. And on the long drive to London, you'd best keep a civil tongue in your head if you know what's good for you. Cynthia, as I've no doubt you've learned to your regret, will cut you down to size as soon as look at you. And I have no intention of protecting you from the sharp edge of her tongue. Remember that!"

Her look of loathing could not have been more marked if she had discovered a cockroach at the bottom of her porridge. "You held off telling me all this, deliberately, didn't you?" she accused. "You knew that wild horses could not drag me to the altar if I had known that you meant to serve me such a backhanded turn."

It was true, of course. But he wasn't about to confess that he had done wrong when he had meant everything for the best.

186

"I thought you would be in a better frame of mind to accept things after we were married," he admitted angrily. "You'll be mistress of Crammond. And one day of Dunsdale. What can Drumoak signify compared to *that?*"

"For all I care, Crammond and Dunsdale can sink to the bottom of the ocean and Cynthia with them. Especially Cynthia," she shot back.

They were nose to nose, glaring balefully into each others stormy eyes, their voices gradually rising to a pitch that was audible to the coachmen. The coach rolled on its springs. A horse whinnied. Deveryn became aware of the impropriety of their position. Maddie did not care. He descended the carriage steps and shut the door with a clatter. Through the open window he said in a terse undertone, "I'd be obliged if you would send the coach back for me in the morning with my valet and a bag. Martin will know what to pack. Expect me in two days, three at the most. We'll talk of this later."

At his word of farewell, she managed a cool, distancing nod. She heard his command to the coachmen with unmitigated relief. As the horses moved forward, she sank back against the squabs and closed her eyes, thankful that there was no one present to witness her misery.

She spent the next two hours reviewing the progress of her courtship with Deveryn. The shadow of her father seemed to haunt her reflections. At one point, she turned her head into the cold, misted windowpane and cried softly, "What have I done? Oh what have I done?"

Memories flooded her mind, intensifying her sense of guilt and shame. She remembered her father taking her up in front of his mount before she was old enough for her first pony; she remembered learning to swim in the Forth with her father's strong, dependable hands holding her up; she remembered her father's pride when she took her first fence, and his presence in the sickroom when a bout with pneumonia threatened her life. Later, there were other less happy memories, but she did not dwell on those. She consoled herself with the thought that no one was perfect. She never pretended that her father was. But she would permit no one to speak ill of him.

Her own sorry predicament she blamed on herself, though, to be sure, Lord Deveryn did not escape his share of censure.

187

Habitually used to having his own way in everything, he had, she decided, taken advantage of her inexperience. He was odious, selfish, arrogant and . . . old. No doubt he would try to rule her with a rod of iron. He would never be given the opportunity, she promised herself.

Pleasant reveries floated at random through her mind, relieving, in some small part, her feelings of impotent rage. She imagined herself saddling Banshee and melting into the hills until such time as Deveryn and her stepmother removed their hateful presence from Drumoak; she saw herself conferring with her solicitor demanding that he procure an annullment of her odious marriage; she pretended that she was eloping with Malcolm to the Continent where they would live happily ever after and thumb their noses at Lord Deveryn across the safe distance of the English Channel.

The outcome of this fanciful form of cognition was predictable. Maddie arrived home in a state of acute nervous exhaustion. She longed to confide in someone. It was not in her power. Deveryn had constrained her to silence. In the privacy of her own chamber, frustrated anger gave way to despair.

A sleepless night did nothing to restore her equilibrium or assuage her feelings of ill usage. On the contrary, the evasions she was forced to practise on her aunt intensified her shame. The marriage to all intents and purposes might never have taken place. She did not even have a ring to show for it. Deveryn, Maddie decided, might very well be an unprincipled rogue. She'd heard of men of that ilk from the girls at school.

Towards noon, after a listless morning of packing her few belongings, Maddie was called to the front hall. And into her hand, unexpectedly, fortuitously, fell the power, in some small measure, to decide her own fate.

Within the hour, under the escort of her grandfather's emissary, Maddie was en route to London.

Chapter Twelve

The small, restless sounds of the audience as they made themselves comfortable for the duration gradually faded. The conductor raised one arm imperceptibly. The baton descended and the opening strains of Handel's Water Music, measured, graceful, a perfect complement to the elegant and spacious Georgian interior slowly wafted through the ground floor rooms of the Earl of Bessborough's commodious town house in Cavendish Square.

Under the brilliant glare of the crystal chandelier, Lady Bessborough surveyed her guests with unmitigated pleasure. Her husband, the earl, was expected to put in an appearance later in the evening when the House retired for the night. She caught the eye of her second son, Freddie. He was deep in conversation with a very pleasant looking young woman— Samuel Spencer's granddaughter, as she remembered. She supposed that Freddie was regaling the girl with the gory details of his near demise at Waterloo. He and his friend, Captain Gronow, had dined out for the last several months on the stories of their alarming though sometimes amusing exploits while serving with Wellington. Her ladyship smiled fondly at the favourite of her brood. A moment later, her eyes were anxiously scanning the room. Thankfully, Lady Caroline Lamb, her ill-starred daughter, was nowhere in evidence. The girl's disastrous affair with Lord Byron was long over, though not forgotten. That degenerate, fortunately, was safely married, though to be sure, rumour was rife that all was not well in Byron's household. She shuddered to think what

189

mischief Lady Caro might get into if Byron should ever give her the nod again. The Countess silently deplored the blatant indiscretions of the younger generation, conveniently forgetting that in her salad days she herself had set the ton on its ear. Her long-standing affair with Lord Granville, sadly now at an end, had been conducted with far more circumspection than she was formerly wont to employ.

Her eyes wandered to the Duke of Raeburn. She eyed him speculatively. Now *this* was something. What, she wondered, could have dragged such a recluse from Raeburn Abbey? Matchmaking, of course. He'd been a widower for all of two years and was but newly come into the title. Now who . . . ? Surely not Spencer's granddaughter? Poor Freddie! He looked to be completely captivated.

His Grace, the Duke of Raeburn, negligently crossed one silk stockinged ankle over the other and made a mental note to reprimand his valet for the something less than mirror shine on his best pair of evening pumps. He did not think that the trifling awkwardness of not having paid his retainer for some few months merited such lackadaisical service. After all, he reasoned, his pecuniary embarrassment was of a temporary nature. His eyes travelled to the pretty little thing who was to be the source of his future prosperity. His spirits flagged.

Madeleina, he refused to call her by the undignified diminutive, was wrapped up in the music. It took very little to please the child, so he had discovered—a posy of flowers, a book of poems, a drive in his carriage. Her delight in such trifles was gratifying. Still, there was something obscene in a man of his years, he could not say experience, offering for a girl who was of an age with his own daughters. Thankfully, they were still in the schoolroom with their younger brother, the heir, a boy of fifteen.

In another year or two, the girls would be of marriageable age and angling for a Season. Worse, a Court presentation was obligatory, and the expense of such a venture was mindboggling, especially when the treasury was empty. With a *moue* of distaste, His Grace thought fleetingly of his departed father. If only the old sod had gone to his just reward before he had time to empty the Raeburn coffers. A taste for fast horses, faster women and deep play with the Devonshire set had been

190

his ruination. And it stood to him, George Darnley, as head of his House, to rectify matters. Since the death of his dear lady wife two years before, his fate had been predictable—marriage to some heiress or other.

But damn if he wanted to get shackled! Women were intimidating. Beautiful women even more so. A comprehensive glance in the girl's direction confirmed his suspicion. In a year or two, Madeleina was destined to be one of the beauties.

The dismal prospect of life with a beauty passed before his eyes—balls, routs, soirees at Carlton House, musical evenings such as the present boring affair at Lady Bessborough's, the Opera, the theatre, a full calendar of social engagements during the Season, for what beauty could forego the pleasure of displaying her one claim to fame? None of his acquaintance. And it went without saying that for every public appearance, there would be a visit to some fashionable and expensive mantua maker. Good God! In all probability, the girl would expect *him* to turn into a fashion plate.

He raised his quizzing glass and sadly surveyed the occupants of the room, particularly the gentlemen. Egad! But he didn't know what the younger generation was coming to! It was all Weston tailoring and those damned pantaloons, a relic of Wellington and his armies which the Corinthian set had taken up. "Trousers," some called them. Before Waterloo, a gentleman would not be caught dead in such casual attire in a lady's drawing room. Breeches and silk stockings were *de rigeur,* now, regretfully, worn only at court or Almack's Assembly rooms, or by ancient relics such as himself. Even Wellington had adopted the current mode.

He let the quizzing glass drop to his chest and gave his attention to the music, his expression stoic. When the last few bars of the overture came to an end, he applauded with gusto. Duty served, he did not remain for the rest of the programme, but made his apologies to his neighbours as he scraped back his gilt-edged chair, and made for the library on the heels of several other retreating gentlemen.

Maddie watched the departure of the gentlemen with a derisory twitch of her lips. Napoleon had disposed of the angry mob with one burst of grapeshot. In England, a few bars of Handel, and the rout was equally effective. She said as much to

191

Freddie Ponsonby, and was rewarded with an appreciative chuckle. His mother, Lady Bessborough, riveted her son with a stern eye and the young man sobered.

The musical programme came to an end. The great doors were thrown open by liveried footmen, and by degrees the guests began to idle their way in small groups to the supper room. Freddie made his excuses to Maddie. In the absence of his father, he was acting as host and his mother had signaled that it was time to inform the gentlemen that their presence was required.

As Maddie rose from her place, she said in an amused undertone, "We've lost our escort. Raeburn has deserted us."

Miss Spencer acknowledged Maddie's words with an unladylike snort. "And so has every other gentleman in the room."

"Where have all the gentlemen got to?"

"The library, I've no doubt. It's not uncommon at this kind of do. If our hostess had engaged to have an opera singer to do the honours, especially one with a pretty face, the gentlemen would have stuck to their places like glue."

"What has the library got that's so attractive?"

"Not books. Of that you may be certain. Now, my dear, I think it's time to circulate. Ah, here comes Raeburn to do the honours."

Maddie smiled shyly as His Grace made his way toward them. In his beige satin breeches and matching waistcoat with plum coloured brocade cutaway coat, she thought him very elegant for an older gentleman. She judged him to be something under fifty, though she knew herself to be shockingly inept at placing the ages of those she numbered among the elderly. Youth made her blind to what other ladies present were not slow to remark. The Duke was of athletic build, carried himself well, had a healthy crop of dark brown hair distinguished with grey at the temples, and possessed an uncommonly handsome pair of intelligent hazel eyes. Maddie looked unseeingly at the aristocratic features and thought merely that the hooded eyes gave His Grace an air of one who was either perpetually bored or sleepy.

She angled a sideways glance at her aunt. That lady's expression was inscrutable. For that matter, the Duke's

FREE

B O O K C E R T I F I C A T E

ZEBRA HOME SUBSCRIPTION SERVICE, INC.

YES! Please start my subscription to Zebra Historical Romances and send me my free Zebra Novel along with my first month's Romances. I understand that I may preview these four new Zebra Historical Romances Free for 10 days. If I'm not satisfied with them I may return the four books within 10 days and owe nothing. Otherwise I will pay just $3.50 each; a total of $14.00 (a $15.80 value—I save $1.80). Then each month I will receive the 4 newest titles as soon as they come off the press for the same 10 day Free preview and low price. I may return any shipment and I may cancel this arrangement at any time. There is no minimum number of books to buy and there are no shipping, handling or postage charges. Regardless of what I do, the **FREE** book is mine to keep.

Name _____

Address _____

   (Please Print)

City _____ State _____ Zip _____

                                        Apt. #

Telephone ( ) _____

Signature _____

           (if under 18, parent or guardian must sign)

Terms and offer subject to change without notice.

MAIL IN THE COUPON BELOW TODAY

To get your Free **ZEBRA HISTORICAL ROMANCE** fill out the coupon below and send it in today. As soon as we receive the coupon, we'll send your first month's books to preview Free for 10 days along with your **FREE NOVEL.**

GET FREE GIFT

expression was equally bland. She thought the two of them were perfect for each other. Her grandfather had told her that Raeburn was a widower and on the lookout for a wife. In the week since she had been in London, he had been a frequent visitor at the house and an attentive escort. Only one thing could account for it. He had fallen in love with her aunt on the long, wearying coach ride from Drumoak to London.

The thought of her precipitous flight from Drumoak made her smile slip a fraction, and though she was careful to respond to her companions' desultory comments on the room and its appointments, her mind was miles away.

On that morning almost a fortnight before, when she had descended Drumoak's long staircase, the Duke of Raeburn had seemed like a godsend. He had come, he had informed her, at her grandfather's behest to escort the ladies to London. His offer had been accepted with alacrity. Within the hour they had been on their way, taking a polite but distant farewell of Cynthia, who looked glad to see the back of them, and a prolonged and affectionate farewell of Janet, who was not. From Duncan, Maddie would not be parted, nor he from her. He had acted as one of the outriders and now found employment in Samuel Spencer's stables. She suspected that Duncan was no happier than she in the unfamiliar and strangely impersonal environment in which they found themselves.

Her reception by her grandfather had not been an affectionate one. She had not expected affection. They were, after all, strangers to each other. He was everything that was solicitous. And if she now regretted a lack of warmth in his demeanour, she soon perceived that there was nothing personal in it. Samuel Spencer was by nature a cold man. Moreover, he was preoccupied. As a connoisseur and collector of some note, to which fact the house on Curzon Street with its fine furnishings and elegant appointments amply attested, he was frequently away on foraging expeditions. House sales and auctions in and around London, and even farther afield, drew him like a magnet.

In the week since Maddie had settled in, she had seen very little of him, though his presence had made itself felt. From the moment she wakened till the minute her head touched the pillow at night, she had scarcely a moment to call her own. Her grandfather had seen to that. Her days were spent with tutors and dancing masters and modistes. Nothing about her seemed to please. Miss Maitland would have been aghast at the tutoring of her elocution teacher, so Maddie thought, for Mr. Clarke tried to induce her to speak as if she had a plum in her mouth. It simply murdered the clarity of her diction, especially those final consonants. But that was the English for you. Since they couldn't enunciate properly themselves, they didn't want anyone else to. And as for the useless rules on protocol she was obliged to memorize, it would have been laughable if it weren't such a chore. Who in his right mind cared a brass button whether it was proper to introduce a countess to a marchioness, or the other way round? Only the English. If she hadn't known better, she would have suspected that she was being groomed to take her place as duchess, or some fool thing.

Only once, so far, had she come to points with her grandfather. He mentioned casually over dinner one evening that he wanted her out of her blacks. She dug in her heels, pointing out in as reasonable a tone as she could manage, that she wore them out of respect for her father.

The silence pulsed with leashed anger. She watched guardedly as her grandfather brought the linen napkin to his lips. His eyes blazed. Her chin lifted.

It was Aunt Nell who smoothed over what gave every evidence of becoming an ugly contretemps. She tactfully suggested a compromise—half mourning. Though Maddie had no conception of the distinction in mourning dress, the words sounded acceptable. She signified her acquiescence. Her grandfather, after a slight hesitation, followed suit. Which was why, she reflected ruefully, she was wearing a lilac silk which was indistinguishable from the finery of any lady in the room. She conceded that her grandfather had adroitly outflanked her.

His parting comment, "There's a good deal of your mother in you, Maddie," she had not mistaken for a compliment. She suspected that there was a good deal of her grandfather in her as well.

But he was not the sort of man to take into one's confidence. She had reached that conclusion within hours of her arrival. Indeed, her circumstances were so shocking, she did not think she dare confide them to anyone, however sympathetic and broadminded, which her grandfather was certainly not. There was nothing for it but to stew in silence. She felt as if she were sitting on a powder keg. Only one spark was necessary to ignite the conflagration—Deveryn.

Her unhappy train of thought was interrupted by the Duke's exclamation of pleasure.

"Lady Mary. And blooming like the first rose of summer. Marriage would seem to agree with you, my dear. So where is the bounder who stole my favourite niece from me?"

Maddie saw a young woman of sallow complexion whose rather undistinguishable features were suddenly transformed by a singularly charming smile. "Your Grace, how lovely to see you again." Her eyes travelled the diminishing throng of people. "Max is here, somewhere. Possibly in the library." Her hazel eyes lit up with mischief. "Perhaps he can't bear to tear himself away from the scholarly gentlemen who are invariably to be found in the bookroom on such occasions as this."

"Lord Bessborough has a very fine library," admitted Raeburn, with a twinkle.

"But not as fine as his wine cellar," Lady Mary responded in like manner.

Adroitly, His Grace turned the subject to less contentious channels. "Allow me to present Miss Nell Spencer and her niece, Miss Madeleina Sinclair."

It seemed only natural, after the introductions were made, for the group to move as one to the open doors, and even more natural, when they sat down to supper, for the younger ladies to find a place together. The Duke led Miss Spencer to a table not far removed.

"Madeleina seems in somewhat better looks this evening," he remarked conversationally. He was thinking of Maddie as she had been on the tedious, seven day drive from Edinburgh to London. He'd thought her then a rather colourless thing with little animation and even less conversation. She had improved on acquaintance. Still, she could not hold a candle to her aunt when it came to address. Old man Spencer had convinced him that the journey would give him the perfect opportunity to get to know his betrothed, even court her a little. Instead, he'd felt more akin to a nursemaid than a suitor.

Lack of practice, he supposed, and raised his index finger to summon one of the liveried footmen who was dispensing glasses of champagne from a silver salver.

Miss Spencer gratefully accepted a glass from the Duke's hand and permitted a footman to serve her a selection of delicacies. She waited till he had withdrawn. "I don't know which hit her hardest, the tragic circumstances of her father's death or the loss of her beloved Drumoak. I think I told you that to all intents and purposes it belongs to her stepmother now? But Maddie is young. The young have a way of bouncing back from what you and I would go into a decline over. At heart, she's a very sensible girl."

After a thoughtful silence, the Duke said, "Perhaps I'm too old for her. Oh don't look so surprised. The thought had crossed my mind."

Miss Spencer coloured slightly. "I don't think anyone loves Maddie better than I do. And I am persuaded that she's a very fortunate young woman to have attached a gentleman such as yourself."

"You do? Why?" His Grace regarded the object of their conversation through half-hooded eyes. Lady Mary's husband, Max Branwell, had made a belated appearance and was being introduced to the child.

Miss Spencer, normally rather diffident with members of the opposite sex, found to her surprise that the Duke was very easy to talk to. She spoke without reservation. "You're a handsome man, possess a distinguished title as well as superior intelligence and address. Any woman would be flattered by your attention."

"You forgot to add that I'm also as poor as a church mouse."

"Oh money!" disparaged the lady in the manner of one who never had to do without a thing in her life. "My father will settle a fortune on the girl."

"And you don't find that rather . . . crass? Distasteful?" asked His Grace. The infelicity of his remark suddenly struck him, and he said quickly, "I beg your pardon. I spoke without thinking. I meant no disrespect to your father. On the contrary, my disapprobation is all for myself."

Miss Spencer took some few minutes to marshal her thoughts before launching into a reply. "Your Grace, my father and I rarely agree on anything. But from the moment he confided that he had selected you to be Maddie's husband, I found myself in perfect harmony with his decision, though for different reasons. My father, as I've no doubt you've remarked, thinks only of the prestige of the title. It flatters his vanity to think his granddaughter will be a duchess."

Raeburn acknowledged the truth of her statement with an imperceptible nod of his dark head. He refrained from voicing the vulgar suspicion that Samuel Spencer's personal ambitions to rise above his humble beginnings as a silk mercer would also be realised. He'd heard through the grapevine that young Devonshire had been courted but had politely but firmly declined. Devonshire, a bachelor of only seven and twenty, would have suited the old man better. Spencer's great-grandson, in those circumstances, would have been heir to a dukedom. But, as the whole world knew, Devonshire's heart was already given to his cousin, Lady Caroline Lamb. He'd been hopelessly in love with that capricious young woman since he'd been a boy in short coats.

"Your Grace, may I speak frankly?"

"Please do."

The footman returned and diligently refilled champagne glasses and tempted palettes with a selection of dried fruits and hothouse grapes and strawberries. It was some few minutes before Miss Spencer could continue where she had left off.

"You know, of course, some of the circumstances of Maddie's background, so there's no necessity for me to give you a complete biography. However, I think it would be helpful for you to remember that in the last number of years the girl has had a somewhat eccentric upbringing. She's been literally alone in the world, making her own way, managing her own affairs."

"I understood that she was at school." Surprise edged Raeburn's voice.

"Miss Maitland's Academy," snorted Miss Spencer. "I shan't bore you with a description of that establishment. Suffice it to say that Maddie learned nothing of any use to her there. The social graces, those necessary and elegant refinements which ease one's way in our society are somewhat lacking in her."

197

"Yes. I noticed that she doesn't have much to say for herself."

"She's not stupid, by any means."

"Intelligent? A clever girl?"

"Worse. She's had the disadvantage of a singularly masculine education." She looked at him with some trepidation.

Surprise brightened his eyes. "Well, that's something, at any rate!"

"I beg your pardon?"

"My late wife was something of a bluestocking."

"Oh." There was no mistaking that the Duke of Raeburn did not find education for a woman to be an unwelcome accomplishment. Quite the reverse. The discovery left Miss Spencer at a loss for words for some few minutes.

"I understand you had charge of the girl since she left school?"

"More or less. That is to say, I met Maddie by chance two years ago at just such an evening as this. The poor thing was having a miserable time. I found her hiding in the cloakroom. I made up my mind then to do something for the child. We started corresponding and when she left school, I made my home in Scotland to be with her. It was as much as her father would allow from the Spencers. He was still bitter, you see, at the way our family had reacted to his elopement with my sister. My father was . . . is . . . a hard man." Her voice drifted away as if following in the wake of her thoughts. Her expression grew pensive. She came to herself gradually, and flashed her companion a look of apology. "I beg your pardon. Woolgathering is not a habit with me."

"You were remembering less happy times, I collect?"

"I was thinking of my sister and how like her Maddie is. Constance was one of the beauties of her Season. Would you believe that a duke offered for her?"

"Ah! That would explain your father's long standing antipathy to the man who eloped with her."

Miss Spencer's sigh was scarcely audible. "My father hates to be thwarted."

"And you? How is it that you have never married?"

"A not uncommon tale. Because, kind sir, nobody asked me."

"That I find hard to believe." The words sounded like the merest gallantry, though they were sincerely meant.

"I had not my sister's beauty, you see, and . . ." she faltered. She had been about to say that the taint of shop was too strong about her family in those days. She recovered herself quickly and merely observed, "But I have wandered far from my subject. We were talking of Maddie. You will need a deal of patience, but the results will more than reward you. She's like an uncut gem. A little polishing, and she will be perfect for her setting."

The Duke's thoughts wandered to the two uncut gems in his schoolroom at Raeburn Abbey. His daughters, the precocious brats, would require mallet and chisel to chip away their rough edges before they were ready for Polite Society. A happy thought struck him.

"After the wedding, when we remove to Raeburn Abbey, if you wish it, I should be honoured to offer you the hospitality of my home."

"Of course I'll visit. Nothing on God's earth could keep me away."

"No, no! You misunderstand. I mean as a permanent arrangement. My offer has much to recommend it. Forgive me, but I don't think your own situation is a happy one."

"You mean in my father's house? He's not the easiest man in the world to live with, I'll give you that."

"Well then, what could be more natural than for you to accompany Madeleina to her new home when she marries? You would be company for the girl, and, if I may say so, a salutary influence on my own growing daughters."

Miss Spencer went pink with pleasure. "You're too kind, Your Grace. I never thought . . . it never occurred to me. Thank you. I shall certainly consider your invitation."

When the Duke of Raeburn composed himself for sleep later that night, he set himself to dream of the young woman who was destined to be his bride. It was no fault of his that Maddie's indistinct image faded altogether to be replaced by the picture of a more mature lady of handsome demeanour and intelligent grey eyes. His last thought before sleep claimed him was not felicitous. Duty, he deplored, was a hard task master.

Maddie fared little better, for no amount of willpower could keep Deveryn from her dreams. She awoke feeling little refreshed for her night's slumber, and could not throw off the weight of dread which seemed to hang on her neck like a millstone.

She was in the breakfast room when she heard her grandfather's roar of displeasure. The cup and saucer in her hand rattled so hard, she was compelled to set them on the table.

"What was that?" she asked of her aunt in a tremulous whisper. "It sounds like an animal in pain."

"Papa in one of his rages," Miss Spencer replied, and placidly went on buttering her dry toast. "I saw his solicitor, Mr. Gregson, enter his study as I came downstairs. I wouldn't be in his shoes for the world."

A moment later, the same imperious voice bellowed just outside the breakfast room door, and Maddie jumped.

"Maddie? Where are you? Get in here at once, d'you hear?"

"Oh dear!" said Miss Spencer. "I wonder what has occurred to put him in such a taking."

She spoke to air. Maddie's slender form was already gliding through the open door in answer to the summons.

In the study, she found her grandfather, lean and impatient, stalking up and down like one of the caged lions she had once seen in the menagerie at the Tower of London. His quarry, whom Maddie took to be the poor solicitor, was cornered in the lone armchair in the room. She'd heard once that the only way to deal with a ravening beast of prey was to face it down. She discovered that she was not so sanguine.

"You w-wanted me, G-Grandpapa?" she stammered.

His tawny eyes, several shades lighter than her own, pinned her to the wall.

"What's this I hear from Scotland?" he bellowed.

Her knees buckled. Speech deserted her. She could not think how he'd come by the particulars of her pseudomarriage unless Deveryn had divulged their secret. She waited for the axe to fall, the keg of gunpowder to ignite: domesday, armageddon.

"Don't look like that child. I shan't eat you."

She found herself sitting on a straight-backed chair and could not think how she had got there.

As if from a long way off, she heard her grandfather demand, "Why didn't you tell me that I was not named as your guardian in your father's will?"

Evidently, she made some suitable reply, for the next few minutes were taken up with a discussion between the two men on the inconvenience this intelligence occasioned.

Gradually, it was borne in on Maddie that her grandfather was in ignorance of her more pressing dilemma. The wash of relief enabled her to pay attention to what was being said.

"Your father and I had everything settled between us before he removed to Drumoak, or so I thought. I warned him to put his affairs in order before he left town. Gregson drew up the necessary papers. I've since learned that your father never signed them. Did he mention anything to you?"

"About what?"

"Your future."

A vague recollection came to mind, but the edges were blurred and would not sharpen. "Now that you mention it, Papa did intimate that I might be coming here for a visit."

"You were to make your home with me permanently or until such time as you were to marry."

It made sense. Her father had lost Drumoak. Where else was she to go? It must have galled him to come to his father-in-law to beg for favours.

"I don't think my guardian will trouble himself over much about my welfare. I should think Uncle Thomas will be delighted to learn that you've taken me under your roof."

"It's your marriage I was thinking of," said Mr. Spencer crisply. "Nothing can be done without your guardian's consent."

"That scarcely signifies since I'm not thinking of getting married," said Maddie carefully.

"You're betrothed to the Duke of Raeburn," was the short answer.

"Who?" It didn't sound like "Deveryn."

"Raeburn. The man who escorted you to London. You're not averse to him, are you?"

201

"No, but . . ."

"Then it's settled."

Aghast, her thoughts chaotic, Maddie could not find the words to voice her objection. A pit seemed to yawn at her feet. Raeburn. Deveryn. Checkmate!

"I've told you, Scotland won't answer," she heard her grandfather say to the little man who had voiced a timid suggestion. "A peer of the realm must be certain that his progeny are legitimate. Look at Paget. He married his countess in Scotland, but as soon as he could find a cleric in England who wasn't averse to marrying a divorced man, he married her again."

Maddie's ears pricked. "What's wrong with marriages performed in Scotland?" she asked.

"For the Scots, nothing at all. But these quick marriages are scarcely worth the paper they are written on if the parties are domiciled in England."

"Mr. Spencer, I beg to differ," interjected the solicitor. "In a court of law . . ."

"Who is talking about a court of law?" roared Spencer. "We're talking of the ton. We're talking of St. George's in Hanover Square. We're talking of the Prince Regent. D'you think I'd permit my granddaughter to follow in her mother's footsteps? There's nothing for it. The marriage will be delayed until this . . . guardian . . ." he said the word as if he had just swallowed some foul tasting medicine, "this . . . guardian . . . can be found and his consent obtained. See to it for me, Gregson. And don't come back with any more half-cocked ideas like the one you just offered."

Maddie knew that she must be in shock. The craving for one of Janet's hot toddies was overwhelming. She wondered what the penalty for bigamy was, and resolved that she would never find out.

"How did you come to meet my father?" she asked for something to say.

"What? Oh, we met at his club."

For some reason, she had the feeling that her grandfather was hedging. She tried again.

"I'm surprised. I understood that your aversion to my father was fixed. What can have transpired to make you

202

change your mind? You never cared before to know anything of me or my mother. Why is it that having ignored our existence without a qualm for all these years, you suddenly turned charitable?" She had meant to speak calmly, without heat, but was aware that her words came out clipped and edged with acid.

His black brows came slanting together. "You are mistaken. It was your father who kept the estrangement going long after I relented."

"But I always thought . . ."

"What?"

"That it was of your making."

"Who told you that? Your father? Well perhaps it was, at the beginning. But after your mother died, I came to my senses. Unfortunately, your father's pride was greater than my own. He was wonderfully revenged for my former coldness. He kept my granddaughter from me."

He could not know how his words had shocked her. It was not that her father had lied to her. Over the years, her grandfather's name had been scarcely mentioned. She had not even known of her aunt's existence until she had met her by chance at some musical evening or other when she'd been so unhappily first introduced to society. No, her father had told her no lies. But she felt in some sort as if she had been deceived.

She brought her thoughts to the problem in hand and said as mildly as she could contrive, "Grandfather, I don't think I care to marry Raeburn, with or without my guardian's consent."

The eyes he turned on her were hard, though his words remained gentle. "You know nothing of such things, child. Trust me. Everyone's best interests will be served by this marriage."

She'd heard those words, or words like them, before. Deveryn had said them to her. "Everyone's best interests will be served by what I propose," he'd said.

She let her eyes rest on her grandfather's straight figure. By her reckoning, he was close to seventy years old, yet he gave the impression of being younger, though his hair was silver. She thought that perhaps as a young man, his colouring had been similar to her own. She could sense his restless energy.

Already he had lost interest in her. He had spoken. There could be no further argument. The message was conveyed in the set of his features and his slashed brows. Altogether, she thought him an unapproachable, cold man.

There seemed no urgency in standing up for her rights. She did not know how long it would take to get a reply from Canada, but she thought it must be at least three months. She determined that she would send her own letter across the Atlantic begging her Uncle Thomas to withold his consent to a marriage she could not, under any circumstances, enter upon.

In the hour before her tutor was due to arrive, she kept to her room and lost herself in *Media*. The unhappy plight of Euripides's tragic heroine was not comforting. Medea's husband, another Jason, had also said, "Everyone's best interests will be served by what I propose," or words to that effect. And then he had proceeded to make Medea absolutely miserable. That women were regarded as little more than chattels by men was very evident. The significant men in her own life—her father, her grandfather, Deveryn—were perfect examples of this deplorable masculine attitude.

Perversely, she wondered at Deveryn's complacent acceptance of her flight from Drumoak. There'd been plenty of time for him to reach London and seek her out. But he hadn't. She was sure she was glad. Deveryn's offences were not forgotten. He had wronged her father. He had browbeaten her into marriage and then promptly given her birthright to another woman! Unforgiveable!

Henceforth, she decided, no man would mistreat her with impunity. She had meant what she had said to Deveryn. She was perfectly capable of making her own way in the world. If she was pushed to the limits of her endurance, she would prove it. More! She would push back.

Chapter Thirteen

The Viscount Deveryn winced imperceptibly as he descended the steps from his rooms on Jermyn Street. He turned hard right and set off in the direction of his club in St. James, a mere stone's throw from his lodgings. Sheer force of will kept his back straight and an indolent half-smile fixed on his lips. Despite two bruised ribs, and against doctor's orders, he had dragged himself from his sick bed to perform what he considered to be a distasteful though necessary duty. It was his design to face down the cajolery of his peers and squelch the report he half-expected would be circulating, that he had taken Cynthia Sinclair to be his mistress.

The irony of his situation was not lost upon him. Little more than a month before, he had been at some pains even then to conceal the identity of his former mistress. His object, as he remembered, was to spare his mother's feelings. And he had succeeded. How much more imperative did it appear to him now to conceal from Maddie the knowledge that Cynthia Sinclair and he, Deveryn, had been discovered in a compromising position in his bed-chamber at the Falcon in Grantham. And irony of ironies, on this occasion he was innocent of wrongdoing!

He was also furious with Maddie. In some sort, he blamed her for his present predicament, for if she had been present on that long tedious drive from Edinburgh to London, it would have been she in his bed, and this farce need never have run its course! And most iniquitous of all, she had deprived him, the husband who loved her, of his conjugal rights. The long nights of passion which he had anticipated with such pleasure had been rudely snatched from him. He supposed that his disclosure that Cynthia was to be his pensioner had been the prod for Maddie's impetuous flight. Who could say with Maddie? Her thought processes were an enigma to him. Intimidation and brute strength seemed the only means of compelling her attention. When he finally caught up with her, he intended to blister her backside till she could not sit down for a week.

The thought sobered him. When he caught up with Maddie, there would be the devil to pay, no matter which report of Grantham got back to her. Better by far, he grimly decided, that she believe the woman who had been discovered in his chamber was anyone, *anyone* other than Cynthia Sinclair.

He slowly manoeuvered himself across St. James Street and with as light a step as he could contrive, ascended the stairs to the entrance of White's. His eyes flicked to the bow window on his left. Brummel and Alvaney were already ensconced at their familiar posts, lazily surveying the passers-by and the patrons who entered the hallowed portals of White's and the less exalted, adjacent Boodles and Brooks, the Whig stronghold across the street.

In the lobby, he encountered Raggett, the proprietor. Rumour had it that the old man swept the carpets himself in the mornings to retrieve the gold which the patrons had carelessly scattered on the floor during the long night of play. And while they crept away to the house of 'Jew' King in Clarges Street to mortgage their estates, or to 'Hamlet,' the jeweller in Cranbourn Alley to pledge the family silver, he laughed all the way to Ransom, Morland and Co., the bank on Pall Mall. Deveryn completely discounted this scurrilous piece of spite. If Raggett was well-breeched, and it was safe to assume that he was, any fool could deduce the reason why. His pockets were lined from the astronomical fees which White's wealthy patrons paid over annually without demur, and from the atrocious prices for the most indifferent dinners he had ever had the misfortune to sample. The monotonous fare of roast beef, boiled fowl with oyster sauce, and apple tart to follow seemed to suit the older more staid clientele. His set preferred to dine at Wattiers on Piccadilly where the Prince Regent's former French chef, Labourie, knew how to tempt the most fastidious palate.

In the downstairs lounge, he allowed himself a carefully bored perusal of the select company. Argyle was there with Worcester, those intimates of the Beau, and Sefton, already broaching his second bottle of claret, by the look of him. Deveryn heard a burst of laughter from the darker depths of the interior. As if on signal, he began to pick his way through a motley crew of peers of the realm. Though it was only the middle of the afternoon, half of them looked to have already started on what gave every evidence of becoming a long night of dissipation. His progress was slow, for having been out of town for more than a month he was greeted by many acquaintances and was compelled to exchange a few pleasantries before he finally reached the group by the table along the far side of the room.

"Speak of the devil!" exclaimed Toby Blanchard in feigned horror and speedily vacated his seat to make room for the new arrival.

"How are the ribs?" asked Perry Montford, of an age with Deveryn, but as dark as he was fair.

At the sly gibe, laughter, at Deveryn's expense, became general. He eased himself into the straight-backed chair which Toby held for him with exaggerated solicitude.

"Mending nicely, thank you," he managed with a grimace and snapped his finger to attract the attention of a passing waiter.

"Fell off your horse, did you?" Freddie Ponsonby's question was rhetorical. Everyone present knew that Deveryn had sustained his injuries at the notorious Falcon in Grantham defending a lady's honour from a party of drunken bucks who had tried to force their way into the viscount's chamber.

"What are you doing here, Freddie?" Deveryn asked affably. "This is Tory territory. I thought Brooks was your natural hunting ground."

"I'm apolitical, old man," was the airy rejoinder. "I leave politics to the rest of the Ponsonby clan. I'm here as Max's guest."

Deveryn's eyes met those of his brother-in-law, the Hon. Max Branwell. A flicker of something passed between the two men.

Since he'd been laid up in bed for the last fortnight, Deveryn had been forced to take his brother-in-law somewhat into his confidence. Max Branwell, he mused, was a good sort. He'd confirmed yesterday that Dolly Ramides was more than willing to perform this small service for him. Though no money had changed hands, the tacit understanding was that he'd be generous for any inconvenience the lady might be put to on his behalf.

Max had laughed at that. "Good God, Jason, I think the lady cares more for the cachet of having her name linked with yours than she does about the monetary reward. When she heard that your motive was to protect the name of another lady, her disappointment was patent." Max gave his brother-in-law a sideways look. "I don't suppose you'll take me fully into your confidence?"

Deveryn would much rather not. He thought that he cut a ridiculous enough figure as it was without having to divulge that his bride of twenty-four hours had run away from him and shortly thereafter, he had been caught *in flagrante delicto* with her stepmother when he was as innocent as a newborn babe.

He remembered that he'd also been as naked as a new born babe and he shuddered.

A waiter appeared at his elbow.

"Champagne," he told him, "and lots of it."

His words were greeted with wild enthusiasm. When the noise had abated somewhat, Montford asked, "What are we celebrating?"

"The mounting of a new mistress," responded one young buck brazenly. Deveryn silenced him with a withering look from below slashed brows.

"What we are celebrating," he announced gravely, "is the dawn of a new era." He raised his glass. "Gentlemen, I give you 'the estate of matrimony.'" His strategy was well thought out. He meant to sow the seed in their minds that marriage was a distinct possibility in his immediate future.

Blank silence greeted his words. Only one gentleman was seen to follow the viscount's example. Max Branwell drank with gusto.

"The toast is not to your liking?" asked Deveryn blandly,

taking in the startled expressions of his companions. He winked at his brother-in-law.

"I say old chap, you can't expect us bachelors to drink to anything so, well, downright decadent. Might as well ask us to drink to Napoleon's victories in Europe."

"Freddie," responded Deveryn reasonably, "Napoleon is old history."

"And so is the estate of matrimony."

A murmur of assent greeted this bald statement.

A thought occurred to Toby Blanchard. "I say, Jason. You're not thinking of getting leg shackled, by any chance, are you?"

"And if I am?" Deveryn held his glass up to the light and idly watched the bubbles of champagne float to the surface.

"What? After Grantham?"

"What about Grantham?"

There was no menace in the viscount's expression so that Freddie Ponsonby had no qualms in advising, "If I were you, I should wait awhile before offering for some eligible. When word gets out, it is bound to spoil your chances with fond mamas who are protective of their chicks."

"You might try for an orphan," interposed Max Branwell, studiously avoiding Deveryn's hard stare.

A protracted silence fell, each man lost in his own private reflections. It was assumed that Deveryn was bowing to parental pressure to beget heirs. It would happen to all of them sooner or later. Their days were numbered and they knew it. It cast a gloom on what had started out as a very jolly affair.

"Rotten luck, Deveryn," commiserated Montford gloomily, "to be caught with your trousers down just when you meant to do the honourable."

Max Branwell was seen to choke on a mouthful of champagne. He looked sheepishly over the rim of his glass at his stern-faced brother-in-law.

"Can't understand how you could be so negligent," speculated Blanchard. "T'ain't like you, Jason. I would have thought you would have known better than arrange a tryst in such a den of iniquity, and on such a night."

"So you might," agreed Deveryn smoothly. "Then of course, the lady in question was not there by invitation. You

209

need not look so surprised. Give me credit for some finesse. There was a mill in progress. What gentleman would arrange an assignation in such a place in those circumstances? Would you? Would I?" And he wished belatedly that he had obeyed his first, sure instinct to avoid Grantham like the plague and push on to a less notorious resting place. Only the knowledge that the inns and coaching houses for miles around would be choked to the garrets had persuaded him to take the last two rooms in the infamous Falcon, to his eternal regret.

He could almost hear the wheels turning as his companions considered his words. It was Montford who finally challenged him.

"What sort of lady would brave the rowdies of Grantham just for the pleasure of your person?"

"An impetuous one," responded Deveryn.

"Cynthia Sinclair never struck me in that light," mused Blanchard. "I thought her rather cautious in a calculating sort of way, if you know what I mean."

It was Deveryn's turn to look surprised. "Cynthia Sinclair? How did her name get into this conversation?"

Freddie Ponsonby eyed his friend with faint suspicion. "The woman in your bedchamber. My cousin twice removed, Jack Ponsonby, silly young blighter, was one of the rowdies who burst into your room. He thought he recognized her."

It was what Deveryn had been afraid of.

"I'll wager there are more Ponsonbys in England than there are Smiths," remarked Max Branwell idly.

"Yes, the Ponsonbys are prolific, I'll give you that, in or out of matrimony," Freddie admitted freely.

Deveryn ruthlessly brought the conversation round to the subject of Cynthia Sinclair. With studied indifference, he observed, "Your cousin was mistaken. Mrs. Sinclair, as far as I am aware, was nowhere near Grantham on the evening in question."

"What are you up to, Jason?"

"I?" Surprise etched his voice. "Nothing at all."

"Are you saying that it wasn't Cynthia Sinclair with you that night?"

"Dear me," he responded languidly, "I must not have the command of the King's English I once thought I had. In a word, no!"

"But my cousin saw her," protested Freddie.

"What did he see?"

Freddie could not help the leer that spread slowly across his face. "A lot of bare skin, I'll give you that. The lady was as naked as the day she was born."

Deveryn visibly winced.

"Ribs troubling you, old boy?" his innocent-faced brother-in-law inquired with malicious enjoyment.

Deveryn returned a thin smile. As Max Branwell knew perfectly well, it was the recollection of Cynthia Sinclair's attempted seduction which had brought on an involuntary shudder. He did not think he would ever forget the chagrin of that night. It had begun when Cynthia had pushed boldly into his chamber and had begun to disrobe in spite of his protests. His amused tolerance had soon turned to an arctic coldness when he perceived the lady's heedless determination. He could not have felt more embarrassed if Maddie had been in the next room. And when the door had burst open, and he had leapt out of bed . . . The damning picture they must have presented was too disturbing to contemplate.

"She was a brunette; that much even Jack's friends vouchsafe," said Freddie thoughtfully.

"That point, I am willing to concede."

"But Freddie," demanded Montford earnestly, "did he get a good look at her face?"

Freddie's lip curled. "Would you, man, in similar circumstances?"

"Quite." Deveryn raised his index finger and gestured to the footman to refill the glasses. Before he could avail himself of the refreshment, a silver salver was presented. He accepted a note of highly scented paper, quickly scanned the contents and slipped it wordlessly into his coat pocket. Within minutes, he had taken a polite leave of his friends and was strolling indolently out the front door.

His companions, all except Mr. Branwell, crowded the bow window, much to the disgust of Mr. Brummel and Lord Alvaney.

"Good God!" said Montford. "Will you look at that? A lady in an open carriage on St. James Street in the middle of the afternoon. What's the world coming to?"

They watched in stunned silence as Deveryn hoisted himself into the phaeton. He took the ribbons from the lady's hands, said something to the tiger who held the horses' heads, and took off toward Piccadilly.

"That was no lady," observed Toby Blanchard speculatively. "That was Dolly Ramides, the opera dancer."

"Good God. And she's a brunette."

"And impetuous, as Deveryn said. No other lady would dare show her face in St. James Street later than noon!"

Slowly, the gentlemen retired to their places at the far wall, ignoring the sour looks and grunts of complaint from the more staid members of the establishment.

"D'you think he was serious about getting shackled?" asked Montford.

"Of course. He wouldn't joke about a horrid thing like that."

"Wonder who the lucky girl will be?"

One suggestion led to another. By the time Mr. Max Branwell strolled away, the betting book was open and hefty wagers were being placed on the most likely eligible to lead the elusive viscount to the altar. The name of Maddie Sinclair never came up.

Just as Branwell accepted his hat and cane from a liveried footman, the tranquil halls were split by a sudden excited exclamation which tore from the lips of Lord Blanchard.

"Good grief! Dolly Ramides! It's Dolly Ramides! I've won the book! Raggett! Raggett! Where are you? I'm collecting on the old bet I made before Christmas. Dolly Ramides has captured Deveryn!"

By nightfall, it was all over town that the Fallen Angel's new ladybird was none other than Dolly Ramides and that she was the mysterious lady whose honour the viscount had defended with his bare fists.

Only Jack Ponsonby, nursing a broken jaw at his uncle's estate in Surrey, refuted popular opinion. His protestations went unheeded. Everyone knew that the young whelp went delirious when under the influence of strong spirits. Not that his family objected to the quantity of brandy the boy could put away of an evening. It was the ungentlemanly habit of not

212

being able to hold his liquor which invoked their severest censure.

Notwithstanding young Ponsonby, Deveryn took comfort in the knowledge that his strategy had proved effective. But as a victory, it left much to be desired, in that gentleman's opinion. To claim Maddie as his bride at this point in time was unthinkable. The scandal would be impossible to live down. He thought that in a month things would have quietened down and they might pretend to wed with scarcely an eyebrow being raised. In the meantime, he found his position intolerable. Circumstances compelled him to court his own wife as if he were a suitor aspiring to her hand. He hoped that he could get to her before the shocking report of his imaginary liaison with Dolly Ramides reached her ears.

Deveryn's hope, as he suspected, was a forlorn one. It took less than twenty-four hours for the report to reach Maddie's ears. The first obscure reference which was made in her hearing was over tea in the drawing room of her grandfather's house on Curzon Street. Lady Bessborough, escorted by her son, Freddie, was paying a morning call when Lady Mary Branwell entered.

Maddie liked the older girl, though she found it hard to account for her partiality. They had been introduced at Lady Bessborough's musical evening and had spent a pleasant hour in each other's company at the supper table. Lady Mary, whose breadth of experience and circle of acquaintances far surpassed Maddie's, had recognized what the younger girl was at a loss to explain. They were birds of a feather.

She had been struck by Maddie's lack of affectation. Her eyes did not stray to the young bucks when she was in conversation with a lady. Long silences did not discompose her. Neither flattery nor spite had once fallen from her lips. True, the girl had had little to say for herself but, after Max had joined them, her dark eyes had lit up with intelligence and amusement at his clever though rather oblique witticisms. She had boldly come back at him with a devastating rejoinder. That had shocked him. He was used to thinking that only the Verney girls had the wit to appreciate his brand of humour. It had evidently shocked Miss Sinclair as well. After that one sally, she had turned shy. But Lady Mary's interest was piqued.

213

Moreover, her husband had suggested that it would be a kindness to cultivate the acquaintance of the girl since she knew so few people in town.

Lady Mary's glance strayed to Lady Bessborough and her eyes lit up with pleasure. That lady was known to possess one of the most brilliant minds of her generation. Her education was superior and though her morals were questionable, her disposition was sweet and gentle. At one time she and Lady Mary's mother had thought to open a school for girls and give young ladies the benefit of an education grounded in the classics. That venture had been squashed by their respective families. They had vowed, then, to ensure that their own daughters were not deprived of their due. Lady Mary was very glad that her mother had kept her promise.

"Aunt Harriet," she exclaimed and planted a kiss on the cheek Lady Bessborough turned up to her.

Maddie observed the older girl's every movement with keen interest. Her manners were enviable. Her poise, something to emulate. She was glad when Lady Mary elected to take the empty chair beside her own. Though she had thought Freddie Ponsonby an amiable young man, his flowery compliments had begun to grate on her nerves. She cast around in her mind for some suitable topic of conversation that she might introduce. She need not have put herself to the trouble. Freddie took up the slack in the conversation.

He asked gravely after Lady Mary's brother.

Lady Mary replied with a twinkle that he had returned from a mill at Grantham which had necessitated a week long stint in bed under doctor's orders.

Maddie recognized that Lady Mary and Freddie were teasing each other playfully. She listened with half an ear to the snatches of quiet conversation which reached her from the two ladies who were tête-à-tête on the yellow brocade sofa by the long windows. She heard Lady Bessborough mention the word "Deveryn" and Maddie's attention became rivetted. Lady Bessborough imparted some confidence to Miss Spencer. A woman's name was mentioned, "Dolly Ramides," she thought. Restrained laughter followed. Only one phrase carried clearly before their voices dropped to little more than a whisper— "sowing his wild oats."

214

Not unnaturally, Maddie was beside herself with curiosity, but had no means of satisfying it. She forced a smile to her lips when Freddie Ponsonby addressed some passing remark to her about Lady Mary's delinquent brother, but really, she had no interest in the antics of what she presumed to be a young hellion bent on mischief who was in a fair way to turning his mother's hair a premature grey, or so his sister implied. She wished Freddie and Lady Mary at hades, and most of all the young rakehell who was the brother, and wished that she might quiz her aunt on the more interesting topic of Deveryn.

It was not to be. The visitors departed, Maddie engaging herself to Lady Mary for the following afternoon. Before she could corner her aunt, however, her tutor arrived. Maddie watched regretfully as Miss Spencer ascended the stairs, and she turned reluctantly to follow Mr. Clarke into the small yellow saloon on the ground floor. For once, she had a question for him.

"How is it," she asked, "That Lady Mary Branwell's husband is plain 'Mr. Max Branwell?'"

Mr. Clarke, an unprepossessing gentleman of indeterminate years whom Maddie lumped with "the elderly" was gratified to have at last piqued his pupil's interest. He'd thought her a very dull sort of girl who was incapable of learning.

"I'm not acquainted with the lady in question," he intoned in that drawl which Maddie could never quite emulate, "but Lady Mary must be the daughter of a duke, a marquess, or an earl. Evidently, she has married a commoner. You must always address her as 'Lady Mary' and remember that she takes precedence over her husband at all times."

When he saw Maddie's blank look, he sighed and went on slowly and deliberately, "Think of Lady Caroline Lamb. She is the daughter of an earl. Her husband is plain 'Mr. William Lamb.'"

"She's not 'Lady Lamb,' then?"

"No. To address her as such would be to reveal the depths of your ignorance."

Maddie digested this nonsense in stony silence. After a moment, she observed, "I don't wonder that the Americans have chosen to be republicans."

Mr. Clarke laughed. "You won't think so if you marry into

the aristocracy."

Maddie hadn't the heart to argue the point with him.

When Mr. Clarke took his leave, she ate a solitary lunch in the breakfast room then went in search of her aunt. But she was foiled again, for Miss Spencer had taken it into her head to wait on Lady Bessborough that very afternoon, a singular compliment but not unheard of. Maddie suspected that the two ladies wished to discuss the viscount in more private surroundings. It irked her excessively to have to cool her heels when she itched to know what was going on. At a loose end for once, she wandered to the stable block at the back of the house. She felt vaguely guilty for having her days so ordered that she'd had very little time to discover how Duncan was settling in. She hoped the other stable hands were not giving him a hard time. With his thick Scottish brogue and slow, deliberate way of thinking, she thought that they might very easily make him the butt of their sport. If that were so, and her eyes flashed dangerously, they would very soon find themselves dealing with a virago who could equal any of the mythical heroines of antiquity.

Her grandfather kept an immaculate stable and coach house—clean, fresh, and smelling of well-oiled leather, axle grease, and turpentine. The head groom, Mr. Lloyd, directed her to the harness room where Duncan was at work. They acknowledged each other's presence without a word being spoken. Maddie found a stool. She carried it to the warmth of the boiler and settled herself to observe.

Duncan broke a large mass of yellow wax into a black iron pot and set it at the side of the open range to melt. Maddie knew every operation of the task he was engaged in. At Drumoak, she had frequently helped prepare the paste that was so necessary to preserve the leather harness and tack. She waited till he had added the mixture of water and litharge before she spoke.

"How are they treating you?"

A big smile lit up his ruddy face. "A'm no much o' a stablehand, that's for sure."

She nodded in commiseration. "Rotten! Now why doesn't that surprise me? These English think they are . . ."

"Och no, Miss Maddie," he interrupted. "Dinna *fash* yersel'. I've no quarrel with the way I've been accepted, in

216

spite o' my being handless around horses."

"Well, of course," she averred as if she were defending her cub from attack, "you've never had the practice. Drumoak's stable only ever had a couple of horses in its stalls, except for the odd occasion."

Duncan left the range and went to the workbench where he proceeded to set out the stone crocks which were to receive the paste he was preparing. Without conscious thought, Maddie took his place at the range and became involved in stirring the slow bubbling mixture. She removed it to the far edge of the range, away from the heat.

"This stuff is ready. Where's the ivory black?"

He handed her a large tin of black powder from which she spooned several heaped ladles. Expertly, she added them gradually to the pot, beating furiously until she was satisfied with the consistency of the mixture.

"This looks about right." She dragged the heavy pot back to the hot iron plate and stirred furiously till the bubbles told her the mixture was once again on the boil. Duncan, seeing that his mistress had displaced him, resigned himself to being a spectator. He sank onto the stool which Maddie had vacated and watched with mingled respect and admiration. There wasn't a thing the girl didn't know about the management of a stable. Still, he had one little surprise for her which he could scarcely contain for impatience.

"Done," she said finally, and removed the pot from the heat. "We'll give it a few minutes before we add the turpentine."

She turned to look at him. In his extended hand was a dirty, chipped tin mug which she automatically accepted. "What's this?" she asked, and sniffed suspiciously.

"Beer!" he replied with a touch of smugness.

"I don't drink beer!"

"It's no for ye. It's for the harness paste."

His eyebrows lifted a fraction. "Beer? In the harness paste? What an extravagance!"

He couldn't suppress a chuckle. "Och, I've learned a thing or two from these *sassenachs*, Miss Maddie. Each groom has his own secret ingredient to make his harness polish that wee bit different, a'll no say better. A'm told that Mr. Brummel's groom adds a good doze o' champagne."

217

"Go on, you're pulling my leg."

"Och, no! It makes the fine gentlemen feel superior. Here, I'll do that now."

They changed places.

"I wonder," said Maddie with a knowing look in her eye, "I wonder how much beer and champagne finds its way down the gullets of the coachmen and grooms?"

"Aye, there is that. I was hopin' that at Drumoak we might start addin' a wee dram o' Glenlivet." He flashed her a bold smile.

"Bite your tongue, Duncan," she told him with mock severity, "I'm half-persuaded already to make our special ingredient cod-liver oil. How does that tickle your fancy?"

He laughed and shook his head. He donned stout leather gloves for the next part of the operation.

"Keep well back!" he told Maddie. She had no need of the warning. The melted wax mixture could give the worst burn of any. Well out of reach, she watched Duncan carry the heavy pot to the bench and fill the stone jars to the brim. No words were exchanged until the task was completed.

Finally, she asked, "How long will that last?"

"A month or so."

In Drumoak it would do them for a year. Her thoughts strayed to Janet and Banshee and Kelpie, all abandoned in her haste to escape Deveryn. Inevitably, a wave of nostalgia brought the familiar ache, filling her senses with the taste, feel, and sights of home and all the things she loved best in the world.

She could almost hear the roar of the breakers as they surged against the shore, and feel the spray on her face as she rode hell for leather across the sand dunes. Since her arrival in London, she'd been out riding only once. The sedate pace which was permitted to ladies along Rotten Row in Hyde Park was more torture than pleasure to one who had roamed the Forth shoreline and hills of Lothian at will. If there were compensations to living in the lap of luxury, she had yet to discover them. In her own mind she was convinced that nothing could compensate for the loss of Drumoak or the freedom she had enjoyed before Deveryn came into her life. She could never forget that it was by his design that her safe and ordered life had become lost to her.

Her throat seemed to tighten and she could feel the burn of tears at the back of her eyes. Better leave, she thought, before turning into a watering pot. She waited only till she could gain command of her voice.

Before she could do so, the door to the harness room opened, and a young stable boy, a bright-eyed lad of about fifteen summers, came in at a trot. He spotted Duncan, but missed the small, erect figure stationed in the shadows.

"Mr. Ross, Mr. Ross!" he exclaimed excitedly. "The mill's on fer ternight. They've found a real bruiser ter stand up wif yer. Mr. Lloyd told me ter tell yer. Same time, same place."

The boy suddenly noticed that the face of the man to whom he was speaking had gone beet red. He broke off and his gaze followed Duncan's to take in the bristling form of a young lady who stood a little way off behind the open door.

Willie groaned. He knew better than mention the coarse masculine sports in a lady's hearing. Ladies, he knew from sad experience, regarded it as their God-given duty to turn men into milksops. Look at his da.

"Cor! I'll come back later!" he averred, and spun himself about.

A cool, imperious voice nailed him to the floor. "Just a moment, boy! A word with you, if you please."

Willie didn't please, but didn't dare say so. Reluctantly, he turned back to face the pretty young lady whose face seemed to be carved out of granite. He remarked, with some relief, that her glacial stare was trained, not on himself, but on poor Mr. Ross. That giant seemed to have shrivelled by several inches and shrunk by a couple of stone. Women! Da was right. One look from an irate woman, and a man could feel as if he'd been caught with his breeches down. The glacial expression was turned on him, and his hands went automatically to the waistband of his trousers.

"What bruiser? What mill? Where and when?"

Her voice, he thought, could make hell itself freeze over. He was not brave enough to dissemble. Haltingly, he stammered out everything he knew. He couldn't bring himself to look at Mr. Ross.

"Thank you. You may go. And close the door behind you."

He made his escape with unabashed alacrity.

Maddie began a furious pacing. She rounded on Duncan. "What are you thinking of, Duncan? Didn't you learn your lesson, last time, at Balmedie?"

The red tide of colour had faded from Duncan's cheeks to be replaced by a vacuous grin that hovered somewhere between an apology and anguish.

"Och, Miss Maddie, we're no talkin' prize fights. That was when I was a professional. This is strictly amateur."

She stopped in her hectic perambulations. "It is? What's the difference?"

"We're no out tae kill each other. The mill only goes for ten rounds."

"Is that good?"

He pressed the advantage he sensed. "Only ten rounds? I've never fought in anything less than twenty-five in a professional fight. A man can take a hellova poundin' when he's forced tae fight till one or t'other is lying flat on his back."

"A lot can happen in ten rounds. You know what the doctor said. You ought never to fight again." Her voice gentled to a cozening, coaxing lilt. "Have you forgotten how it was last time? Oh I'm not talking about your broken ribs and your other injuries," she said with a swift return of impatience when he tried to break in. "I'm talking about your loss of memory, and oh, that daft look you had in your eyes for the longest time. You're only now coming back to yourself." She gave him her most melting expression. "Duncan, I couldn't bear it if anything happened to you, and Janet would never forgive me."

"Now, now lass," he soothed, "I swear ye're makin' a mountain out o' a molehill. I'm only sparrin' wi' other coachmen, and they couldna fight their way oot o' a lady's bandbox."

"Yes, that's how it begins," she said, turning away wearily, "but one thing leads to another. What I can't understand is how you got started again."

Duncan saw his chance of distracting Miss Maddie's thoughts from their unhappy direction.

"Me and some of m' mates went out to Grantham to watch the mill between Gully and the Chicken. Och that wer somethin' to gladden sore eyes."

"And?" prompted Maddie when she observed the dreamy expression softening her lackey's rocky features.

"Och, well, we were havin' a quiet pint in the taproom at the Falcon after it was all over, when, through no fault of m' own, mind ye, I got involved in a wee bit o' a scuffle."

That intelligence did not surprise Maddie. It was common knowledge that the big mills that took place in and around London often ended in punch drunk orgies of violence.

"I'm all ears. Pray continue."

"Ye'll be rememberin' Lord Deveryn?" He missed the sudden change in her expression. "He got in a wee spot o' trouble, and I took it upon myself to help him *oot* o' it. Now there's a gentleman who *kens* how tae employ his dukes! Aye, he owns the finest pair o' fives I've seen *oot* o' the professional circuit, and that's sayin' something!"

"Lord Deveryn resorted to fisticuffs?" Her tone was patently credulous.

"Och, he didna start it," Duncan hastily explained. "It were a group o' rowdies, drunk as lords but fine young gentlemen every one o' them, who *kent* the crest on his carriage. There was a rumour that he had a woman in his chamber. They were just oot for a bit o' lark." He laughed at some private reflection. "They got more than they bargained for."

"Wh-what happened?"

"Me and m' mates followed them up the stairs. They burst into his lordship's chamber. A moment later they came flyin' oot, and he as naked as the day he was born and roarin' like a lion. Well, it was five agin one. M' mates and me didna like *thae* odds. We had *tae* help him."

"And . . . and was there a woman with him?"

"So they say. I couldna really tell ye."

Maddie knew better. She stewed in silence for some few minutes. She remembered the Falcon. They had given that particular coaching house a wide berth on the last lap of their journey to London. "Too unsavoury," Raeburn had called it. Just the kind of place a man of Deveryn's stamp would seek out to "sow his wild oats," she thought, recalling Lady Bessborough's words of only hours before. She wondered whose field he had been ploughing, and remembered the name

221

'Dolly Ramides.'

"And was he suitably grateful?" she demanded. No doubt he had tried to bribe poor Duncan to silence. But there was no guile in Duncan as Deveryn would learn to his regret.

At the unexpected return of ice in Miss Maddie's tone and demeanour, Duncan blinked rapidly. "Grateful?" he parrotted.

"You did save his miserable skin, didn't you?"

Duncan blinked again. He felt as if he had somehow missed something in the conversation. "His lordship didna see me," he said slowly. "It were dark on the stairs. And I carried two o' them off by their coat-tails."

He didn't care for the angry way Miss Maddie folded her lips together. He sensed a storm coming.

"Next time," she stormed at him, "next time you jump into the fray, kindly remember that Lord Deveryn is the enemy! Have you got that, you dunderhead? Lord Deveryn is the enemy!"

She looked at him in shocked silence. Her hand flew to her mouth. Finally, she said in a low, contrite tone, "Oh Duncan, that was unforgivable! I should not have called you 'dunderhead.' Can you ever forgive me?"

He nodded mutely. Everybody, at least everybody at Drumoak, knew about Miss Maddie's temper. It flashed to a white-hot heat then evaporated into thin air like the brandy which flamed the Christmas pudding. There were compensations. For days afterwards, she would be as sweet as honey.

"We'll talk about this later," she said, visibly striving for control. "I'm not myself. Just try to stay out of trouble. All right?"

Again he nodded.

"Thank you." And she slipped quietly out of the room.

Duncan sank onto the stool. Miss Maddie hadn't given him a chance to explain about his mates being so bowled over by the way he had handled himself that from that moment onward he'd been accepted as an equal. More. He'd earned their respect. He wasn't about to throw it away because of a young girl's squeamishness. One day, he promised himself, he'd make her proud of him.

Chapter Fourteen

The commodious green saloon at the Rossmere's handsome residence in Manchester Square was habitually, on the second Thursday of every month, reserved for what the Countess of Rossmere was pleased to call her "ladies' day." Her husband, the earl, was once heard to affectionately refer to his wife's Thursday gatherings where ladies of an intellectual bent indulged their taste for the academic over tea as "The Bluestocking Brigade." The name stuck.

Maddie made her debut into this august company as a guest of Lady Mary Branwell on the very afternoon following her conversation with Duncan. And she was enchanted.

She found a group of about twenty ladies informally helping themselves to biscuits and tea which had been set out at one end of the room. Some of those present she already knew. The Countess of Bessborough was there as was the reigning beauty of the Season who was nicknamed "The Toast," Lady Elizabeth Heatherington. That she was also heiress to a considerable fortune ensured that the young woman had an enormous following. Lady Rossmere, her hostess, Maddie would have easily recognized as the mother of the girl who had brought her. The connection of these subdued and attractive wren-like creatures to the Viscount Deveryn missed Maddie completely. She had no recollection of ever having heard the names "Rossmere" and "Verney" in connection with each other.

She'd heard of the Bluestocking Brigade from her aunt, Miss Spencer. From what she had heard, she had expected to find herself in company of a group of hatchet-faced dowds whose conversation was too rarified to admit of the commonplaces of ordinary mortals like herself. Nothing could have been further from the truth. The chatter was as typical as was to be found among any group of ladies, with one notable exception. Whenever Lady Mary introduced Maddie to one of her mother's guests, she frequently added a word of explanation.

"Miss Smith's interest lies in Physics. She delivered a paper not so long ago entitled 'The Horseless Age—A Peek into the Future.' Fascinating!"

"Miss Paxton-Brown is an entomologist. She takes her work very seriously. Would you believe that Meg is working on a cure for—now what was it?—oh yes, warble fly? Papa can hardly wait for the results of your experiments, Meg. It decimated his herds last year, you see."

By degrees, they made their way to Lady Bessborough who was in conversation with a startlingly pretty young woman whose vivid beauty put Maddie in mind of home. Complexion like cream, hair like fire, amber-eyed, young Lady Rutherston was the epitome of the fair skinned girls who were typical of the more northern climes. Maddie was conscious that her own more subdued colouring, though similar, lacked vibrancy in comparison.

Lady Mary made the introductions. "Aunt Harriet, you already know Miss Sinclair, I collect."

Maddie curtsied as Lady Bessborough acknowledged the greeting with a friendly smile.

"Catherine, Lady Rutherston, may I present Miss Maddie Sinclair? Maddie, this is my dearest friend. We make up the Classics branch of the Bluestocking Brigade, along with my mother and sisters, of course. Oh, will you excuse me. I think it's time to begin."

Maddie stared unblinkingly at her companions. That two such elegant and formidable lionesses of the ton should share her own eccentric affinity, and, moreover, admit to it, filled her with astonishment.

"Don't be intimidated, child," said Lady Bessborough, mistaking Maddie's wide-eyed look. "We're quite harmless, aren't we Catherine?"

Lady Rutherston flashed Maddie a commiserating smile.

"Of course we are. And we have no intentions of boring you with a subject which is dear to no one but ourselves."

"Oh, but I wish you would! What I mean to say is, I won't be bored."

"You won't?" Lady Bessborough's tone was dubious.

"Harriet," interjected Lady Rutherston, her amber eyes lightening with interest as they surveyed Maddie, "I do believe we've found another sheep for the fold."

"What?"

Maddie stood stock-still as two pairs of eyes became trained on her slight person. In other circumstances, she would have been very glad that she had chosen to wear one of her new morning gowns with its shorter length showing a bit of ankle and horizontal rows of tucks around the bodice and hem. But this unnerving assessment, she knew, was of quite a different order.

Lady Bessborough spoke first. "She's very young."

"So were you, I daresay. So was I. What has that to say to anything?" said Lady Rutherston with a dismissive shrug of her shoulders.

"Are you a classicist, child?"

"Yes." There, it was out!

"What branch?"

Maddie did not hesitate to answer. "Attic Greek."

"Be more specific," Lady Bessborough admonished.

Lady Bessborough could be quite formidable when she wanted to be, Maddie thought. False humility, she conjectured, would not be tolerated in these circles.

"Linguistics, first and foremost."

"Pshaw!" decried the older lady. "I regard that as a branch of the Sciences! It has no soul."

Maddie was enjoying herself enormously. "Very true. But without it, there would be no other branches of Classics. Linguistics is the key to unlocking the body of knowledge."

"Yes, but to what purpose if we don't benefit from that knowledge? It might as well stay obscure for all the good it will do."

"Exactly. And without precise translation, there can be no proper interpretation."

This was argument for the sake of argument, and Maddie

relished it. She had never expected that in London, of all places, among the *crème de la crème* of the ton, she would find any group of ladies with more to their conversation than the latest fashions from Paris, or which hostess gave the most lavish parties and other such commonplaces, though she admitted that these ladies were comfortable in any circumstances, and envied them for it. She thought herself very fortunate to have been taken up by Lady Mary, and wondered at it a little.

As they took their places on chairs set out in a semi-circle around a makeshift podium, Lady Bessborough excused herself and went to greet a young woman who had just entered.

"You said that linguistics was your first love," observed Lady Rutherston in a quiet aside. "What comes second?"

"Greek drama. And yours?"

Lady Catherine smiled confidingly. "The same. Or at least it used to be. But with two babies at home, and another one expected, there hasn't been much time of late to pursue my interest."

Maddie was suitably commiserating.

"I'm supposed to give the paper next month on 'Women in Classical Greece,'" Lady Rutherston remarked.

"I look forward to hearing it," responded Maddie with some enthusiasm.

Lady Rutherston eyed the younger girl speculatively. "You wouldn't care to collaborate with me, would you? I could use the help."

"Oh, I don't think . . . I'm not sure . . . perhaps someone else . . ."

"There is no one else. As you've observed, even as Classicists, we all have our own particular speciality. Lady Bessborough and our hostess are addicted to Plato, with Lady Mary, it's Homer. Of course, we all dabble, but we don't feel competent in each other's field. My husband has offered to help, but he is worse than useless. His thesis is that the women of antiquity were put on a pedestal by their menfolk."

"That's hogwash," protested Maddie. Privately, she thought that Lord Rutherston must be an ignorant clod, and wondered at the waste of the vivacious and intelligent girl who had married him.

"That, my dear Miss Sinclair, by and large, is the typical male attitude, and most of them have some background in the classics. My thesis, on the other hand, is that Athenian women were much like the women of our own day and age."

"Which is to say?"

"For the most part, despised and taken advantage of, except for a fortunate few."

Lady Catherine expressed Maddie's own sentiments exactly. It seemed foolish to let false modesty stand in the way of what might well turn out to be a very pleasant exercise.

"I'll do it," said Maddie, evincing more confidence than she felt.

"Good girl! We'll talk about it later. Here comes our hostess with the guest of honour."

As it happened, the Countess of Rossmere had secured a compatriot of Maddie's for her guest speaker on that particular Thursday. Maddie's eyes followed the tall figure of Walter Scott as he limped his way toward the podium. He was a familiar figure to her, for she had seen him often enough as he went about his business in the streets of Edinburgh. She wondered at the odd turn of events that had thrown them together now, when they had been near neighbours but almost strangers in their native land.

The man was held in the highest esteem, even in England. The Prince Regent was his most devoted admirer. It was commonly believed that Scott was the author of the Waverley novels, though he steadfastly disclaimed that honour. Only one poet surpassed him in popularity—Lord Byron. Yet, there was no envy there. The two literary giants were reputed to be the best of friends, in spite of the disparity in their ages and the dissimilarity in temperament. Scott was an acknowledged philanthropist, inclined to be abstemious and utterly without malice. Byron, as everyone knew, was the opposite.

Mr. Scott had chosen for his subject, "Waterloo and its Aftermath," which surprised Maddie a little. She had expected the man of letters to hold forth on some literary topic. But it seemed that Scott had visited the famous battlefield six weeks after the event and had been deeply moved by the experiences which many of Wellington's officers had related. As for the Duke, Scott extolled him as the most sensible and plain person he had ever met, and regarded his friendship as the highest distinction of his life.

He held his listeners spellbound to the last word. He called for questions.

One young woman was on her feet, a little in front of Maddie, to the right.

"Mr. Scott," she said in a peculiarly light and breathy tone, "today you have said some very unflattering things about Napoleon Bonaparte. Your great friend, Lord Byron, on the other hand, admires him to excess. Will you admit, for once, to being at odds with this *bête noir* of our society?"

The question was patently emotional in character. Maddie craned her neck to get a better look at the lady who had asked it. At her back, she heard someone murmur the name "Caro Lamb." The girl on her feet was slight of form with wisps of blond curls framing a small gamine face. It was easy to see how she had come by the nickname, "the Sprite."

Mr. Scott seemed to weigh her question for a moment. Maddie thought she saw a softening in his piercing grey eyes. "Lady Caroline," he said at last, his rough Scottish voice smoothing to velvet, "I'm delighted to see you again. Your brother continues to mend, I trust?"

The reference, Maddie knew, was to Freddie Ponsonby who had been gravely wounded at Waterloo. His sister, Caro Lamb, whom he adored, had rushed to Brussels to care for him through a long convalescence.

"Thank you, yes," intoned Lady Caro in the same breathy tone. Maddie wondered if it was affectation. "Will you answer the question please, Mr. Scott?"

There was a faint stir in the audience, but the man of letters gave no indication that Lady Caro's needling had ruffled his feathers. Quite the reverse. He answered her question civilly and gravely, and with an unmistakeable thread of compassion in his voice.

"On the question of Napoleon, Lord Byron and I have long since agreed to differ. On our muse, however, our opinions are remarkably alike."

"And what about your views on men who mistreat women?" persisted Lady Caro. "Did you know that Lady Byron has

228

deserted her husband and charged that the man is impossibly insane?"

From the corner of her eye, Maddie saw Lady Bessborough rise and move toward her daughter. Her expression was stricken. The girl seemed to struggle, then suddenly crumpled into her mother's arms. She was led out sobbing incoherently.

"What was that all about?" Maddie asked Lady Rutherston in a soft undertone.

"Scott and Byron are devoted to each other. I think it's a case of the attraction of opposites. Caro Lamb would like to see Byron sent to oblivion. She should be pleased. He's almost sunk that low now. He can't afford another scandal."

"She looked so . . . distraught."

"Don't worry about her. Her mother will see that she's all right. As for her husband, William Lamb, he is an absolute paragon."

The awkward moment was soon smoothed over, too smoothly in Maddie's opinion. She'd heard all about Lady Caro Lamb and her disastrous affair with Byron. But that was long over. Public opinion had not been kind to the girl who had once been the darling of society.

With characteristic indifference, she had broken one of its cardinal rules. She had flaunted her indiscretions. Some said her excesses were mere affectation, that Caro Lamb would rather be infamous than anonymous. Maddie was not convinced. She thought the girl looked to be on the verge of a nervous breakdown.

With the departure of Caro Lamb, relief became almost patent. The questions were lively, but not argumentative. The nature of Scott's address was not of the sort to spark debate. Maddie wondered if it had been a deliberate ploy on his part.

She managed a few words with him before she was surreptitiously but determinedly edged away by other ladies.

"You spoke at my school on Founders' Day," she told him shyly. "Miss Maitland's Academy for Girls in Charlotte Square."

His pleasure was gratifying. "You're a graduate of Miss Maitland's? Now there's something to be proud of! You'll have one of the best groundings in the classics outside of St. Andrews University. My lack in that respect has been one of the great regrets of my life, though I've no one to blame but myself."

Mr. Scott, unlike Lord Byron, was reputed to admire clever women, or so he said. Still, it was common knowledge in Edinburgh that his own daughters had enjoyed a very indifferent education.

"You spoke to us about the Scottish regalia and their mysterious disappearance during the last century. Are you still hunting them down?"

His grey eyes took on a fervent glint, "Aye. And one day, God willing, I'll find them, and Scotland will once again glory in its rightful insignia of state."

She believed he would. An elbow caught her in the ribs, and she regretfully gave way to another lady eager for a word with the great man.

Lady Mary had overheard the few words she had exchanged with Mr. Scott.

"What regalia?" she asked, and led Maddie to the tea table where the scones and tea had been newly replenished.

"The Scottish regalia? You might call them the crown jewels —you know, the royal crown, the sceptre and the sword of state. No one knows what happened to them, whether the Scots themselves hid them or whether the English spirited them away from Edinburgh Castle after the Jacobite Rebellions."

"Oh. Is it important?"

"Mr. Scott thinks so. I wish I'd had time to quiz him some more. He's very eloquent on that subject. He has a theory that they're still in the Castle."

"You'll have your chance to quiz him later in the week," said Lady Mary, studiously involved in stirring the silver spoon in her teacup. "He's to be at a small house-party my mother has arranged at our country estate in Oxfordshire. As I understand, your grandfather has accepted an invitation on your behalf."

Maddie was quite overwhelmed at this signal honour. She scarcely knew Lady Mary, yet the girl was cultivating her acquaintance. Her pleasure could not have been greater if she had been invited to Carlton House by the Prince Regent himself.

It was her first glimpse of Dolly Ramides which robbed her of her newfound equilibrium. She had been prevailed upon by Lady Elizabeth Heatherington, she who was known as "The Toast," to go riding in Hyde Park at the fashionable hour of five o'clock in the afternoon. Although the girl was an acknowledged beauty, Maddie could detect no affectation in her, and she did not hesitate to accept the invitation. Like Maddie, the girl sat her mount as if she'd been born in the saddle and complained of the decorous pace and the two grooms who kept a wary eye on their charges. It amused Maddie to see the court which Miss Heatherington attracted, an honour she was given to understand the young lady heartily despised. It seemed that they could not walk their horses a few paces before they were halted by some admiring beau or other.

And then, just as suddenly, they were deserted. The throng of admiring cicisbeos showed the two ladies their heels as they spurred their mounts across the turf to a dashing phaeton which had drawn up at their approach. The sole occupant of the carriage was young, strikingly beautiful, and so elegantly attired that Maddie, in her spanking new chocolate brown riding habit, felt suddenly like a little brown wren.

"Well!" exclaimed Miss Heatherington in affronted accents. "Those beastly fribbles! There's only one thing you can depend upon in the male animal and that's his monumental inconstancy!"

"She's very beautiful," murmured Maddie. "Do you know her?"

The beauty tossed her head. "I know her. You might say that she is my counterpart in the demi-monde."

"I beg your pardon?"

"Dolly Ramides. She's an opera singer, and as I hear, the toast of that other world in which our menfolk are so much at ease but to which we ladies are not privy. She's Deveryn's lightskirt. I'll wager that that phaeton cost him a pretty penny or two. We should be grateful to Miss Ramides. She makes an excellent diversion. What do you say we put these sway-backs through their paces and damn the consequences?"

"I'm game," declared Maddie, suddenly reckless.

It was wasted exercise as the two girls later agreed. The mounts which their respective guardians' grooms had seen fit to provide for them could easily have been outrun by any old lumbering Clydesdale straight off the farm.

"A tortoise could have shown a better leg than this old slug," complained Maddie to Duncan as she slapped the reins into his hands before stomping into the house.

But her temper, she knew, was not ignited by anything so paltry. Deveryn had done this to her. Fickle, fickle Deveryn! He might at least have had the decency to wait till the irregularity of their situation was sorted out. She was glad that their marriage had been kept secret, else she would have been the laughingstock of the town! Insufferable man! If she never saw him again, it would be too soon for her. When she found her thoughts speculating on what the viscount might have been up to in the month since she had seen him, she lost patience with herself.

There was plenty to occupy her, and for the day or so that remained before her departure for Oxfordshire, she spent every spare minute working on the paper Lady Rutherston was to give at the next meeting of the Bluestocking Brigade. She found numerous examples in her reading to support Catherine's thesis that the lot of women in classical Greece was not a happy one, and not substantially different from the unhappy fate of the women of her own class and era. Her studies did nothing to lesson her ire with her so-called "husband."

It was with something akin to relief that she greeted the day of her departure for Oxfordshire. Lady Mary and her husband, Mr. Branwell, collected Maddie in their own comfortable carriage. The drive down was uneventful, though pleasant, the countryside rather drab as was to be expected for February. She thought Oxfordshire rather pretty, but nothing to write home about. She hoped that one day she might say as much to Deveryn.

The Rossmere's house, on the other hand, quite bowled her over. She had seen grander houses, but nothing to compare with it in charm and comfort. The room which was assigned to her could not have pleased her more. French doors gave onto a pretty wrought iron balcony, very small and of little use in winter, but in the summer months she could imagine it filled with crocks of flowers. She thought the influence probably Italian. A Romeo and Juliet balcony, she decided. But wonder

232

of wonders was the door to the right of the French windows which gave onto a small closet with its own tiny window high on the wall. Here was housed an elaborately carved mahogany commode. Under the lid, she discovered the ubiquitous chamber pot. Nothing in the house was ever to impress Maddie as much as this one small indication of gentility. At Drumoak, the chamber pot was kept under the bed. In her grandfather's house in Curzon Street, each bedroom had a commode which was sheltered by a silk screen. But this—this was luxury on a scale she had never imagined.

The rest of the house, what little she saw of it before retiring, pleased her almost equally as well. She thought that a week in such pleasant surroundings would prove an agreeable respite from the woes that plagued her. In her mind's eyes, she consigned to perdition the men who sought to order her life— Deveryn, her grandfather, and, in some unspecified way, even her father. She went to bed with an easy mind for the first time in weeks and tumbled quickly into sleep.

When she descended the stairs the following morning, her step was light, her smile sunny. She was neither surprised nor dismayed to learn that she was the first to be up and about. At Drumoak, she'd been accustomed to being out on the links with Banshee before the house stirred. A footman directed her to the stable block. She hummed a little tune under her breath as one of the grooms led out a gentle-eyed chestnut with a flash of white between her ears. Until she proved her mettle, Maddie knew she would rate only the most docile mounts for her enjoyment. One did not argue with one's host's head stud- groom. She thanked him prettily, and decorously used the mounting block to hoist herself onto the mare's back, then waited demurely till an undergroom led out his own mount.

"Flash," as the little mare was predictably named, might not have been the equal of Banshee in stamina and speed, but oh! it was glorious to feel the motion of the mare beneath her and hear the pounding of hoofbeats against turf as they sped across the wide expanse of parkland. Only the roar of the sea in her ears could have improved on what was almost perfection.

Up and up they raced toward their goal: Duncairn at the summit of the broad and fertile valley of the Rossmere estate. They slowed to traverse the home wood, then Maddie gave her mount its head as they crested a series of gentle rises, swiftly approaching the stone cairn which marked the summit. The wind in her face, the smooth motion of her mount, the sunshine beating on her back, all combined to make Maddie forget that she was in unfamiliar territory. As Flash's long limbs stretched out to crest the final rise, Maddie did not think to slacken her pace. She heard the groom's warning shout at her back. Almost simultaneously, she saw the low wall of a ruin dead straight ahead. Too late to rein in, she dug in her heels and prepared to make the jump. Flash decided otherwise. The mare plunged and stamped and came to a sudden quivering halt and Maddie went sailing over her mount's head to the other side of the wall.

Strong arms gripped her shoulders. "You little idiot! Don't you know better than to go charging blindly into the unknown?"

She knew that she was dazed. The groom's rough voice sounded remarkably like Deveryn's. She blinked up at him.

Strong fingers moved over her limbs, testing for broken bones. "For God's sake, say something."

There could be no doubt. The voice belonged to Deveryn. She tried to speak, but the fall had winded her. When the air finally rushed into her lungs, she said weakly, "She's no hunter, is she?"

He laughed, a sound of mingled relief and exasperation. He hauled her to a sitting position and propped her against the wall. "Wait here," he ordered.

His instructions were redundant. Maddie was too sore to do more than breathe, and even that was painful. When he returned, her eyes were closed and her head lolled back against the stone wall.

"Sweetheart!" he said urgently. "Say something."

She opened her eyes slowly and felt the cool of his wet handkerchief as he bathed her face.

"What happened to the groom?" she rasped out.

"I relieved him of his duty almost as soon as you left the stable yard. You never once looked back to see who was following you."

He bathed her face with almost lover-like tenderness. By degrees, Maddie came to herself. Breathing became easier, her

234

thoughts clearer. She struggled to free herself of his clasp.

"Don't tell me you're one of the guests for this house party?" she groaned.

He sat back on his haunches, studying her. It was evident she had suffered little hurt from the tumble she had taken. The softened expression grew harder.

"No, I live here," he said.

She looked at him blankly for a long, unfocused moment. "Dunsdale, as I may have told you, is the family seat of the Earls of Rossmere."

He could almost see her mind making connections as first disbelief, then doubt, and finally comprehension illumined her dark eyes.

"Then Lady Mary is . . ."

"My sister," he finished for her.

"And this is all a . . . hoax—a ploy to get me here?"

"Not exactly. I arranged for you to be included on the guest list. Everything else is just as you surmise."

She'd thought for an awful moment that they were to be the only two people on the estate.

He rightly interpreted the relieved expression and said dryly, "I only wish! For what I have to say to you, madam wife, is not for the tender ears of gentlefolk." His voice rose to a roar. "You damn well deserted me! And that I should have to resort to subterfuge to get my own wife under my own roof is beyond anything! I knew you would not come at my invitation. And you can wipe that look of martyred innocence from your face! I have every right to be angry with you, and you know it."

Though she flinched, she said with only a barely perceptible tremor, "Whether or not I am your wife is debatable. Furthermore, I did not desert you. I had no choice but to obey my grandfather's summons since you warned me that our marriage should be kept secret, or don't you remember?"

"Gammon! You could have delayed till I returned from Edinburgh. You could have left a note. You were punishing me for Cynthia."

She was struggling to her feet, pushing away his hands as he made to help her. Her voice came back to her in full force. "I'm not punishing you, Deveryn, I'm severing the relationship. Those marriage lines aren't worth the paper they're written on, and you know it."

"We sealed the bargain with our bodies, or had you forgotten? That means we truly are married." His voice was dangerously quiet.

"Piffle! If that were so, you would be married to half the ladies in London! Yes, and the ones who aren't ladies either."

She caught the slight widening of his eyes, and the hint of a snarl behind the teeth bared in a grin.

"You're addiction to hyperbole would be laughable if it weren't so vulgar. No one has ever accused me before of being a womanizer."

"Before what, Deveryn? Before Grantham?" she recklessly challenged. Damn! She hadn't wanted him to know that his tryst with another woman affected her with anything stronger than bored indifference.

He surveyed her for a long moment through narrowed eyes. "It never ceases to amaze me how you gently bred girls contrive to pick up any dirt that is going. What have you heard?"

She didn't want to talk about it. What she wanted was a warm bath and a hot toddie and Janet's shoulder on which to cry. But the wall was behind her and Deveryn blocked her line of escape. His hands clamped on her shoulders.

"I got it from an eye witness," she blurted out.

"Who?" His fingers tightened on the soft flesh of her arms.

"From Duncan. He was there, at the Falcon. You should be grateful to him, you and what's her name, Dolly Ramides? He stopped two of them before they could tear you apart. Don't worry! I've warned him in future not to interfere in what doesn't concern him."

A flicker of something came and went in his eyes. The fingers which had been digging into her arms relaxed their cruel pressure. The thin line of his mouth softened. He released his warm breath on a whispered sigh.

"Oho! So my bloodthirsty wife would like to see me torn limb from limb would she? Little savage!" His thumb brushed the mutinous set of her lips.

Some day, he promised himself, some day he would confess the whole, when Maddie had learned to trust him implicitly. They would look back and laugh about the episode at

236

Grantham. But for the present, it behooved him to proceed with the greatest caution. "Maddie, listen to me please." He chose his next words with care. "The lady," he said vaguely, "was not there by invitation. She bribed the landlord to gain entrance to my room. She had scarcely entered when Jack Ponsonby and his cronies came charging through the door. Nothing happened. Nor would it have. I'm a married man now. That means something to me. Why would I even want another woman, when I have you as my private possession? I'm not fickle with my friends. Do you suppose that I would be any less loyal to the woman I have chosen for my wife? Trust me, Maddie, and I'll never give you cause to regret it."

Orpheus could not have played his lute more sweetly to beguile the shades in the Underworld, thought Maddie, than Deveryn plied his voice to charm her from her humour. Everything about him was mesmerizing—the liquid harmony of his accents; the fall of wheat-gold hair across the brow giving him that attractively boyish aspect; the transparency of blue eyes, hiding nothing, like a Scottish loch, still, deep, and clear down to its rocky bottom; and that smile—slow and utterly winsome. The whole effect was devastating . . . and as smooth as the polished granite sink in Drumoak's kitchen. She didn't trust him.

"Miss Ramides is only a drop in the bucket. An ocean separates us, Deveryn." The words came out clipped and bitter when she had hoped for a semblance of serenity.

"You are my wife. Nothing can change that fact," he answered evenly.

She picked nervously at a loose thread on the seam of her glove. "I wouldn't count on it. I understand a little about these marriages of declaration. The parties are supposed to set up house together. In our case that didn't happen. Perhaps, if you applied to the solicitor . . ." Her gaze drifted to his and the fury she saw building there brought her to a sudden halt.

He lifted her in his arms, none too gently, and hoisted her over the wall as if she had been a sack of coal.

"Mount up," he told her curtly a moment later and cupped his gloved hands for her booted foot. She vaulted into the saddle without a murmur, though every bone and muscle in her body made known their displeasure.

When they came to the edge of the park, he reined in and turned in the saddle to face her. She felt the probe of his eyes like a violent attack. His voice, when he spoke, held none of the warmth which had earlier charmed her.

"Make up your mind to it, Maddie, we are married, period. Need I remind you that our marriage was thoroughly consummated? Furthermore—don't say a word," he threatened when he saw her lips begin to move. "Furthermore, if I were to marry any other woman, the legitimacy of my future heirs would be forever called into question. You are my wife. Only my sense of decency has prevented me from descending on your grandfather and carrying you off by the scruff of the neck as you deserve. Argue with me on this point one more time and I'll make you regret that you ever learned to talk!"

"Who's arguing?" She could not resist the taunt.

Fleetingly, his eyes warmed. "You always have to turn every conversation into a debate! But on this subject, madam wife, I intend to have the last word!"

"It's yours," she needled.

He shot her a look of amused indulgence. "There's only one sure way to silence you," he said. "I was saving that pleasure for later. But if you go on like this . . ."

A cry rang out across the park, and both riders turned in the saddle to observe a horse and rider making in their direction.

"Sophie!" said Deveryn. "We'll talk of this later. For the present, we'll go on as we were before. Be on your best behaviour and take your cue from me."

Maddie did not mistake the softly spoken imperative for anything less than it was—a threat. Still, his words reassured her a little. "We'll go on as we were before," he had said. A temporary respite was better than nothing at all, she reasoned.

As Deveryn's young sister drew level with them, Maddie pinned a smile of greeting on her lips. She had stumbled into a tortuous maze. Until she could see her way out of it, it were prudent, she decided, to play the game as Deveryn wanted. When she extended her hand to Lady Sophie as Deveryn made the introductions, Maddie's manners could not have been faulted.

Chapter Fifteen

Deveryn was in a foul humour, which was nothing out of the ordinary of late, he told himself violently, as he allowed Martin to ease him into his black tailored evening coat. Ever since he'd met the prickly thistle from Scotland, his peace had been cut to shreds. But now he tottered on the brink of disaster, and all because of that one act of defiance on the part of the impetuous chit. Her fiery temper could damn well plunge them both into a scandal to rock Court circles, as well as bring infamy upon his family name. Damn her to hell!

The valet was dismissed with a curt word of thanks, and Deveryn subsided into a capacious wing armchair. The cheroot he had been smoking earlier was on the stand at his elbow. He picked it up and inhaled deeply, his thoughts drifting to the conversation he'd had earlier with his brother-in-law. Max was a barrister who was speedily making a name for himself in his field. As a younger son of a younger son, he'd been forced to take up some profession or other and claimed that it was no hardship, since he was fascinated by everything connected with law. Deveryn had quizzed him about marriages performed in Scotland, particularly marriages of declaration. Max had thereupon embarked on a long and complex tale of Robbie Burns, Scotland's Bard, whose wife had repudiated a similar type marriage and in so doing had borne bastards to the poet until such time as he'd persuaded her to a more regular union. The story made Deveryn's hair stand on end.

Since he had no desire to take Max fully into his confidence, he'd thought it expedient to turn the conversation. It was evident, however, that his brother-in-law's curiosity was at bursting point. In the end, Deveryn had made up his mind that the only safe course was to write to the solicitor in Edinburgh as soon as he returned to town. He could not credit that Mr. Forsythe would have loaned his support to anything irregular. Of course, it could be that Maddie was right in her conjecture and that until they openly cohabited and let the whole world know it, the legality of their marriage would be in question.

His lips compressed into a tight line as he remembered that it was only an hour ago that he'd decided he was done with playing a waiting game. The talk about Grantham paled into insignificance in light of what Max had disclosed. With Samuel Spencer's blessing, he'd thought he could damn well force Maddie to set up house with him. Where else could she go? And he was certain that once the facts were laid before Samuel Spencer, he'd have the announcement of their marriage in the *Gazette* before he, Deveryn, could change his gloves. He was a damn good catch. He knew it. The girl couldn't do better.

Or so he'd thought till he had been rudely jolted out of his complacency by a few distracted words of his mother's as they ascended the stairs to dress for dinner.

"Did I mention that Uncle George will be joining us for dinner? He arrived this afternoon, but he'll be gone by tomorrow, so I shouldn't think you need consider his preferences for this houseparty you've planned."

"For dinner?" he'd replied absently. "What could possibly drag him away from Raeburn Abbey?"

"Mary's friend, what's her name? Oh yes, Miss Sinclair. There's a betrothal there in the offing, so I am given to understand. I feel rather sorry for the girl. Though I'm devoted to my cousin George, of course, it's my experience that these Spring and Autumn marriages are rarely happy."

He'd spun to face his mother. "What?"

His mother's look of surprise had quickly given way to speculation. "Uncle George. He's courting Miss Sinclair," she clarified.

"Over my dead body!" he had bit out vehemently, and had spun on his heel to stalk to his own chamber.

It was this intelligence which shook him more than anything, for he did not know if Samuel Spencer would settle for an aspiring earl when a full-fledged duke had fallen into his lap. And as for his mother's cousin, Raeburn . . . who could tell? Heiresses were not to be had growing on trees, and Uncle George was known to have inherited a pile of debts when he succeeded to the title. To lay the whole story before Samuel Spencer now while Maddie still kept him at arm's length was not to be thought of. It was necessary to make their marriage incontrovertible fact before taking others into their confidence.

He threw the stub of his cigar into the smouldering fire with an angry motion of his wrist. The whole enterprise pivoted on Maddie! Not that he would be fool enough to let her know it. In her present frame of mind, she might very easily send him to the roustabouts with a snap of her fingers. He was not forgetting her antipathy based on his past actions with respect to her father. Add to that, Cynthia, Drumoak, and Dolly Ramides and his offences in her eyes must be serious indeed.

He'd been dealt a poor hand, there was no getting round it. Somehow, he had to better the odds. He examined the problem from all angles and came full circle to his original conclusion. Everything pivoted on Maddie. The thing could be settled quietly and without scandal if she would only admit to being his wife.

This last thought roused him to cold anger. There were dozens of women he could name who would give their eye teeth to be in her position. Why the hell did it have to be *her?*—a woman, a girl really, whose experience of the world was so slight that she could not recognize the good fortune that had befallen her? The word "love" he discarded as too common-place to describe their condition. This was Fate; Answered Prayer where no petition had been made; divine intervention; The Doctrine of Grace in comprehensible form. Maddie was too ignorant to recognize it for what it was. And that made it *hell* for him. Her mind was bent on tallying accounts, calling in debts, vindicating her position. He wanted simply to immerse himself in her, blending body and soul till it was impossible to tell where one began and the other ended. A year ago he would have laughed himself silly if any of his friends had confided such maudlin sentiments to him. Unmanly, Jason, he told himself sadly. Also, undeniably true.

241

He rose and took a turn around the room, his brow creased in thought. Martin walked in a moment later to hear his master's lips whistling the refrain of some bawdy drinking song he had not heard in an age. His own lips lifted slightly.

"My lord?" he intoned mildly, and he began to fold away the pile of discarded clothes which were thrown on the bed.

"You wouldn't believe it if I told you, old chap," answered the viscount as he slipped through the open door. The thought that he was about to embark on his delayed honeymoon had cheered him considerably.

Maddie was not slow to remark the viscount's cocky smile as they sat down to dinner. There were fourteen at the table, some few with whom Maddie was unacquainted: her host, the Earl of Rossmere, whose likeness to the viscount had tied her tongue in knots when they had been first introduced; Mr. William Lamb; Lady Sophie; and her governess, Miss Trimmer, an elderly dragon whose sharp eyes missed nothing. For the first time, Maddie was very glad that she'd had the benefit of Mr. Clarke's tutoring.

She found herself agreeably placed between Mr. Lamb and Mr. Branwell. Deveryn sat opposite, slightly to her right, between his sister and Lady Caro. Freddie Ponsonby and Toby Blanchard were there as well. On her host's left was "The Toast," Lady Elizabeth Heatherington. The Duke of Raeburn, whom Maddie was not at all sure she was pleased to see, was seated on his hostess's left hand. The guest of honour, Mr. Scott, naturally, on her right.

Maddie's eyes surreptitiously swept the table. She'd been told by Lady Mary that at the Countess of Rossmere's board, manners were very informal. She could tell at a glance, however, that there was nothing informal about the order in which the countess had placed her guests. Protocol was observed to the letter. She thought that her tutor, Mr. Clarke, would have been unconditional in his praise. It took her only a minute or two to work out that she was at the very bottom of the ladder. The thought was lowering.

As if sensing her slight pique, Mr. Branwell intoned in her ear, "Mr. Scott may be the guest of honour, but the menu has been chosen with you in mind." At her look of surprise, he explained, "Lord Deveryn's doing."

Her eyes swung to Deveryn. He was watching her with a bemused expression on his face, though his head was inclined toward Lady Caro as if every word that fell from her lips held him spellbound. Very easily, and openly, he raised his wine glass in a salute and brought it to his lips.

Until the first course was served, Maddie was beside herself with apprehension. When the footmen began to serve Mulligatawny soup her sigh of relief was almost audible. Naturally, Deveryn would not serve such exalted company so base a dish as porridge. She chided herself for her wild fancies and remarked to Mr. Lamb on her right, that the soup was of a very high order. What she did not say, but might very easily, was that the stock was obviously boiled from whole fowl, when the bones would have done just as well. She thought that if Janet were let loose in the kitchens of Dunsdale, she could save her hostess thousands of pounds a year. Not that the countess would thank her for it.

The second course was not quite so acceptable—cod's head smothered in a smooth lobster sauce. Her glance flashed to Lord Deveryn.

"Have you tried this dish before, Miss Sinclair?" he asked from across the table.

Maddie scarcely knew where to look. Her tutor had warned her in no uncertain terms that to talk across the table was considered particularly ill-bred. Nobody at the countess's table, however, seemed to take exception to Deveryn's breach of etiquette, unless it was Miss Trimmer whose lips tightened imperceptibly.

"No," said Maddie, "I've not had that pleasure."

"It's an English delicacy. May I suggest that you spear it with your fork and hack it to bits with your fish knife as if it were . . . a battle axe?"

She managed a thin smile.

"Don't you have cod's head in Scotland?" asked Mr. Branwell, to make conversation.

"Yes, but we boil them for fish soup then feed them to the stable cats," she answered absently. She particularly disliked the way the cod's eye gazed at her unblinkingly from the middle of her plate, and wondered if it were by design or ill fortune that the head had fallen to her lot. "What do you do with the body?" she asked.

Deveryn caught her remark. "What else? We boil it for fish soup then feed it to the stable cats." He positively purred. "You Scots always get everything backwards."

The guests, all intimates of the Rossmere household with the exception of Maddie and Lady Elizabeth, became alert. Cutlery was laid aside. Footmen were called to refill wine glasses. It was evident that one of the famous Verney dinner debates had just been launched. The subject under discussion was not in question: Scotland Forever versus England and St. George.

Lady Caro caught her brother's eye and said distinctly, "We Ponsonbys are Irish. Naturally, our loyalties are with the Scots. Right Freddie?"

"I'll say. Anything to take these arrogant English snobs down a peg or two."

All eyes turned to Maddie as if waiting for the next salvo. She looked around the table. Her eyes dropped to her plate. She picked up her dessert spoon and very deliberately covered the cod's head with a mountain of lobster sauce. "The least we can do," she said in a pronounced Scottish accent, "is give the *puir* wee beastie a decent burial."

Her supporters were not slow in following her example: first Lady Caro, and very quickly thereafter, Mr. Scott, Freddie, and belatedly and a little sheepishly, Toby Blanchard.

"Toby!" exclaimed Deveryn. "You turncoat!"

"Nothing of the sort! I've always detested cod's head, but have never been brave enough to say so. If I can get out of eating it simply by kissing the Scottish flag, then what I say is—lead me to it."

"The odds are still uneven," remarked Lady Mary. "I don't know who to cast in my lot with. I'm afraid I don't know much about Scotland except that the climate is rather cold."

"Watch it, Mary," admonished Deveryn. "The Scots will stand anything but an attack on their climate. There never would have been a Jacobite rebellion if some poor English sod in an Inverness tavern hadn't complained that frostbite was a communicable disease and its origins were in Scotland."

"What has England got that Scotland hasn't got?" asked Maddie on a note of belligerence.

"Summer," stated Deveryn emphatically, "and with enough

heat to ripen fruit."

"We have fruit, too!" she exclaimed.

"Oh, yes," interposed William Lamb, stirring himself from his natural indolence, "I remember very well. I should. I spent two years at Glasgow University after I came down from Oxford. I distinctly remember that in a remarkably warm summer there, I tasted peaches that could very easily have passed for pickles, and it is upon record that at the siege of Perth, on one occasion, the ammunition failing, your nectarines, Miss Sinclair, made admirable cannon balls."

"Have you done?" asked Maddie in frigid accents.

"By no means," interjected Deveryn with relish. "I still suffer nightmares when I remember the North Sea winds. Even experienced Scottish fowls don't dare try to fly across the streets of Edinburgh. Have you seen them, William? They sidle along, tails aloft, and would rather succumb to the deprivations of prowling alley cats than chance the violence of the gale."

"Gentlemen, gentlemen," interposed Mr. Scott from the far end of the table, "plagiarism does not become you, and you, passing yourselves off as fine English gentlemen." His tone was sorrowful.

The gentlemen in question exchanged sheepish grins.

"Plagiarism, Mr. Scott?" asked Lady Rossmere, who had been observing the byplay with a benevolent eye, and more particularly the interesting interplay between Miss Sinclair and her son.

"The words more or less are stolen from the mouth, or perhaps I should say 'pen' of my dear friend and colleague, Sydney Smith." He smiled benignly at Mr. Lamb and Lord Deveryn in turn. "Gentlemen, you won't be denying that you subscribe to the *Edinburgh Review*. Aye, I thought as much."

"Shameful!" said Freddie Ponsonby, rubbing his hands gleefully. He'd never been to Scotland, hoped he never would, and could not think why he'd permitted himself to be roped into a cause to which he hadn't a word to contribute.

"The truth still stands," responded Deveryn airily. "And who can name one thing that Scotland has that England hasn't got?"

"My heart, for a start!" Maddie shot back with alacrity.

"Oh that!" Deveryn immediately responded, ruthlessly cutting off Toby Blanchard who had been desperately trying to get a word in edgewise. "Women are so fickle. I don't doubt that in another month or two, your heart will be completely converted to everything English."

"Don't bet on it, Deveryn!" she retorted.

"There's one thing that impressed me about the Scots," said Lord Rossmere musingly, and the only one at the table to calmly continue eating his dinner.

"What's that, dear?" asked his countess.

"Even the lowest menial knows how to read and write. Whereas here, well, you know how it is. Nobody troubles. The attitude is, why bother when the local priest will do it for you?"

"Aye," agreed Mr. Scott, "but that's because in Scotland every man sees himself in some sort as a *lad o' pairts*, an educated man, that is. Whether it is true or not, we believe that education is the great equalizer. Take my shepherd, for instance."

The argument continued unabated for the remainder of the meal. The footmen removed course after course with scarcely a person present aware of the excellent dinner cook had prepared at the express wish of the winsome young master. Only two of the countess's guests remained aloof from the general frivolity—the beautiful Lady Elizabeth and the Duke of Raeburn. But since these worthies had the distinction of sitting on the left hand respectively of the earl and his lady, there was never any slack in the conversation.

When it was time for the ladies to leave the gentlemen to their port, both sides agreed that the honours were even. As the dining room door was closed upon them, William Lamb's voice was heard to say, "Good, now we can talk broad."

Maddie thought little of it, but Lady Caro, who was just ahead of her, turned and said in a voice vibrant with scorn, "Philistine!" and she picked up her skirts and went racing up the stairs.

"The girl's moods are like quicksilver," said Lady Rossmere. She stood undecided for a moment. "I'd best go after her. No telling what she may get up to, and I promised her mother . . ." The words were lost to Maddie as the countess ascended the stairs.

When she entered the drawing room, Maddie thought at first to place herself beside Lady Elizabeth. The beauty, however, gave her a cold stare. Lady Mary's smile was much more to her liking, and Maddie accepted the tacit invitation. Within minutes, the countess returned with Lady Caro whose disposition appeared to have had a turn for the better. Her gaiety was infectious, and she kept them amused till the gentlemen joined them.

When the piano lid was opened, Mr. Scott invited Maddie with a twinkle to join him in singing the odd Scottish ballad for the erudition of their English friends. Their object was soon devined by Deveryn, for though the Scottish words were incomprehensible to English ears, he had heard Maddie sing them at Drumoak and knew they were songs of wild Scottish victories against their ancient foe. They paid the penalty for that piece of spite, for Deveryn and young Sophie knew as many ballads which extolled English victories, and sang them with gusto.

Mr. Scott listened attentively as he idly sipped a double dram of Scotch whisky. Suddenly, he cried out, "Glenlivet! I'd know it anywhere!"

"What?" the exclamation came from Lord Rossmere who had been tête à tête with Raeburn in a quiet corner of the room.

"Glenlivet?" asked Deveryn, his eyes endeavouring to catch Maddie's frantic gaze which wandered everywhere except in his direction. "The finest Scotch whisky there is to be had? How do you come by it, sir?"

His father looked down at the glass in his hand. He put it to his lips and slowly savoured a mouthful of the amber liquid. "By George, so it is. Miss Sinclair brought it with her. Thank you, my dear. It's almost impossible to come by south of the border. I gather you brought it with you when you left Scotland?"

"Hum . . . yes," confessed Maddie, not daring to look Deveryn in the eye.

She managed to avoid him for what was left of the evening, and when she retired for the night, she was careful to mount the stairs in the company of one of the other ladies. It happened to be Caro Lamb.

They reached the head of the stairs, and, without preamble,

Lady Caro suddenly asked in a small intense voice, "Whom do you imagine I consider the most distinguished man I have ever met?"

"Lord Byron," said Maddie without thinking, and could have bitten her tongue out.

She need not have distressed herself. The answer brought a small, satisfied smile to Lady Caro's serious expression. "No, my own husband, William Lamb," she answered quietly, and left Maddie to stare after her.

She was still staring when she heard Deveryn's amused voice at her shoulder. "I love the way you roll your 'r's' when you're in conversation with a fellow Scot. You should do it more often, Maddie."

"What?" Her hand whipped instinctively to her bottom. "Roll my arse?" And for the second time in as many minutes, she wished she could bite off her tongue.

There was that devilish glint in his eye. "Your 'r's,' Maddie. I wish you would roll them for me. I adore your Scottish burr." And he walked away with the confident swagger she knew so well.

"Philistine!" she hissed after him, but her own eyes held an irrepressible twinkle.

It took only a few minutes to complete her ablutions and ready herself for bed. Lady Rossmere had kindly loaned her the use of a maid. But Maddie felt awkward about being fussed over. The offer to brush her hair she declined kindly but firmly, and watched from her chair at the lady's dressing table as Rosie scooped up her discarded silk gown and carried it off to be brushed and pressed and returned in the morning.

It was terribly stuffy. The fire in the grate had been banked up to last through the night. And it was a *coal* fire. She didn't know whether to be appalled or overwhelmed by such a show of luxury. A moment's reflection persuaded her to amend her opinion. The Rossmeres didn't give a straw for luxury. The whole house was a statement in comfort. It must be nice, she thought, to be so situated that one could indulge one's preferences without counting every penny. If she ever found herself in such a fortunate position, the first thing she would do was prohibit the making of porridge in her kitchen. It was mere whimsy, of course. Should she ever be so fortunate as to be mistress of a home of her own, she would . . . A new train of thought insinuated itself in her consciousness.

She didn't think she was pregnant, but how could she tell? Her cycle had always become irregular at any crisis in her life, and there had been many of those in the last month or two. Hopefully, in another week or so, everything would be back to normal. Pregnancy was not to be thought of! She tried to stifle the leap of joy which started her pulse racing when she thought of having *his* baby growing inside her. Her thoughts drifted.

She remembered the day Malcolm's mother had told her that she'd left childhood behind and was now capable of making babies. After that, she'd had the typical girlish fancies—a house filled with love, laughter, and her own babies, and in the background, almost as an afterthought, a masculine presence, the shadowy figure of some male or other who would make it all happen. That had been the part of the fantasy which had been least welcome. To permit a man such intimacies with one's person seemed indelicate, undignified and absolutely terrifying. How men could even wish for such a thing had been beyond her ken. But that was before Deveryn. The very thought of him brought her body alive with an achy awareness.

She didn't like it. She palmed her breasts over her cotton night attire, and tried to placate the throb of the nipples suddenly grown sensitive. It wasn't fair! For a whole month she'd been mistress of her body. She'd subdued it with scarcely an argument. But all it took was a few hours in Deveryn's discomposing presence, and every pore, every fine hair, every drop of blood, skin, muscle, bone rebelled against her as if *she* were the enemy.

"It's wicked," she said aloud, and flattened her breasts as if she would erase her femininity. "We're not even married."

Her body evidently did not share her scruples. She was hot. She was restless. She needed a cool draught of air to instill some sanity into her rioting senses. She reached the French doors onto the little balcony just as they opened, and there stood Deveryn, framed in the doorway, as if her body had conjured him up out of thin air.

She stumbled back with a cry. He swiftly drew the curtains together and turned to face her. A roguish strand of blond hair fell across his forehead.

"What are you doing here?" she asked, controlling the warble in her voice with super-human effort.

He cocked one eyebrow as he moved farther into the room, his hands automatically going to the intricate folds of his neckcloth. Maddie bustled away. The back of her legs hit the bed and she fell against it.

"It's been a month," he said. "What did you expect?"

He discarded his garments with easy grace till he was down to his trousers. His potent virility hit her like a tidal wave, flooding every pore on the surface of her skin. She could sense them opening to get more of him. With a little cry of rage, she shot to her feet. She wasn't about to forget all the man's iniquities in spite of the messages her traitorous body was trying to feed her.

"You've got the wrong room, Deveryn," she sneered. "I'm not Cynthia or Dolly what's-her-name. You should have stayed in London. I don't think you'll find any lightskirts among your mother's guests. Perhaps if you try below stairs."

Her angry tirade broke off abruptly as he reached her in one lithe stride. Strong fingers encircled her throat, squeezing gently.

"You're my wife."

His eyes held hers. She could hear the frightened rush of air from her lungs as her breathing became more difficult. His eyes dropped to her parted lips. She tried to close them, but breathing became intolerable. His eyes lifted to hers and she could see the subtle change in his expression. She recognized the look. A cry tore from her lips the second before his mouth covered hers.

His kiss was smothering, cutting off air till she thought her lungs would burst. Her mouth went slack beneath his, giving in to the implacable demand that she surrender everything to him. She felt a rush of cool air on her shoulder as he pushed her wrapper aside to slide in a tangle at her feet.

He released her lips to say hoarsely, "Maddie, put your arms around me."

She stood hesitating for a split second then took a step backward only to find herself pinned against the smooth polished wood of the bedpost.

"Don't," she pleaded, but his arms were already wrapping

themselves around her, one hand splaying out to bring the lower part of her body into intimate contact with his. Her hips arched into the heat of his arousal even as she uttered the weak and wholly ineffective denial, "No."

Tongue and lips washed the protest from her mouth, flooding her with his essence, filling her with the rhythm and beat that her inflamed senses instantly recognized. Everything inside her went liquid with wanting. Her hands went to his shoulders, then crept round his neck, and her fingers lost themselves in his hair.

Through the thin cotton of her gown, he took the weight of one breast in his hand. She leaned into his palm, firing him to a rougher, more abrasive contact. His tongue trailed hotly moist from the pulse behind her ear to her throat.

"Maddie, touch me," he breathed, even as his fingers deftly undid the row of buttons that opened her gown from throat to waist.

"Touch me," he repeated, and his warm breath fanned one swollen nipple as he pulled the gown from her arms.

Her arms spread out over his shoulders and he jerked slightly at her first tentative touch. The pads of her fingers grew sensitive, absorbing the sensation of powerful masculine muscles, tensed, straining to gentle his virility lest his mate recognize her weakness and imagine herself in jeopardy. The picture flashed to her fingertips and they lifted from his feverish skin.

His head rolled back. "Maddie . . . please . . . more," he pleaded.

Her delicate touch descended, and with almost detached interest, she touched them to the pulse beating wildly at his throat. A shudder shook his frame, vibrating beneath her damp palms, and she could feel heat leaping to life between her thighs.

She stilled, waiting for the moment to pass, and his head descended. The tip of his tongue traced a lazy path round the hardened bud of one nipple, evading the throbbing peak, deliberately heightening her anguished pleasure.

"Jason," she begged, "don't!" The torment of anticipation was almost too much to bear.

He pulled back and she was shocked at the hard glitter

blazing from his eyes.

"Jason, don't what?" he raged. "Why won't you give in to me? Why won't you admit you want me as much as I want you? Your body knows it, even if you don't. Shall I prove it to you?"

She shook her head. It was unnecessary to prove something she already knew. But he mistook her meaning. With a muttered oath, he stripped the gown from her till she was uncovered to his hungry gaze.

"Maddie, you are so beautiful. I'll never get enough of you," he murmured softly. His eyes lingered on the auburn triangle at the juncture of her thighs and she felt as if he had caressed her there, intimately, and with voluptuous abandon. She made a slight, evasive movement and both hands were captured behind the bed post. He restrained her easily. The will to fight him had been lost before he'd even stepped into her chamber. But he wasn't to know that.

His eyes held hers in their heated, passionate embrace. In the charged silence, she could sense the movement of his hand as he released himself from his trousers.

The tempo of their strident breathing increased, its sensual rhythm filling the room. Her body quivered, the tension of waiting for what he would do next bringing her to fever pitch.

He freed her hands and dragged her closer, one palm at the small of her back, bringing her hips forward.

"Open your legs for me," he whispered thickly.

Of its own volition, her body answered him. His fingers slipped inside her, and her muscles tightened involuntarily.

"Maddie," he groaned, "why do you put me through such hell when . . ."

She felt him poise for entry. Her fingers dug into his tensing shoulders. He thrust into her and with a soft cry she arched back in mindless ecstasy.

One arm wrapped around her waist, his hand against her back, preventing her from falling. The other hand curved around her hips, controlling her movements, arching her to meet each hard thrust of his loins, and his mouth closed over one tortured nipple, suckling hungrily as if he would fill himself with her. Maddie could no longer stifle the pleasure sounds that seeped from her throat. As the pleasure mounted, so did the pitch of her anguished wails.

She heard his deep throated chuckle before he lowered her to the bed. "Maddie, you'll rouse the whole house."

But a groan of pleasure was torn from his own lips as she wrapped her legs around his flanks.

With ruthless control, he stilled her writhing movements and levered himself from her. Slowly, dazed, her eyes languid with passion, she tried to focus on his face. He gave her a moment to come to herself.

"Jason?"

His voice was unbending. "Tell me you want me."

Her eyelids drooped as she tried to fathom his sudden coldness.

"Tell me!" he ordered.

"I want you."

"Now say that you're my wife."

"I'm your wife."

"Maddie," he breathed, coming into her fully, "I love you."

She repeated the words only a breath after his passionate avowal. He seemed to understand the sudden rush of tears that drenched her cheeks.

"It's all right, love. Everything will be fine," and he set himself to reward her reluctant confession with the worship of his own adoring body.

At the crest of their pleasure, his hand reached blindly for her mouth, stifling her piercing cry of anguish, and he pressed deeper, deeper, fervently blending his body into hers, smothering his own hoarse cry of triumph against her throat.

They lay spent in each other's arms. "Maddie," he said, but could not find the words to tell her of the awe he had experienced at their joining. "Maddie," he said again, and fell silent, contenting himself with the feel of her in his arms.

His sated indolence was rudely dispelled when Maddie pulled from his inert clasp and shrugged into the crushed wrapper which had been discarded on the floor at the foot of the bed. He raised on his elbows and watched her curiously as she stationed herself at the fireplace, staring into the fire.

"Are you all right, love?" he asked.

She spun on him, and he could tell at once from the set expression on her face that she was far from all right.

"What is all this supposed to prove, Deveryn?" she

demanded in a tight, little voice.

"So we're back to 'Deveryn' are we?" he asked, his lips compressing. "Am I only to hear my name on your lips when we're in the throes of passion?"

Her velour wrapper, he noted dourly, was belted tightly at her waist. He began to fasten the buttons of his trousers, and realized, belatedly, that he hadn't even removed them to make love to her. A moment's reflection, and he philosophically absolved himself for a lack of his habitual finesse. He was as much of a novice as Maddie. He'd never been in love before.

"Deveryn, you told me once that you knew, you knew . . ."

"Yes?"

". . . how to prevent conception," she finished in a rush. "Did you? Is it possible that I'm . . ."

He scowled at her. "Of course I didn't, and it's very possible," he retorted baldly.

"But why?" she wailed.

"Because," he answered with ruthless honesty, "It's beyond my power to withdraw from you once you start your caterwauling."

"What are you talking about?"

"Your pleasure sounds."

"I? I make sounds?" she asked indignantly. Her cheeks were pink with embarrassment.

He was totally captivated. "I assure you, darling, I've already decided that the only suitable place for our bed-chamber is at the top of the house and well away from the nursery and the servants' staircase. You see, I want to hear you when I don't have my hand over your mouth."

A fiery bloom flamed from her hairline to her bare toes. "You're . . . you're disgusting!"

"No," he said, and extended his hand palm up. "Only a very hot-blooded husband who happens to be in love with his wife. Now come here."

"What for?" she hedged.

"Maddie," he warned, "just do as I say.

She crossed the room with slow, halting steps, and came to stand just out of arm's reach. Wordlessly, he raised his open palm. She edged closer, assessing the determined set of his mouth. With a little sigh of resignation, she placed her hand

254

in his. He pounced on her and dragged her across his lap, stifling her startled squeal of fright with a hard kiss.

His eyes mocked her. "May I be permitted to say, Lady Deveryn, that I love the way you roll your 'r's' in bed?"

"No, you may not! And you're a d—"

Again, he kissed her into silence.

He drew back his head and observed with a smirk the brown eyes pooling to black as he filled his hands with her breasts.

"Jason," she murmured, "what did you mean when you said that you couldn't withdraw when I made those sounds?"

He wasn't about to tell her. The minx could persuade him to anything if she put her mind to it. Almost. But never that, he resolved.

He fumbled for the belt of her wrapper and eased it open, bending her head back over one arm, exposing the hardening peaks for his delectation.

"Bite your tongue, Lady Deveryn, and roll your 'r's,'" he said suggestively.

Within minutes, his hand was cupping her mouth.

Chapter Sixteen

The first wave of morning sickness hit Maddie minutes after Rosie had delivered her pre-breakfast cup of hot chocolate. She put it down to fatigue. There had been little respite, during a long night of passion, from the sensual delights Deveryn had been so eager to teach her. She'd been no less eager a pupil, if truth were told, though she'd tried not to show it. He had said as much. She'd protested quite long and eloquently. She might have saved her breath to cool her porridge. At the thought of such unpalatable fare, her stomach heaved and she made a dash for the commode in the closet.

When Rosie returned some time later, she found Maddie huddled in bed. The cup of chocolate was on the bedside table, untouched.

"It must have been something I ate at dinner," said Maddie, though she couldn't remember a thing after the cod's head.

Rosie, a motherly type, was in her element. The young miss was in no position to argue when she began her fussing. She banked up the fire. She bathed Maddie's hands and face with a washcloth wrung out in tepid water. At Maddie's request, she went to the kitchen and fetched a glass of hot water and salt so that Maddie could gargle and clean out her mouth. On her own initiative, she brought along a carafe of lemon and barley water and urged Maddie to drink it. Maddie gratefully accepted Rosie's ministrations. Before she drifted off to sleep, she asked the maid to tell her hostess only that she'd had a restless night and would sleep till luncheon.

Deveryn heard the tale from young Sophie as he prepared to

mount up with the earl and lead a party of riders on a tour of the park and its environs. Maddie had not appeared for luncheon, but that meant little. She might have been anywhere in the house or grounds and dinner was the only meal with any semblance of formality where everyone was expected to dine at the same time.

Not finding her with the others in the stable block, he anxiously scanned the surrounding park. He was not forgetting Maddie's near disastrous fall from her horse the day before.

"She's feeling a bit under the weather."

Deveryn quickly glanced around and caught Sophie's innocent expression. One brow arched. "Who is?" he asked with a carefully blank expression.

"Miss Sinclair. I've just come from her room. She had a restless night. She's still sleeping."

"Miss Sinclair? Ah yes! That would be Mary's friend," he said with affected indifference, and had the presence of mind to turn away to conceal the flicker of a smile which twitched his lips. He busied himself tightening 'Thelo's girth.

"Oh oh!" exclaimed Sophie *sotto voce.* "Here comes 'The Toast.' What a disagreeable girl! I can't think what Maddie sees in her."

Deveryn rested one hand on the pommel of 'Thelo's saddle and turned slightly to take in the arrival of the tardy beauty. He'd never really given Lady Elizabeth a second glance, but Sophie's words had piqued his interest. Lady Elizabeth owed her invitation to Dunsdale to the strength of her friendship for Maddie. Yet, if his mother was to be believed, the girl's manner toward Maddie had inexplicably turned cool.

Through the veil of his thick lashes, he watched the beauty's approach. Dolly Ramides, he mused, could not have demonstrated better stage presence than Lady Elizabeth Heatherington as she accepted the homage of her court. She was flanked by Toby Blanchard and Freddie Ponsonby who positively fawned each time she batted her eyelashes and flashed her brilliant smile. When her eyes lit on Deveryn, the smile became dazzling. He recognized the studied allure behind the quickly averted gaze.

Max Branwell approached the viscount and said conversationally, "I see the Beauty has recovered from her fit of the sullens."

"It would seem so. What brought them on?" asked Deveryn carelessly.

"Miss Sinclair stole her thunder."

"What?"

"Oh, it was done unconsciously, but very effectively. It won't be soon forgiven. She has claws, that one. I hope she doesn't sink them into Miss Sinclair."

"Let her try!"

"Oho!" laughed Max. "It's like that, is it?" He ignored his brother-in-law's tightening jaw. "If I were you, old boy, I'd set up a mild flirtation with the lady. That would be Miss Sinclair's best protection, in my humble opinion."

Deveryn answered noncommittally, but as he rode out over the cobbled stable-yard, he reflected on the mystery of what attracted a man to a particular woman. Why Maddie? Why not Lady Elizabeth? She was the daughter of an earl, uncommonly beautiful, possessed a certain intelligence, knew her way about Society, and—his eyes flicked to her slender form sheathed in an olive green riding habit—and her dress sense was impeccable. But the sum of the various parts amounted to nothing, excited him in no wise. Cynthia Sinclair was preferable. Dolly Ramides even more so. And these ladies had lost their allure. But Maddie—the very thought of her made the blood drum in his veins. Unpredictable Maddie with her fiery temper, tempting him with her worldly innocence, crossing him at every turn, compelling him to laughter with her ready humour, taking him down a peg or two with her sharp tongue.

Ten minutes out, and he leaned low in the saddle and whispered the word of command in 'Thelo's ear. The gallop became an awkward lope, and suddenly the big stallion sank to its knees. The other riders caught up to them.

"You go on, sir," he called to the earl. "'Thelo has developed a limp. I'd best have it seen to."

"Rotten luck!" someone commiserated.

"I'll go back with you," offered Max Branwell with a curiously bland expression.

Lady Mary, fortunately, came up just then. "He's not a baby, Max. Stop fussing. Do let us go on."

Deveryn waited till the line of riders had crested the first rise. He patted 'Thelo affectionately and turned back toward the house. 'Thelo's limp was nowhere in evidence.

There was no question, in broad daylight, of gaining entrance to Maddie's chamber by climbing the branch of the old laburnum tree that just grazed the iron railings of the balcony. He entered the house and made boldly for her door. He tapped once. No answer. He turned the doorknob and entered. He was careful to lock the door behind him.

She was stretched out on top of the bed in chemise and drawers. The quilted coverlet had slipped to the floor. Laid out on a chair was her brown riding habit, stockings and stays. Maddie had evidently planned to go riding and thought better of it.

He crossed to the bedside table and lifted the glass from the top of a half-empty carafe of some cloudy liquid. He sniffed. Barley water. He replaced the glass. Some ladies claimed that they owed their fine-pored complexions to the harmless and utterly tasteless swill. It was the first sign of vanity he had detected in her. He smiled.

He dropped a kiss on her nose.

"Rosie," she crooned, "you're so, so good to me." But she did not waken.

He straightened. Silently and without haste, he undressed himself, carefully arranging his garments on the chair by the dressing table. He padded back to the bed and climbed in beside Maddie.

He brushed the backs of his fingertips against her nipples through the fine linen chemise. The nipples puckered. Maddie purred—but slept on.

He untied the strings of her drawers and eased them open. His hand slipped inside and brushed lightly against the amber silken screen that hid her secret core.

"Mmm," she moaned, and her knees fell open.

He waited till the pounding in his loins had become bearable. "Wake up, Maddie," he whispered, his voice rough with passion. Maddie's sigh was low and languid.

The tips of his fingers found the entrance to her body and slipped inside.

"Maddie, you're so soft," he murmured in her ear. "Your heat draws me like a moth to flame."

"Henry?" she purred dreamily.

"Henry?"

He drew back and glared down at her. Her eyes were tightly closed, and her lips were turned up at the corners. She opened one eye.

"Fee, fie, fo, fum," she chirped. "I smell the blood of an Englishman," and she convulsed in silent laughter, hiding her face in the pillow.

"You witch!" he groaned. "I'll teach you to play games with me."

He dragged her drawers to her ankles and her chemise over her head, stilling her movements with his powerful body.

"Jason," she protested weakly, "Rosie will be back any minute now. Cook is coddling an egg for me. You really must go. It was only a joke."

He had her exactly where he wanted her—astride his lap. "Sweetheart," he murmured, "this is no joke. See," and his fingers curled round the back of her hand, and he brought it to the proof of his desire for her.

"Oh," she said, and involuntarily curled her fingers around the throbbing length of his shaft. Deveryn moaned and threw back his head.

The doorknob rattled. Maddie clutched convulsively at Deveryn.

He sucked in his breath, and between pain and pleasure he ground out, "For God's sake, woman, have a care," and he dragged her frozen hand from his manhood.

"It's Rosie," she mouthed silently.

"Get rid of her," he mouthed back.

"How?"

"That's your problem. The joke's on you. Tit for tat, darling."

"What?"

"You'll see," and he flashed her a salacious grin.

An impatient rap on the door had Maddie go rigid.

"Yes?" she warbled.

"It's Rosie with your coddled egg, Miss Sinclair. But the door's stuck. I can't seem to open it."

"Put your hands on my shoulders," said Deveryn, and Maddie did.

"Rosie, I've changed my mind, thank you, but I don't think I could face a coddled egg at the moment," Maddie's voice held an edge of desperation.

"Lift up," murmured Deveryn in her ear.

"What?" She was totally distracted by having to carry on two conversations simultaneously.

"Lift up," he commanded softly.

Maddie obediently rose on her knees.

"Are you all right, Miss Sinclair?" came Rosie's muffled voice through the locked door.

"Perfectly, thank you. I thought I'd get dressed and go for a breath of fresh air."

"Well, if you're sure. Oh, by the by, you haven't seen anything of Lord Deveryn from your window, have you? Her ladyship thought she saw him approaching the house."

Maddie looked down on a perfectly nude Lord Deveryn.

"No, no, I haven't seen any of him, I mean *anything* of him at all!" she quickly corrected.

Deveryn's hands on her flanks inexorably urged her down. Her silent struggles to evade his intent were unavailing. Inch by slow inch, he eased himself into her body.

She cried out and clung to his neck.

"What was that, miss?"

"I . . . I stubbed my toe."

"Mm!"

After a moment, Rosie's footsteps could be heard retreating down the long corridor.

"You devil!" Maddie groaned. "Have you no shame?"

"You misjudge me," he groaned. "You always wanted to ride roughshod over the English. Now's your chance."

He used his hands on her hips to hint her into motion. She caught on quickly.

"Maddie, this is . . . this is . . . agony."

His features were carved in sensual lines, his eyes half closed. Perspiration beaded his smooth upper lip. Under her hands, the muscles of his shoulders strained taut.

"Good Englishman," she taunted. "I want you to suffer. I'm not forgetting all the points you scored last night at the dinner table. Besides, there are centuries of old scores that have still to be settled."

262

She came down on him slowly, showing no mercy. *"This,"* she said, "is for Sherrifmuir, and *this* is for Harlaw, and . . ."

"Maddie, Maddie," he protested through gritted teeth, "those were only skirmishes."

"Oh, very well then. Though I'd thought to save the battles for later. *This* is for Flodden Field, and *this* is for Culloden, and *this* is for Wexford."

His fingers sank into her flanks to still her movements. "Maddie," he said hoarsely, "that last was in Ireland."

"Oh, I'm broad-minded," she crowed.

Without warning, he hooked one powerful arm around her waist, and he swept her beneath him, their bodies still coupled. He took his weight on one hand, and carefully swept tendrils of unruly locks from her face. Their breathing was ragged. His eyes were soft with emotion.

"Maddie," he said, "you're doing this all wrong. Let me show you. *This,"* he said, and buried himself inside her, *"this* is because I love you, and *this* is because I love you, and *this* . . ."

"Jason," she said, "Oh Jason!"

He took her pleasure cry into his mouth.

Maddie's morning sickness continued to assail her for the first hour or two immediately after waking. As a result she took to eating sparingly and changed the hour for her daily ride to early of an afternoon. The nausea conveyed little to her except perhaps that the change of cuisine at Dunsdale was in some perplexing way upsetting to her digestion. Only Rosie was privy to the discomfort the girl endured, and since Maddie was an unmarried lady, or so Rosie thought, she said nothing that might have alerted her to the proper origin of her bothersome disorder.

Deveryn, who might have divined the cause of Maddie's complaint at once, was not in a position to know, for although he came to Maddie's chamber every night to exercise his conjugal rights, he was careful to leave long before the first pale shaft of light lit up the eastern horizon.

Before long, Maddie began to dread his nightly visits. She soon came to feel that no pleasure on earth could ever compensate for the distress she experienced with Deveryn's relations. With Lady Mary and Sophie, she was able to be natural, but with the earl and his countess, she felt tongue-tied and utterly wretched as if she had in some sort betrayed their trust, which she felt she had. Her wretchedness was compounded by the fact that Lady Rossmere seemed to go out of her way to make her feel at home and invited confidences. Maddie could not conceive a happier home nor a more convivial family, and the more she came to like and respect the Verneys, the more odious did she judge her own conduct. She took to avoiding her hostess's presence whenever she could do so without giving offence. If Lady Rossmere noticed, she did not remark upon it.

Deveryn brushed off Maddie's misgivings with an indifference which she could not like.

"Don't you feel any guilt at all for what we are doing?" she asked him one night as he methodically removed his garments.

"What are we doing?" he asked.

"We're deceiving your family."

His eyes caught and held hers in the dressing table mirror. She could not read their expression. She laid aside the comb she had been idly pulling through her hair when he came to stand behind her. His hands cupped her shoulders and he dragged her back against his thighs. He leaned over and brushed her lips with his own in a long lingering caress.

"Come to bed," he said.

"You haven't answered my question."

"It won't be for much longer. Now come to bed. I've been impatient for you since the moment I left you this morning."

"Is this all you can think about?" she asked, but she allowed him to lead her to the bed just the same.

"Yes," he said simply. "Does that shock you?"

It did, but he did not wait for her answer, and very soon thereafter, it was all that Maddie could think about as well.

Deveryn's devotion to Maddie in the long hours of the night was matched by an equal indifference which he displayed on other occasions. His neglect was a small source of irritation, not least because he seemed to have attached himself to Lady Elizabeth's court of admirers. It would have surprised Maddie to learn that only two people present misconstrued the viscount's mild interest in the beauty—herself and the lady

264

in question.

Lady Elizabeth's glacial reserve seemed to have melted at the edges, but Maddie could not be comfortable with someone whose regard was demonstrably fickle. And since Lady Elizabeth's preference seemed to be for masculine society, and she was scarcely able to show her face before one or other of the gentlemen attached himself to her person, Maddie's dislike was very easily concealed.

She threw herself into all the entertainments which were laid on and particularly enjoyed an excursion to the university town of Oxford, only an hour's drive away. She remembered that Malcolm had complained that his year at the university there had been a waste of time and that the undergraduates spent more hours in bawdy houses than they did at their studies. Her eyes avidly scanned the red bricked buildings but could detect nothing that did not appear eminently respectable.

The week drew quickly to a close and the houseparty began to break up. Mr. Scott was the first to take his leave. The other guests were due to leave on the Monday morning, but Mr. Scott had a boat to catch. He could never endure the tedious carriage ride from London to Edinburgh and was in the habit of taking the boat trip from Leith to Wapping whenever there was reason to come to London, a much more comfortable means of transportation as well as speedier, so he informed Maddie. He adjured her to try it some time and she promised to give it some thought.

She was sorry to see him go and thought that the dinner conversation would be predictably flat without his rapier intelligence and store of anecdotes to entertain the company. She had come to look upon the unusual Verney dinner debates as the high point of the day. She never knew what to expect. The subjects varied from the sublime to the ridiculous, but were unfailingly entertaining. Sometimes, where she felt she had some competence, she argued her point of view with vigour. At other times, she sat in silence, absorbing everything and filing it away for future reference.

It was a remark of Lady Caro's which got them started that evening. Apropos of nothing, she shocked the table by observing, "I have no creed. Truth is whatever I think it is."

The debate that raged after that deliberated challenge was fast and furious. Maddie listened in silence for some time and lost her patience. It seemed to her that everyone was talking in circles.

At one point, she struck in, "Lady Caro is right in this, at least: if there is no God, then everything is permissible. The fault in her logic is when she says that she has no creed. That *is* her creed."

"D'you mean," asked Toby Blanchard in some perplexity, "that if there is no God, then there is no right and wrong, and we can each go our own way?"

"Certainly, I do," Maddie stated unequivocally.

"Oh, I say, that's a bit far-fetched."

"If there is no God," challenged Maddie, "we are each free to go to the Devil in whichever way pleases us."

The counter-attack was instantaneous.

"What about common decency?" someone interjected.

"And a gentleman's code of honour?" said another.

But Maddie stood her ground. If she did not come off the victor, she took some comfort in knowing that she had at least fought her adversaries to a standstill.

"My dear," said the countess in a lull in the conversation, "where did you learn your philosophy?"

"From my minister, Mr. Moncrieff, Sunday by Sunday, as I listened to his sermons."

"I think I see your object, Miss Sinclair," said William Lamb with a thinly disguised sneer in his voice. "You would have us all become 'enthusiasts.' Is that not so?"

There was no more derogatory word he could have chosen. To be called an "enthusiast" was tantamount to being labelled a fanatic, or worse—a Methodist.

"No," demurred Maddie. "That was not my object. If anything, I merely wished to provoke you into thinking where your creed might not ultimately lead you."

"I salute you," he returned in the same disparaging tone. "And I envy you your principles. To be so absolute in one's conviction of right and wrong must have its own compensations. You will not take offence, I trust, if I continue to prefer my consolations?"

"Oh no," she responded, affecting a light tone to cover the

prick of conscience his words had suddenly evoked. "Theory and practice are two different entities. We are not so very different, after all." She studiously avoided Deveryn's gaze and became absorbed in pleating and unpleating her discarded table napkin. She was glad when Freddie Ponsonby turned the conversation into less argumentative channels.

"Good grief, Jason," he exclaimed, "I'd no idea one could get an education merely by attending church. Remind me sometime to take it up."

"I'll remind you now," said the viscount. "Tomorrow is Sunday. Naturally, there will be services in the chapel."

Freddie groaned and joined in the hilarity that was made at his expense.

Maddie chanced a quick look at Deveryn. He gazed at her dispassionately for a long moment then turned his attention to Lady Elizabeth. Maddie saw his lips move, but his words were drowned out by the heated conversation that was taking place between Freddie Ponsonby and Max Branwell. The beauty listened in silence as Deveryn concluded what he had to say, then she angled her head back and gurgled with laughter, her eyes slicing to Maddie. Maddie gave them both the back of her head.

Lady Caro sought her out later in the drawing room. She looked a little shame-faced.

"Sometimes," she said, "I say things just to shock people. I really am a believer, you know, and quite, quite devout."

"I guessed as much," said Maddie.

Lady Caro edged closer, endeavouring to make their conversation as private as possible. "Your Mr. Moncrieff sounds quite out of the ordinary. I wouldn't mind having him for my spiritual advisor. As it is . . .." she flashed a quick glance at her husband who, along with most of the gentlemen, including Deveryn, was paying court to Lady Elizabeth, "as it is, William just confuses me. It is he who has no creed, you know."

Maddie murmured something appropriate, but she felt far from comfortable at being cast as the recipient of Lady Caro's confidences. She sensed that the older girl looked to her for some sort of direction on the strength of the stand she had taken at the dinner table, and she felt like the worst sort of hypocrite.

When Deveryn came to her that night, he found her standing in the middle of the room, tears streaming from her eyes. He'd been expecting something of the sort after the conversation at the dinner table.

"There's no need for tears," he said, cradling her gently in his arms. "And they won't change my mind."

"What we're doing is wrong," she choked out.

"No."

He lost no time in undressing them both and leading her to the bed.

"Jason . . . please . . . don't."

His mouth cut off her weak protest, and his hands soon flamed her to a quivering, eager passion.

He used her as he'd never used her before, as if her initial reluctance had roused some demon in him that demanded she yield him the total control of her body.

"Tell me now," he said through deep, harsh breaths, his voice almost savage, "tell me now that you don't want this," and he held her at bay with one palm against her breasts, pushing her into the pillows, and he stroked her voluptuously to a mindless, rapturous climax.

It was only the beginning.

"Every inch of you belongs to me," he told her at one point and proved it to her by slow, possessive touches and profuse kisses where she had never imagined a man would kiss a woman. She was beyond shame. Her body had become an instrument for their mutual pleasure, and he let her know it.

When he finally came into her, the temper of his lovemaking changed. "Sweet Jesus, Maddie, when will you learn to give in to me? I'm your husband. I love you. You have no right to turn me away as if I had no claim to your affections."

Afterwards, he lavished her with tenderness. She fell asleep weeping into his neck.

She met him next as she descended the long staircase the following morning just before chapel services. He came out of the library as her foot touched the bottom step and she knew intuitively that he had been watching for her. She was aware of her heightened colour and could not bring herself to look directly into his eyes.

His voice was strained. "Take my arm. We'll go together."

She laid her fingers gingerly along the sleeve of his immaculate dove grey cutaway morning coat and allowed him to lead her to the private chapel in the east wing of the house. She had not forgotten that he'd promised to give her a wedding ceremony in Dunsdale's chapel if it would satisfy her scruples. She wondered if he remembered.

When they reached the double oak doors with their small leaded windowpanes, he turned aside to look out one of the long windows that gave out onto the park, as if he were about to show her something of interest. But he said under his breath, "Maddie, about what passed between us last night . . ."

"Not now, Deveryn!" she cut in, afraid that she might disgrace herself by bursting into tears. "There's no need to apologize for what happened."

His voice was rough with impatience. "I wasn't about to apologize for what happened last night. I did nothing to you that could conceivably be called wrong between a man and his wife. My offence, if offence it was, was in initiating you into too much and too quickly. It would have happened sooner or later. It will happen again." His voice gentled as he saw the blush that crept over her cheeks. "Maddie, I know how your mind works. I won't have you flay yourself for the natural expression of the affections we share as husband and wife. You're going to enter that chapel with a clear conscience, at least with respect to what we do in the privacy of our bedchamber. Do you understand?"

She could only nod her assent.

With the back of his fingers, he lightly brushed her cheek, a surreptitious movement that was private and very intimate. It made her feel warm all over.

"Good," he said, and rewarded her with one of his rare, unconsciously tender smiles.

As they entered the centre aisle, she dropped his arm. They walked past the rows of pews filled with servants to the family pews at the front of the chapel. At the altar, Deveryn genuflected. Maddie refrained. It was not part of her church tradition. He stepped aside to let her enter the pew ahead of him.

The countess turned her head as Maddie and Deveryn took

their places. There was a knowing gleam in her eye as she acknowledged their presence with a careful inclination of her head. Maddie felt suddenly conspicuous. All the Verneys occupied the first pew, except for Deveryn. That he had deliberately absented himself from his habitual place to sit with her was a calculated honour.

She stole a quick glance at him. His eyes were serious, his expression remote. She folded her hands in her lap and gave herself up to silent contemplation.

The service began. At the first prayer, everybody but Maddie sank to their knees. In her own church, she would have been standing. She felt awkward and did not know what she should do. Deveryn decided the matter for her. His hand closed round her wrist and he tugged her down to kneel beside him.

The experience of kneeling in God's presence at the side of the man who might or might not be her husband left her deeply shaken. A thousand damning thoughts seemed to circle in her head. She had given Deveryn the possession of her body, and he had used her with more intimacy than she'd ever thought possible. If he were not her husband, then she was no better than a Magdalena. She did not know how she could pray and by degrees, her chin sank to her breast.

She became conscious that worshippers were going forward to the altar rail to receive the elements of the Eucharist. Deveryn went with them. Maddie hung back. She felt herself to be in a state of sin and unworthy to take the sacrament. She wished she had never set foot in the chapel, and could not think how she would explain her reluctance to Deveryn when the service was over.

As Deveryn turned from the altar rail, his eyes fell on Maddie. She was still on her knees. It was evident that she had not thought of availing herself of the sacrament. As he drew near, he noted the long spikes of eyelashes, like fans against her cheek, beaded with moisture. The others would surmise that she had refused to go forward because of her Scottish tradition. He knew better. As he took his place beside her, he lashed her with silent, bitter reproach.

Maddie felt the chill of that censure and tried to convey with her eyes her anguished apology. She was met by an impenetrable wall of ice. At the chapel door, he deserted her and mingled with the other worshippers, the epitome of charm and affability. She could not help noting that it was Lady Elizabeth who had his arm as they idled their way to the dining room.

After a miserable lunch where Maddie was subjected to the indignity of watching Deveryn flirt outrageously with Lady Elizabeth, she wandered disconsolately to her chamber. She thought that Deveryn was wonderfully revenged. He had stolen her home, then her heart, and finally her honour. He swore that he loved her, yet it seemed that he had only one use for her. She wondered at her own love for a man she knew only superficially. And from what little she knew of him, she was sure she did not like him. But then love and liking, like theory and practice, were two different entities.

She wished there was some older and wiser lady whose counsel she could call upon. But her situation was so far beyond the pale that she knew she could never bring herself to confess any of it to anyone. Only to Deveryn, and he had shown a complete disregard for her feelings.

If they truly were married, as Deveryn said, and if he kept his promise to let her have a minister of the church perform a proper religious ceremony, she thought that honour would be satisfied. Only then would she be able to look the Countess of Rossmere in the eye.

Her spirits brightened a little at the thought, and she determined to broach the subject with Deveryn at the earliest opportunity.

The opportunity to speak with Deveryn was not to be hers. She learned from Lady Mary that her brother had taken it into his head to visit an old school friend who happened to be visiting mutual friends in Oxford, and that he was not expected to return till the following morning. Something in her expression, she thought, must have conveyed her distress, for the older girl added gently, "He promised Mama that he would be here to take his leave of her guests before they removed to town."

Maddie waited for him long into the night. Her vigil was in vain. Eventually, she blew out the candles and slipped into bed. Sleep was a long time in coming.

She awakened the second before his mouth covered hers.

The darkness was velvet, the heat of his body close to hers, like a warm blanket. His breath filled her mouth with the taste of brandy and stale tobacco smoke. But it was the scent on his skin which brought her rudely from the dark depths of slumber. He was drenched in the scent of some cheap, cloying perfume. Her fingers tangled in his hair, and she put every ounce of her strength into hauling his head back.

"You drunken lecher!" she cried out. "You stink of other women. You're not welcome in my bed, Deveryn. D'you understand? Go back to your lightskirts. Just leave me alone."

His hands closed round her wrists like iron manacles. She winced and thought that he would snap her fragile bones. The struggle was unequal. She released him and lay panting.

"Don't think I don't want to!" he told her savagely. "And don't think I haven't tried! An honest whore's welcome is preferable to what I get from my own wife."

"I'm not your wife," she shouted, struggling in earnest now to be released from his punishing hands. "And I'm glad that I'm not."

"Then what does that make you?" he sneered. "You're no better than the whores I've come from."

He regretted the words almost as soon as they fell from his lips. He'd had a hellish day. His night had been no better, not since he'd ridden out in a foul temper, vowing to himself that he'd give his little puritan wife something real to be sorry about.

He'd been taken aback by the remorse he had read in her whole demeanour when they had been in the chapel, and he'd damned her for it. Whilst he had been on his knees thanking the Deity, or Providence, or the Powers That Be for his good fortune, she had been prostrate with guilt. He'd known it when she had refused the sacrament. He'd seen it in the tear-bright eyes and head bowed in shame. Her unhappiness was a bitter rebuke to him.

In a mood of heedless anger, he had attempted to forget his sorrows in the time honoured way of gentlemen. But the inferior brandy and sensual delights of Mrs. Chapelstow's superior bawdy house had lost their efficacy. He had wanted to punish Maddie. He had ended up by punishing himself.

He had tried to stay away from her. It was beyond him. She

drew him like a magnet. He longed for the solace and reassurance that was to be found in her arms. Her rejection had cut him to the quick and had brought forth the spate of ugly words spilling from his own mouth.

"Maddie," he said, his voice deep, unsteady. "Try to understand. It's been hell for me. Those women . . . they're unimportant. They mean nothing to me."

With a tortured cry of rage, she flung herself at his head and lashed him wherever her nails fell, flaying him with her anger. He rolled on top of her and grasped her wrists, pinning them above her head. Her breasts and shoulders heaved with her furious sobs of impotence, but he held her down, compelling her to listen to him.

"Maddie, please," he begged. "It was a mistake. Nothing of any significance happened—nothing that makes one jot of difference to us. It's you I love. I'll be . . ."

"Don't!" she cut in furiously. "No love words, Deveryn. No remorse. I couldn't stand it. Just leave me alone. Everything is wrong for us. It has been from the first. Please, just go away."

She sensed his hesitation as he pulled back slightly. He released her wrists. A moment later, she felt the roughness of his thumb as it traced the path of the hot tears which spilled from the corners of her eyes and became lost in the tendrils of damp curls clinging to her cheeks.

"Don't cry, love," he said, expelling a ragged breath. "You can't know what it does to me."

She was ashamed of those telling tears, and that shame fueled her pride. Without thinking of the consequence, she surged against his chest and pushed him backwards, twisting and sliding her body from beneath his, desperately lunging away from him. Her chin and one shoulder were captured in a relentless grip and he jerked her back, controlling her effortlessly with the press of his weight.

The silence pulsed with leashed violence. His mouth was only inches from hers. She turned her face into the pillow to evade the flood of his breath as it broached her parted lips. His fingers sank into her hair and tightened cruelly as he dragged her head up. She tensed, waiting for his kiss.

It came—hot, open, demanding and blatantly aggressive— the primitive male subduing his mate. She fought him like

273

a jungle cat, clawing, kicking, bucking, rolling, arching away. He was implacable.

She kissed him back: hard, angry kisses, yielding him nothing. His tongue invaded her mouth and she fought to master it. He freed her wrists, and she wound her fingers into his hair, dragging him deeper into the embrace. His hands slid to the opening of her gown. Buttons scattered as he wrenched it open from throat to waist. His hand slipped inside and cupped one breast and his thumb grazed the swelling nipple, brushing it again and again with tantalizing butterfly strokes till Maddie moaned her anguished pleasure cries into his mouth.

He released her lips. Their breathing was harsh, erratic, laboured. He touched her in the most intimate way a man can touch a woman and she arched into the caress.

"Maddie. Let me love you," he pleaded.

She found it almost impossible to answer him for choked tears. Finally, she said, "I've no use for your love, Deveryn." And she lifted her head from the pillow to take his lips in a hungry demand, showing what she wanted from him.

He gave her his passion. He wanted to give her so much more. But her small rigid body lying silently beside his in the darkened room would permit no tenderness to pass between them. He left her long before daybreak.

Chapter Seventeen

Maddie had not been back in London for more than a fortnight before it was borne in upon her that she was with child. It was the little chambermaid who cleaned out the grates, a girl of no more than thirteen summers, who revealed what she had only begun to suspect.

Libby was as bright as a button and a bit of a chatterbox. She was also new to domestic service and had yet to acquire that impassive and wooden countenance which was so indispensable to those who wished to take up service in the stately homes of the Upper Ten Thousand.

She stopped in her labours as she heard Maddie retching behind the ornate silk screen. She sat back on her heels and wiped her grimy hands on a cloth which was tucked into the waistband of her bib-front apron.

Maddie appeared and groped her way to the bed. "I'll be as right as a trivet in a moment," she said, noting the small frown of concern which furrowed Libby's normally smooth brow. "A few mouthfuls of barley water usually settles my stomach," and with a small grimace of distaste she drank greedily from a glass which had been set on her bedside table.

"That's three days in a row," said Libby.

"Longer than that," corrected Maddie. She sat down on the edge of the bed and pinched her cheeks to bring back the colour. "My digestive system seems to be in a bit of an uproar. I can't fathom what could be wrong." She grinned at Libby to divest her next remark of any real malice. "England must not agree with me."

"If yer were m' ma, I'd say yer was in the family way," said Libby with characteristic forthrightness, and turned back to the empty grate to continue with the tedious task of blackening the iron grilles. She missed the sudden bloom of colour which flamed in Maddie's cheeks.

Maddie watched the maid's vigorous movements for some few moments. When she thought that the colour in her complexion had faded, she said carefully, "Libby, do you have many brothers and sisters?"

"There be eight little 'uns after me," said Libby without turning.

"Oh, you must know all that there is to know about having babies from watching your mother."

"I would say so."

Silence.

"I don't know anything at all, and I'm much older than you," said Maddie cautiously, striving for a neutral tone.

Libby's head swivelled round. She gazed at Maddie's slightly pink cheeks for a long considering moment. Comprehension slowly dawned. Her little flat chest puffed with self-importance. Brushes were downed and she settled herself to give the older girl the benefit of her superior knowledge.

"Arsk away," she said, and grinned like the cat that had just swallowed the canary.

"How does a woman know when she's in the family way?" asked Maddie without further encouragement.

"That's easy. First she gets sick somethin' awful; then she get's to wearin' a special dress; then she gets as round as a barrel."

"A special dress?" asked Maddie in some confusion.

"Yer can always tell," nodded Libby. "Next ter bein' sick, it's the best sign. Me ma always wears 'er blue dimity. That's why a'm 'ere now in service." She saw Maddie's blank look and said by way of explanation, "Last time she put it on, I said, 'Eer, we're not havin' another young 'un in the 'ouse are we? A'm sick an' tired of havin' babies ter look after.' Well, that did it. Me ma said 'twer time I was out an' earnin' a livin'. Now me younger sister stays 'ome an' 'elps take care o' the young 'uns.'"

"What if your mother didn't want to have babies. How

276

would she go about it?"

"Yer can't *not* 'ave babies if yer a married lady," said Libby in a superior tone, much in the manner of Maddie's tutor when his pupil was proving to be particularly obtuse. "Only if yer *not* married, and me ma told me afore I came into service 'ow ter keep meself from gettin' in the family way."

"How?" asked Maddie without prevarication.

Libby's voice dropped an octave, and she said slowly and deliberately, "Yer must never let a lad put 'is 'and on yer knee!"

"What?"

"It's what me ma told me," said Libby sagely. "He can 'old yer 'and, but yer must never let 'im put 'is 'and on yer knee."

Maddie regarded Libby's wise little face and said at length, "That's excellent advice, Libby. See that you follow it and no harm will come to you."

"Don't worry, miss, I will," averred Libby fervently. A sudden thought struck her. "'Ere, miss! You didn't let a lad put 'is 'and on *yer* knee, did yer?"

"Oh no, Libby," she answered, not quite truthfully, "never on my knee."

Libby nodded her silent approval. "Well then, yer all right, ain't yer?" and she went back to her blacking.

Maddie was only a little the wiser until she made a call in Berkley Square to confer with young Lady Rutherston about the paper on which they were collaborating for the next gathering of the Bluestocking Brigade.

"You're very good with the language, but I suppose you know that," said Catherine, slanting an admiring look at Maddie. "I'm going to feel like a fraud taking credit when you're the one who has done all the work."

"Think nothing of it," responded Maddie, idly polite, her thoughts grappling with the problem of how to introduce a subject which was of far more immediate importance to her. "You have children. You have other things to do with your time."

"It's nice of you to say so, but, as we both know, one can always find the time to do what one really wants to. I suppose I've developed other interests."

"And you're expecting another child," said Maddie,

doggedly following the scent which interested her. "Nausea is no laughing matter."

"What? Oh, I see. No, that's long since over. It only lasts for two or three weeks in the second month or so. I'm five months now."

Maddie's eyes surreptitiously swept over Lady Rutherston's slender figure.

"I see that surprises you," said Catherine. "That makes me feel so much better, especially since I've had to drag out this old thing to disguise my blooming proportions." She fingered a green silk frock with a rather full gored skirt which Maddie thought must be in the height of fashion. "I'll be tired to death of it before my confinement is upon me, and though I have others, they're all of them instantly recognizable."

Lord Rutherston chose that moment to put in an appearance. He intimated that he was on his way to Tattersal's in Hyde Park to look over some horseflesh. A few pleasantries were exchanged. He was more than politely interested when Catherine explained the reason for Maddie's visit.

"Miss Sinclair has come up with an interesting shade of meaning on some words which throws an unusual light on *Medea*," his wife told him.

"I'd like to stay and hear what you have to say," he said, turning his grey eyes upon Maddie. "Unfortunately, I'm bidding on some horses, and can't delay. Perhaps some other time?"

"That would be lovely," said Maddie, knowing intuitively that his words had not been uttered as a matter of form.

He bent his dark head and brushed Catherine's cheek with his lips. Maddie barely caught his murmured, "Your gown is very becoming. Now where have I seen it before?"

Lady Rutherston's reply was indistinct, but it startled a wicked bark of laughter from her husband.

When the marquess had taken his leave of the two ladies, Lady Rutherston turned back to Maddie and spoke in a musing tone. "You know, we could do it together."

"I beg your pardon?"

"This paper that I'm to present at our next meeting. We could do it together. How would it be if I gave a general perspective and you concentrated on *Medea* in particular?"

"I don't think that would be wise," Maddie prevaricated.

"Are you afraid to nail your colours to the mast?" asked Lady Rutherston quietly.

"What?"

"I think you know what I mean, Maddie. You're afraid to let it become general knowledge that you're an intelligent, educated young woman with a scholarly bent. I quite understand if that's what makes you hesitate."

"Oh no," she quickly denied, then considered Lady Rutherston's words more carefully. After a moment's quiet reflection, she looked up and said with a rueful grin, "D'you know, I think you're right. That's exactly what I'm afraid of. I don't think the world is ready yet to accept our breed of woman."

"It never will be until women themselves are willing to fly their true colours. It takes courage, I know."

Her look was so full of understanding and so expectant, that the words, "I'll do it," were out of Maddie's mouth before she could stop them.

"Good girl. And you're not wholly right about the world, you know. Some of it has already been converted. Take my husband, for instance."

Maddie gave the matter some thought as she made the short walk to her grandfather's house on Curzon Street. The Marquess of Rutherston must be an exception indeed if he did not find clever women an abomination. She wondered about Deveryn's father, the Earl of Rossmere. All the Verney women were clever, so Deveryn had once told her. She remembered that his tone had been faintly disparaging, conveying, to her ears, that amused masculine tolerance which she found so obnoxious. She did not think his father shared his sentiments, else his own daughters would have been raised as intelligent widgeons, which Lady Mary and Lady Sophie certainly were not. Her own daughters, she quickly resolved, would have the benefit of their mother's tutoring, whatever their father might have to say on the subject.

This proved to be an unhappy train of thought, for it was by no means certain that she'd decided to acknowledge the father of her unborn child. She'd scarcely had time to consider the implications of her momentous discovery, and the future was

279

something she preferred not to think about. She did a quick calculation and reckoned that she was about two months gone. Prevarication was a luxury she could no longer afford. One way or another, she had to make a decision about Deveryn.

She'd thought, when she'd left Dunsdale, that nothing on God's earth could ever induce her to come within hailing distance of him again. On that last morning, moments before she'd stepped into the carriage which was to take her back to London, he'd descended the front steps of the house and had mingled with the departing guests. She'd been shocked to see one side of his handsome face disfigured by deep scratches which puckered his skin from eyebrow to jawbone. Her own bruises were artfully covered by a silk scarf which she'd tied securely under her chin. But she'd felt self-conscious when she'd heard the ribald laughter of some of the gentlemen as they conversed in undertones as they had clapped him on the shoulder with something like amused envy. It was an acid remark from Lady Caro which had put her wise. His friends assumed that the scratches were the result of a wild night of carousing and wenching in the fleshpots of Oxford. The insight had done nothing to improve her temper. Her leave taking of the viscount was as chilly as she could make it, and he had not lingered by her side.

On the long carriage drive home, there had been plenty of time for reflection. His professions of love, she'd decided, were next to worthless in light of his subsequent actions. And she'd damned herself for a fool for allowing herself to succumb to his powerful attraction. Try as she might, she had not been able to prevent herself from dwelling on the intimacies they had shared as lovers. From there, it had been only a step away to imagining him sharing the same intimacies with the nameless, faceless women to whom he had gone in Oxford for his pleasure. She supposed, since they were women of experience, that he'd found her own artless responses somewhat lacking in comparison. Her thoughts had been torture to her. They still were.

Jealousy, she'd discovered, was the demon of all emotions, capable of afflicting its victims with a pain that was almost palpable. Deveryn was a devil. It was in his nature to have a roving eye. Women looked at him boldly and he returned their stares. She'd seen it at Drumoak with Cynthia. She'd observed the same phenomenon at Dunsdale with Lady Elizabeth. Even Lady Caro had not been averse to flirting with the rakish viscount. Flirting was one thing, thought Maddie, but she'd be damned before she'd put up with a "husband" who came to her with the scent of other women on his *skin*.

She'd made up her mind, on the long drive home from Oxford to London, that one way or another, she'd root him out of her heart. She'd tried to convince herself that she never wanted to see him again and hoped that their so-called "marriage" would be invalidated. She dwelt at length on all his iniquities, beginning with the fact that he'd cuckolded her father and given her home to his erstwhile mistress. She discovered that she hated him with a passion, but even that could not eclipse her love. She'd thought herself then the unhappiest and most ill-starred of women. That thought came back to torment her as she turned into Curzon Street. Pregnancy was a complication on which she had not counted.

When she entered her grandfather's house, she made straight for her chamber. Once there, she sat down at her elegant escritoire and extracted a sheet of paper from a drawer. At the top of the page, in pencil, she wrote the word, *problem* and underneath, the word *baby*. Her mind then grappled with solutions. After half an hour, she'd come up with ten, all recorded neatly. One by one she eliminated the more far-fetched ideas till her list was reduced to four: Tell Deveryn; Tell Grandfather; Marry Raeburn; Go home. After a moment's reflection, she eliminated a further two. That left her with "Tell Deveryn" and "Go home."

She crumpled the paper into a ball and tossed it in the fire, watching till the flames licked round it and burned it to white ash. She began again with a fresh piece of paper. This time, she wrote only one word at the top of the page—"Home." She stared at the word for a long time before that sheet of paper was also discarded and tossed on the flames.

She had no home. Even if she went to Scotland, without Drumoak, she had no means of supporting herself and could not now, in her condition, find employment. Furthermore, she would have to go into hiding since she was still under age. She wondered fleetingly at a country whose laws permitted a woman, on the one hand, to marry the man of her choice when she was sixteen years old, and on the other, kept her a minor till she was one and twenty. But then, Deveryn had never been her choice, not really. There were no laws, as far as she could see, which vouchsafed any kind of liberty to a woman if some man wished to flaunt them.

Tell Deveryn. Tell Deveryn—the words seemed to drum in her head. What choice did she have? Without a penny to call her own, she was stymied, and she knew it. For all her fine clothes and grand style of living, she might as well have been a pauper. She'd heard herself called an heiress. That was a joke, only she did not feel like laughing. A woman never had control of her own fortune. And like her property, she too would be passed from the control of one man to another—her father, her guardian, her husband. She supposed that when she was old, and if she outlived her husband, her sons would have the management of her person and property. Intolerable!

To escape her unhappy thoughts, for the next day or so, she immersed herself in preparing her paper on *Medea*. There was the odd outing in Raeburn's carriage, Miss Spencer always in attendance to Maddie's great relief, but there was little offered in the way of more elaborate entertainments. The Season was not yet in full swing, and Maddie's engagements in society were confined mostly to musical evenings and small gatherings in the homes of ladies whose acquaintance she had made through the offices of her aunt.

Her first party of any major consequence was scheduled for Saturday night—not a ball by any means, but a glittering affair for all that. They were invited to attend a soirée in the Prince Regent's private residence, Carlton House. Maddie had heard from the little housemaid, Libby, that all the great town houses in Mayfair were in a state of readiness for the return from their country estates of the blue-blooded aristocrats who were fortunate enough to secure one of the invitations to so illustrious an event. She wondered if Deveryn would be there, and what she should say to him if he were.

By the time Saturday night rolled round, her nerves were on edge. She paced her room, rehearsing for the thousandth time in her head what she would say to the father of her unborn child. She did not think she could bring herself to the point unless she had some assurance that he would be a faithful husband. And then she thought that there was nothing he could say, in light of his history, that would ever convince her of his fidelity.

She was saved from further gloomy reflection by the entrance of the upstairs abigail whom she shared with her aunt. Over Bertha's arm was the dress that Maddie was to wear at the Carlton House soirée that evening. Of pale lavender silk tissue and heavily embroidered at the square cut bodice and hem with silver thread, its resemblance to mourning dress, in Maddie's opinion, was slight. She had a leisurely bath, and allowed Bertha to dress her without a murmur. She was putting the finishing touches to her toilette when a velvet box was delivered to her bedroom door. Inside was a rope of diamonds for her hair and diamond droplet earrings to match. On the note which accompanied it, in her grandfather's spidery scrawl was written, "Wear these just for tonight. They were your grandmother's, and it would please me to see them on you."

How could she refuse? She thought that it would be a very long time, if ever again, before her grandfather would be gratified by anything his granddaughter might do. Obedient to his wishes, she allowed Bertha to adorn her with the priceless gems.

They were the first thing that drew Deveryn's eye as Maddie entered the octagonal vestibule of Carlton House on her grandfather's arm. He had positioned himself on the gallery above so that he could watch for her entrance. Though all the rooms of state were on street level, some upstairs chambers had been reserved as cloakrooms and retiring rooms. It was inevitable that Maddie cross the marble floor of the Octagon to reach the Oval Staircase. When she did, Deveryn was there to feast his eyes on her.

He thought that he had never seen her look more beautiful. In the months since he had known her, she had allowed her hair to grow. It was no longer an unruly mop of curls but the elegant coiffure of a lady of fashion with wanton tendrils artfully brought forward to frame her face. Under the brilliance of the gilt chandelier, her tresses shone like burnished copper. As her head moved, diamonds flashed in her hair and at her ears. Her skin, he thought, looked as soft as the silk of her gown which showed at the edges of her dark mantle. Though she was smiling, it seemed to him that there was an aura of sadness about her. He had thought, once, that he could banish that look forever.

Maddie's eyes swept up and travelled the press of people in the gallery. They alighted on Deveryn and passed on, then quickly returned. He tried to capture her gaze but only succeeded in driving down the long sweep of her lashes, like shades on windows, blacking out the probing rays of the sun.

As she brushed past the scarlet and gold draped curtains of the arched entrance to the Oval Staircase, Maddie's steps slowed to allow her aunt to catch up with them.

Miss Spencer was in transports. "This is beyond anything. No wonder Carlton House is extolled as the finest royal residence in Europe. And we haven't even begun to see its treasures." She drew in her breath. "So this is the famous Oval Staircase. It's . . . it's . . . ," she floundered for words, her eyes darting up the long graceful sweep of granite green walls with decorative arches in intricate white and gold plaster work.

"Magnificent," supplied Samuel Spencer, "also Baroque. Don't miss the Rococo pedestal clock on the landing below. I was instrumental in acquiring that little piece for His Highness."

As they followed the press of people up the cantilevered staircase, Maddie listened with half an ear as her grandfather drew the ladies' attention to various architectural details, and she dutifully let her eyes wander up over the sumptuous blue and gold lace-like balustrade and beyond, to the glazed dome high above in the roof. Inwardly, she was striving for composure for that first face to face encounter with Deveryn since Oxfordshire.

When they stepped into the gallery, her eyes could not find him. Her first feeling was one of relief. A moment's consideration, and her relief was replaced by unease. Deveryn, it appeared, was trying to avoid her.

Her unhappy thoughts stayed with her until she stepped into the Crimson Drawing Room on the ground floor.

"It's . . . it's . . . ," she stammered.

"Magnificent," supplied Miss Spencer with a touch of smugness.

Samuel Spencer merely murmured, "Save your superlatives, Nellie. You'll need them for the Circular Room." He spoke in Maddie's ear. "Who do you think supplied the crimson damask?"

The walls, the windows, the upholstery were all done in crimson satin. Maddie looked a question at her grandfather.

"Yes, yours truly," he replied with more than a hint of pride. "And it's British through and through, specially woven for the Prince in one of my own factories. And the Rubens on the wall over there," Maddie followed her grandfather's gaze to one of the many gilt-framed masterpieces which adorned the walls, "I got that for him at Christie's for a veritable song. Yarmouth was beside himself."

Like her grandfather, the Earl of Yarmouth was a collector and also acted for the Prince Regent in finding and purchasing acquisitions for Carlton House. Though there was a certain rivalry between Samuel Spencer and the younger earl, as was only natural, they were often to be seen in each other's company at Christie's and at house sales in and around London. Maddie listened attentively as her grandfather drew her attention to other *objets d'art* which he had procured for his Prince.

She knew that her grandfather considered his presence at Carlton House that evening as the acme of his ambitions. He had confided his sentiments when the gilt-edged invitation card had arrived in Curzon Street. Though he'd been often in the Price Regent's private residence, and had the Prince's confidence to some extent, his lack of gentle birth had precluded his entry to the more select affairs in mixed company. In short, as he'd told Maddie, though he found a warm reception at the Prince's levees where only gentlemen were present, he did not aspire so high as the drawing rooms where their wives and daughters mingled with the *crème de la crème* of Polite Society.

"And d' you know why all doors are now open to me?" he'd asked.

"No," she'd answered cautiously.

"Because of Raeburn. The duke may not have a feather to fly with but he's accepted everywhere. And he'll soon be part of the family. That's why."

She'd been on the point of disputing her grandfather's assumptions, and then had thought better of it. It was an argument she was quite sure she could not win and might lead her into all sorts of difficulties. Some part of her brain—the craven part, she'd admitted guiltily—had decided it was better for the moment to let sleeping dogs lie. The thought of confiding to her grandfather the intelligence that she was with child to a man who might or might not be her husband was enough to give her hysterics.

She tried to put the conversation from her mind as they approached the black and gold doors which gave entrance to the Circular Room where the Prince Regent was receiving. She'd been told that the party that night was to be very informal. Even so, butterflies began to stir and flutter in her stomach. She hoped that when she was presented, she would not disgrace herself or forget everything she had been taught by her tutor.

The blaze of crimson and gold suddenly gave way to the more muted and restful tones of blue and silver. A forest of dark crimson Ionic columns seemed to hold up the ceiling which was painted to resemble the blue vault of the heavens. The brilliant glare from the several elaborate crystal chandeliers was reflected from an equal number of long pier glasses which adorned the walls. Though the motif of the vast chamber was predominantly Greek, Maddie felt that the emperor Nero could not have found a more suitable setting.

She regretted that uncharitable thought a moment later. The Prince, she decided, was no Nero. He exuded charm and affability and was everything that was gracious. As for herself, she could never afterwards remember whether she had curtsied or uttered a single word to any of his pleasantries. Her grandfather showed more presence of mind. He made some complimentary remarks about the latest renovations to the house and His Highness could not have been more gratified.

Their time with the Prince was very brief, and soon they were free to wander at will. Scarlet and gold liveried footmen, like a regiment of well-trained dragoons, dispensed a selection of beverages from silver salvers. And for those who wished to sample the culinary delights for which Carlton House was justly famous, tables loaded with every kind of delicacy were laid out in two of the ante-rooms.

Maddie had just accepted one of the beverages, ratafia to her great disappointment, when the Duke of Raeburn approached. She gave him a civil though cautious welcome. Her aunt was more effusive. He engaged to show the ladies the treasures of the house, particularly the paintings, since Samuel Spencer had been waylaid by Lord Yarmouth. It was to Miss Spencer that he offered his arm. Maddie tagged along behind, as if she had been a chaperone.

It was inevitable that they became separated, for the crush of people exerted an irresistible pull. Maddie scarcely noticed. Her eyes travelled the assembly with avid interest. She had the pleasure of meeting many acquaintances, though there was one whose society she later wished she had avoided.

She had wandered up to the gallery which overlooked the Octagon. Lady Elizabeth Heatherington was at the rail waiting, so she informed Maddie with an arch smile, for Lord Deveryn to procure her a glass of champagne. Maddie resisted her first impulse to disappear into the crush. She'd made up her mind to speak to him. And though the setting was too public to allow of any prolonged conversation of a personal nature, it would take only a moment to arrange a more suitable time and place for a private interview.

"I had the pleasure of meeting a relative of yours," said Lady Elizabeth, carefully avoiding Maddie's eyes. "Lord Deveryn made her known to me."

Maddie asked the question though she already knew the answer. "Who might that be?"

"Your stepmother, Cynthia Sinclair."

"How nice," said Maddie. She knew that something more was expected of her, but just to hear Deveryn's name linked with her stepmother's opened an old wound. She did not think she could speak without betraying herself.

Lady Elizabeth was not to be deterred by Maddie's reticence. "The poor woman is quite friendless. If it weren't for Lord Deveryn, she would be isolated in that house on Baker Street."

The reproach in Lady Elizabeth's tone was thinly veiled. Maddie bore it with iron restraint.

"I collect you've made a friend of the lady," she said, studiously neutral, though a thousand suspicions were

287

churning in her mind. Deveryn and Cynthia together in London when all the time she had thought him still at Dunsdale! Her isolation in Curzon Street, so it would seem, had not the power to move him as . . .

"It was the least I could do in the circumstances," said Lady Elizabeth breaking into Maddie's train of thought. "Jason asked me to keep an eye on her, introduce her a little into society. I was happy to be in a position to oblige him in this small favour."

Maddie managed a convincing smile. "Does Deveryn have a particular interest in my stepmother, then? Is there a wedding there in the offing, d'you suppose?" She had no idea what had made her say those words.

Lady Elizabeth was genuinely shocked. "Good Lord, no. Cynthia Sinclair, as you well know, is in mourning. Deveryn was an intimate of her late husband. He has a strong sense of obligation for your father's widow." Her tone suggested, thought Maddie, that her lack in that respect left much to be desired.

"You would seem to be in his lordship's confidence," Maddie suggested.

"I suppose I am."

Maddie felt the covert scrutiny of a pair of cool blue eyes, not the opaque and intense blue of Deveryn's, but a polar hue, like, she surmised, the Arctic Ocean. Intuitively she recognized that the beauty's dislike of her had become immutable. On first acquaintance, she had been of a friendlier disposition, and Maddie wondered if it was Deveryn who was responsible for giving Lady Elizabeth this barely concealed disgust of her.

"I no longer see anything of my stepmother," she said at last, breaking the silence.

"No. So Jason tells me," returned Lady Elizabeth.

Annoyance licked through Maddie like flaming brandy. She felt the grind of her teeth and made a conscious effort to relax her stiff jaw. *What did you expect?*—she jeered at herself inwardly—*discretion? loyalty?* That Deveryn, she would not deign to give him his Christian name, had dared to mention any of her circumstances to a stranger was not to be borne. One word and she could exonerate herself and blacken her stepmother's character beyond redemption. She wanted to say that word and could not think what prevented her from doing so.

The first wave of her anger ebbed, leaving her shaken and vaguely self-contemptuous. From the corner of her eye, she saw Deveryn approach holding aloft two champagne glasses. Her first thought, that blonds looked marvellous in black, brought a quick resurgence of anger. He was too masculine, too handsome, too graceful, too urbane, too confident. Everything about him was exaggerated, and most of all the brilliant smile he flashed her when Lady Elizabeth's attention was distracted. The urge to bait him was irresistible.

"Lady Elizabeth tells me you've more or less taken my stepmother under your protection," she murmured provocatively and raised the glass of ratafia which she'd been clutching in her hand. She avoided his eyes and let her gaze wander to the elegants who crisscrossed the floor of the Octagon below.

"It's not necessary to thank me," he answered quietly and with equal provocation. "It was the least I could do. The lady's circumstances are not happy."

"So I'm given to understand," she replied, and sipped delicately from the crystal glass in her hand. To be drinking ratafia when the two sophisticates at her side were enjoying champagne irked her beyond reason. A sideways glance at Deveryn's roguish grin convinced her that her "husband" knew exactly what was going through her mind. When she could unclamp her teeth, she said with only the merest trace of venom in her voice, "It's very good of you, Lord Deveryn, to stand in the role of a *brother* to my father's widow."

He did not answer and she allowed her eyes to lift innocently to his. She was prepared for a sudden blaze of anger, and was surprised to see him looking grave and with something like regret in his expression.

Lady Elizabeth, detecting a slur in Maddie's last observation, but by no means sure what was implied, hastened into speech to demolish the chit who dared fence with a gentleman in whom she had developed a proprietary interest. "Cynthia Sinclair," she said succinctly, "is in mourning. Naturally her friends wish to comfort her in her time of grief," and her eyes made a critical survey of Maddie's lavender silk and the diamonds at her ears and in her hair.

A flush heated Maddie's cheekbones. The insolent perusal and veiled reference to her own lack of mourning dress could not have been more cutting. Nor would she or could she defend herself from such barbs without revealing the intimate details of her personal life. Her composure was badly shaken. She covered it by calling one of the liveried footmen and placing her half-empty glass on the tray on his arm. When she turned back to her companions, the flush had faded from her skin and a polite half-smile was in place.

"Charmed to see you both again," she murmured. "Pray excuse me. My grandfather must think I've become lost."

She had no thought now of arranging a quiet tête à tête with Lord Deveryn to inform him of her unhappy plight. Quite the reverse! Nothing could prevail upon her to take him into her confidence. Women were obviously his weakness. Cynthia Sinclair in particular. She herself was just another conquest whom he'd "married" out of a sense of obligation. She had too much pride to put herself in the position of suppliant to his benefactor. He could have Cynthia Sinclair and Lady Elizabeth and all the women he wanted with her goodwill. But he would never have her. And because she knew that her angry thoughts were nothing but bravado, she grew more vexed than ever.

She had no idea where her feet were taking her. They moved, and she followed. Half a dozen steps took her through the arch to the Oval Staircase. Some of the guests were descending the stairs intent on taking in the famous conservatory on the garden level in the basement. On Maddie's left, the stairs continued up, though they were roped off. Without thinking of consequences, she unhitched the rope, quickly replaced it and went sprinting up the stairs. At the head of the staircase, she came out onto the upper gallery. It was lit by two ornate lanterns which cast deep shadows in the several decorative arched alcoves. There was no exit that she could see. Maddie moved to the centre rail and looked down. Two floors below, she could see people moving about in the Octagon. One floor below was the gallery she had just fled. Lady Elizabeth's dark head was bent over the railing. If Deveryn were there, Maddie did not see him. Cautiously, she stepped away from the balustrade.

Without warning, an arm clamped around Maddie's waist. An involuntary scream rose in her throat, but before she could utter it, a smothering hand covered her mouth.

"Don't be alarmed," an amused masculine voice said in her ear. "It's only your husband," and he spun her to face him. "Maddie," he said, "it's over. The waiting is over."

"You can go to . . ."

He stopped her with a kiss. Unrepentant. Proprietary. And with an unmistakable command that would tolerate no argument.

He caught her off guard. She was a seething cauldron of raw emotion. She longed for a safe retreat. Deveryn was anything but safe. He was the source of her most bitter unhappiness. She loved him. But in that moment, she hated him more.

Angry fire raced along her spine; it cooled to ice, then heated to boiling point. She slammed her fist into his ribs, desperate to be released from the unwelcome sorcery of the lips and tongue that so skillfully robbed her of reason. He gave no sign that he'd felt the slightest twinge from the force that she'd exerted. Her capitulation was sudden. She felt the comfort of his strong arms wrapping themselves around her and she could no longer fight what she really wanted. Like melting wax, she clung to him, pouring herself over his hard length. Without breaking the kiss, he placed her arms around his neck. When he felt her clenched fingers uncurl and catch in his hair, he traced a path with his palms from her fine boned wrists to her elbows, smoothing them over her kid gloves, and down to the swell of her breasts.

There was nothing comforting in the touch of his sensual caress. Cold reason intruded. She broke away from him, her eyes shadowed with the confusion of her emotions.

"Not that way, love. We'll be seen from below," he said with a smile in his voice, and he captured her wrists and dragged her into one of the darkened alcoves.

"Jason, I'm warning you," she managed to get out before the blond head descended, blocking everything from her but his own faintly menacing presence.

He took his time, subduing her slight show of resistance with slow, compelling kisses, savouring the feel of her in his arms. The rebellious words were easily ignored when her pliant body

291

gave him a different message. He filled his hands with her, boldly taking possession of every curve and contour, touching her intimately, stroking her ceaselessly till he could feel the surrender in the small quivering body that was held so closely to his own.

He buried his face in her hair, his laugh unsteady as he said, "Maddie, we must find some other way to make you listen to me. This is sheer agony."

He released her slowly, steadying her with one hand against the small of her back. With one long finger under her chin, he tipped back her head. Her eyes were closed.

"Look at me," he said softly.

Her eyelashes resisted his command then slowly lifted to unveil her dark eyes, slightly disoriented. Her skin was flushed, her lips parted and swollen from his kisses. She came to herself by degrees.

Even in that dim light, she could see the gleam in his eyes, brilliant with masculine satisfaction. Her own eyes narrowed in displeasure, but before she could find her voice, the look was carefully erased from his expression.

"At last, I've got your attention," he said with a chuckle, and cupped her chin, holding her immobile when she would have turned her head away. "Maddie," he murmured, "everything is all right. I've had confirmation from Edinburgh. We really are married."

A burst of laughter from the floor below wafted up the wall of the gallery. With sudden clarity, Maddie became conscious of the impropriety of her position.

"We shouldn't be here," she said, and struggled free of his arms. He let her go. "I shouldn't be here with you, like this," she said with more force.

"No," he agreed amicably and adjusted the bodice of her gown as if, thought Maddie, he were her lady's maid. She didn't think to object. "Where we should be and will be soon, and would have been long since if you had controlled your ferocious Scottish temper, is in our own house doing exactly what we have been doing but in the privacy of our own chamber." He took a step back and examined her critically. "One look at you and everyone will know that I've been making love to you. It can't be helped. Listen carefully."

His playful mood changed abruptly to a more serious vein. His hand cupped her elbow and she allowed him to lead her to the stairs.

"I shall call at Curzon Street first thing Monday morning to speak to your grandfather. As soon as he is told about our marriage, whatever happens, you are leaving with me and that's flat. You can pack your trunks or you can come to me in your shift. It's immaterial to me. But you had better be there or I'll tear the house apart looking for you."

He left her at the gallery rail where he had been stationed when she had first caught sight of him when she'd entered the house. Not another word was spoken between them. Nor did he look up to acknowledge her presence when he strode through the Octagon to the front entrance, though Maddie was certain he knew she had not moved from where he had left her. As usual, she thought with a stab of irritation, not a word of explanation had been offered for his continuing involvement with her stepmother.

Chapter Eighteen

She really was married to Deveryn. The thought revolved in her mind as she lingered over her toilette that night before retiring to bed. She was married to Deveryn. And suddenly she could no longer deny that, deep down, she knew she was glad. Not in high alt, she admitted with a faint sigh of regret—there had been too much between them for that—but bone deep, achingly, sadly, glad.

Thoughtfully, she removed a lace-edged handkerchief from the top drawer of a tall ivory inlaid rosewood dresser which stood against the wall. It had been some time since she had examined the favours which had fallen to her lot on Christmas day. She touched each one reverently, remembering with vivid recall, the last meal she had shared with her father and how it had been he who had given her the angel—a slightly tarnished angel—into her safekeeping.

Superstition, of course. It was only coincidence that events had turned out as the Christmas favours had predicted. She touched her finger gently to the small silver trinkets which lay in the palm of one hand—the angel, the baby, the ring. Only, she did not have a ring.

She was married to Deveryn. He would not have said so if it had been otherwise. And she knew that before she could go to him with a free heart, she would have to put behind her forever the unhappy circumstances of their past.

Another soft sigh fell from her lips. She folded the trinkets into the handkerchief and replaced it in the drawer. She shut the drawer and thought that the action was symbolic. She would try, no, she must shut the door on the past—on Drumoak, on Cynthia Sinclair, on her father, on her jealousy—if her marriage to Deveryn was to have any chance of success. She was beginning a new life. The seed of that new life was already in her body. Her child. Deveryn's child.

Sleep was impossible. Restlessly, she roamed the room, unconsciously running her fingers through her hair. She halted in front of the looking glass on the dressing table, and stared at herself for a long moment. With unblinking eyes, she tried to penetrate the depths of the fathomless dark eyes of the girl reflected in the mirror. Maddie Sinclair, she acknowledged, was a mass of contradictions. Even to herself, she was an enigma. There was no explanation for how, against honour, against logic, against her own will she had tumbled into love from the moment she had walked into a stranger's arms on a stormy night outside Inverforth's parish church.

Deveryn. She had wanted to hate him. It had been beyond her power. She had discovered that at Dunsdale. And though she did not think they had one thing in common, one mutual interest, one compatible characteristic, she knew beyond doubt that he was as irresistibly drawn to her as she was to him. It was a mystery she could not plumb.

Absently, she touched her fingers to the crystal bowl on her dressing table. Brittle. She felt as brittle as the glass beneath her fingers. She thought that it would take very little to shatter her into a thousand slivers that could never be restored. He could break her very easily if he chose to. And she would be a fool to let him see the extent of his power.

She shivered and turned back to the bed. He would come for her on Monday. She would tell him about the baby. *Everything will be fine, everything will be fine.* She repeated the words over and over, like a litany, trying in vain to lull herself to sleep.

On Monday morning, Maddie waited in trepidation for the summons that would call her to the drawing room and Deveryn. She expected him to be annoyed when he heard that her grandfather was not at home. She herself had been less than happy when her aunt had told her at the breakfast table that he'd gone off, on impulse, with Lord Yarmouth to look over the contents of a house near Canterbury which had just come up for auction.

"When is he expected back?" she'd asked, unable to keep the note of alarm from her voice.

Her aunt had been engrossed in reading the latest stack of invitations which had just arrived by morning post. "Who can say?" she'd answered idly. "Perhaps tomorrow, or the next day."

Maddie tried to tell herself that a day's delay was a minor irritation, and one, moreover, for which she was not responsible.

Nevertheless, when she walked into the drawing room, she could not prevent herself from flinching when she came under Deveryn's turbulent eyes.

"Get a warm pelisse," he told her harshly. "We're going for a drive."

"My grandfather isn't . . ."

"I know where your grandfather is," he cut her off with a show of impatience. "I met Lord Hertford last evening in my mother's house. They're neighbors."

"Lord Hertford?"

"The marquess. He's Yarmouth's father. He told me that he'd gone with your grandfather to Canterbury. Now get that pelisse and leave word that you're going for a drive to Richmond. That gives us at least an hour."

Within five minutes, Deveryn was handing her into his curricle. In another few minutes, Maddie knew that their destination was not Richmond. The curricle came out onto Wigmore Street and turned east then north.

"Where are you taking me?" she asked in an undertone, keeping her voice low so that Deveryn's groom, perched up behind, could not hear their conversation.

Deveryn smiled in that way which always made Maddie fear the worst. "For a walk in the country," he returned with no attempt to keep their conversation private. "It's a nice day for some exercise."

Within another five minutes, Deveryn was checking his team of horses at the end of a country lane. He assisted Maddie to alight, and signaled the groom to take over the ribbons. The groom saluted his employer and drove off at a spanking pace.

"Now, we can talk," said Deveryn, and with a firm hand he led her to a gap in the privet hedge which bordered the lane.

"How shall we get home?" she asked with a backward look at the disappearing curricle.

"My man has instructions to return within the hour. Watch your step."

She carefully avoided a puddle as she negotiated her way through the hedge. She looked about her and came to a halt. A small, two storey, whitewashed house with a thatched roof nestled invitingly in the middle of an orchard. From the tall chimney, the wind caught a curl of smoke and drew it playfully into a frothy wake.

Deveryn's hand urged her forward. "Don't be shy," he said. "There's no one about."

"This . . . can't be proper," she protested weakly.

They entered the unpretentious building by the back door. "What's proper between a man and his wife?" Already his hands were at the fastenings of her pelisse and he was drawing it from her shoulders. "As I told you at Carlton House, I've already had confirmation from your solicitor that we are positively, indubitably, irrevocably married. I have every right to be alone with you. We have an hour, and I for one, don't intend to waste a minute of it."

He had taken her by the hand and was half-leading half-dragging her up the narrow, steep staircase. Before they reached the top, it came to her what Deveryn's purpose was. She dug in her heels and brought him to a standstill.

"Deveryn," she said, her voice tight. "I don't wish to go any farther."

The words were scarcely out of her mouth when an arm was wrapped tightly around her shoulders. Her head was tipped back and her bonnet deftly removed and sent sailing over the balustrade.

"I thought you might be difficult," he said on a soft laugh, his warm breath fanning her hair. "It's up to you. You can come with me now, this minute, openly, as my wife, to my lodgings in Jermyn Street, or we can discreetly play out this farce until your grandfather returns and I can explain our situation. Either way, Maddie, I intend to have some time alone with you."

Her assent was taken for granted, for he grasped her hand and moved ahead, and like an idiot, thought Maddie, she followed without a murmur.

They came onto a small landing. Deveryn opened a door and stood back for her to enter. She hesitated.

"Maddie," he said, brushing her hair with his lips, "give me some credit. I've kept my distance for two whole weeks until I knew for certain that we were wed. Perhaps it was wrong of me to insist on my conjugal rights when we were at Dunsdale, knowing as I did how upset you were at our situation. Try to understand how I felt. I had my wife living under my own roof. How could I possibly have been expected to keep away from you? And when you spurned me, naturally I was angry. Whilst I needed you so damn much, you could turn me away without a flicker of regret. I behaved abominably. You have my apologies, though I'd probably do the same again. But now, to be told that your grandfather has gone off for an indeterminate number of days is more than I am willing to tolerate. An hour of my wife's time surely isn't too much to ask?"

There it was again, that amused tolerance which she so much detested. "There's more to marriage than bed, Deveryn," she said with a flash of temper and smacked her reticule against the hard muscles of his abdomen. He grunted and released her. She stepped into the room.

Maddie took one look and sucked in her breath. Deveryn, at her back, emitted a strangled, "Oh my God," then burst into laughter.

The room was done in purple and crimson, the walls draped with heavy damask to give the effect of an Eastern potentate's palace. Gilt-edged mirrors were everywhere, but it was the one on the ceiling strategically placed above the enormous purple satin draped bed which had Maggie's eyes round with astonishment. Her mouth gaped, then closed, and finally drew into a thin line. She turned her stormy gaze upon Deveryn's carefully impassive countenance.

"A love nest," she purred, dangerously calm.

He threw up both hands in a placating gesture. "This is not my house, I swear it. I borrowed it from a friend. He might have told me what to expect."

"Don't you have a love nest, Deveryn?" she inquired, her voice coated with sugar.

He flashed her a taunting smile. "No," he replied

emphatically. "I decided when I returned from Scotland that I had no more use for it. Besides, I was almost never there. It lay empty for almost a year. 'Love nests' mean long term arrangements. They've never been my style. Does that satisfy your wifely curiosity?" He closed the door softly behind him and propelled her forward into the centre of the room.

He wandered around examining first one thing, then another, and finally moved to the bed where he stretched full length on top of the luxurious feather mattress. Locking his hands behind his head, he watched Maddie curiously.

She was standing where he'd left her, in the centre of the room, motionless, her head tilted up, gazing steadfastly at the mirror on the ceiling. With a sudden flurry of movements, she came to life and began to strip the gloves from her fingers.

"Fine! Fine!" she muttered under her breath. "Why am I surprised?" and she crossed to the dressing table in three angry strides. She slapped her reticule and gloves on the cluttered top, scattering a swansdown powder puff and several small black beauty patches. Maddie left them where they fell, her temper in no way improved by these relics of another lady's occupancy. She turned on her heel to stare at the man whose brilliant blue eyes mocked her so patently. He was idly surveying her from beneath half-hooded eyes.

Her own eyes heated and sent sparks shooting at him.

"Well, what are you waiting for?" she demanded. "Let's get it over with. I haven't got all day," and she stalked to the Oriental silk screen which stood, for some odd reason, a good six feet from the wall. Her fingers began to fumble impatiently with the tiny row of buttons on her bodice, slipping them quickly from their button holes till the bodice gaped open. Angrily, she dragged the hem of her brown kerseymere frock over her head, unwisely forgetting to undo the buttons on the cuffs of the long-sleeved gown. In a matter of seconds she was in a hopeless, smothering tangle of folds and cursing vehemently as she tried to fight her way free of the morass of constricting fabric.

It was Deveryn who extricated her from her unhappy predicament. "Hold still," he said between laughter and delight, and skillfully slipped the buttons which impeded her movements.

Her cheeks were flaming when she finally dragged the frock over her head. "Thank you," she said between her teeth.

Deveryn sauntered away and Maddie threw her frock over the top of the screen. After a moment she took a quick peak at Deveryn. He had retired to the bed where he reclined at his ease, an indolent smile of expectation playing across his handsome face. He hadn't so much as removed his neckcloth. She gritted her teeth together and began on the strings of her stays. The edges parted and Maddie pulled the garment over her head. The fine lawn chemise was similarly dealt with. She was down to her drawers. Her actions were meant to be a calculated insult and she refused to draw back so late in the game. She stifled her pangs of modesty and shimmied out of the drawers. Only then did she look around for a robe or a towel to cover her nakedness. Unfortunately, there was nothing. A movement caught her eyes and she looked up. She bit back a moan of mortification when she caught sight of herself reflected from various angles in the several mirrors around the room. But it was Deveryn's image which covered her with chagrin. He was cooly taking advantage of every view that was presented. She cupped her breasts and with a cry of rage swooped around the screen. Little angry puffs of breath fanned her lips.

"A veritable dragon," murmured Deveryn, and inched away as she sailed over to the bed.

"Well?" she railed at him. "This is what you wanted, isn't it?" and she kneeled on the purple counterpane and loomed over him with as much menace as she could muster.

One strong arm caught her waist in a loose clasp. His eyes were gleaming with laughter. "Actually, Maddie," he said, "I only wanted to talk. But I'm quite willing to gratify my wife's passionate nature. After all, what are husbands for?" And he looked past her stormy face to gaze enraptured at the ceiling. Maddie twisted her head and followed the direction of his eyes. She'd forgotten about the mirror over the bed.

"Oh no," she groaned and put out a hand to cover her posterior.

One small shake was all it took to have her sprawl against him. "I'm quite overcome," he said, and flashed her a frankly sensual grin. "D'you know, this is the very first time that you've been the one to make the overtures? My pet, how can I refuse you?"

"You let me think . . . you made me, you . . . ," she began, but he grasped her shoulders and quickly tumbled her beneath him where any resistance could be more easily quelled.

His lips sank into hers in a slow, proprietary kiss, taking his fill of everything she had to offer. "I lied," he said, and his lips descended to brush the sensitive spots he knew from experience were particularly pleasurable for Maddie. "Of course I meant to make love to you. But I thought I'd have to persuade you with passion. Who would have believed that I could goad you into taking off all your clothes? You're not very wise when you're in a temper, are you? I must remember that." And he laughed.

Her small, infuriated movements of outrage made no impression on him. The stroke of his tongue at her shoulder, on her throat, lightly, lightly against a swelling nipple before he took the peak into his mouth was enough to open her to his more urgent, passionate possession. When it came, she was as hungry for it as he. Only then did he divest himself of his garments.

She cried out when he brought himself fully into her. He stilled, then thrust deeply to make the possession as complete as he could make it. She was like melting honey beneath him, enveloping him in her warmth, clinging to his driving body, returning every brush of his hand, offering touch for touch, kiss for kiss, setting him on fire with the soft pleasure sounds she made against his throat.

In husky, erotic whispers, he told her how he loved her body open and vulnerable to him, her softness, everything that was feminine in her accepting his maleness and his claims to who and what she was. His words became more blatantly sexual and he could feel the heat rise in her, wantonly, like wild fire.

Again and again, he brought her close to climax, then deliberately delayed her pleasure, forcing her to confess that she craved his love, his touch, his passion, everything he was doing to her. Her words were like a spur to his bridled ardour. Unchecked, he rose above her, bracing himself on his arms, fusing their bodies with a deeper, surer penetration. She cried out and reached for him, and the sudden blaze that ignited them brought them to a shuddering, mindless rapture, till there was nothing in the world but themselves and the demanding beat of their locked bodies. At the last, came Maddie's animal cry of fulfillment. To Deveryn, it was the sweetest sound on earth.

In the gentle wash of receding pleasure, his fingers idly brushed her hair. They lay silent for a long while, the only sound in the room the tempo of their breathing as it slowed to normal.

Maddie turned slightly, curling into him. She thought it strange and rather wonderful that in the act of love a subtle shift in power took place between them. She did not know why this should be so, but she was aware that Deveryn's gratification was dependent, to a greater degree, on the pleasure he brought to her. She touched a hand to him with affected negligence, covertly savouring the ripple of powerful muscles on the sleek and damp torso beneath her open palm. He was so blatantly masculine—frighteningly so. And yet, that essentially brute strength was ruthlessly tempered to a becoming gentleness whenever she gave herself completely into his hands. Surrender, she thought. She had surrendered to him and he had rewarded her with unlimited tenderness. But then, hadn't he also surrendered to her? There had been moments when she'd thought she was the one who wielded the power. She was replete, happy and touched by his gentleness. It seemed the perfect time to tell him about their babe, confess her own pleasure in being his wife and the mother of his unborn child.

He laughed. "I think I'm beginning to learn the trick of managing you," he mused carelessly. "I should chain you to my bed. It's the one place where you finally admit who's master," and he turned his sparkling gaze upon her.

Maddie felt as if she had been slapped. "You put too much stock in what we do in bed," she told him, and would have slipped from his arms.

He jerked her head back to the pillow and studied the belligerent tilt of her chin, the flush on her cheeks, the stubbornly averted eyes. "What we do in bed will be at the heart of our marriage. Don't ever forget it," he told her, and he let her go.

They scarcely exchanged two words on the drive back to Curzon Street. He sent his coachman ahead with the curricle and walked Maddie to the door.

"You're wrong, you know," she said, as she made to ascend the stairs. "It takes more than a tumble in the hay to make a marriage."

She would have given him her back, but he captured her hand and brought it to his lips as if to kiss it lightly. Instead, he nipped her sharply with his teeth.

"Nevertheless, I'll call for you some day soon, Maddie. See that you're here." His eyes were deep and fathomless.

"And where," she asked with thinly veiled contempt, "do you intend to take me?"

He smiled tolerantly. "Oh," he said with a drawl that set her teeth on edge, "we'll cover the same ground as before and I may introduce you to a few paths you've never been down. It would take a lifetime to explore all that the park has to offer, don't you agree? And I intend to become familiar with every inch of it."

And he left her staring.

She spent a few, uncomfortable hours regretting the impulse that had prevented her from confiding fully in Deveryn. She told herself over and over again that she'd been a fool to take umbrage at his careless remark. He'd meant nothing by it. She herself might just as easily have taunted him with the very same words. Why hadn't she teased him back? Laughed it off? Silenced him with a kiss?

The answer was not hard to find. She could do none of those things because she was quite simply and unequivocally unsure of him. Though she'd been gratified to hear that the reason he'd kept his distance from her for two weeks was out of respect for her scruples, she could not prevent herself from wondering how much of that time had been spent in her stepmother's company.

Cynthia Sinclair. Why was it that everything always seemed to come back to her stepmother? *Let it be, Maddie,* she told herself. *You know that you are jealous of the woman, which is irrational, all things considered. Deveryn loves you. You love him. Shut the door on ancient history. Give him a chance.*

She felt the vague discomfort of a headache coming on.

Though she had no real inclination for fresh air, she made up her mind that a ride in the park was just the thing to clear her mind.

Once in the stable block, she looked around for Duncan. Her mount was led out by an undergroom she did not recognize.

"Where's Duncan?" she asked.

His averted head and shifting stance roused her suspicions at once.

"Dunno, miss," he answered.

"Who does know, then?" Fear lent a sharp edge to her words.

But the groom had no answer.

It was at that moment that the young stable boy, Willie, chanced to come out of the building. Maddie called to him. Recognition flashed in his eyes. He threw away the broom in his hand and gathered himself as if he would bolt.

"Willie!"

Her tone was peremptory and boded ill if he should disregard the summons. Willie resigned himself to his fate. She questioned him closely, and within moments had dismissed both groom and mount and was following a vaguely reluctant Willie up the outside iron staircase to the grooms' quarters above the coachhouse. Nor would she allow him to escape when he opened the door to Duncan's small cell of a room. She pushed him ahead of her and shut the door firmly.

Duncan, fully clothed, lay on top of a small cot. His face was almost unrecognizable. Besides a mass of cuts and abrasions and two black eyes, the flesh beneath the puffy skin was swollen almost shapeless. At their entrance, he turned two vacant eyes upon them and stared without recognition.

Maddie did not need to be told how Duncan had come to be in such a sorry pass.

"How many rounds did he go to?" she asked, and moved to the cot to take one of Duncan's bruised hands between her own. She put it to her cheek.

"Twenty-six, miss," answered Willie. Then, as if to compensate for Duncan's sorry condition, he added, "If you think Mr. Ross is in a bad way, you should see the other bloke. He had to be carried off in a stretcher. Mr. Ross is only a little bit groggy and the doctor says he'll be as right as a trivet in a day or two."

Maddie knew better, but she saw no point in correcting Willie's misapprehension. At least they'd had the sense to get medical attention.

"Go and fetch Mr. Lloyd," she said. "I'd like a word with him."

For some reason Willie could not fathom, he felt a rush of guilt as if he had been the one to lay Mr. Ross flat on his back and put those tears on the young lady's cheeks. "I'm very sorry, miss," he said, and shot her a consoling look.

"What? Oh, there's nothing you could have done, Willie. I'm the one who could have put a stop to it. It's because of me that—oh, never mind. Just be a good boy and fetch Mr. Lloyd."

Before Willie could do as he was bid, Mr. Lloyd himself, a dapper, little man in his early forties, pushed through the door. He had been, at one time, a jockey to which occupation his slight and supple frame was admirably suited. From his slightly scandalized expression, it was evident that the groom had already given him the report of the unheard of intrusion of a lady in the grooms' quarters.

Willie eyed the two silent figures and on signal from Mr. Lloyd slunk through the open door. His heart was unaccountably heavy. Only an hour before, he'd been on top of the world, boasting to the stable boys of the other great houses in the neighbourhood that no less a personage than Big Duncan was one of his intimates.

Inside Duncan's room, Mr. Lloyd voiced a quiet and respectful protest at Miss Sinclair's presence in a stablehand's chamber. Maddie ignored it.

"He's going back to Scotland," she said, "just as soon as I can manage it. Until then, I shall be obliged if you would warn the grooms that I shall be spending a good part of each day with Duncan."

Mr. Lloyd remained uncomfortably silent. In his long career, he had never known one of quality show such an interest in a mere underling.

"Well?" demanded Maddie, her eyes narrowing on the silent figure beside the door. She made an effort to soften her expression. She admired Mr. Lloyd. He was as honest as the day and an industrious employee. Her grandfather was lucky to

306

have him in his employ. The condition of the stables and carriage house were their own recommendations, and as far as she could tell, relations among his under grooms were harmonious. Even Duncan, who had never before been out of Scotland, had been happy here.

"Mr. Lloyd," she said persuasively, "Duncan needs familiar faces around him. Believe me, I know. I shall stay with him till he's well enough to travel to Scotland. He has relatives there who know how to care for him."

The groom stepped to the narrow cot and made a careful study of Duncan's inert form. His eyes lifted to Maddie's. "Surely, miss, that's not necessary. The man took a beating, but no bones were broken. I know he looks awful, but those cuts and bruises will soon heal." His voice became even more heartening. "He's only a little bit groggy, miss. In a day or two, he'll be as right as rain. Just you wait and see."

Maddie began to explain carefully and patiently about Duncan's early career as a pugilist and how in just such a manner it had come to an abrupt end. "So you see, Mr. Lloyd," she went on, "this 'grogginess' as you call it, may take weeks to clear up. Even months. He needs constant care. There is nothing you can say to make me change my mind. You may expect my presence here until he leaves for Scotland."

Mr. Lloyd looked to be dubious. "It's a long, uncomfortable drive. Do you think he's up to it?"

"No. And he's not going by road. There's a boat that does the run from the docks at Wapping to Leith," she said, remembering Mr. Scott's stated preference of travel. "That's how he'll make the journey. Of course," she mused, "he can't go alone. Perhaps Willie or one of the grooms can go with him." She wondered how she could afford it, and thought she might ask Deveryn for the money.

Mr. Lloyd surprised her by saying, "Then I'd better give you his purse. I've had it locked away for safe keeping."

He excused himself and returned within minutes.

"What's this?" asked Maddie, accepting a plump leather bag which the head groom held out to her.

"Duncan's winnings. Be careful. There's as much as five hundred pounds in that wallet."

For a moment she was speechless.

"He earned this much in just one fight?" she asked. A school mistress earned less than one hundred pounds per annum.

"Not quite. Some of it is from wagers he made on himself. There's good money in fighting if you have talent."

That there was also a good chance of ending up as witless as a widgeon, Maddie forebore to point out.

She devoted what was left of the day to Duncan, even going so far as to eat her meals with him. Her aunt looked in once and accepted Maddie's desertion with good grace. Willie was assigned by the head groom to keep an eye on the big man and call one of the grooms if it proved necessary. The task was not onerous, nor did time hang heavily on his hands for Miss Maddie told one story after another, all Scottish in origin, of strange creatures called banshees and kelpies and selkies whose malevolence towards unwary mortals made his straight hair curl into ringlets. He was sure he would not sleep for a week for nightmares, but could not drag himself away from the hushed accents that told the horrible tales with such relish. Intermittently, she spoke of the old days, and of a place called "Drumoak," and promised Duncan that he would soon see and smell the familiar sights of home. Surprisingly, at one point, Duncan laughed. Willie turned to look at Maddie, a grin of relief lighting up his small, square face. She turned her head away, and he knew that she wept silent tears.

"Miss?" he asked in an urgent whisper. "Is Mr. Ross . . . worse?"

She answered with a vigorous shake of her head, and, much to Willie's discomfort, she covered her face with her hands and wept in earnest.

By the time Mr. Lloyd had returned with the intelligence that passage had been booked for Duncan on the schooner that sailed from Wapping to Leith on the Friday, Maddie had fully recovered and since Duncan had fallen into a deep sleep, she was persuaded to return to the house.

She was back early the next morning and was greeted with the news, given with excited impatience by Willie, that Duncan was up and about and had spoken a few words. This stunning revelation did not produce the effect he had hoped, for though Miss Maddie laughed, he remarked the flash of tears before she turned away.

But her tears proved to be only temporary, for Duncan was more like himself and almost childishly happy when told that he would set sail for Scotland on the Friday. Maddie covered her sadness well. One part of her wished that she too might make for home, the other desired to be only wherever Deveryn was. *A heart divided*, she thought, and wondered if she would ever be whole of heart again.

Chapter Nineteen

Melbourne House was the home of Lady Melbourne and her daughter-in-law, Lady Caroline Lamb. The former was the wife of the Viscount Melbourne, confidante of the Prince Regent, and a Whig hostess of considerable political influence in her own right. Though she shared her home with her son, William Lamb, the heir to the title, and his wife, Lady Caro, it was widely known that there was little love lost between the two women.

Miss Spencer proposed to Maddie that they make a call on this unusual household. Though it was only a short walk between Curzon Street and Whitehall, the sky was overcast and she wisely ordered the carriage, overriding Maddie's protest that she be allowed to remain with Duncan.

"You need to get out more, Maddie, and enlarge your circle of acquaintants. Oh, not that Caro Lamb's society is going to make a jot of difference to you. She's almost ruined her chances of being received in the best drawing rooms. Still, Lady Melbourne suggested that your friendship might be a salutary influence on the girl. It seems that Caro Lamb has taken a liking to you. But be careful, dear. Her affections are known to be fickle."

"Are you an intimate of Lady Melbourne, then?" asked Maddie.

"Not particularly. But your grandfather regularly supports Whig causes. William Lamb, so he seems to think, has a future in politics, or he would have if his wife could be constrained to temper her excesses. She may very well turn out to be the proverbial millstone around his neck."

Both ladies were at home when Maddie and Miss Spencer presented their cards, and whilst Miss Spencer was shown to Lady Melbourne's drawing room on the ground floor, Maddie followed the footman to Lady Caro's upstairs suite of rooms.

Maddie could not be other than gratified by the effusive welcome she was given. Lady Caro, it seemed, was in one of her 'spritely' humours. She presented a young gentleman of decidedly foppish dress and manner whom she introduced as a young cousin, Jack Ponsonby.

It seemed that they had just partaken of tea and sandwiches. A cup was soon procured for Maddie, and she accepted one of the small, bite-sized cucumber sandwiches for which, she had observed, the English had a passion.

Her eyes followed Lady Caro as she moved about the room. Although the girl was as graceful as a dancer, there was nothing restful about her. On this particular occasion, she seemed to burn with an inner excitement.

"In another week or so," she said in her peculiarly breathy voice, "I'll have my busybody of a mother-in-law exactly where I want her. I'm going to make her sorry for every vicious lie she's ever spread about me."

Maddie did not know how she should reply. Though she found Caroline Lamb as appealing as she was unpredictable, these frank confidences always left her at a loss for words. Her mind groped for some suitable reply, but she was saved from her embarrassment by the interjection of Lady Caro's cousin.

"Take a damper, Caro. The old dame has been more than generous to you and William. You have your own suite of rooms here at Melbourne House and the use of Brocket whenever you want to rusticate in the country. What more could you want?"

Though the words were addressed to his cousin, it was on Maddie that he trained his lorgnette, lazily and quite brazenly giving her the once over.

Dandy, thought Maddie, and affected an interest in the cup and saucer which she balanced in her hands. She wondered how soon she could make her excuses.

"Revenge is what I want," said Lady Caro, her eyes taking on a fanatical glitter. "And I've found just the way to set the old harridan back on her heels, yes, and pay off old scores on every last one of my enemies."

The quizzing glass swivelled to Lady Caro as she did a little pirouette before falling gracefully into an overstuffed armchair where she convulsed in giggles. Her lightning changes of mood, thought Maddie, were fascinating to watch, but she had no doubt that to live with them would drive any sane person to Bedlam.

"Do tell, Caro," droned the young fop as he sprawled inelegantly, one arm thrown along the back of the satin brocade settee. "Byron, I presume heads the list?"

"Need you ask? But my mother-in-law comes a close second. Then," she mused, "there's William."

"William? You mean your husband?"

"The same."

"Good God! That's shocking! William Lamb is a paragon! He must be. He tolerates your indiscretions which, I may add, are legion."

Lady Caro stamped her foot. "Fustian! William does not 'tolerate' my indiscretions. He's completely indifferent. And if it had not been for the fact that he keeps a string of women, there would *be* no indiscretions."

"A string of women? What has that to say to anything? A wife shouldn't trouble herself about such things," said young Ponsonby negligently.

Maddie, who had just calculated by the ormolu clock on the mantel that her courtesy call had lasted no more than five minutes and that it would be impossible to extricate herself from this painfully embarrassing conversation for another ten minutes, suddenly turned to confront the unsuspecting gentleman. Her voice was chilling when she addressed him.

"That attitude, sir, went out with panniers and hooped skirts. Why should a gentleman take more liberties than he is willing to permit his wife? That would be rankly unjust."

Again the quizzing glass was raised and an indolent perusal made of the indignant young lady. "True," drawled Ponsonby. "But men have nothing to lose. An unfaithful wife runs the risk of being divorced."

"In Scotland," gritted Maddie with a becoming flush across her cheekbones, "an unfaithful husband runs the same risk."

313

Young Ponsonby's eyebrows shot up. "Barbaric!" he murmured dismissively.

"Well, I think it's capital," exclaimed Lady Caro. "In England, however, a woman has to be more inventive if she wants justice. And I," she intoned, "I have found the perfect method of exacting retribution."

"How?" asked Ponsonby bluntly.

Lady Caro's voice dropped to a whisper. "May I rely on your discretion?"

Young Ponsonby gave her the nod, but Maddie could only stare and listen with horrified fascination.

"I've written a novel," confided Lady Caro. "All my persecutors are in it, and easily recognizable, though I've had to change their names, of course. My publisher thinks it will be sold out as soon as it comes off the presses." She clapped her hands looking, thought Maddie, like a child who had just been given a treat.

"Have a care, Caro. You'll be the butt of vulgar gossip and ridicule when the book comes out," said the cousin.

"Much I care for that! Besides, what more can they do to me? I'm already banned from Almack's. My mother-in-law has tightened the purse strings. William doesn't take me anywhere." She slanted him a speculative look. "Come to think of it, Jack, you're the last person to talk of ridicule and gossip. Do tell what really happened at Grantham. I've heard a dozen different versions of the story." She winked at Maddie before continuing in the same bantering tone. "Is it true that in a fit of jealousy you broke into Deveryn's room and tried to take Dolly Ramides away from him?"

Jack Ponsonby emitted a vulgar expletive and threw a glowering glance at his cousin's laughing face. "No," he answered with ill-concealed temper, "and if Dolly Ramides was anywhere near Grantham that night, my name is not Jack Ponsonby."

"Then who . . . ?" asked Lady Caro.

Maddie had to bite back the very same question as it sprang involuntarily to her lips.

"That," said young Ponsonby with a secretive smirk, "would be telling. Suffice it to say that if my friends and I had known that Deveryn was entertaining a lady—a real lady, that

314

is—in his chamber that evening, we would not have subjected him to our silly prank. Still," he said thoughtfully, "he wasn't much of a sport. I was lucky to get away with a whole skin."

The conversation with Lady Caro and her cousin burned in Maddie's brain long after she had taken her leave of Melbourne House. She reminded herself, over and over again, that she had made up her mind to shut out the past and make a new beginning with Deveryn. She'd known, after all, that he'd had a woman with him at Grantham. Only now she was almost certain that it was Cynthia Sinclair. The wound, she discovered, was far more devastating than when she'd believed that Dolly Ramides was the woman in question.

By degrees, she managed to control the pain of her discovery, and she decided that she would never refer to it. The past was forgiven. She only hoped that one day it could be forgotten. She was to remember the irony of those thoughts some hours later when her grandfather returned from Canterbury.

She was in the drawing room making notes on the text of *Medea* for the paper which she was to present on the following Thursday at the meeting of Lady Rossmere's Bluestocking Brigade. By and large, her paper was ready. All it lacked was a little polish. She was not averse to the task since she found that it deflected her thoughts from more disturbing channels.

From time to time, she answered her aunt's quiet monologue as that lady sat meditatively at her tambour frame, occasionally setting the odd stitch in what was to be a needlepoint cushion cover.

Maddie became more involved in her work. Though she was a little nervous about standing up in a room full of strangers and delivering her address, she was not new to the experience of public speaking. At Miss Maitland's Academy, she had been a member of the Literary and Debating Society. All the senior girls were obliged to participate. She knew first hand about the thrust and parry of public debate. Still, she felt herself to be more than a trifle rusty, and wondered a little at her own temerity in putting herself forward in this way. It was, however, too late to draw back.

Her powers of concentration, as Miss Maitland had once remarked, were extraordinary. Samuel Spencer had already entered the room and barked his greeting before Maddie became aware of his presence. He said a few sentences which at first made no sense to her, then spun on his heel and was gone.

Maddie's eyes flew to her aunt's. Miss Sinclair had gone as white as a sheet. Only then did the significance of her grandfather's few words penetrate. His voice could be heard outside the door issuing orders to sundry servants. Maddie threw aside her notes and went sprinting after him.

She caught him as he was about to descend the main staircase. "Whose engagement is to be published on Friday?" she asked breathlessly, laying a detaining hand on his sleeve.

"Your engagement to Raeburn," he replied, and would have continued on if Maddie's hand had not clamped convulsively on his arm.

"No," she said, then again, more forcefully, "No. It's out of the question."

She felt the colour recede from her cheeks, and knew that her lips had developed a betraying quiver. She pressed them together to stop their trembling, waiting with fragile control for the explosion that would blow her away.

It seemed as if they had become rooted to the spot, so long did they stand there staring unblinkingly into each other's eyes. It was Maddie who broke the silence.

"Grandfather, I must speak to you," and without waiting to see if he followed, she picked up a candelabra and led the way to the downstairs library.

She moved like a sleepwalker to one of the straight-backed chairs and could not say whether she was more relieved or frightened when her grandfather stepped into the room. Without glancing her way, he lit a taper from the candelabra she had set on the mantel and proceeded to light several branches of candles around the room. Only then did he turn to face her, his feet splayed out on the hearth, his hands clasped behind his back.

Refusing to be intimidated, she took the initiative, beginning with the least contentious issue. "You said that you were going to Paris. When?"

His stare unnerved her, but he answered her question

without hesitation.

"Tomorrow morning, at first light. There's a sale or two in Paris that Yarmouth and I happened to hear of while we were in Canterbury. I should be back within the week."

Nervously, she licked her lips, and pressed on. "Why is it necessary to publish the announcement of my engagement to Raeburn when you're away?"

"Why not?" he asked.

She let his question revolve in her mind and tried for a calm she was far from feeling. Finally, she said, "The duke has not asked me to marry him."

"Nor shall he. My dear, what did you expect? This is an alliance negotiated by lawyers." His tone gentled. "I would not have accepted Raeburn's suit, however, if I had not thought that he would make you an admirable husband. You must rely on my judgement."

"You are not my guardian," she said doggedly. "You have not the right to dispose of my future."

For the first time, she felt the flash of his anger, though not a muscle betrayed him.

"A minor matter," he argued. "As I've said before, what guardian would cavil at the offer for his ward from a duke? Besides, the marriage itself will not take place until we hear from Canada. Does that satisfy you?"

There was only one more argument she had yet to use. "I don't wish to marry Raeburn."

She could not be other than grateful for his restraint. In fact, she was almost persuaded that her avowal had been long expected. Quietly, reasonably, he began to use every argument at his disposal to convince her of her good fortune.

Tell him now that you are married to Deveryn, one part of her brain told her. But instinct overrode logic, for there was something about his eyes, something about his stance, which warned her to be cautious. If Deveryn had been with her, she thought, she might have had the courage to confront her grandfather with the ruin of his ambition. Without Deveryn, she felt like a sparrow in the shadow of a soaring, predatory hawk. She could not do it.

He said something which dispelled the fog of her meandering thoughts.

"My father?" she questioned. "What has he got to do with my marriage to Raeburn?"

"It's what he wanted—agreed to, in fact."

"Are you saying that my father wanted me to marry the duke?"

"Indubitably. It was part of our bargain."

"Bargain?" She thought her voice sounded like the echo in the game she had once played in the granite quarry she'd been taken to see when she was a child.

"The bargain we made about your future before he left for Scotland and the accident which claimed his life. I had thought to spare you the details. Not that there's anything to hide, you understand. It just seemed more expedient—better," he quickly corrected, "that you remain in ignorance of the terms of our agreement."

She felt suddenly overly warm and was surprised when she shivered. Her eyes met her grandfather's hard scrutiny with unwavering intensity. "What agreement?" she asked in sudden trepidation, and knew by the way his eyes narrowed that he had determined to be brutally honest.

"For a price, your father gave his consent to your removal to my house and your future marriage to Raeburn."

She could only stare.

"Oh, don't look so stricken," he said irritably. "It's not so cold-blooded as it sounds. He was desperate for money. I proposed a brilliant match for you and an end to our estrangement. It was all done for your own good."

There was logic in what he was saying. She could sense it all through her body.

"Do you say that my father came into some money?"

"A fortune," he answered dryly.

She laced her hands together and stared at them blindly. Some part of her refused to accept the harsh reality of her grandfather's words. With a flash of bravado, she burst out, "Why should I believe you? There was never any love lost between you and my father, and I shall never be persuaded that he would put me up for sale as if I were a piece of prime horseflesh at Tattersal's."

Her bitter words apparently left him unmoved. "You're letting your imagination run away with you, Maddie," he replied evenly. "You have no reason to doubt my words. I tell you, your father and I settled our differences. You should be grateful. For once in his life, he was putting your interests above his own."

"You said he sold me for a price."

He grew impatient. "All right, all right! If that's the way you want it! He sold you for a price. Does that satisfy you?"

"I won't believe it. My father was a gentleman. He loved me. He would never have been a party to such a proposal."

It was when she saw the dark flash of colour on her grandfather's cheeks that she realised she had inadvertently insulted him in the worst possible way. She had implied that he was not a gentleman. In actual fact, he was not, for Samuel Spencer was not of gentle birth. In the circles in which he moved, such a circumstance put him at a disadvantage. It was something he concealed as much as possible.

The words of apology trembled on her lips, but before they could be uttered, his voice slashed the silence.

"Your father may have been a gentleman, but he was not above compromising his honour for a price. We can settle this argument very easily. Before he left for Scotland, he went on a spending spree, everything of course charged to my account as we'd agreed. The unpaid bills are still accumulating. I've instructed my solicitor to pay off every last one of them. You may see them if you wish."

She was beyond words and simply stared at him through the gathering mist which clouded her vision.

"As you wish," he said, his voice devoid of expression. "I shall leave word for Gregson to come by some time tomorrow so that you may peruse the cancelled debts at your leisure. But prepare yourself for a shock."

He had moved to the door and held it open. It was obvious that he regarded the interview at an end. Maddie slowly got to her feet and obeyed his silent command.

"You'll find out, Maddie, that your father was a profligate as well as an inveterate gambler. Money slipped through his fingers. One can tell a lot from a man's bills and bank statements. You'll discover that you were very low on the list of Donald Sinclair's priorities. I shall be back within the week. For the moment, I defer to your wishes on the announcement of your engagement. But it's only a postponement. Remember that. It's too late to withdraw now. We shall talk of this later when I return."

There could be no discrediting her grandfather's disclosures when on the afternoon following their conversation, Mr. Gregson himself delivered the bills into Maddie's hands. Most of the accounts were for garments from expensive modistes, a few were from prestigious jewellers for costly trinkets, and one, a ninety-nine year lease was for a house in Baker Street made out in the name of Cynthia Sinclair. Donald Sinclair had been a devoted husband evidently, thought Maddie. At the very bottom of the pile was a gaming debt in the amount of ten thousand pounds. Maddie knew that what she held in her hand was her father's vowels—an I.O.U. made out in his bold script to one Jason Verney, the Viscount Deveryn. She looked at the name and the sum of money involved for several long minutes, and a deathly stillness seemed to creep into the room.

In a sudden, heedless passion, she slammed her fists into the inoffensive, Louis XV escritoire where she sat, oblivious of the raw pain to her knuckles where they'd scraped the smooth mahogany of the desk. She palmed her eyes and tried to calm herself.

Memories, hedged in by a newer loyalty, suddenly burst the dam and sucked her into a raging whirlpool of disillusion and anguish. Deveryn and Cynthia. Behind her closed eyelids, she could picture them perfectly. And where memory failed, imagination ran riot. Scene after scene flashed before her eyes, torturing her with the spectacle of Deveryn and Cynthia in moments of intimacy. A little sob shook her suddenly.

Deveryn and Cynthia—together, like two sides of the same coin—a nemesis for the House of Sinclair.

"Ah, Papa," she murmured out loud, overwhelmed by a sudden surge of pity for the father who had failed her. Deveryn and Cynthia, driving him to ruin with a carelessness which seemed more callous than premeditation. Besotted by his young wife, indulging her with every extravagance to buy her love, Donald Sinclair cut a pathetic figure. *As I do*, she thought, and felt the pain for both of them in every cell in her body.

Like a marble sculpture, she sat without moving, her hands

cupping her eyes. She lost track of time. When she came to herself, she was completely disoriented, and for a moment could not think where she was. Then her eyes fell on the bills which lay scattered around on the carpet.

She picked them up and went through them methodically. By her reckoning, her father had run up debts, including his debt to Deveryn, to the staggering total of twenty thousand pounds. Drumoak was the least of Donald Sinclair's losses, for she did not think that it would fetch as much as a tenth of that sum. She stared dry-eyed at the bills in her hand, smoothing them again and again with trembling fingers.

When she left her chamber to go to dinner, she was very calm, very composed and frighteningly empty of all emotion.

For two days, it rained solidly—a not unusual circumstance given the geography and the time of year. Foreigners to the capital, and there were many since the publication of Princess Charlotte's engagement to Prince Leopold, might have been excused for thinking that the natives were strangers to the phenomenon, so loudly and pithily did they voice their displeasure.

Maddie was not one of them. The vagaries of the English climate gave her a reprieve from Deveryn's demands, since a drive in the country, or even in the park, was no longer an adequate subterfuge to permit him to pursue their clandestine marriage.

The viscount, on the other hand, complained as much as any man, and with more reason, in his opinion. The unrelenting rain had very effectively kept him from his wife.

He was stationed at the window in his mother's drawing room overlooking Manchester Square, mulling over in his mind how he could circumvent the proprieties and steal more than two minutes alone with Maddie.

"Damn the rain!" he said, and abruptly turned back into the room.

"What?" The Earl of Rossmere's eyes continued to scan the headlines of his morning *Times*.

"The rain, sir," answered Deveryn. "It makes travel almost out of the question."

"Who's thinking of making a journey? You've only just got here."

There was no reply to this idle observation, and after a moment the earl's eyes lifted to study his heir from behind the screen of his thick lashes. "So you *are* anxious to get back to Crammond," he murmured, as if to himself. "I had wondered at this absence from town. Your mother tells me that you've been provisioning the place and have gone so far as to hire a full complement of retainers. If I didn't know you better, my boy, I'd say that you'd taken it into your head to settle down."

Max Branwell, the only other occupant of the room, turned away to hide a smile. "I'll ring for more coffee," he interposed diplomatically, and half rose from the comfortable gold brocade side chair which was pulled close to the blazing fire.

"Don't trouble yourself, Max," said the earl. "I'm perfectly certain that her ladyship has commandeered every last lackey in the house. No one is going to answer that bell-pull till after our guests have departed."

"What? Oh, quite."

Mr. Branwell sank back in his chair. He'd forgotten that the place would be teeming with people. The countess was hosting the annual open house for her Bluestocking Brigade where, for once, gentlemen were permitted to attend. Some, like himself and present company, were under orders to show their faces since there were always a few lively bucks in attendance who thought it great sport to bait the girls. The countess relied on her male relatives to lend moral support and smooth things over if the debate degenerated into an exchange of personal insults, which was more than likely since the countess invariably elected topics for discussion at these mixed affairs which fanned the flames of the proverbial war between the sexes.

The earl cocked a meaningful eyebrow at his son. "Well?" asked Lord Rossmere, pointedly.

Deveryn could not prevent the boyish grin that spread across his face. "In a day or two, sir, you may expect to offer your felicitations. For the present, I am not at liberty to say more."

Lord Rossmere folded his newspaper without haste and carefully set it on the small side-table which flanked his chair.

"You surprise me, my boy," he said in that same pleasant manner from which nothing, it seemed, could ever provoke him.

Deveryn stiffened imperceptibly. "Sir?"

Mr. Branwell became conscious of the subtle change in the atmosphere. With studied casualness, he again rose to his feet. "I'll swear," he said in a casual tone, "that a ball would require less fuss and bother than this do, yes and be much more enjoyable besides. I promised Mary I'd be there for the start. I'd best be getting on down."

Neither of his companions made the least attempt to detain him. Nothing was said until the door closed softly at his back.

"Do take a seat, Jason," said the older man, gesturing to the chair which Mr. Branwell had newly vacated. "I feel somewhat at a disadvantage when you stand towering over me. That's better," he went on when the viscount, after a slight hesitation, followed his father's suggestion.

The earl's blue eyes, deceptively lazy, studied the younger man for some few minutes before he offered, "Your mother has been a trifle anxious about you of late."

Deveryn, equally casual, ventured, "How so?"

"She's taken it into her head that you've become something of a libertine."

The viscount laced his fingers together and quirked one questioning eyebrow in a manner which was singularly reminiscent of his sire.

A small smile touched the earl's lips when it became evident that the younger man meant to preserve a noncommittal silence. "You don't deny it?" he asked at length.

"I thought I had when I admitted that I was on the threshold of matrimony," was the cool rejoinder.

"Which is precisely what has your mother in a pucker."

"I would have thought, sir, that the report of my nuptials would put her into transports. It's what she's been angling for these last several years."

"Very true. But some gabblemonger has frightened her into thinking that the lady you are about to offer for is, to be frank, quite unsuited to be the next Countess of Rossmere."

The eyes of the two men met. "By a strange quirk of fate," said Deveryn in a tone that belied the rigid set of his jaw, "the girl I happen to love is, in my opinion, eminently suitable to take her place in our family. However," and here he leaned forward as if to emphasize his point, "should it have been otherwise, if Maddie . . . if the lady of my choice had been, by birth, an unsuitable candidate, it would have made not a jot of difference. Nothing on God's earth could ever make me give her up."

The earl, having heard what he wished to hear, visibly relaxed. "Maddie? That would be Miss Sinclair. So . . . your mother thought as much when you were at Dunsdale. But since then there have been all sorts of disquieting rumours."

The viscount ignored this last comment and, picking up a discarded letter opener which he appeared to examine with some interest, said mildly, "So mother guessed it was Maddie?"

"Apparently. I thought perhaps the Heatherington girl?"

"She was never in the running."

"Ah, throwing sand in our eyes? It's as your mother suspected. Which brings me to something else she happened to mention. Your uncle Raeburn I'm told is courting the girl."

"He's decided to withdraw from the field," said Deveryn, and he carefully replaced the letter opener where he'd found it.

"Has he, by Jove! And how did you manage that, may I ask?"

Deveryn glanced at the earl from under his lashes. "I merely . . . explained the situation," he said gravely.

The earl's eyes were brimming with suppressed laughter. "And Raeburn stepped aside because he did not wish to stand in the way of true love? How very commendable!"

"Something like that," answered the viscount without elaboration.

A considering silence ensued as both men became lost in private reflection.

Deveryn's thoughts drifted to Raeburn Abbey and the interview which he'd had with the duke. He'd gone down almost as soon as he'd had confirmation from Edinburgh that his marriage to Maddie was binding. He'd half expected that the issue would be settled over dueling pistols. Raeburn, as he'd remembered, had seemed almost relieved when he'd told him bluntly that Maddie Sinclair was off limits to every man by virtue of her marriage to himself. The duke had assured him that he could count on his discretion, and had agreed to leave everything in his hands. He'd thought then that the whole matter could be settled very quickly and easily. And so it would have been, if Samuel Spencer had not disobligingly gone off to Paris on the spur of the moment.

"Mmm . . ." said the earl reflectively. "Why is it that I have this feeling you're concealing something behind that inscrutable expression?"

Deveryn assessed his sire with fathomless blue eyes which had deepened to indigo. "Soon, sir," said the viscount, "very soon, I shall be in a position to satisfy your curiosity."

"My boy," disclaimed the earl, "I hope I am not so vulgar. It's merely that . . ."

"Yes, I know. Mother!"

The two men exchanged amused glances.

"You see how it is," said the earl at his most laconic. "She can never be persuaded that her cubs neither need or want her protection. I've repeatedly told her that you've been through a war and know how to look out for yourself." The earl paused and chose his next words with care. "Much good it does. She seems to think that you've landed in a quagmire."

Startled, Deveryn sliced a glance at the older man. "A quagmire?" he repeated blankly.

The earl's voice was as smooth as satin. "I did mention, did I not, that several rumours are circulating? You must know, surely, that your name has been bruited about with that opera dancer's—what's her name?—not that *that* signifies in the least. No, it's the other dasher that's set your mother's teeth on edge."

"Dasher!" exclaimed the viscount, thinking of Maddie.

"Worldly widow, then," drawled the earl, relishing his heir's sudden loss of countenance. He could not resist adding another promising faggot to the blaze. "D'you think it's wise, my boy, to be so patently dabbling in the petticoat line when you hope to secure the hand and affections of another lady? Or perhaps Miss Sinclair doesn't mind? One can never tell with these modern misses."

A warm tide of colour heated Deveryn's normally saturnine complexion. Not since he was a boy in short coats and caught out in some devilment had he felt so acutely embarrassed. And, he thought, the implied rebuke in his father's words was so unjust. His converse with Cynthia Sinclair since arriving in town had been of a strictly business nature. He'd only been to the house on Baker Street a time or two, and at the lady's request to explain some minor matter of business respecting her income from the property in Scotland. He'd been careful, on every occasion, to take along Freddie Ponsonby and Lady Elizabeth Heatherington so that the proprieties had been observed.

That the two women had become fast friends had surprised him almost as much as it had gratified him. It was a friendship that he had encouraged since it relieved him of some of the burden of responsibility he felt for the lady's unfortunate circumstances.

It was also unfortunate that Maddie could not be persuaded to view the whole matter dispassionately. Even now, he'd heard the odd comment which suggested that people were curious about the lack of converse between the two women. He would not tolerate such vulgar speculation once he had his wife under his roof. Maddie would be civil to Cynthia Sinclair or he would play the heavy-handed husband. On this, there would be no compromise.

He became conscious that the earl was watching the play of emotions on his unguarded features. In stilted accents, far removed from his habitual nonchalance, he embarked on an abridged explanation of his involvement with Donald Sinclair's widow. His father cut him off in mid-sentence.

"No need to explain your conduct to me. Good grief, when I was your age—well, that is neither here nor there. At any rate, I put all that behind me when I wed your mother."

"Yes," interposed the viscount with an oddly twisted smile, "I had heard something of your unusual courtship, though, unlike you, I don't put much credence in rumour."

The earl shrugged negligently. "That's old history. What I did, I did for your mother's own good."

"It's true then?" asked Deveryn.

"Possibly. What have you heard?"

In other circumstances, the viscount would have had more respect for his sire than to confront him with ancient gossip which showed the earl in a bad light. Since he himself, however, felt somewhat put out by his father's blunt taunts, he saw no reason not to return the compliment.

"That you abducted my mother at the altar as she was about to repeat her vows to another man," he stated baldly.

"A milksop," averred the earl with a shudder of revulsion. "He would never have made her happy. Unfortunately, she would not admit to it. I was forced to take extraordinary measures to prove that I was the better man."

"Good God! Surely you didn't, I mean, you did wait till you were married before . . ." He faltered before the earl's stern eye.

"That, my boy, is none of your business."

Deveryn looked at his father in shocked silence. "And to think," he murmured, "that I . . ." He shook his head and then offered by way of explanation, "I can scarcely take it in, sir. You don't give the impression of being such a hot-blooded creature, and as for my mother, she hardly seems the type to inspire a man to such passion."

"One's children," droned the earl, "are always inclined to see their parents with blinkers on. However, to return to the object of this discussion—your mother."

"I was under the impression that I was the subject of this discussion," quizzed the viscount.

"Were you? Oh no! I don't hold with meddling in the affairs of one's own grown children. But your mother's peace of mind—that is a different matter. I may rely on you, I trust, to do everything in your power to alleviate her distress?"

"Quite."

"Thank you, my boy. Unfortunately, you see, she has this notion that you are your father's son. It has been known to keep her awake at night. To be frank, I don't like it when she's troubled."

"I'll lay her fears to rest," averred the viscount with filial piety and a sincerity that was later to be proved entirely misplaced.

Chapter Twenty

When Maddie entered the portals of Lady Rossmere's house, she balked at the unexpected crush of people, many of whom were gentlemen. The answer to the terse question which she directed to her companion, Lady Rutherston, did nothing to soothe her overstrung nerves.

"Open house?" repeated Maddie, her mind going blank.

Catherine's eyes warmed with concern. "Does it make a difference?" she asked gently. "I never thought to mention it."

"I don't think that what I have to say will be received warmly by our opposite gender," disclaimed Maddie in a small voice.

Catherine's clear laugh rang out. "Don't let that weigh with you. This is our one chance a year to give these arrogant coxcombs a well deserved set-down. Even Richard, liberal as he is, verges sometimes on the condescending. The male animal, as I make no doubt you've learned to your regret, considers himself the superior of our species."

"I heard that," said Lord Rutherston coming up behind them. "Mind your manners, Catherine, or you'll find out soon enough just how superior this condescending male animal can get." And he chucked his wife under the chin in a condescending manner which Maddie eyed with marked disfavour.

By the time they had availed themselves of the refreshments which were laid out in adjoining rooms, Maddie had begun to get a hold of herself. She scanned the crowd for a glimpse of

Deveryn's blond head. When she could not find him, her confidence increased. Max Branwell, however, soon disabused her of the notion that she could avoid her husband's presence.

"If you're looking for Deveryn, he'll be here directly," he told her with a knowing smile.

"How . . . nice," she murmured inanely.

At two of the clock precisely, Lady Rossmere opened the meeting to standing room only. The two speakers were introduced and took their places at a long table facing the audience. Maddie listened as her friend began, a little hesitantly at first, then gradually with more confidence, to argue her thesis, namely, that the golden age of Athens was golden for only half its citizens—and that the male of the species.

Maddie's eyes travelled the room, absently noting the members of the audience with whom she had an acquaintance. In the front row was Caroline Lamb flanked by her husband and her mother, Lady Bessborough. Lord Rutherston was off to the side. She might have been mistaken, but Maddie thought his eyes glinted with more than a little pride as Catherine carefully and persuasively made her presentation. Freddie Ponsonby was stationed near the entrance, his head inclined to catch something that Lady Elizabeth Heatherington was whispering in his ear. Lady Elizabeth turned to the side revealing the presence of another lady. Cynthia Sinclair, stunning in black, inclined her head gravely in Maddie's direction. Maddie, equally polite, returned the gesture, and wondered if the pomona green silk which she had donned that morning could legitimately be regarded as half-mourning.

Catherine's discourse drew to a close. Her parting comment was that women throughout recorded history had been relegated to a low place in the scheme of things by men.

"How low is a pedestal?" demanded Perry Montford in a stage whisper, eliciting a host of appreciative, masculine chortles.

Lady Rossmere was on her feet, explaining with a cautionary glance at the offender that the question period would be deferred until the second speaker had had her say. There was a polite round of applause.

Her palms were damp; her throat was dry. Maddie reached

for the glass of water which had been thoughtfully set out for her, and sipped slowly.

According to the gospel of Miss Maitland, the besetting sin of orators was a failure to capture the interest of their audience. "For what's the point," she was used to demand of the senior girls, "of wasting hours and hours in doing your research and even more hours in fashioning your facts into a logical exposition if nobody pays attention? From the moment you open your mouth, you must get their interest and hold it." She had not told them what to do when their minds went blank.

Maddie carefully replaced her glass on the table and rose to her feet. She looked out at a sea of expectant faces. She opened her lips and tried to speak, but her tongue seemed to be glued to the roof of her mouth. Her heart hammered wildly against her ribs, and quite literally, her knees knocked together. Stage fright, she thought, and gripped the edge of the table till her knuckles showed white.

At the entrance to the library, two latecomers paused to take in the scene. It was the younger, taller gentleman which riveted Maddie's attention. Deveryn took one step into the room and caught sight of her. Maddie could almost feel the shock of recognition as it rippled all through his body. For a moment, he looked to be bewildered. His eyes roved the room and then returned to the speaker's table. After a moment, a smile of mingled surprise and comprehension gentled his features.

The audience grew restive, and some turned to stare at the gentleman who had captured the attention of the guest speaker. Deveryn, conscious of several speculative glances, turned aside.

His appearance acted on Maddie like a douse of cold water. She expelled a great shuddering breath and, to her great relief, finally found her voice.

"What is the worst thing that can happen to a woman?" she asked her listeners in an arch tone.

It took a moment for the audience to realise that the question was not rhetorical. She repeated it, and one of the bolder debs, who was known to be in her fourth Season and the despair of her parents since she frustrated their ambition to marry her off to some eligible gentleman, answered boldly,

"To remain unmarried, or so I've been told since I was in the cradle."

A gale of feminine laughter swept the audience. The gentlemen remained predictably stoic.

"And what," asked Maddie, in the same bantering tone, "is the worst fate that can overtake a *married* woman?"

Maddie's design was caught by some of the brighter ladies. Several voices called out at once.

"To be barren."

"Not to have children."

"To produce only daughters for her lord and master."

Maddie put up a hand to halt the spate of excited chatter. "My next question is this—who told you so? Who decreed that that's the worst fate that can befall a female?"

"Men, of course!" someone instantly responded.

"You've got the picture," said Maddie. "Shall we ask the gentlemen the very same question? Gentlemen, what is the worst fate that can befall a male?"

From the back of the room, a young buck challenged, "You surely don't expect a *gentleman* to answer that question in mixed company?"

Hoots of masculine laughter greeted this not so oblique sally. A few of the ladies were seen to be blushing. Lady Rossmere threw a look of anguished appeal at Maddie.

"We'll excuse that last remark," said Maddie, flashing her heckler a smile of patient amusement. "Mr. Shea is not long down from Oxford. He has, as I understand, just turned twenty. Little does he know that his days are numbered."

More laughter followed, this time from both sexes.

"What Mr. Shea has yet to discover, or perhaps won't admit to," said Maddie lightly, "is that men—want—heirs. A man's ambition is centred on his sons. With sons, a man reaches for posterity. He can found a dynasty. Establish his house. Continue his name. Deprive him of those heirs and you rob him of his life's blood. Sons are, at one and the same time, his greatest strength and his most profound weakness."

She paused and allowed her eyes to roam the room. "What man," she said softly, "has not regretted at some time or other that women are a necessry tool in begetting his heirs?"

She waited till the laughter and cat calls had died down

332

before continuing. "Women, you see, are the weak link in the chain of his ambition. A clever woman, if she wants to, can use that weakness against him.

"Euripides wrote a play entitled *Medea*. It's a cautionary tale for all men who would underestimate the power of a defenceless female. For Medea, a wronged wife and without recourse to law or kin, exploited her husband's weakness to exact her own retribution, and in so doing she brought his hopes to ruin. Gentlemen, in the name of self-interest, you had better pay attention to Medea before her influence spreads to your own wives and daughters."

The silence seemed to pulsate with tension.

For the first time since she'd begun to speak, Maddie looked directly at Deveryn. Their eyes locked.

She's as fragile as porcelain, he thought.

Then Deveryn blazed with sudden, heart-stopping comprehension. *Is it true?* his eyes hotly demanded.

He saw her poise as if to take flight, sensed each panicked heartbeat, felt every difficult breath, but he refused to release her from his unrelenting gaze until she answered him.

Her eyes blazed a reply. *Yes, it's true.*

He felt himself stagger as if she had reached out and struck him. By the time he'd recovered, she had withdrawn, her head studiously averted. She did not look near him again.

He bided his time with diminishing patience as he waited for her erudite and humourous exposition to reach its conclusion. When the question period became prolonged, his annoyance intensified. But when the thing was at an end and no one showed any sign of going home but hedged her about, his temper became explosive.

"What a jewel," breathed Max Branwell in exaggerated accents, his eyes following Deveryn's gaze as they traced Maddie's path through the crush.

The viscount betrayed no interest in this observation save perhaps that his expression became a trifle more haughty.

Nothing daunted, Mr. Branwell continued in the same mischievous vein, "Poetic justice, old boy. Who would have believed that the fallen angel would have fallen victim to an ardent bluestocking? I'm sure I've listened to a score or more of your scathing diatribes on the folly of clever women. Quite

Byronic, I thought, if you don't mind my saying so! I say, this is famous! I can scarcely wait for your intended to make an appearance at Sunday dinners. D'you think you're up to it, Jason? A word to the wise—better start now, brushing up your Greek and philosophy, and so on. The girl is positively brilliant. Your mother and sisters are going to be hard pressed to look to their laurels. Don't tell me—I get it—the countess, herself, hand-picked the girl for you. Well, it stands to reason. Who else would fit into the family as if she's been bred to it? D'you know—something tells me that this is all a shock to you? I collect that the females in your family have been holding out on you, Jason. Sue 'em, that's my advice. I'll even act for you if you like." He slapped his brother-in-law consolingly on the shoulder. "It couldn't happen to a more deserving fellow!" And having delivered himself of this left-handed compliment, he gave a bark of laughter and sauntered off.

But Mr. Branwell was far off if he supposed that the viscount was out of countenance because his wife had turned out to be more than he'd bargained for. Deveryn could not have cared less, so he told himself, if Maddie's interests ran to mountain climbing, or balloon flying, or pearl fishing, or tight-rope walking. None of that signified because, naturally, whatever interested Maddie would also be of interest to him. He'd make it so. And as for the scathing diatribes on clever women in which he had formerly, quite sincerely, indulged, he dismissed them all as the arrant nonsense of a mere male uninitiated in the mysteries of love. Maddie and he had a lifetime before them to discover what made each of them unique. He looked forward to it. But of far more import at that moment was the reason for his wife's evasive tactics. She had not wanted him to know that she was with child—he had seen it in her eyes. Even now, he could tell that she was conscious of his every movement and anxiously waiting for her chance to come when she could break cover and make a run for it.

Ostensibly relaxed, he watched the proceedings from behind the veil of his lashes. When he observed that the crowd around Maddie was thinning, he made his move. Like a ravenous, prowling lion, circling, feinting, with consummate skill and unnerving speed, he cut her out of the herd.

"You're hurting me," she hissed at him, trying to shake free of the clamped hand on her elbow.

Deveryn's smile was everything that was cordial though the glance he threw at her could have melted an iceberg. "This way, Miss Sinclair. It won't take a moment. It's a very old scroll, and I'd like your opinion of it."

Maddie recognized the ruse for what it was, but short of creating a scene, she was powerless to gainsay him. She thought he would break her arm if she as much as blinked an eye.

"Smile," he growled, and without thinking, she obeyed him.

He adroitly avoided the stray well-wisher, but at the door their exit was blocked by a very determined figure sheathed in black satin.

Maddie felt Deveryn's hand tense then relax. "Cynthia," he drawled, "how . . . pleasant to see you again. I'd no idea you had an interest in the scholarly."

The two ladies exchanged frigid bows of greeting.

"Put your mind at rest, Jason," said Cynthia Sinclair with an intimate smile that did not include Maddie. "I make no pretense of being other than I am. You, of all people, should know where my interests lie."

Maddie made a small sound that might have been a cough or a snort of derision. Deveryn was far more sanguine.

"I haven't forgotten," he interposed and flashed a disarming grin which carefully included Maddie. "I'd be happy to lay your bets for you when I'm next in Newmarket."

The widow looked faintly amused and boldly suggested, "When you're next in Baker Street, I'll be happy to follow your lead. There's not much you don't know about riding and . . . horses."

"Delighted to be of service," said Deveryn amiably, and forcefully propelled Maddie round the obstacle which Cynthia presented. "I shall bring Maddie. It's time she expanded her horizons. A steady diet of oatmeal and classics has quite put her in the doldrums," he interpolated, as if an explanation of Maddie's frankly polemic expression was necessary.

The foyer was almost empty of people. In two strides they came to a short flight of stairs. He began to descend, dragging Maddie behind him.

"Where are you taking me?" she demanded and stumbled after him.

"To the powder room."

"The what?"

At the foot of the stairs was a door. He opened it, pushed her through and closed it firmly behind him. The room was no bigger than a closet, the only light from one small window. It was bare of furniture.

"What's a powder room?" she prevaricated.

"You know, for gentlemen of a former era when they wished to powder their wigs or hair. And stop evading me."

Suddenly he swooped down on her, and her small cry of fright was smothered as his lips took hers in a hungry kiss. His hands were everything, touching, testing, boldly claiming every curve and hollow, and finally came to rest on the swell of her stomach.

"Maddie," he groaned, his lips skimming over every exposed part of her skin above her collar, "why aren't you happy about this?" and he pressed his hands lightly to her abdomen.

He didn't wait for her to answer but swooped again, cutting off her breath in another demanding kiss.

With arms and elbows flying, she struggled free of him. "Deveryn!" she sputtered. "You're no better than an animal. I'd feel safer with that lion—what's-his-name in the Tower menagerie."

He spread his palms on the wall on either side of her head. "So you would be," he agreed, offering a cozening grin. "Nero is an old dog who's had his day. I'm just coming into my prime—lucky for you. Now answer my question. Why aren't you happy with this new thing that's happened to us?"

For a moment she thought she might cry ignorance. But one quick look at his knowing eyes and the temptation died stillborn.

"Who says I'm not happy?"

His hand cupped her neck, kneading the taut muscles that told against her.

"Then what's wrong?" he asked softly. "Maddie, tell me."

"What could possibly be wrong?" she demanded.

"Don't lie to me, Maddie."

"Oh, I'm a liar, am I? Look who's calling the kettle black.

You're the most consummate liar in all of England, and that's saying something."

"When have I ever lied to you?"

"When have you not? You lied to me about Grantham, didn't you?"

His hand lifted from her neck in one heartbeat of a pause, then descended and began a slow, soothing massage.

"I've never lied to you."

"Haven't you?" she asked, trying to sound arch and managing to sound pathetically close to tears. "I beg to differ. In fact," and she hauled herself out of his arms, "I don't think you know the meaning of the word 'honesty.'"

He stood with folded arms, observing with something like long suffering patience as she gave him her back and stared resolutely out the small window. After a few minutes of this unnatural silence, he began to look merely amused.

"Do you often stare at brick walls, Maddie?" he asked.

"What?"

"The brick wall which has captured your attention. I believe it's the west wall of the wash house should you wish to know."

She rounded on him in pent-up fury. "You talk to me of brick walls when I'm calling you a liar?"

"How did I lie to you?" he asked calmly.

"You told me that the woman in Grantham was that . . . that opera dancer. But she wasn't, was she Deveryn? She was my stepmother."

"I told you no lies. You jumped to conclusions—as you're doing now."

"Do you deny that Cynthia was the woman who was discovered in your chamber at the Falcon?"

"I told you the truth. The lady was not there by my invitation. Nothing of any significance happened. That's all you need to know."

"Was she or was she not Cynthia? A simple 'yes' or 'no' will suffice. Don't bother with the lecture. Well?"

A pulse beat furiously in his cheek. "Yes," he stated.

"Then why did you let me think it was someone else?"

"Because you have this irrational antipathy to Cynthia Sinclair. My God, look at you. You're almost foaming at the mouth. For God's sake Maddie, calm yourself. You'll harm the child."

Maddie was, at that moment, at the end of her tether. Seething with mingled outrage and anguish since she'd taken possession of her father's cancelled debts; haunted by a resurgence of remorse for having in some sort betrayed him by her marriage to Deveryn; weakened by a habitual morning sickness which she could not shake; stung by her stepmother's graphic taunts of a few moments before, she heard Deveryn's unfortunate choice of words and her control broke.

"Irrational! Irrational antipathy! Inmutable loathing, more like, and with good reason," she shrilled at him in a voice that the fish-wives of Edinburgh would have eschewed.

He reached for her and she jerked her arm from his grasp. "Don't touch me! Don't lay a hand on me. Liar! Adulterer! Cheat! Murderer!"

The venom in her voice shocked him as much as the words. Stung to a passion almost as great as her own, he grabbed her shoulders and roughly shook her.

With a menace she could not mistake, he said, "Speak to me in those tones again and I'll lay the lash to you. Now explain yourself, madam, and keep a civil tongue in your head," and administering one last shake, he abruptly released her.

She stumbled back and, straightening, shot him a look of furious contempt. Her voice throbbing with suppressed emotion, she said, "Deny it if you dare, Deveryn. My father lost not only Drumoak to you at the gaming tables, but also the sum of ten thousand pounds."

"I don't deny it. Get to the point."

For a moment, she was at a loss for words. She'd had it on the tip of her tongue to convict him of his denial with the evidence of her father's cancelled debts. She'd never expected him to admit to her accusations.

"Well?" he demanded.

Rallying, she went on. "My stepmother did almost as well. Between the two of you, you bilked my father of close to twenty thousand pounds."

"I see. And I take it you have newly come by this information."

"Two days since, when my father's cancelled debts came into my hand."

He made a gesture of impatience. "Though I don't expect you to believe me, I'll say it anyway. I never expected to collect on that gaming debt. It was my man of business's doing. I gave him leave to act for me when I was in Scotland. He found your father's vowels and presented them to your father's solicitor here. There was nothing I could do. But I wish you would believe that I have invested every penny in Drumoak. And even if I did win such a sum of money from your father, I wish you would tell me how that makes me a murderer."

She tried to match his control but failed miserably. "It's not hard to figure out," she said with a break in her voice. "Consider that my father was infatuated with his young wife. She takes a lover. In very short order, my father loses the wife whom he adores, his estate, and . . . and the whole of a legacy to which he had newly come into. Like a wounded animal, he makes for home." She paused to steady her breath, then said very softly. "Do you truly believe that my father lost his life in an accident? I tell you . . ."

His fist slammed into the wall and the spate of accusing words froze in her throat.

"Why am I to blame?" he thundered, his mouth contorted in fury. "Why not your father? I wasn't the one who allowed my wife *carte blanche* so that any man thought that she was his for the taking; I was not the one who gamed away your precious Drumoak; I was not the one who wagered his last groat on the turn of a card. If your father did take his own life, and I can scarcely credit it, how am I to blame? The man was a weakling, without character. He gave not a second thought to your unhappy fate!"

"You're a fine one to talk of character!" she railed at him, angry past caring. "You stole a man's wife; forcibly dishonoured his daughter; what more can you do to him unless you mean to visit your vendetta on the next generation of Sinclairs!" She tossed her head and stared at him with defiance smouldering in her eyes. "I'd be a fool to let you get your hands on my child."

His face went starkly white and his hand clenched as if to strike her. She noted the gesture, and her eyes widened with sudden knowledge of the jeopardy she had brought upon herself.

339

Shaking, visibly controlling his temper, he said, "You may well flinch from me, madam wife. What you have said is unforgivable!"

Long moments passed, Maddie not daring to flex a muscle so threatening did Deveryn's presence seem in that small room.

Finally, he smiled, then laughed. "What a performance!" he exclaimed softly and shook his head at the spectacle she presented. "Melodrama does not become you, Maddie. I think your study of Greek drama has mounted to your head. This is England, or had you forgotten?"

Keeping his eyes locked with hers, he murmured, "For a clever girl, you're not very sensible. Have you considered that you're not in a strong position? What are you to do? Where can you go? To whom can you turn? Certainly not to your grandfather! He's more like to beat you senseless when he hears of the hoydenish escapade you've involved us both in. In a very short while, you will come to know how much authority a husband wields over a rebellious wife. Use the wits you were born with, Maddie. Swallow your bile and sue for terms while I'm still in a humour to be reasonable."

He smiled ironically in that twisted, satanic way which had earned him the soubriquet "the fallen angel."

Maddie goaded, but still deathly afraid, challenged cautiously, "Are you th-threatening me, Deveryn?"

He laughed, and let her go. "No. I'm telling you what you may expect. You've been spoiled past redemption. Oh, not in any material sense, but by virtue of the fact that you've been free these many years past to go your own way. From now on, you'll learn to accept the bit between your teeth, or you'll suffer the consequences. Do I make myself clear?"

Staring doggedly into his face, she said, "I think you must not have been listening when I gave my address in your father's library."

"What? That faradiddle about the power of a defenceless woman?" For all that his voice was soft and silky, it grated on her ears. "Maddie, admit it. You can't do a damned thing. Do your worst. I dare you!"

"W-Watch me, Deveryn," she said, then again, with more conviction, "Just you watch me!"

* * *

In his lodgings in Jermyn Street, at three o'clock of the morning, having broached his third bottle of burgundy, the Viscount Deveryn found to his annoyance that he still could not banish from his mind the picture of Maddie as he'd last seen her, like a furious, helpless kitten, spitting her impotent rage at him. One part of him wanted only to stop her mouth with kisses and love her into silence; the other, and the one which surfaced most often, wanted to tumble her skirts above her ears and lay the whip to her bare bottom.

He could not believe that she would speak to him in such terms after everything that had passed between them. "Liar! Adulterer! Cheat! Murderer!" He was none of those things! How dare she fling such baseless accusations in his teeth when he was the one who was more sinned against than sinning? It was *he* who was the victim of them all—Cynthia Sinclair, Donald Sinclair, and most of all, Maddie Sinclair. He wished to God he'd never heard the name Sinclair, had never come into Scotland, had never put his heart into the hands of the little spitfire. They were ruthless hands, as his bruised heart could testify.

And that last cut—*that* was the most wounding of all! He did not think that he would ever forgive or forget the manner in which he had been left to discover for himself that he was to be the father of her child.

"Women!" he said aloud, conveying, in that one word, all the scorn of the bewildered male for an enigma which could not be grasped by his superior intellect.

"Yes, my lord," murmured his valet noncommittally, and unobtrusively went about removing the remains of a late supper which it was evident his lordship had scarcely touched.

"Where was the champagne? Where were the soft words?" demanded Deveryn rhetorically.

"Quite so, my lord," responded Martin, with the merest hint of ingratiating sympathy.

The viscount stared morosely into space, moodily reviewing the besetting sins—and there were many—of the love of his life. Maddie Sinclair Verney might be a brilliant scholar, but as a wife she was positively brainless.

His thoughts wandered to Maddie as she had been that morning, articulate, lucid, and so endearingly humourous as she had delivered her address, a set-down really, to the complacent males in her audience. How startled they had been! How proud he had been of his clever, little wife! But dammit if she had not meant every word for *him!* It was so unjust! He was a broadminded fellow—liberal to a degree. How dare she lump him with men in general as if his ambition stretched no further than the begetting of heirs. He was sure he scarcely gave a thought to the succession.

"Should she give me a son, no doubt I shall be expected to weep buckets of crocodile tears and go about Friday-faced for the rest of my miserable existence," he told his valet.

Martin's stoic demeanour suffered a momentary lapse. He recovered quickly and managed a toneless, "Quite."

"It's not as if I don't like girls, you understand," said the viscount conversationally. "She's welcome to fill my house with 'em. After all, my mother's a female, and so are my sisters. Nobody has ever accused me before of not being fond of the softer sex. But dammit, man, she has no right to keep me from my sons."

Martin had no ready answer for this intelligence, but a more sober eye than Deveryn's would have noted that the colour had receded somewhat from the valet's normally sanguine complexion.

"Mark my words, Martin," continued his lordship, waxing belligerent, "there isn't an ounce of romance in a woman's heart. Bookkeepers and bankers, every last one of 'em! Debits and credits—that's all they understand. What's the matter with you man? You look to be three sheets into the wind. Oh, stop fussing and go to bed."

Martin, wisely, gave every appearance of obeying his master's bald command. An hour or so later, he returned with a blanket which he threw over Deveryn's softly snoring form after having first removed his master's immaculate boots.

At noon the following morning, Deveryn wakened, his head throbbing savagely, his bones aching from having spent the night in the cramped confines of his favourite armchair.

Almost immediately, his eyes lit on a silver salver on which reposed a single folded sheet of paper. He reached for it and studied the several Greek characters which were written in a bold hand across the top of the page. They formed his name. He knew at once that it came from Maddie. Inside were two short

342

sentences, again, in Greek letters.

Perhaps it was the effects of his night of dissipation, perhaps it was because the viscount had scarcely glanced at Greek since his Oxford days. Whatever the reason, it took him a full five minutes to work out that he was not reading Greek words but a mere transliteration of English words into Greek letters.

The note was short and cryptic. He read, "Medea Part Two begins. I hope you are watching, Deveryn."

He reached Curzon Street within thirty minutes, having bathed, shaved, and changed his garments. He was not surprised to find Maddie gone and the house in an uproar.

The Countess of Rossmere silently remarked that her son was not in his best looks. To be frank, and the countess was nothing if she was not frank, she thought the same might be said of any of the several persons who graced her drawing room on that particular cold and blustery Saturday evening. Only her husband, the earl, gave the appearance of being totally unaffected by the events which had overtaken them in these last several hours.

Her eyes wandered to Samuel Spencer, and her heart softened. He looked to have aged ten years since she had last spoken to him at Carlton House—was it only a week or so since? A flash of irritation showed itself in a small frown which clouded her smooth brow. It was intolerable that the men of the Verney family should conduct themselves with so little propriety, as if beneath the veneer of their impeccable manners, they concealed their true nature—something wild and savage beyond taming. Though her mother's heart went out to her son since she knew that he was wretched beyond permission, her sympathies were mostly for the girl. No one knew better than she how ruthless a Verney male could become when thwarted in love. Her own male relatives—and she sliced a glance to her cousin, Raeburn, who was tête à tête with Miss Spencer—were gentle and chivalrous creatures. Why couldn't the Verneys be more like them?

It was inconceivable that any one of her male relatives would browbeat a young girl into a clandestine marriage and then proceed to exercise his conjugal rights given the unhappy situation in which the girl found herself. She was sure she had been ready to sink when, in reply to his father's pointed enquiry about the consummation of the marriage, Deveryn had tersely admitted that not only had he been on the most intimate terms with his wife in Scotland, but also at Dunsdale, and in London besides. Small wonder that Maddie had bolted when she discovered that she was pregnant! Still, her mother's intuition told her that the viscount had not divulged the whole story. She could not believe that he'd held off from making his marriage public until he'd had a reply to a letter he had sent to Maddie's guardian in Canada. She could not believe it because it was so untypically Verney to wait on any man. She suppressed a shudder. She did not see how things could be worse than they were.

She gave the signal and the two footmen who had been stationed by the door moved quietly into the room and removed the remains of a cold collation of which only the earl had eaten heartily. The door closed upon the departing servants and several voices rushed into speech at once. Only Deveryn, slouched in a chair, his legs stretched out before him, maintained an aloof and forbidding silence.

It was Lord Rossmere whose commanding tones, all the more menacing since he rarely raised his voice, cut across the flurry of recriminations and comment.

"Mr. Spencer," he said in a voice that was wont to send his servants scurrying for cover, "these senseless recriminations are redundant. Why my son and your granddaughter chose to marry without your consent has already been gone into. She had no guardian in England to whom application might be made for her hand. Oh, I agree that Deveryn has much to answer for, but I, for one, am wearied to death of rehashing old issues. If there is anything new to be said on the subject, I am willing to listen. If not, I suggest we let Jason get to bed. He has an early start ahead of him tomorrow."

From the depths of a commodious wing armchair, Miss Nell Spencer offered tremulously, "I think that Maddie was not happy when my father informed her that her betrothal to Raeburn was to be published in the papers."

"Well, of course she wasn't happy," exclaimed Spencer, patently annoyed. "What a dim-witted thing to say. How

344

should she be when she was already wed and expecting another man's child?"

The Duke of Raeburn reached across and clasped Miss Spencer's trembling hand in his own strong one and squeezed in a comforting gesture. "Why was I not advised that the betrothal was to be published so soon?" he asked coldly, looking at Spencer.

Samuel Spencer shot His Grace a withering look. "Where were you, Raeburn, these last few weeks? We scarce saw you in Curzon Street. And when you did come, it was Nellie to whom you paid court. Good God! In my day, we knew how to sweep a lady off her feet. Yes . . . well . . . we all know which gentleman beat you to it. I thought merely to put things on a more regular footing. Some silly fop had already approached me about offering for Maddie. The girl stands to come into a fair bit of money. I'd no wish to have a stream of suitors camping on my doorstep once she increased her circle of acquaintances. The announcement of your betrothal would have put a stop to all of that."

The earl approached His Grace and proffered a crystal glass of ruby red liquid. "What? A reluctant swain, George?" he quizzed in a soft undertone. Raeburn disengaged his hand from Miss Spencer's clasp and accepted the glass without comment.

Deveryn, adjusting his long body in his chair, said with the first interest he had shown in the last hour, "But there was no announcement of the betrothal in any of the papers."

"No," admitted Spencer grudgingly. "Maddie and I had words on the subject. I agreed to defer the publication till after I returned from Paris. Only see what a bumblebroth awaited me today when I stepped over my threshold."

"Be thankful for small mercies," drawled the earl. "Deveryn remained here in London until you should arrive from Paris so that he might explain in person the unhappy circumstances of your granddaughter's disappearance. If he'd gone tearing after her, as he wished to do, think of the torment you would have endured not knowing the why or wherefore. As I understand, the several messages she left behind were remarkably uninformative."

"Why didn't you go after her at once?" demanded Spencer. "You've given her a good two days headstart as it is."

345

Deveryn shrugged. "Speed is not of the essence in this instance. I can't overtake her as I would surely have done if she had travelled by coach. And there's not another packet going to Leith for several days. At least we know her destination. I'll catch up to her soon enough."

The countess tilted her head to one side and, addressing Spencer, said softly, "You said that you and Maddie had words. What does that mean, precisely?"

Mr. Spencer gave a short, deprecating laugh. "I know what you're thinking, but you're very far off. Good grief, don't you think I learned from my mistakes with Maddie's mother? I tell you, nothing of any significance happened. I did not lose my temper or threaten the girl in any way, shape or form. On the contrary, I let her have her way about the announcement to the papers."

"And so you did," said the countess soothingly. "Why don't you just begin at the beginning and tell us what was said?"

Though it was evident that Samuel Spencer thought he was embarking on a useless exercise, after a few false starts, he gave an abridged account of his last conversation with Maddie.

"Naturally, I tried to persuade her to fall in with my designs," he said, unconsciously truthful. "I thought if she knew her father had been in favour of the match, she would have been more open to Raeburn's suit." He seemed to lose interest in what he was saying to follow some private train of thought.

"But she wasn't, was she?" observed the countess gently.

He fixed his gaze upon her. "No," he stated. "And now we know why," and he shot a truculent look upon Deveryn's harshly carved features.

"There's something more, isn't there?" intoned the countess in sudden intuition. "Something perhaps which you feel has no bearing on Maddie's disappearance and which you don't feel comfortable confiding to strangers. But you know, Mr. Spencer, it were wiser if we knew everything that happened that night."

Mr. Spencer's eyes dropped to his clasped hands. At length he said, "I did lose my temper, though I'm perfectly sure not one angry word passed my lips. But . . ." He hesitated.

"Yes?"

"I behaved unforgivably. We got into an argument about her father. I had not meant to say anything against him, but she provoked me. I'm afraid I tried to discredit him in her eyes."

And with a great deal of circumlocution and a little patient questioning by the countess, the whole story came out.

"Are you saying," asked Lord Rossmere, carefully neutral, "that for the sum of twenty thousand pounds the girl's father gave up all rights to her?"

A dark tide of colour rose in the other man's cheeks. "No," he answered curtly, then with more belligerence, "the sum agreed upon was fifty thousand pounds. Donald Sinclair had thirty thousand waiting for him. He never came back to claim it."

Deveryn felt, at that moment, as if a dead weight had been lifted from his shoulders. "Thirty thousand pounds still to his credit!" he exclaimed softly, and he shut his eyes as the implications filled his mind with stunning force. By degrees, the tension eased from his body. He opened his eyes and looked directly at Spencer.

"But Maddie thought . . ." he said.

"What did she think?"

"Maddie thought that her father had used up every last groat of the money you'd given him—oh, not that she told me the whole story. She said that he'd come into a legacy and lost it all. It half convinced her that . . . well, that he hadn't had much to look forward to."

"Oh, Donald Sinclair had plenty to look forward to. That was only the down payment. In addition, I undertook to settle an income of five thousand a year upon him."

"Good God," exclaimed Raeburn. "What a mercenary fellow he must have been."

Spencer shook his head. "No, no. You don't understand. To be fair, he only wanted me to settle his debts. The rest was my own doing. And no, I am not generous as a rule. Oh, call it conscience money! Call it whatever you like! But he was the man my daughter once loved and married. He was the father of my only grandchild. For the first time, I had him where I wanted him. But, do you know, the taste of revenge turned to ashes in my mouth."

A thoughtful silence ensued. At length, some desultory conversation followed on the journey that Deveryn would be embarking on at first light.

"I should arrive in Edinburgh in five days," said Deveryn in answer to his father's query.

"That's going some!" remarked the Duke of Raeburn.

"I'll be travelling light," responded the viscount, "and I've already sent out my grooms with a string of fast mounts to await me at the posting houses."

Miss Spencer intoned quietly, "Why don't you delay and come with the rest of us aboard your yacht? Maddie will be safe enough at Drumoak for the extra week that's involved."

The viscount shook his head. "No, I've already wasted too much time as it is. I'd go mad sitting in town, twiddling my thumbs, till the repairs to my yacht are done."

"Besides," interposed the countess, "I expect my other daughters will be anxious to make the acquaintance of their new sister-in-law. They'll want to come with us. It will be several days before we're all ready to make the journey to Scotland. Think of it as a holiday."

With rapidly diminishing patience, Samuel Spencer expostulated, "What I don't understand is why we have to go to Scotland at all. Why not simply let Deveryn bring Maddie back to us?"

The countess riveted him with a piercing look. "Nothing," she said with frost in her voice, "nothing could be more certain to make the girl dig in her heels. Furthermore," she went on, her accents becoming decidedly more arctic, "to drag her from everything familiar would be the worst form of cruelty. You need not come with us if you don't wish to. But there's no saying how long it might be before you see Maddie again."

She glanced up as her husband came to stand over her. He bent his head and kissed her very swiftly on the brow. For her ears only he murmured, "History has a way of repeating itself. Don't take on so, my love. Everything will be just as you wish it."

She flashed him a grateful look.

After that, conversation ceased altogether. The countess looked at her watch and exclaimed at the late hour. As her guests rose to take their leave, she begged her son in a quiet aside to wait on her in her dressing room.

As Samuel Spencer reached the head of the stairs, he turned to the countess and said pleadingly, "I swear I meant everything for the best. It's these modern manners I'm not accustomed to. In my day, marriages were arranged, and very happy they were, too. I don't doubt, Lady Rossmere, that you were never given the choice of whom you would wed."

"Certainly not," she exclaimed, and shot a very telling look at the earl, who merely returned an enigmatic smile.

Deveryn caught that silent exchange between his parents. It was a look he'd often surprised on their faces, but never until that moment had he understood to what it referred. Damn if he did not feel himself blushing.

"In our day," said the countess without blinking an eyelash, "marriage came first, and love came afterwards. But you see how it is with our young people. They're in love, or at least Deveryn loves Maddie. We have only his word for it that she loves him, too. And really, Mr. Spencer, there's no reason why we should withhold our blessing from this union, is there?"

"No, no. I'm too old now to hold grudges. Only a fool don't learn from past mistakes."

He thrust out his hand. Deveryn took it in a firm clasp.

His voice visibly shaking, Spencer said, "I only want what's best for her. And if she's set on you, I won't stand in your way. Oh, if only I had said words like those to Maddie's father, so many years ago, how much pain and misery we might all have been spared! I'll do better with my granddaughter in future. I give you my word."

"As I shall," said Deveryn, visibly touched by the old man's tortured expression.

Miss Spencer slipped a comforting hand into the crook of her father's arm. "Come along, father," she said. "You mustn't take all the blame on yourself, you know. In our several ways, we've all been guilty of pushing Maddie into what we thought was best for her. She's a redoubtable girl. And Duncan is with her. I have perfect confidence in her ability to take care of herself. Good God! Think how she managed Drumoak!"

"It's not that," disclaimed Mr. Spencer, the slump of his shoulders more betraying than any words. "It's just that she could be anywhere."

"Nonsense," intoned Miss Spencer, marshalling her confidence. "Maddie is like a homing pigeon. She won't be far from Drumoak. Deveryn will find her. You can count on it."

The countess and the earl paid their guests the singular compliment of walking them to the front door. Deveryn made his way to his mother's dressing room to await her pleasure. He'd seen that look in her eyes. He expected a very uncomfortable interview, and unconsciously squared his shoulders. Mothers, he had discovered to his regret, had no qualms about meddling in the lives of their grown children.

Chapter Twenty-One

The journey by sea from Wapping to Leith took all of five days. In under half that time, Maddie was wishing that she had elected to go by coach. A coach might very easily be pursued and overtaken. A runaway wife might just as easily, if she had a change of heart, instruct her coachman to turn the coach around and return to their point of departure. Such was not possible in the situation in which she had placed herself. She had crossed the Rubicon; burned her bridges behind her; cast the die; and she was miserable. She did not think Deveryn would ever forgive her.

These unhappy reflections were mitigated by only one consolation. Duncan had apparently suffered no irreversible injury from the prize fight. His recovery had been swift and complete, so much so that Mr. Lloyd had voiced the suggestion that a removal to Scotland was no longer necessary. Maddie's opinion, however, had prevailed. Ostensibly, she wished to remove Duncan from temptation. Privately, she was furious with Deveryn for taunting her so mercilessly and wished to teach him a lesson. When she had boarded the schooner with Duncan and sent a protesting young Willie back to Curzon Street with her several notes of farewell, she had felt an overwhelming sense of relief to be shot of the lot of them— Deveryn, her grandfather, and Raeburn to boot. She was done with being the pawn of the male animal! Even her father . . . but that did not bear thinking about. Only the thought that her actions were bound to occasion pain and anxiety to Miss Spencer had made her falter in her resolution.

But by the time her anger had abated, leaving her in a more rational frame of mind, it was too late to turn back. She felt herself to be the most wretched of creatures and did not see how a graduate of so venerable an establishment as Miss Maitland's Academy could conduct herself with so little reference to the logic she had been taught to revere.

"I have a ferocious temper," she blurted to Duncan as they stood on deck waiting for their first sight of the Scottish coastline.

Guilelessly, he nodded his agreement.

She was moved to lay a hand on his arm. "Have you been a victim of my temper too?"

He turned twinkling eyes upon her mournful expression. "Black Douglas's famous fives canna match the wallop frae that wee tongue o' yours," he said.

"That bad, mmm?"

"Aye. But then Black Douglas never apologizes."

"I hope I always do," she said softly.

"Och, Miss Maddie, there's nothing sweeter than yerself when yer doin' penance."

She wondered what form of penance an irate husband might deem appropriate for a runaway wife. Her reveries left her more dejected than ever. Worst of all was the terrible suspicion that Deveryn would leave her to her own devices. She was sure that by a husband's reckoning it was no less than she deserved.

The growing conviction that she had not conducted herself wisely or justly did not act on her conscience as might have been expected. By degrees, a more rebellious spirit revived. If her conduct was questionable, Deveryn's was infamous. If her actions could be said to be rash when her temper was roused, his were abominable. Moreover, there were no skeletons in her closet; in his, he kept a veritable cemetery.

By the time the ship docked in Leith, Edinburgh's port, she was resolved to continue with her original plan. A coach was soon engaged to drive them the short distance to Miss Maitland's Academy in Charlotte Square in what was commonly referred to as 'The New Town.' The Academy, which never had an enrollment of more than 40 girls at one time, most of them day students, comprised two houses in a Georgian Square designed by a native son, Robert Adam. The coachman was instructed to wait. It took Maddie less than five minutes to pen a note which she left with the doorman advising Miss Maitland that Miss Sinclair had returned to Lothian and deemed it an honour to accept the invitation to help put the finishing touches to *Medea* in preparation for Founders' Day. This done, she returned to the coach and gave the driver instructions to take the coast road to Inverforth and Drumoak.

The day was fine and, as usual, blustery. Maddie remarked that it was good to fill one's lungs with the invigorating air of Caledonia.

Duncan said nothing, but held the flapping plaid on his shoulders a trifle more securely to his chest.

Truth to tell, Maddie was not as unequivocally happy with the sights and sounds of home as she had expected to be. For one thing, she had forgotten, if she had ever been aware of it, that a perpetual gale blew off the North Sea. The effect was like a douse of cold water. "Invigorating," she had called it. "Penetrating," would have been more apt. For another thing, she had grown accustomed, in the few months she had been in England, to the softer, prettier, more cultivated landscape. The trees and flowers which braved the untamed coastal climes of home were few and far between. She tried to shake herself of her vague feelings of disappointment and began to point out landmarks to Duncan, exclaiming enthusiastically on the splendid view across the Forth estuary to the distant shores and hills of Fifeshire.

It was the familiar sight of Janet's diminutive form as she turned from the black iron stove with spurtle in hand which evoked in Maddie's breast her first real sense of homecoming. The aroma of ginger and stewed rhubarb was distilled on the air, a delectable reminder that the first jams and jellies of the season had been newly preserved.

"Janet," Maddie cried out, "we've come home," and she promptly dissolved into tearful laughter.

The bout of weeping was a momentary lapse, occasioned more by happiness than misery, and was soon put to rout by Janet's practised manner of dispensing, in equal parts, a rough sympathy and scalding hot tea. Her shrewd dark eyes darted from Duncan and though she made perfect sense of Maddie's disjointed explanation for their sudden appearance at Drumoak, she was in no doubt that things were far from what they seemed.

It was only when Duncan rather sheepishly made his excuses and wandered off that Janet voiced her anxieties.

"And what did Lord Deveryn have to say when yer grandpappy tried tae marry ye off tae that duke?"

Maddie's eyes widened then fell away. "Nothing. What should he say?"

"Where is he?"

"In London, I presume."

"Ye left him tae the wiles o' that *beesim* just tae gang and play school with Miss Maitland?" demanded Janet, as if Maddie had confessed to some mortal sin which put her beyond the pale.

At her loftiest, Maddie responded, "I won't stay at Drumoak, and Miss Maitland will take me in till I hear from Uncle Thomas. He's my real guardian, not Grandfather Spencer. Furthermore, the whereabouts of my stepmother and Lord Deveryn are of the supremest indifference to me."

"Tush," said Janet, not the least abashed by Maddie's chilling manner. "Yer temper got the better o' ye again, I make no doubt. Here, make yerself useful," she ordered and pointed to the apron which habitually hung from a hook on the back of the kitchen door.

For the next half hour or so, Maddie, as she had so often done in the past, put the finishing touches to Janet's labours. On each small pot of jam which stood cooling on the plain deal kitchen table, she placed a small circle of oiled paper and topped it with tissue paper which had been dipped in the white of an egg. Last of all, she bound the covers securely with string.

"Ten pounds," said Maddie, counting the jars, "and a little left over for a fresh batch of scones." Her eyes lit expectantly upon Janet and the corners of her lips turned up.

"Hurmph! In the food press," muttered Janet, endeavoring in vain to resist the cozening smile which Maddie had perfected since she'd been a child in leading strings. From a large black kettle on the stove, she poured boiling water into the copper preserving pan, but her eyes carefully followed Maddie as she disappeared into the pantry next to the scullery. Moments later Maddie returned.

"Shortbread, oatcakes, and scones," she said wiggling a

plate under Janet's nose. "D'you know how long it is since I've tasted any of these treats? I didn't know it before, but this is what one misses the most."

She sat at the kitchen table with her back to the wall and watched Janet's familiar and comforting movements as she wrung out a dishcloth in cold water from the pump at the kitchen sink.

"Scones?" asked Janet.

"No! The foods one loved as a child and some special people with which to share them. I can scarcely wait till tomorrow. Shall we have Scotch broth, and sheep's head with trifle to follow?"

As soon as she had said the words, she had a vivid impression of the dinner she'd taken such pains over to impress Deveryn when he'd first come into Lothian. Much good it had done her. He'd been seduced, even then, by a siren's lips and a bunch of hothouse grapes. Men!

"The English," she said disparagingly, "have a fondness for cod's head. Can you believe that?"

Janet calmly proceeded to wipe down her hot stove. "The *puir* man's dinner," she observed. "And they turn up their noses at porridge." Her eye held a teasing gleam.

Maddie ignored it and opened her lips to gobble a piece of Janet's melt-in-the-mouth fresh butter shortbread.

"Dinna dare!" exclaimed Janet.

Maddie's mouth instantly closed and the shortbread dropped from her fingers. Obedient to Janet's warning, she broke off a piece of dry oatcake.

"D'you know, Janet," she said at last, "you and my tutor, Mr. Clarke, have a great deal in common. Like you, he is an absolute stickler for form. The problems you both present are similar in nature. With you, it's whether or not one should reach first for the oatcake or the shortbread. With Mr. Clarke, it's whether to make your curtsey to a countess or a marchioness."

With arms akimbo, Janet turned to face her young mistress. "And I would hope that ye didna disgrace the name o' Sinclair and Scotland when ye were in England."

"Good heavens! Nothing like that!" returned Maddie in mock horror. "I'm a walking book of correct etiquette. I'd never let the side down. Auld lang syne and Scotland forever rolled into one—that's me."

She reached for the dish of leftover rhubarb preserves and assiduously, though fastidiously, deposited a spoonful on the corner of her plate. "See?" she asked lightly. "I've got it down pat, just as you and Mama always instructed," and she spooned the merest smidgeon of jam on the corner of a half scone and nibbled delicately.

"So," said Janet sagely, "ye dinna care tae be a fine lady."

"Frankly, no. Janet, you know nothing about fine ladies and gentlemen. I could tell you stories that would make your hair stand on end." She was thinking of herself and Deveryn. "Oh, their manners are impeccable, I'll give you that. But one daren't look too closely at their morals."

"Aye," said Janet with more shrewdness than Maddie could safely tolerate, "Lord Deveryn, is it?"

"Why must you drag Deveryn's name into this conversation?" asked Maddie crossly. Her fingers began to drum an idle tattoo upon the tabletop. As abruptly as she had begun, she ceased. "All right! All right!" she said with an air of abstraction. "Lord Deveryn it is! He's not the man I thought him." She was sorry that she had said as much and snapped her teeth together.

"Never say he's put an unholy hand upon ye!"

"An unholy hand?" Maddie said uncertainly. Comprehension suddenly dawned and colour flooded her cheeks. She made a little choking sound deep in her throat and managed a tremulous and not quite truthful, "Janet! Would I permit it of any man?"

Like the cozening smile, the look on Maddie's face was one with which Janet was all too familiar. "Ye've been a bad girl," she said, and gave Maddie one of her hard, Presbyterian stares.

Maddie tried to look discouragingly aloof, but succeeded in merely appearing absurdly guilty. Unconsciously, with the tip of her tongue, she licked her dry lips.

Janet's eyes narrowed. "If ye've done something wicked . . ."

"Not wicked, Janet! How could you even think so?"

"Well?" There was no give in Janet.

Maddie offered a crooked smile. "Only an eeny-weeny, teeny bit naughty." She suppressed the childish urge to cross

356

her fingers behind her back.

"Lord Deveryn . . ."

"Don't!" expostulated Maddie. On a calmer note, she said, "I can't explain. Please don't ask me. I know you always liked him. He's done nothing to forfeit your good opinion. Really!" She gave her attention to the last piece of scone on her plate. "A lovers' quarrel," she finally got out. "That's all."

"Mmm!" said Janet. She took the teapot from the table and filled it from the kettle that perpetually simmered on the stove.

"Give it a few minutes tae *mask*," she said, setting it on the table by Maddie's elbow. She seated herself on a chair opposite.

As though to change the subject, she offered, "There hae been *mony* a change since ye were last here at Drumoak."

"What changes?" asked Maddie, carefully pouring herself a cup of weak tea. She knew that Janet preferred stronger brew, and set the teapot down without offering it.

"Masons, slaters, plasterers, painters hae been in an oot o' the *hoose* for the last *twa* month."

"Slaters?" asked Maddie, looking up. "Are you saying that there's a new slate roof on the house?"

"Among other things. Also, for the first time in years, an agent to see that things get done. Mr. Milne is his name."

"Oh?"

"Ay. Frae Edinburgh. He tells me that he's in Lord Deveryn's employ." Maddie made no comment and Janet went on, "Lord Deveryn seems to be paying the piper."

"Yes, well, the house belongs to Cynthia now, more or less. I'm sure Deveryn is acting for her."

"Ye're as daft as they come," muttered Janet under her breath, and reached across the table for the teapot.

Maddie recognized the taut expression on Janet's thin face. She braced herself mentally for the dressing-down that it signified would follow, and wondered, dejectedly, why in the world she had ever thought she would be coming home to hot-toddie and sympathy.

At last, the harangue began. "Och, I thought ye would be wed tae the man *lang* since. Ye're bonnie. Ye've got brains. A body with eyes in her head could see that the man wanted ye like a bee wants honey. He's poured money into yer *hoose* which is more than yer faither did, even when his pockets were well-lined. And dinna tell me that Drumoak belongs tae yer stepmither! Lord Deveryn himself told me about Cynthia's provision under the terms o' yer faither's will."

"He did?" For a moment, Maddie thought that Deveryn had confided the whole sorry business, but Janet's next words reassured her.

"Aye. When she weds, everything reverts tae ye. And wi' a woman like Cynthia Sinclair, I dinna doubt that she'll shackle some *puir* unsuspectin' male afore the year is oot."

"You do?" Now that was interesting.

"I was hopin'," said Janet meaningfully, "that it wouldna be Lord Deveryn."

"She's trying," agreed Maddie, and leaning one elbow on the table, cupped her chin in her hand.

"And?" asked Janet.

"And what?"

"And what are ye doin' tae see that she disna succeed?"

Maddie's expression turned stubborn. "If he wants her, he can have her," she said, and bit down on her lower lip to quell its betraying pout.

"He can have her," repeated Janet slowly. "Och, it's just as well. A man like Lord Deveryn needs a woman who kens how tae hold him." She chuckled. "In my day, I . . . och, well, that's neither here nor there. It's tae be expected that the ladies will a' be flapping about him like moths tae the flame." And she slanted a glance at her pensive companion.

"You don't know the half of it," said Maddie, and stared morosely into space.

A reflective silence descended.

"Will he come after ye, d'ye suppose?" asked Janet at length.

"Oh yes, I think he must." But then again, she silently reasoned, he might just as easily decide to divorce her from England. For all she knew, it might be possible to do it in secret. Then no one would be the wiser about their clandestine marriage. Except, of course, that in another month or so, fingers would be pointing at her and she would be referred to as a "fallen woman"—which was exactly how she felt. She sniffed.

"Have I ever told ye the story of how yer mammy swept the

field o' her rivals when she first came to Drumoak as yer faither's bride?"

"Frequently," said Maddie discouragingly. It was one of the myths she'd been raised on and, child-like, had never tired of its telling. She knew it by heart.

"What did I tell ye?"

"You know. How mother was young and beautiful but with a beastly temper, like mine. And when she discovered that Papa was a bit of a ladies' man before they were wed, there was a terrible quarrel and she went off in a huff to Edinburgh."

"And?"

"What? Oh yes. Papa had a temper, too, and to spite Mama invited all the most beautiful ladies around Drumoak to a party. Mother heard about it and came storming back with whip in hand and drove them out of the house. Papa had never been more proud of her in his life, and so on, and so on, and so on. Of course, it wasn't true. A lady does not take whip in hand and drive her guests from her home however much she might wish to do so. Still, it was a charming tale."

"She disna? Then what does she do?"

"She asks them to leave, politely, of course."

"That's all ye ken! I told ye no lies, though I didna mayhap tell ye the whole of it. It was no polite party yer faither put on that night but a drunken orgy. And thae were no ladies o' quality yer mother took her whip tae, but, if ye'll excuse my French, barques o' frailty."

"What?"

"Ye ken, bits o' muslin."

"D'you mean 'lightskirts?'"

"Doxies, trollops, Cyprians, every last one o' them," said Janet with the merest trace of smugness on her thin lips.

Maddie's face was a picture of incredulity. "You're pulling my leg! Papa wasn't *that* sort of man. I don't believe he would have served Mama such a turn."

Janet answered at her bluntest. "Every man is o' *that* ilk, given the opportunity. Yer mither was wiser than ye are. She made damn sure that Donald Sinclair was never again presented wi' temptation. Maddie, ye ken fine what yer faither was afore he wed yer mammy. Aye, and became again, once she was gone. But I swear tae ye, in a' the years o' their marriage,

359

he made her as happy as any woman has a right tae be. She kent that it's the woman who *maun* make sure that her man keeps tae the straight and narrow."

Maddie digested this homespun philosophy as she absently nibbled on a piece of shortbread. At length she asked, "Did Papa ever take up with any married ladies?"

Janet's laugh was more like a cackle. "Only the wicked ones wi' complacent husbands. Och, but yer mammy put a stop tae his philanderin' frae the minute she got his ring on her finger."

"Men!" interjected Maddie with obvious revulsion. "Why, Papa was no better than . . ." She almost gave herself away.

"Aye," said Janet, her shrewd eyes regarding Maddie steadily, "no better than Lord Deveryn."

Maddie suddenly realized that she was down to her last bite of shortbread. She studiously chewed on it and affected an interest in the remaining crumbs on her plate.

At length, she offered, "My mother was an exceptional woman."

"Aye. Things might have been different if the Good Lord had spared her."

The words, though sad in themselves, opened the door to happier reminiscences. Thoughts of Deveryn faded, and Maddie conversed happily and easily about earlier days when her mother was alive and it seemed that all her memories were bathed in sunshine.

They talked long past bed-time. There had been only a few changes in neighbouring families to occasion much interest. "Hatches, matches, and dispatches," as Duncan referred to them with a smile when he entered later to bank up the kitchen grate with several blocks of peat.

The intelligence about his purse from the prize fight he had won occasioned only a tepid interest. It would buy a few luxuries. But what was there to spend it on? Drumoak was their lives. Maddie gave a careful accounting of every last penny she had spent to finance their trip to Scotland. It was accepted, as she knew it would be, without demur. On her diffidently applying for a small loan to tide her over for a short stay in Edinburgh, Duncan instantly and gratifyingly assented. Janet looked as if she might argue the point.

"With or without the loan, I am accepting Miss Maitland's

invitation to stay until Founders' Day," Maddie informed Janet with an uncompromising set to her little chin.

Janet sighed. "Ye've no been listenin' tae a word I've said."

"Dear Janet," said Maddie, lifting the other's calloused hand and putting it to her cheek. "I have been listening to your every word, and believe me, I understand perfectly what you are trying to say. It's just that . . . well . . . there are things you know nothing about. Besides," she said more briskly, "in my book, it's the knight who's supposed to fight for his lady— not the other way round."

"Fairy tales," said Janet with a dismissive shake of her head. "That were yer mammy's doin'."

"I like happy-ever-after stories," responded Maddie with a teasing gleam in her eye. "As a child I went to sleep well content having listened to tales of King Arthur and his knights. Whereas, your Highland tales of magic kept me awake long after bedtime."

"So ye'll no bide till Lord Deveryn gets here?" said Janet, bringing the subject of their conversation ruthlessly round.

"You know, he may not come."

"He'll come."

"I'm not keeping my direction a secret. Miss Maitland's Academy is not so very far away."

"Ye'll be makin' him go the extra mile? And I thought that ye were a good Christian lady, as yer mother brought ye up tae be. Ye've grown hard, Maddie."

Janet's parting words revolved in Maddie's mind, nagging her relentlessly in moments of solitude. She contrived to put them from her when she led Banshee out the following morning and rode at break neck speed along the soft sands at the edge of the receding tide. For the hour that she rode, with Kelpie at her heels, unrestrained, racing the wind, exulting in the feel of blood and bone beneath her, she contrived to banish all unpleasant thoughts. But the moment she dismounted and began the slow walk home, they rushed in to plague her.

"I wish I *were* hard," she confided in Banshee's ear. "If it were true, I'd be a far happier girl. D'you think I'm hard?"

Banshee's ears pricked and she nuzzled Maddie's shoulder.

"Well, of course, even murderers have been known to be kind to animals," she went on, retrieving a lump of sugar from her pocket and offering it to Banshee's eager lips. "I'm afraid, in a court of law, your opinion wouldn't count for anything. Have I been hard on Deveryn, d'you think?"

She stopped to watch the spectacle of Kelpie trying to shepherd a flock of seagulls. "I'm too soft on that dog. She's getting fat. She ought to be put to work."

She put two fingers to her mouth and whistled. Kelpie came streaking back on the instant.

"Good girl," said Maddie approvingly as the ball of black fur came to a stop at her feet. Alert brown eyes gazed up at her, waiting for the next command. Maddie looked into the distance, noted the piece of driftwood, and pointing with one finger gave the command, "Fetch!"

Kelpie took off.

"I've done a good job with you two," said Maddie thoughtfully. "What a happier place the world would be to be sure if only husbands could be so easily trained." She sighed, then sighed again. "D'you think I'm at fault for not keeping my husband on the straight and narrow? You'll be telling me next that Cynthia was one of those wicked married ladies that Janet mentioned, and that Deveryn did no more or less than my father would have done in his place. You know, I don't think, deep down, I like men very much. But then, as I've said before, liking and love are two different entities. Now if only men could be more like women, the world would be . . . You're right. It would be different and not nearly so interesting. Perhaps I should try to become more like my mother."

Banshee whinnied softly and nudged Maddie's pocket.

"Oh, so you think that note I left Deveryn was cold and unfeeling? You may be right. But you must own that the provocation was great. 'Do your worst!' Those were the words he flung at me. And I did. I don't think that proves that I'm hard, necessarily. It's just this beastly temper of mine! Was it my fault that I could not turn the boat around and go back to him? Oh, you think it was? Deveryn very likely agrees with you! Good girl, Kelpie. What an interesting piece of driftwood."

She stopped to admire what had evidently been the branch of a tree, and Kelpie, impatient for more fun, cocked her head to one side and barked ferociously. Obedient to her dog's command, Maddie flung the driftwood from her.

"I can always count on you and Kelpie coming to me when I whistle," Maddie said confidingly to Banshee. "If only I could be as sure of Deveryn." She placed thumb and ring finger in her mouth and emitted a piercing whistle. "D'you think he heard me call for him? I hope so. And if he comes—*when* he comes—what should I say to him?"

But on that subject, both Banshee and Kelpie were distressingly silent.

As Maddie had hopefully surmised, Lord Deveryn reached Drumoak the day after she took up residence in Miss Maitland's Academy. The report reached her through the good offices of Janet who sent Duncan into Edinburgh on the pretext of procuring the freshest cod and oysters to be had for his lordship's dinner.

Cod's head, conjectured Maddie. *That will please the servants. They'll eat like royalty on the leavings as long as Deveryn is in residence.*

In the course of conversation, Duncan guilelessly let slip that a large party of Deveryn's friends was expected to reach Leith the following week, conveyed in his lordship's private yacht, no less, which was normally docked at Deal. The house was a beehive of activity. Extra staff had been taken on; beds and bedding were being aired; the stables were to have a fresh coat of whitewash; a ton of coal had been ordered; and, in short, Drumoak was preparing for its first house party of any significance since Donald Sinclair's marriage to Cynthia.

"To what purpose?" asked Maddie, catching a glint of something under Duncan's lashes which she did not like.

"A betrothal, I think," he said with marked uneasiness.

Maddie caught her breath. She could not believe that Deveryn would be so base as to pay her back in such coin.

"Whose betrothal?" she demanded through set teeth. But to that pointed question, Duncan would not dare give an answer.

The exchange with Duncan left Maddie shaken. Fortunately, however, there was little time to be wasted on useless speculation, for Miss Maitland had arranged matters so that Maddie was fully occupied in the preparations for Founders' Day.

A full rehearsal of *Medea* was scheduled for that afternoon.

Though Maddie thought that the girls did an excellent job, she was not surprised that the interpretation of the play was strictly conventional.

Miss Maitland, eagle-eyed, erudite, and, when the occasion merited it, appallingly eloquent, was in attendance.

"Well, what d'you think?" she asked in her no-nonsense style.

There was never any point in euphemisms with Miss Maitland, thought Maddie, and liked her the better for it. "Very, very competent, and . . . a dead bore." She spoke in an undertone so that the sharp ears of the girls could hear nothing.

Miss Maitland's slow smile softened what was essentially a face as no-nonsense as her innate character. On the wrong side of fifty by a year or two, she had only one vanity that Maddie was aware of. Her pale green, almost transparent eyes were fringed by the longest curling eyelashes that Maddie had ever beheld. They were thick and sooty by virtue of the fact that Miss Maitland darkened them. At the end of the day, the blackening had a tendency to weep and form puddles. This entirely human and feminine trait made the lady irresistible.

"They're all yours," she said to Maddie cheerfully. "I have the supremest confidence in your ability."

At the door, she turned. "A word of advice, my dear. I know you won't mind my mentioning it. You sound as though you have a pebble under your tongue. Spit it out, there's a good girl. There's no excuse for less than perfect diction, you know." Miss Maitland never saw the need to keep her conversations private. The girls' ears picked up every word. Maddie was aware of a few commiserating glances.

"Too many cooks spoil the broth," said Maddie darkly, but when she addressed the girls, she rewarded them with a brilliant smile. "Very, very competent," she told them with as much warmth as honesty. "Miss Maitland has prepared you well. Bear with me a little as we try, together, to effect something a little different."

"Medea," she said, addressing the girl who played the role of Euripides's unhappy heroine, "you are a very pretty girl, very feminine and look to be a heart-breaker." "Medea" did not mistake Maddie's comments for flattery. At Miss Maitland's, there were never any gratuitous compliments.

"But don't forget that when this play was first performed, all the parts were played by men. In fact, you would have been, quite literally, a man in woman's clothing. Moreover, Medea had those attributes which were essentially thought to be masculine. Well, can you imagine Medea domesticated and at her embroidery?"

Her faint sally was greeted with gurgles of laughter.

"Efface your femininity, Medea! Exult in those qualities which have been supposed, wrongly, to belong solely to the male. You are clever, brave and audacious. You need all your wits about you. You are about to do what few women before or since have ever attempted. You are about to cross swords with your lord and master. And you, Medea, will come off the victor."

Maddie's impassioned monologue was interrupted by a slow handclap. That it was derisory, could not be doubted. She spun to face her mocker.

"Jason Verney at your service," said Deveryn at his most debonair, and he slowly sauntered into the room. Maddie's bracing speech, taken to heart so sincerely a moment before, was instantly discarded as the viscount's eyes boldly made love to every female they encountered. In that moment, Maddie knew that every feminine heart, her own included, was beating just a little faster. She could not help herself. She just stood there, grinning like a monkey. Deveryn, she thought, had that effect on women.

"Miss Sinclair," he said suavely, bending over her hand. She heard the sighs of several of the girls and snatched her hand away as if she had laid hold of an asp.

"Lord Deveryn," she said. "To what do we owe the pleasure?"

He did not answer, but strolled among the players, acknowledging first one then another of the girls. He looked, thought Maddie, as if he were Gabriel straight from heaven.

"Is Miss Sinclair leading you astray?" he inquired of "Medea," taking her hand in his. "I'd be delighted to act as antidote," and he winked rakishly.

"Medea" giggled and blushed, and looked to be entirely smitten.

Deveryn came toward Maddie and offered his most disarming grin. "Don't get yourself in a pucker, Miss Sinclair. I'm just passing through and thought I'd look up old friends when I'm in the neighbourhood."

His words shook her. Surely, *surely*, he would not abandon her to her unhappy fate?

"Personally," he said, addressing the girls, "like most men, I always thought that Medea was a prime candidate for Bedlam. But what do I know? I bow to Miss Sinclair's superior knowledge of the female psyche. However, the male psyche is well within my province. I should like to address a few remarks to those of you who play the parts of the gentlemen in this play. You there! Medea's husband. What's your name again?"

"Jason," muttered Maddie.

"Yes?" asked Deveryn.

"No! No! Jason is the name of Medea's husband."

"Is it indeed?" he said softly. "I had forgot."

Maddie studiously avoided his eyes.

"You there, Jason," he said. "Don't ever think to cower before the spleen of any woman, no matter how formidable her cleverness, her courage, or her audacity. For you have that one quality above all others which the impassioned Medea lacks. You personify cool logic, an attribute which, in my experience, is rarely to be found in the female of the species, present company, one hopes, excepted. Think on these things, ladies, as you go over your lines. You're dismissed, unless of course, Miss Sinclair, you wish to say a few words to the chorus?"

"No," said Maddie, "the chorus is unexceptionable."

"My sentiments exactly—a group of admirable ladies who possess all the virtues of the softer sex. Ladies, you are excused."

The girls, with much uncharacteristic batting of eyelashes and gurgles of laughter, slowly and reluctantly made their exit.

"And now, Lady Deveryn," said the viscount in an imperturbable tone, "Take my arm, if you please. There are a few words I have to say for your ears only."

Chapter Twenty-Two

They took a turn in the square.

"Charming," said Deveryn looking about him, "and quite reminiscent of Bath. I'd no idea Edinburgh had an elegant side to her."

"Oh yes," said Maddie, more than a little eager to keep the conversation in neutral channels, "this is the New Town, built in the last century, by Adam and Craig. There are many fine squares besides this one, as well as crescents and . . ."

"Maddie," he interposed gently, "Why did you run away?"

"Because," she said, and could not think what to say next.

"Can't you tell me?"

She looked at him blankly as if she had lost the thread of their conversation.

"Don't you know?"

"Yes," she said, her voice low and throbbing, "I . . . I wanted . . . revenge." It sounded so petty when baldly stated, and she could not prevent the blush that stole over her cheeks.

With something like pain in his voice he observed, "I suppose I deserved that. But . . . well, where there is love, there can be no question of revenge." After a moment he went on in a steadier tone, "My sins must be grievous indeed."

There was no answer. He sliced a look at her. She was staring at him as if, he thought despairingly, she were a fawn and he the hunter who had cornered her to move in for the kill.

"For God's sake, don't look like that!" he said roughly. "I won't hurt you. How can you even think it?"

Her eyes fell away and he was moved to speak more gently.

"Maddie, we haven't dealt very well together in the past. My fault, I own it. But . . ." he exhaled a long breath, "I'm wiser now."

He was remembering that last interview with his mother on the eve of his departure for Drumoak. Her tongue had been scathing as she'd recounted scandal after scandal involving generations of the Verney men. "Congenital savages," she'd called them. He'd been truly shocked at her disclosures until she'd very gently but persistently forced him to examine his own conduct with respect to Maddie. He counted it a small mercy that his mother did not know the half of it!

He'd given a solemn undertaking that when he had his wife under his hand, he would conduct himself in the manner of a true English gentleman. He was, when all was said and done, as much a Darnley as a Verney, or so his mother told him, and with a little practice he might very easily cultivate some of the softer virtues which would endear him to a wife.

It was only by the greatest force of will that he could hold himself to that promise. For when he looked at Maddie, knowing that she belonged to him, he was seized with the almost overpowering urge to make his claims upon her in the oldest way known to primitive man. He ruthlessly restrained himself.

With a calm that he was far from feeling, he said, "You have made your sentiments very plain. Forgive me for not heeding your words sooner. I promise that things shall be just as you desire, from this moment on."

Whatever Maddie had expected of Deveryn when he caught up to her, it was not this resigned almost indifferent gentleman who walked at her side. She thought, then, that she would welcome a tongue lashing, a beating—anything but this annihilating civility.

Miserably she answered, "Thank you."

"May I say something in my own defence?"

She signified that he might.

"About your father, Maddie . . ."

"Yes?"

"I cannot believe he took his own life. I made some enquiries, you see. He'd made some . . . investments. He wasn't destitute, as you seem to think. You can verify this very easily for yourself with his man of business in London."

She stored the information away for future reference. Whether or not she had ever truly believed that her father had taken his own life was highly debatable.

"It . . . it doesn't signify," she said, trying to convey that, in spite of everything, she still loved him.

To Deveryn's ears, her words were damning. He stiffened but doggedly pursued a subject that he had long rehearsed. "For my past, I make no apology, though I never was, as you seem to think, a libertine of the first order. But I swear that since I met you there have been no other women in my life, in spite of appearances to the contrary. Maddie," he went on, a little more desperately when she remained discouragingly mute, "I swear I have been a faithful husband."

His tone of voice, his whole demeanor was so forbidding, that she took no comfort from his words. She would have forgiven him a hundred women, a thousand, if only she could have her old Deveryn back. She divined his object. She was to be made to realise how much she was losing by her rash behaviour.

More miserable than ever, she remarked, "You owe me no explanations."

If there was any hope for her, he would order her to pack her bags and haul her off to Drumoak. She waited for his command in vain.

Abruptly, he asked, "Have you heard anything from Caro Lamb?"

The sudden change of subject confused her. "Caro Lamb?" she repeated.

"Did you know that she was writing a book?"

Cautiously, she answered, "Yes. What of it?"

"It's out. *Glenarvon,* she called it. *Lord Byron* more like. It's touted as a novel, but every character is recognisable, even poor William. He hadn't an inkling what she was about. Did you know, Maddie?"

"Yes," she answered in a very small voice.

"And you never thought to tell me so that I might warn William?" he reproved.

"She told me in strictest confidence. Besides, William Lamb is a complacent husband. Nothing Caro does ever shakes him

369

from his habitual indifference."

"He's shaken now. His family is pressing him to seek a legal separation. I think he may."

Her steps faltered and she turned to him with a troubled expression. "But why, now, when before he permitted Caro to go her own way and when he indulged her every whim, yes, and condoned every indiscretion?"

"Who can say? There is only so much that even the most complacent of husbands will permit, after all."

She heard his words as the death knell to all her hopes. "Oh," was all she could think to say but thought that she and Caro Lamb must be the sorriest women in Christendom and they had brought it on themselves! She was not conscious of the telling sigh which she exhaled on her next breath.

Deveryn squeezed her hand gently. "Don't repine. William, I am persuaded, still loves Caro in spite of everything. Do you think there's a lesson there for us, Maddie?"

All she could think of was "legal separation," and could scarcely hold back the tears.

Gradually she became aware that Deveryn had embarked on a spate of commonplaces. She listened in deepening gloom as he paid tribute to the beauties of Scotland.

"What a difference a few months make," he remarked, putting his head back and inhaling deeply. "Marvellous! This sea air really blows the cobwebs away. It's as good as a restorative."

"Quite," agreed Maddie.

"When this is all over, I thought we might do a bit of touring—Inverness, the Highlands and so on."

"I didn't think you cared much for Scotland," she said, and let her thoughts drift to Oxfordshire and London, where the air was softer and already the blossoms were on the trees.

"What of my grandfather and Aunt Nell?" she asked at length. "Were they very vexed with me?"

"No," he said shortly. "How could they be? You were not there, I was." His look spoke volumes. "You shall have the pleasure of meeting up with them very soon. I expect them some time next week."

Striving to appear as composed as he, she said, "Oh, I had heard something to the effect that a party of your friends was arriving by sea?"

"You heard correctly," he replied without elaboration.

"And . . . and that there was to be a betrothal party at Drumoak."

"Oh? So you've heard?"

So, it was true! And now she could congratulate herself on being at long last shot of him. When she was sure that she had command of her voice, she said, "Will . . . will Cynthia be there?"

"No," he said, evincing some surprise. "She wasn't invited."

"But . . . but it's her house!"

He seemed to lose patience with her. "The house is not Cynthia's. It belongs to you and your heirs. I've told you so before. If Cynthia cares to make her home at Drumoak until such time as she marries, she is free to do so. But she never will. She detests Scotland."

There was only one other lady she could think of who stood to fill the void—Lady Elizabeth Heatherington. The prospect was only marginally less harrowing.

Through a veil of misery, she listened to the viscount converse on the various members of his family and wished with all her heart that she might have been the one to be welcomed into its ranks. She was sure she did not know what the Verney ladies would make of the "Toast," whereas she, Maddie Sinclair, was a bird of the Verney feather and would soon have found an agreeable patch for herself.

Their walk had taken them quite round the square. At the door to Miss Maitland's he took his leave of her.

"I want your word on it, Maddie, that you won't run away from me again."

"You have it," she said, her eyes fixed on a point above his head.

"Don't look so bleak, my dear. Everything is going to be just as you wish it."

"Is it?" She would have given anything if only they could go back to the beginning and start over. It was not possible, and it was very evident that Deveryn had judged her and found her sadly wanting. She did not blame him.

"I'll take care of all the arrangements."

His words had the ring of finality. No one of her acquaintance had ever been divorced before. What did she know of it? Perhaps, like her clandestine marriage, all that would be required was a simple declaration before witnesses. *I, Maddie Sinclair, do declare that I divorce* . . . She could never say those words—never.

"A week, Maddie," he said softly, "only a week, and then you need never again be plagued by my . . . unhallowed affections."

It was to be one of the wretchedest weeks of Maddie's life. Her dreams were invaded by the weirdest images of herself, whip in hand, scourging a bevy of alluring beauties who thought to steal the affections of the rakish viscount. And damn if he didn't seem to be enjoying every minute of it! It left her quite vexed with him.

And if that nightmare were not bad enough, she was plagued at other times with the spectacle of Bedlam. She seemed to move at will in and out of its awful chambers. But she was ever drawn back by Caro Lamb who, for a lark, had decided to take up residence. There were horrible sights of inmates chained to the walls and ferociously devouring, quite literally, the pages of Lady Caro's novel. Maddie tried desperately to persuade the other woman to come away with her, but no argument she put forward made the slightest dent on Caro's airy refusal. She appealed to a flock of birds which had found perches on the branches of an avenue of oak trees—birds, which had very oddly assumed the identities of the Verney ladies. She wakened every morning with a throbbing head and her nightgown soaked with perspiration.

Nor was she served any better during the daylight hours for to wrestle with Euripides's *Medea* had suddenly become a terrible trial to her. Truth to tell, she longed to march into the drama as if it were reality and take Medea by the shoulders and shake some sense into her. She thought that if she never again heard the name "Medea" it would be too soon for her comfort, and wondered, horror of horrors, how long it would be before the wretched woman took to stalking her in her dreams.

Not unnaturally, as a result of these conscious and

unconscious cogitations, Maddie's conviction that she had conducted herself with all the aplomb of a featherbrained nodcock became firmly fixed in her mind. She was too bright a girl not to discern the message that came from her dreams. That she wished that she could be more like her mother was very evident, but that she feared that she was too much like Lady Caro was no less so. She discovered that she pitied that lady who, like Medea, was wonderfully revenged upon her enemies, but at an astronomical cost to herself and those she loved. The pity of it was that she had not seen it sooner.

Deveryn was right, she decided. Where there was love, there could be no question of revenge. And that she loved him went without saying. She thought that the honourable thing to do was to step aside and leave the field open for some other, more conformable lady who would make him happy. She could not do it. Deveryn belonged to *her,* and she could not, with anything resembling equanimity, see him go to another.

There was only one thing to be done. She must attach him to herself before it was too late, before his betrothal was made public. There was no time for long involved explanations or persuasive appeals. Necessity demanded that she take the most direct approach. Seduction became her object.

It was, however, a full week before she was to see him again. The girls had just filed out of the room when the door opened and the viscount entered. That he left the door open, circumspectly, she took as a bad omen.

"My yacht docked yesterday," he said and moved to the centre of the room, keeping his distance.

This would never do. "Will you excuse me for a moment," she said, and slipped into the corridor to make sure that the coast was clear. When she came back into the room, she carefully and deliberately closed the door. He was lounging against her desk, going through her notes. He looked up and smiled, just so. Her heart turned over.

She pinned what she hoped was a seductive smile to her lips and slowly advanced upon him. He straightened, instinct making him cautious.

"They're at Drumoak, now," he said, his eyes narrowing speculatively.

"Are they?" she asked, and was surprised at the huskiness in her voice.

He looked at her oddly. "Maddie, what are you up to?"

It was now or never. "Jason," she said, and threw herself into his arms. Her hands caught in his hair and pulled his head down. For a moment, he went rigid, but in the next instant she was crushed to his chest and he was kissing her passionately. Her joy was to be short lived. He reached up and dragged her hands from his neck and held her at arm's length. His voice, unsteady, low, vibrated with emotion. She thought it might be anger.

"Now, you come to me—*now*, when to take you would be so wrong."

"Jason!" she cried out, and put out her hands to draw him back.

He stepped away from her as if she were temptation personified. "No! It is not seemly! How can you ask it of me? It is out of the question."

"Why is it wrong?" she said, moving closer.

"Maddie, I'm warning you, keep your distance." And he ranged himself on the other side of the desk. "You can't understand," he told her roughly. "I gave my solemn word, as a gentleman."

"You promised not to kiss me?"

"Oh, nothing personal," he replied with a flash of his old humour. "I'm under a vow of celibacy, that is all."

She stared at him with eyes widened in horror. "Jason," she whispered, "you're not . . . you haven't . . . oh, my God, you're not thinking of converting to Catholicism?"

"What?" Her words mystified him.

"A priest?" she whispered hoarsely.

Bright laughter spilled from his lips. When he could contain himself, he said, "Maddie, use your God-given wits. A priest! I? The Viscount Deveryn?"

"Oh," she said, and, feeling her legs buckle under her, weakly slumped into the nearest chair. "Then why?"

"It was a promise I made to a lady," he said. He studied the droop of her shoulders, the mist of tears in her eyes. His expression gentled. "I've brought your wedding dress," he said. "Will you wear it for me?"

"I'm to wear my wedding dress?"

The words seemed to be dragged out of him. "Only if you wish it."

She gazed into his inscrutable expression and knew that everything was lost. From depths she did not know she possessed, she dredged up a watery smile. "I shall wear it with pleasure," she said mendaciously.

He visibly relaxed, as though, she thought pettishly, he was relieved that she had yielded so graciously. What did he expect? Tears would avail her nothing. And she had too much pride to beg. But oh, she was sure that her broken heart would never mend again.

"It's fixed for tomorrow," he said.

"It is?"

"They'll all be there."

"Fine." She had no clear idea what he was talking about. She was sure she did not care. Her voice had become very unsteady, and she could not trust herself to speak.

"Tomorrow, Maddie, before breakfast. Be ready for me," were his last words to her.

She was wakened by one of the maids long before the breakfast bell was sounded. "Lord Deveryn is downstairs," said Sally when Maddie finally stretched and moved to get out of bed. "He asked me to give you this," and she set down a large box at the foot of the bed. Inside, beneath layers of tissue paper, was Maddie's wedding gown.

She donned it with trembling fingers and was not surprised when she could not do up the top buttons at the back. Fortunately, the matching spencer was looser, and modesty was served. At the door, she hesitated and turned back into the room as if under some compulsion. From her dresser, she removed the lace handkerchief which concealed her three lucky charms—the angel, the baby, and the ring. She tried to shake off the strange humour that had come upon her, but to no avail. Without understanding why she was moved to do so, she tucked them inside her glove and felt oddly comforted.

As she descended the stairs, her heart was in her throat. Deveryn came forward to take her arm. In his buff coloured knee breeches with matching waistcoat and dark coloured coat, she thought he looked as formal as she had ever seen him.

A terrible suspicion took root in her mind. "Deveryn," she

said, "have you seen the solicitor?"

"You look . . . enchanting," he murmured, and kissed her gloved hand. "Yes, I've seen the solicitor. Everything is just as it should be."

She absorbed his words, numbed, stricken to her very soul. They were in the closed carriage and in George Street before she had gathered enough courage to say "Is . . . is Lady Elizabeth Heatherington to be there?"

"No. I never thought to ask her. Shall you mind?"

"Good God, no!"

Hope sprang up in her heart then almost immediately died. What did it matter who the lady was? It was not *she,* and nothing but pain and misery could attend her going to Drumoak under such circumstances. She tried to imagine how she might conduct herself when the announcement was made. The picture which came to her mind was so horrifying, so mortifying, that it did not bear contemplating.

They were at the village of Inverforth before Maddie took her courage into her hands. She cut across Deveryn's spate of small talk with an anguished plea. "Jason, please!" she begged. "I don't know if I can go through with this."

He turned eyes as blue as cornflowers upon her, eyes as enigmatic and inscrutable as those of a marble statue. Her nerve faltered under that impassive stare.

"We're here," he said, as the coach rolled to a stop.

She sat in misery looking down at her clenched fists.

"It's where it all began, Maddie," she heard him say with so much tenderness in his voice that hope kindled in her heart once more. "For auld lang syne. I thought it fitting somehow. Don't say you've changed your mind!"

He assisted her to alight.

"Inverforth Parish Church," he said.

For long, mesmerizing, timeless moments, they stood transfixed, as if all had receded and they were seeing each other for the first time. He had come to her in the night, out of the dark storm, as she had come to him. There had been magic in the air. A benign providence had been at work and had taken the sad, ugly circumstances which surrounded them and shaped them to a kinder end.

He was her destiny. She was his. What matter the how, the

why, or the wherefore? Her fingers closed on the silver symbols inside her gloved hand. He was her destiny. She would never let him go.

With one long finger, he tipped her chin up. "Maddie, love," he said softly, "it's not too late to change your mind. Tell me now if I'm still unforgiven, if your father still stands between us, and I swear I'll take you wherever you wish to go and see that you're well provided for." He took a deep, steadying breath, and spoke almost as if from memory, "I'm not proud of the way I used you at Dunsdale, and as for London . . ." he broke off. "Oh hell, Maddie, I know I've been an abominable husband! You must think that there's one thing ever on my mind. I swear it is not so. I shall try to be worthy of you, I promise, if only you'll give me another chance. Maddie," he said persuasively, possessing himself of her hands, "we shall make our home in Scotland, if you like—Africa, for all I care." Misunderstanding her silence, he asked in a despairing tone, "Maddie, don't you love me? Don't you want me? Have I destroyed every hope for us?"

Laughing and crying on the same breath, she finally got out, "Jason, oh Jason, you incorrigible man! I've suffered agonies thinking that you no longer loved *me*. I was sure you were taking me to Drumoak to announce your betrothal to some other lady. How should I *know* what was on your mind when you've been so . . . so *odiously* indifferent that I scarcely recognized you?"

Her words seemed to appall him. "Betrothed? When I'm a married man? I thought you had guessed. It's Raeburn and Miss Spencer who are betrothed. Surely that does not surprise you?"

"So that's it," she said, covering her eyes with her hand. "Oh Jason, if only you had told me! You have no conception of where my flights of fancy have not led me! But Jason, you were so damnably *vague!*"

"But you must have known, when I asked you to wear your wedding gown, what was in my mind?"

"Then why were you so beastly *indifferent* to me?"

"*That* was not indifference."

He had taken her by the shoulders and he administered a rough shake as if to bring her to her senses. Maddie was too happy to make the least objection to this lover-like sign of his devotion.

"What you are pleased to call my 'indifference,'" he said between exasperation and laughter, "was a show of gentle-manly behaviour to persuade you that I could use you as befits a gently-bred girl."

"Well how was I to know? I was half frightened to death! You've never shown me that *horrid* side of your character before."

"Maddie!" he protested.

"Just funning, my love. Can't you take a joke?"

He kissed her very swiftly and when he drew back, she murmured, "Jason, what *was* I to think when you kept yourself from me for a full sennight!"

"There was nothing else for it. You may recall that I've been under a vow of celibacy? To be near you was too great a temptation to resist. So I stayed away."

She could not help frowning at this. "And who is this lady who so constrained you?"

"My mother, of course," he said, and kissed her frown away. "I was supposed to prove to you that I could be as gentle and as restrained a lover as you could wish."

Into the lapels of his jacket, she murmured, "Jason, how soon . . . what I mean to say is, when will your vow . . . oh, you know what I'm trying to say."

With a grin of pure devilment, he answered, "I'm released from my vow as soon as I get my ring on your finger."

"Oh, Jason," she breathed.

His eyes searched hers, questioned, and read their answer. Wordlessly, he drew her hand through the crook of his arm and escorted her along the flagstoned path. The great doors of the church stood open.

In the narthex, she came to a halt. Lady Sophie, in a pale daffodil muslin came forward. At her skirts clung two pretty little girls clad in white. In their hands, they carried baskets of flowers.

Sophie smiled shyly at Maddie. "Children," she said, addressing the two diminutive flower girls, "make your curtsey to your Aunt Maddie. These are two of your nieces, Penny and Meg."

378

Maddie just stood there staring. Deveryn took her hand and curled it around a slim ivory bound volume.

"Your grandmother's catechism," he said, "and inside, a sprig of white heather, for luck. I remembered, you see."

"Are we . . . are we to be married?" she asked, her eyes blinking rapidly as young Sophie removed her bonnet, and smiling, fixed a white satin ribbon to her curls.

"No. We are already wed, as I've pointed out to you on numerous occasions. I've prevailed upon Mr. Moncrieff to solemnize the declaration we made before witnesses. However, to all intents and purposes, the service will proceed just like any ordinary wedding. Are you ready, love?"

"And shall we say our vows?"

"Yes, my darling, we shall say our vows, and God help either one of us if we don't live up to them."

She removed her kid gloves and set them aside. With heartfelt reverence, she opened her grandmother's catechism and carefully placed her three precious tokens inside the leaves—an angel, a baby, and a ring. To Deveryn's questioning look, she said, "These will become family heirlooms. It's a long story. Oh my love, we never had a chance."

He smiled at that, and offered his arm. "You're mine already," he told her with a show of his habitual, outrageous possessiveness. "I'll have no man give away what already belongs to me."

As in a dream, she allowed her husband to escort her the length of the centre aisle, her bridesmaid and flower girls following in their train. Shyly, with happiness shining from her eyes, she forced herself to meet the steady looks of the assembled guests. She feared to see reproach in their eyes. Her glances met only with warmth and understanding and more.

From her grandfather, a plea for forgiveness.

From Aunt Nell, a blessing.

From Lord Rossmere—was it admiration?

And from the countess—Maddie looked again—a wink and a smile of congratulation, as if she, Maddie Sinclair Verney, had just done something terribly clever. She winked back.

At the communion table, they halted and the service began. When it came time to exchange their vows, Deveryn sank to his knees. Maddie followed suit. She had not the heart to tell him that he was following the English tradition.

He slipped his ring on her finger and with more gratitude than she could bear, more happiness than she deserved, she heard his voice, low, unsteady, repeat his vows.

"With this ring, I thee wed; with my body, I thee worship; with all my worldly goods, I thee endow."

And when she thought that the service was over, that there could be nothing more to complete her joy, the minister offered them the sacrament of communion, and she knew that it was at her husband's instigation.

With trembling fingers, she cupped the silver chalice and drank the wine. She offered it to Deveryn, and when he raised his eyes to hers, she could have wept for joy at what she read there.

They came out of the church to bright sunshine. The village children had gathered at the wrought iron gates. As she stepped under the arch on Deveryn's arm, he reached in his coat pocket and withdrew a fistful of silver coins. He threw them high in the air, and the children went scrambling after the treasure trove with shouts of glee.

"To handsel our marriage," said Deveryn. "Janet told me." And he handed her into the carriage.

"We're not going to Drumoak?" she asked when the carriage made a turn at the end of the high street.

"No." He cradled her against him. "We're going to my yacht for our belated honeymoon. Shall you mind?"

"Sounds wonderful," she murmured, snuggling closer. "Where are we off to?"

"I thought I told you." He turned her face up for his chaste kiss. "At first tide tomorrow, we're sailing for Inverness. You see, my love, you've converted me to everything Scottish."

Moments later, there was a hint of apology in his voice when he said, "You'll miss Founders' Day and the performance of *Medea*. Shall you mind very much, my love?"

She could scarcely suppress her shudder. "I'll get over it," she said handsomely, and then to turn the subject into more convivial channels, "Does your yacht have a name?"

"Destiny," he said, and kissed her again.

The name didn't surprise her in the least.

*   *   *

She came to him that night as he had so often dreamed she would, without shyness, without fear, and without shame. The cabin was drenched in the lambent glow of moonlight, touching them with a sense of mystery, and magic, and awe. Their lovemaking was more than the joining of their bodies, more than pleasure, though it was the sweetest pleasure he had ever known. There was a benediction in her kiss, catharsis in her cry of ecstasy. When it was over, he felt absurdly and deeply happy. With infinite tenderness, he laid his hands against her swelling abdomen. For a moment, he was too choked with emotion to speak. She lay curled trustingly against him, one leg thrown over his hips. He could feel the wet of her tears against his neck—a lover's baptism, he thought.

"Maddie," he said, "tell me why you love me."

She cupped the face that was so very dear to her in both hands and brushed his lips with her own. "Oh my love," she said, "there's no saying why. I could name you a dozen attributes and still not fall in love with the man who possessed every one of them. But you, even when I thought I despised you, quite stole my heart away."

He stroked her throat softly with the back of his fingers. "Do you know, I shall be roasted unmercifully when word gets out that I've fallen for a bluestocking? Who would have believed that a freckle-faced innocent, and a Scot to boot, would have toppled me from my unassailable perch?"

For that piece of malice, she nipped him ferociously on the earlobe. "Aristophanes had the right of it," she said. "We are two halves of an entity. Apart, we're simply not whole. There's no other explanation."

"If that is so, then you are my better half," he answered with feeling.

But she would not allow it, and to stop her protests, he began to make love to her in earnest.

"Jason?" she murmured throatily as he laid her back on the narrow bunk.

"Mmm?"

"Now that our lovemaking has been 'hallowed,' so to speak . . ."

"Yes?" He brought his head up and surveyed her through eyes half-hooded with passion.

"Do you suppose that you could teach me all those *wicked,*

wicked things you introduced me to at Dunsdale?''

For a moment, he stared at her in shocked silence. Maddie covered her face with her hands. When no sound came from him, she slowly and carefully brought them down. She caught the flash of his teeth in the moonlight. Damn if he wasn't laughing at her!

"Well, Jason Verney?" she demanded.

She discovered that he was a patient teacher.

He learned that she had a natural aptitude.

They wakened to a furious pounding on the door as the sky in the east lightened to dawn. Maddie rolled to her stomach and buried her head under the pillow. Deveryn pulled on his breeches and went to investigate. By degrees, she became aware of a subdued commotion on the deck above. She had just slipped into her dressing-gown when her husband strode through the cabin door.

"We set sail in ten minutes," he told her, and sat down on the bunk to pull on his boots.

"What's going on?" she asked.

His face was a picture of suppressed mirth. "Your guardian has arrived poste-haste from Canada. He's at Drumoak now. Duncan has this minute brought a note from my father."

"Well, that's capital. It's years since I've seen Uncle Tom." She could not think what he found to laugh at.

"And will be many more before you see him again, if I have my way."

"What?"

"He's as mad as a hornet and threatens to have our marriage annulled. Would you believe, there's a suitor in Canada he has all picked out for you?"

"Oh," she said, and sat down beside him. "What's to be done?"

"We're eloping."

"What?"

"To England." He was shrugging into a seaman's coarse jacket. "We're to be married at Dunsdale by my mother's chaplain. My father is on his way there at this very moment. He'll arrange things."

"But we *are* married," she exclaimed.

"So I should hope," he retorted, and planted a kiss on the small swell of her abdomen. "But there are some who will refuse to accept it until it's done English style. Maddie, I'm thinking of the child."

For a moment, her expression turned mulish, and he thought that he might have an argument on his hands. But all at once she said, "Oxfordshire!" and smiled a secret smile to herself.

"I know it's not Scotland," he commiserated.

"Very true," she demurely concurred.

"It cannot compare in grandeur or," he waved his hands vaguely, "or in majesty to this wild Scottish landscape."

"Quite," she said simply.

"But . . ."

She looped her arms around his neck. "But you will be there, my darling. And where you are, my heart will be also."

It was obvious that her words affected him deeply.

"It won't be forever," he promised.

"We'll come back for holidays," she allowed.

It wasn't as if she was really, *really* deceiving him, she told herself. Dishonesty was not in her nature. But for a Scot to admit to a preference for anything English—*that* came too close to treason for comfort. Perhaps, given time . . .

He grasped her small chin and turned her face up to catch the pale morning light which streamed through one of the small porthole windows. "Maddie," he said, "I swear I'll make it up to you."

Naughty thoughts, deliciously wicked thoughts, came tumbling into her mind. It would be a very long time, she decided, before he would pry the truth out of her. She tightened her hands on his shoulders. "Deveryn," she said, "you're on."

He held her at arm's length and studied her carefully innocent expression. "Madeleina Sinclair Verney," he exclaimed, "you fraud!" And with a great whoop of laughter, he tumbled her in his arms and kissed her till the lady cried "mercy."

SURRENDER TO THE
PASSION OF RENÉ J. GARROD!

WILD CONQUEST (2132, $3.75)
Lovely Rausey Bauer never expected her first trip to the big city to include being kidnapped by a handsome stranger claiming to be her husband. But one look at her abductor and Rausey's heart began to beat faster. And soon she found herself desiring nothing more than to feel the touch of his lips on her own.

ECSTASY'S BRIDE (2082, $3.75)
Irate Elizabeth Dickerson wasn't about to let Seth Branting wriggle out of his promise to marry her. Though she despised the handsome Wyoming rancher, Elizabeth would not go home to St. Louis without teaching Seth a lesson about toying with a young lady's affections—a lesson in love he would never forget!

AND DON'T MISS OUT ON THIS OTHER
HEARTFIRE SIZZLERS FROM ZEBRA BOOKS!

LOVING CHALLENGE (2243, $3.75)
by Carol King
When the notorious Captain Dominic Warbrooke burst into Laurette's Harker's eighteenth birthday ball, the accomplished beauty challenged the arrogant scoundrel to a duel. But when the captain named her innocence as his stakes, Laurette was terrified she'd not only lose the fight, but her heart as well!

Available wherever paperbacks are sold, or order direct from the Publisher. Send cover price plus 50¢ per copy for mailing and handling to Zebra Books, Dept. 2654, 475 Park Avenue South, New York, N.Y. 10016. Residents of New York, New Jersey and Pennsylvania must include sales tax. DO NOT SEND CASH.